ANNUAL #1

MW01222052

Contents

Fiction

Poetry

Publisher and Executive Editor
John Gregory Betancourt

Editor
Doug Draa

Consulting Editor
W. Paul Ganley

Production Manager
Steve Coupe

A Note from the Editor

I'm writing this on the first day of Autumn and in little over a week begins the most wonderful time of the year! Nope not Christmas. I'm talking about October and Halloween! And since it's such a special time of year we decided to reward our readers with something special. Most of you probably already know that Weirdbook has gone quarterly. Well. we realized that that still doesn't bring enough weirdness into the world and have decided to squeeze in one more issue. Now this isn't simply your average run of the mill extra issue. Nope, from now on, if sales support it, there will be a yearly themed annual and the theme for this year is, in honor of All Hallows Eve, Witches! This issues table of contents contains many names familiar and quite a few that might not be so familiar. You can rest assured though that each and every contributor is a master/ mistress of the strange, the bizarre, the frightening, and lastly, the ENTERTAINING!

And two last things before I go. Wildside Press (www.wildsidepres.com) is now offering subscriptions to Stateside customers at a significant discount over single issues. And don't forget that Weirdbook #37 will be available in late November. Take care and Happy Halloween!!

—*Doug Draa*

Thou Shalt Not Suffer
by Matt Neil Hill

I can tell what my father's thinking just by looking at his fists: that only a boy as willful and ungodly as me could bring a damp book of matches to his first witch burning.

I close my eyes and feel the ghosts of those fists come crashing in, the same lesson over and over. My sins marked out in chipped teeth, bruised flesh and aching bones—my deepest transgressions a constant discolouration, irredeemable. So I'm told. I've tried, thought I'd been careful. Triple-checked the tools needed to start the fire. Sure as I could be I was ready to face my coming of age. But no—I am incapable of directing my life towards the light.

When I pry my lashes apart I find I've turned away from my father at the head of the convoy and now face the pyre directly. If I cannot make it burn I will never see my thirteenth year, never become a man.

Three witches stand before me in the palsied noon light, held up by iron stakes hammered into the ground. They peer out at me from a tangle of timbers ripped from nearby buildings mixed with branches from the dying trees encircling this abandoned retail park. No birds sing for them in such a lifeless place—England's land no longer green or pleasant—a shrine to the old world now only good for feeding the flames. I trod the shopping centre's lonely hallways earlier in the day, too-big coat pulled tight around me as I dragged my feet through its piles of plastic dolls and smashed electronics and let its useless diamonds and gold trickle between my chapped fingers. Ghosts may have watched me, may have called my name. When I emerged from the shadows the accused had been made ready for me, to prove that I'm more than a child.

Through the gaps in the branches I can see their staring eyes and crudely shaved scalps. Their gaze hovers over the clammy cardboard between my fingers, swoops up to my face. My crow-black hair and moss-green eyes were a regrettable gift from my mother, but I have no kinship with these creatures, whatever certain members of the convoy might whisper behind my father's back. The hope in their eyes is a waste of time.

My mother drew her last breath just after I drew my first. What family remained for me was a father who showed his unquestionable love through violence, and a sister five years my senior who despised me for robbing her of our mother. She never missed an opportunity to convince me the victim of my matricide would have hated me too. The convoy's extended family is no comfort, pitying and loathing me in equal measure. My father blamed the rise of the witches for my mother's death, turning their extermination into his remaining life's work. The burden left him scarred, but he has always borne it without complaint. I think he must blame me too, but I will never ask him for the truth. I have since witnessed the traumas surrounding childbirth first hand, seen how complicated and fragile a thing it can be. My sister knows it too, losing the child she carried for eight months only a few days ago. She was distraught, of course, but spitefully chose to reject the comfort I offered. Her sole purpose from the fatal moment of my birth was to torture and torment me, her greatest desire my degradation. I have watched other families cling to each other in the wreckage floating on the surface of the past, trying desperately to keep from going under. My sister and I only held on to drag each other down.

I focus on the match still trapped between my finger and thumb—fragile as a mouse's rib, crumbled red dust around its tip like flecks of meat. I let it fall. Four remain in the matchbook's wet carcass—the image of a stag on the cover above a redundant phone number for a looted pub—four between me and death. A hundred eyes pierce me with their judgement. This has become my world.

Born in the same month the witches first appeared, I was spared the affliction of remembering those early years. Any understanding I have of what came before is sourced from the convoy's campfire tales, my sister's gleeful recollections of extinct treasures, and from my face buried in encyclopaedias or the bible, either willingly or with the weight of my father's calloused hand against my neck.

He says the advent of the witches was slow, but that civilisations always did die gradually. Too many people turning away from the word of God, forgetting the pain this brings. The faith of the righteous spread too thin while others turned to darker practices and prophets, false gods or none at all. Free will divorced from the one who granted it. Not even those who proclaimed themselves witches could have known how many of their ravenous sisters were waiting to join them.

I know that Witchfinder General Matthew Hopkins executed 300 witches in two years in the 1600's. Hundreds more perished in the adjoining centuries—*thousands*. All of those damned souls waiting in a hellish afterlife, unquenchable hatred grown around their hearts like mould spores, filling their bodies, choking, overflowing as they clawed at the looking glass between our two worlds until it finally cracked, weakened as it was by our own transgressions.

It was us who let them through.

Their infiltration was gradual, like a virus amongst the lost and the weak until enough of the population was too seduced to stand against them. Then came the death spells, slave spells, rampant child abductions and barren earth. They drifted unhindered through the corridors of power—the majority of our leaders already too corrupt or hamstrung by obscure laws to oppose them—whispering in the right ears when they could, turning to more direct methods when they encountered resistance. The Houses of Parliament were the first icon of the old world to burn, the charred and poisoned corpses of the people's representatives clogging the Thames for weeks, no one in authority left to remove them and the military in disarray. Their power grew, only those with God on their side left to fight them.

We have far fewer laws now in our new world, and really only one that matters—the avenging spectre hanging over us all. Over me now most of all.

Thou shalt not suffer a witch to live is the letter of that law.

Burn or be burned its spirit.

Beneath my scuffed boots, lines of faded paint segment the tarmac, numbered spaces hungry for the cars that will never return. Dark green thistles force themselves up through the rust-red skeletons of overturned shopping carts in an attempt to reach the occluded sun, the miasma of their slow rot acrid upon my tongue. My sinuses itch with the fumes from the carefully rationed petrol splashed across the outermost reaches of the pyre, the sour odour of the condemned women's piss and fear-sweat nothing but a memory. We came to burn them on a wasteland not accommodating enough to swallow me whole in my hour of defeat. As I look back up at the pyre I know what I am supposed to see.

Whenever I blink or sleep I see forests in darkness, roads choked by camouflaged vehicles with uniformed men poisoned or gibbering within them, survivors crawling the ditches missing tongues and eyes and genitals. Horizons lit with burning skylines. Seasons disrupted and the sun's power diminished. Nothing but spoiled crops and soured milk bitter in our throats. Our country's physical borders—closed many years before my birth to insulate us from the endless tide of the foreign—choked with toxic green smoke capable of stripping the skin from any foolish enough to enter its cloud, an enormously powerful spell no man has the knowledge to undo. Father says the fight against evil united us as a people, but I don't know. My sister and I still wish each other dead after all.

I have only ever truly seen one witch up close, when I was barely six years old. We had camped one night in a farmhouse abandoned by all but the rats and spiders, the faint aroma of their shit and venom. I had left windows open so many times in our travels—cursed by a terrifying claustrophobia if I couldn't feel the movement of air on my face—that no one would have believed it was actually my sister instead of me. I awoke burrowed into my sleeping bag, a weight on my chest. Breath in my ears not my own. Moonlight across the intruder's face, eyes and teeth glistening black like sump oil in her grave-grey face, hair spun from cobwebs laced with tiny eggs. My thighs stinging with the wet, ammonia-scented escape of my fear, hammering heart blocking out every other sound in the world. Her fingers creeping towards my face, petrified snakes seeking out the tiny pink morsel of my tongue.

And just as quickly gone, torn away from me by the vengeful giant that was my father. Still deafened by terror, I watched the crone's pantomime destruction, the rhythmic fall of his axe rending her flesh long after her spirit had departed. Her blood, dripping from my hair and eyelashes, smelled of rotting fish and stagnant water. When I finally closed my eyes the after-image of her skin was scales, her insides become indecipherable writing scrawled across faded wallpaper of roses in bloom.

I try to keep my eyes open and only see what's in front of me these days.

Sometimes the witches are witches, but often they are only women who have earned the displeasure of the herd. More and more so these days, I think. The disobedient, the dishonest, the diseased and the deranged—there is no shortage. Wives cheat. Mothers leave. Sisters try to murder their brothers. The three destined to die today were betrayed to us by villagers too afraid to do the work God demands of them. Years of fear and mistrust have instilled in us a fevered desire to see all those who sin against us held accountable, yet, even now, not everyone has the stomach for it. The covens have torn the world apart and it is no wonder we see them everywhere, however well they conceal themselves behind fair brows and pretty smiles. Vengeance may belong to the Lord, but He had been so terrifyingly absent when the darkness came that its execution fell to us. So we set them all aflame, their screams our way of flinging prayers to the impassive heavens, their blackened bones a tribute to our silent Lord. Father always tells us God will welcome the innocent into His kingdom and grant forgiveness to those who dispatch them there in good faith. I think it's something he made up to comfort himself in his quest for vengeance, but I never really cared if what he says is true. Why should I? God doesn't seem to care. The flames certainly don't. The flames punish the flesh regardless of whether the soul beneath is good or evil, unbiased in their purity of purpose.

In the end, all witches burn.

As I rip the next match from the book I watch the women begin to struggle. Their hands are tied so they cannot escape, their mouths gagged so they cannot enchant us with their spells. I hold my breath and try to light the match but the head disintegrates, a useless puff of sulphur its only exhalation. Three left, like rotten teeth in a broken jaw. Before I close my eyes I can see the women's bruised and lacerated bodies through the gnarled bars of their cage. In the darkness behind my lids it is not them I see.

My sister and I traded many blows over the years, the pain no deterrent but rather an exhortation to further violence. She was always more devious than me and knew not to leave marks, so as to not be punished. There were times I was certain she poisoned me, each concoction of roots and weeds and berries an experiment to see how far she could go. I suffered fevers and bleeding rashes, bouts of vomiting and diarrhoea throughout my childhood—the stench of me becoming who I was—lost blood but survived. Our father refused to believe me when I told on my sister, pointing his finger instead at my own carelessness and stupidity. I know that she must have felt justified—to risk being accused of witchcraft showed how desperate she was to hurt me. I needed to see the mark on her though, the scratch or the bruise. And they were more than worth the beating our father gave me, a score of trophy wounds for every one I wrought on her. Something about her injuries spurred me on, the sight of her discoloured flesh allowing me to feel at peace for a short while.

I remember following her to the water's edge one time, when I was perhaps eight or nine, creeping breathless through the night to see the sinuous curves of her pale body drawing my eye to the pile of clothes at her feet, shed like a viper's skin. Bathing herself beneath the witch's moon, a dangerous flirtation with the forces sent to destroy us. Watching her from the shadows, the blood drained from my stomach and legs. A moan left my slackened mouth and gave me away, my sister turning unerringly in my direction even though I hid. I watched her squint into the gloom, a smile creasing her sly lips. She nodded once—an almost imperceptible movement—and then made as if to cover herself as she opened her mouth wide, her screams fit to cleave in two the bright rock hanging in the sky. My heart pounded faster, its violent thudding in my ears so out of time I only realised the frenzied beats had been our father's footsteps crashing through the undergrowth when he set upon me. It did not occur to me until much later quite how quickly he had arrived at the scene, given the distance between the stream and the camp.

I watched my sister's face between the blows. A light broke behind her eyes, a beacon to illuminate the power she might have over me and my father both. I had recognised the way he looked at her as she grew to womanhood, sure she must have seen it too. I wondered if this was a part of why she hated me so fiercely—for not just killing my mother's body and soul, but for ending the protection against our father her life afforded—but our enmity would have prevented me from asking her, even if I had cared enough to do so. As far as I was concerned she deserved every bad thing that befell her. I know she had come to look uncannily like my mother from the lone photograph I had found within the pages of my father's bible. Fingers that had stroked the edges of her image with love and longing gathered together and struck at me again and again, bursting blood vessels and shattering small bones, punishing me for what I had thought was only a boy's curiosity. He tutored me thoroughly then—as he has on so many occasions since—about how mistaken I was. Whatever his sins might have been clearly paled in comparison to my own and I dared not confront him about how his might be absolved. I was *rotten* with sin, salvation only possible through the abasement of my flesh. As tears and blood pooled in my eye sockets I caught one last blurred glimpse of my sister before night engulfed me—infected moonlight flashing from her teeth as her face broke apart in a hideous smile.

The cries of the convoy call me back from my reverie, everyone grown impatient for the fire. What little wind stirs in this forgotten place carries the perfume of bodies ripened beneath layers of leather, wool, and frayed synthetics, all pitiful defence against the forever-winter sky. The pervasive stink of the last few vehicles running on diesel is overlaid with the stench of animal shit so rich it's almost visible. Behind the crowd our tattered and hard-won ark of horses, goats, chickens and pigs, snuffling and clucking, protected by our silent pack of shepherds, staffs and retrievers, the cats never ours but only their own, sullen, hissing shadows in cages, used as my father told me men once used canaries in coal mines, held at arm's length before us as we walk through the noxious wasteland the covens have made of the world.

My fingers tremble against the remaining matches, icicle sweat in my hair. My chances for redemption are running out. I imagine being grabbed by people I have known for years and being gagged, tied and set beside the condemned. Picture the relief on their faces as they watch the sin boil away from me in greasy, blood-black clouds.

I turn my back on the pyre once more and stare at my father.

I remember him many years ago, dragging a witch from the blazing ruins of a church, no holy place sacred to them, her clawed finger caught in his eye socket, his face streaked with gore. I watched him pound her screaming mouth into a gravestone until all trace of who she had been was removed. He is not that man today. Today his face is filled with more disappointment than I have ever seen, and this from one who has had to beat me almost every day of my life for the failings I refuse to abandon. The difference between the examples is clear. The only punishment to definitively end the repetition of sin is the one that brings the death of the sinner.

I start to walk towards him but his hands come up, palms toward me. He shakes his head, eye aflame. Extends one finger towards the pyre. I must do this alone, no help from him. The faces of the convoy confirm it—those not already turned away in disgust. If a man doesn't have the wherewithal to burn a witch, he cannot be called a man.

The ground beneath me persists in its refusal to swallow me whole as my sister emerges from our father's shadow.

When our eyes meet I understand why I've failed. We've come too far along our particular path into the darkness to turn back. She stands at our father's blind side, as she so often contrives to do, hand cradled around the slack mound of her empty belly, eyes full of secrets. She *knows*. I recall her arms around me a short eternity ago, her whispered *good luck,* gestures so unlike her in their generosity, an act I'd been too preoccupied with my destiny to decipher. She has no need to reveal herself and wave the matchbook's dry twin at me, tiny stag and unusable numbers safely hidden away. It is her parting gift, not to me, but to herself. A way to mark an end to all the black, brackish spite flowing between us, since the very hour I was dragged, bawling and forever blamed, from our dead mother's womb.

A year after the night at the water's edge—a year filled with countless taunting glimpses of her flesh as my sister's new method of torture—I finally succumbed. We were on the road a lot then, living out of cramped motorhomes. She pretended sleep, pushed the blankets from her snake-like pallor, stretched and groaned. I approached her bed, drenched with perspiration, both sickened and aroused. I had barely pressed my lips upon her thigh when her eyes sprang open, her smile just as slight and fleeting as it had been before, her screams again loud enough to crack the sky. Loud enough to alert our father, the door wrenched almost from its hinges to reveal me paralysed, lust disappeared but my guilt still clear. He yanked me by my hair and dragged me naked for a hundred yards across gravel and broken glass with the taste of her still coiled on my tongue, half the community watching, marking his territory with my blood. My scorching embarrassment nothing compared to the heat of my skin flayed against the rough ground, cold sweat boiled away. The farther he dragged me the more my back felt like it was actually on fire, a livid brand created to show the world my sin.

That I should be burned again as a result of my sister's deception turns my gut to crashing surf. To suffer as a result of my legion of failures, of the wellspring of sin I'm told I carry but not *this:* not because my sister couldn't bear to be parted from her mother, she cast for all time as the bereaved angel and I the demon seed. I have trespassed against her with the bitterest intent these last few days, I know, but it was she who began a war with an infant free of any purpose of his own. In my short life no one but me seems to have considered the possibility it was *she* who was tainted and *I* the angel. An angel sent to deliver our mother from the burden of caring for a daughter too corrupt and hateful to deserve her. And now she has taken things too far and engineered the end of my life with a childish trick, when all I had done in playing the previous turn in our eternal game was to save a new innocent from falling under her spell, an innocent who could only have been conceived in sin, given its mother and father.

For he that soweth to his flesh shall of flesh reap corruption—the bible's message had been made clear enough to me; it was our father who had ignored it.

My sister is not the only one to have learned what combination of plants can cause a fever or render sleep, nor which ones might purge a child from the womb and leave no trace of their workings, nor how to administer them without arousing suspicion. Not every wound must leave a visible scar, nor every act of revenge or rebellion be played out in public.

The acid boiling in my stomach flows to my heart, devours its spasming chambers and spills across my tongue. My sister, my tormentor, my murderer...do we not share the same crow-black hair, the same moss-green eyes? Is the skin stretched over our lean bodies not of the same pale cream? When we are wounded, do our bruises not blossom to the same sultry purple of dusk and fade to the same forlorn yellow of dead flowers?

But so what?

We could have united against him, I suppose, had we not relied on his brute strength for our survival. What's more, neither of us could ever put aside their hatred of the other. Our father laid his hands on both of us, but more than his hands on her. The Good Book tells us to honour our mother and father and so we did, each in our own way.

I close my eyes and her face disappears as if I had already cast the dirt across her open grave.

I will not be ended by one such as her.

I relive the distance my father dragged me, the heat of it. Think again about the thicker planks ripped from the retail park to sustain judgement's flames. Look down at the matchbook's pathetic inch of sandpaper half the width of my thumbnail.

My sister calls for me to be added to the tally of those we burn today.

I turn and stride the few steps to the pyre. The witches rattle against their bonds. I focus on the length of splintered timber propped between them. The shouts of the convoy begin. The lesson I learned through layers of flayed skin is my only chance. I gulp down accelerated breaths. The world inside the pyre's confines is so small, so close. I burrow in. Twigs and branches scratch at my face, prick my eyelids. Blood comes. As I insinuate myself between the branches, the crowd gets harder to hear, but I can still make out my sister's demanding screech, my father's bellowed dismissal. My grip on the matches whitens my knuckles.

The witches scream at me from behind their gags as they try to free their hands. The iron stakes tremble only slightly in the tarmac. Like the haunted forests of my dreams, the branches are so densely packed as I force myself closer to the centre my feet almost leave the ground. I stretch my arm until the tendons wail, tremors wracking my lungs. I stumble forward, coat caught up before I slip halfway to my knees. Far enough—too far: *buried.* The timber is within my reach, dry and rough enough I hope. The stink of petrol beneath me, blood in my mouth from my bitten tongue.

Lightheaded in this suffocating tomb, I stand as best I can, reaching as high up the plank as possible. I press the match heads against the wood. The women buck and slither in their bondage. They are all I can hear now, their muffled cries a plea meant either for me or the shadows, I cannot tell which. My own plea—for this to work, for me to live, for the chance to repay my sister for her latest and most heinous trespass against me—is not solely for the ears of God. I cannot afford to pray only to Him, if He has abandoned me. All that matters now is my survival.

I keep the matches pushed into the timber all the way down and feel the friction begin to blister my thumb and even as I wonder if it will be enough to kill the moisture there is a sudden hissing burst of light and I drop the flame instinctively, down towards the film of petrol on the ground and the flames catch and bloom and rush up against my chest, my face. The branches begin to crackle immediately and I thrash against their embrace. I look up into the eyes of the nearest woman at the very moment she rips her bleeding hand free of her ties and sinks her nails into my shoulder. True self revealed, those eyes are solid black now, deeper than death. She scrabbles for purchase on the muscle beneath my smouldering coat, bolts of arctic pain driven into my bones. Gag spat out, the screams pouring between her soot-black teeth begin to sound like laughter. The same flames licking at my belly begin to ascend her thighs. Her grip tightens and I grab at her hand. My vision blurs. I cannot move.

The witch and I scream at each other, with each other—our kinship finally exposed. Joined in fire, her hand beneath mine. We will choke on the smoke as we burn and whoever our prayers went out to will leave us here to die.

Sometimes though, rare as a good night's sleep, prayers are answered.

I would know the hands that grab at my ankles anywhere. I know every calloused inch of them and the salvation they bring. All I can see is smoke and fire, three writhing towers of blackening flesh above me. The witch's hold is broken and I see the sky, birthed into the world a second time through a lacerating tunnel of thorns. Father's face above me, good eye shaky with tears, iron mouth calling for aid. Everything goes dark as he smothers me with his coat and I think maybe he will end me, end the pain we've always shared. As the sky reappears I wonder if I am dead or driven mad when I see a thin ray of sunlight piercing the clouds.

I struggle against the hands that would help me, no longer fists though their touch still wounds. I squirm in the dust to find the spot where the hallowed light falls. Father tries to still me, but I am a man now and will not be stilled. I scrabble for purchase, blistered fingertips scraping the tarmac.

Beyond the baying mob the blade of light stabs at the desolate earth, lone figure illuminated at its point, one hand at her belly and one at her heart, salt-slicked face turned to me with all its snarling teeth on show. The light marks her out, banishing the greatest shadow cast across my life, showing me my course, giving me permission, granting grace. I will not believe the heavenly glow casts her again as the angel; *refuse* to believe God would be so blind. There is only one meaning I will allow to make sense.

It's so hard to pull the air into my lungs, to stop my raging flesh from shivering. So hard to hear my father's words above the entwined choruses of the witches and the crowd. So many agonies to suffer before I can fulfil the law naming the one thing I should never have suffered at all. My answered prayer a debt that can only be repaid one way.

As the pain becomes too much and the ground beneath me finally consents to swallow me whole it is her name I have upon my lips, the real name for what she has always been.

Witch.

And when, as it must, the dark veil lifts from my eyes and I awake I will finish what God means me to finish. Only the death of the sinner ends the sin.

It has been the lesson of my life.

In the end, all witches burn.

No Holds Bard
by Adrian Cole

Venner studied the open plan office. He felt good today. His recent promotion, after a protracted boardroom battle with one of his closest rivals, was particularly satisfying. Difficult not to feel a little smug. Mustn't show it, though. He walked through the office, a vast affair, filled with busy staff, beavering away on their machines. Most of them kept their heads down, not eager to attract the attention of the new Head of Exports. Some glanced up, rewarded with a benevolent smile.

"Come in, sir," said Morrison, opening the door of his glass office as he saw Venner about to tap on it.

His superior did so, nodding, his eyes taking in the sweep of the city's heart so dramatically visible beyond the window. It affirmed Venner's mood. So satisfying to stand over it all, knowing he controlled a lot of what went on there and now would extend that power into Europe and beyond.

"Congratulations," said Morrison as Venner sat.

"Thanks, Tom."

"No more than you deserve, if I may say so."

Venner smiled. Tom Morrison had been a loyal supporter for a long time. He'd get his reward. "I'll probably be spending more time abroad. Just thought I'd have a good look round before I go. Particularly at the development upstairs. How's the rebuild going?"

"Come and see for yourself, sir. Everything's bang on schedule."

Venner allowed himself to be ushered out. They went to a lift. It took them up a few floors. As they emerged, they heard the sound of pneumatic drills somewhere overhead. The corridor they were in was partly lined with old filing cabinets, all marked for disposal. Venner put a hand on one, feeling its dust.

"Where would we have been without our filing cabinets? I assume these are all for scrap?"

"Everything transferred on to electronic files. We're slowly junking everything out. These'll go abroad, along with all the older machines."

"Good. I hate to see anything go to waste."

"We'll need to go up three flights of stairs, sir. And we'll be asked to wear some protective gear. Health and safety." Morrison looked mildly uncomfortable at having to bring the issue up.

"Fine," said Venner.

They walked along the corridor. The offices to either side were empty, their equipment smothered under white sheets, the only light coming from the far windows. Once the major overhaul was completed, they'd be buzzing again.

One office, however, did show signs of life. The two men heard voices and a quick inspection revealed three women working at their pcs. As soon as they saw Venner, they stood up, almost to attention.

"Good morning, Mr Venner, Head of Exports!" they said in perfect harmony.

Venner was slightly taken aback. Were they ribbing him, or was this genuine respect?

"Mr Venner, Chief Executive of Zennor Industries. Mr Venner, who'll be Chairman of the Company!"

Venner's face clouded. Now they were being impertinent. He was neither Chief Executive, the post currently held by another of his rivals, Nigel Burgundy, nor was he likely to become Chairman.

"Who are you people?"

Normally when he used his voice in a certain way, his employees tended to shudder, even though he was renowned for his even-handedness. Not these women. Venner studied them. They must have been with the company for some time—all of them were over fifty. Their clothes were smart but plain, their hair immaculate, and makeup minimal. They probably belonged to an earlier era, he was thinking. Started out on manual typewriters. Surprising they were still with the company, which tended to move people on, bringing in fresh, younger blood regularly.

"Answer Mr Venner, ladies," said Morrison.

"Good morning, Mr Morrison!" they chimed. "Not as important as Mr Venner, but more so, through your children."

Venner turned to his companion, who looked slightly aghast. "Is this some sort of farewell surprise?"

The women were giggling as they left their desks and went to a door at the back of the office, going through and closing it. Morrison was gawping at the space they'd left.

"I don't mind a bit of fun," said Venner. "But you'd better look into that, Tom. I daresay you'll find a bottle or two of sherry in one of those desks."

* * * *

"I think you were more than lenient, darling," said Clarissa Venner, sitting back comfortably in one of her plush new chairs and sipping at her customary after-dinner glass of wine. She smiled at her husband's recounting of the events of the day. "You should at least have given them a good telling off. Whatever were they thinking?"

"I suspect it was a bit of a prank that backfired. No harm done. Tom'll sort it out. Besides, I've got other things to think about. Not least Hong Kong."

"You're too soft. That's why they love you, I suppose."

Venner was about to comment further, when the phone behind him on a small table rang. He reached around and lifted the handset. "It's Tom Morrison," he grunted, reading the name on the phone's screen.

"Well answer him!"

"Hello, Tom. What's wrong?" It wouldn't be a social call. No one called Venner at this time of the evening unless it was to do with work and a necessary interruption to his private time.

"I'm sorry to disturb you, Michael, but it's bad news, I'm afraid."

"Oh?" Venner leaned forward attentively. Morrison didn't call him by his Christian name unless it was something personal.

"It's Nigel Burgundy. He's had a heart attack."

Venner grunted again. He was no great friend of Burgundy's, and they'd clashed heatedly in the boardroom more than once. "Is it serious?"

"Well, yes, I'm afraid so. Actually, he's dead. It's chaos here. The Chairman rang me. I don't suppose you could come in, could you?"

"Of course. Give me half an hour." Venner put the phone down.

"Whatever is it, darling? You look as if you've seen a ghost."

"Not quite." He gave her the news.

"Nigel Burgundy's dead?" she said. "Well, he's no loss. I'm sorry, but he was a pain in the backside, and he's blocked several of your ideas in the past. Now what have I said?" She refused to be cowed by her husband's strange expression.

"Not you, darling. Those—women. I told you, they called me Chief Executive."

Clarissa sat up slowly, savouring the title. "Yes, you said. So, if Nigel's dead, who gets his post? You've just been made Head of Exports, so it won't be you."

"Well actually—it could be. If that's what the Board wanted."

"You'd better get to that meeting. Are you sober?"

He nodded. Oh yes, he was sober all right.

* * * *

"Dreadful business," said Sir Frederick, Chairman of Zennor Industries. He was looking round at the group of Board members, most of whom had been his colleagues for many years. "I knew Nigel had been ill, of course, but I thought he had it under control." His face was ruddy, his frame larger than was good for his own health, but his eyes retained the old glimmer that his business rivals had known for decades. When he went down, it would be with all guns blazing.

Venner used the uncomfortable pause. "Is Emily all right? It must have been a shock to her." He hardly knew Nigel Burgundy's wife, but she seemed a pleasant enough person.

"Yes, thank you, Michael. She's with her family."

There was another pause. Everyone knew the issue of the Chief Executive's role needed airing quickly, but no one, least of all the hopeful candidates, wanted to be the first to broach the subject. The Chairman, however, hadn't become ruler of his empire by standing on ceremony.

"We'll need a re-think," he said. "For the time being, however, I'd like to put a temporary measure in place, to ensure good continuity. I suggest we appoint Michael to the post of Chief Executive. It'll mean a stay on that visit to Hong Kong, but we can cover that for now. Michael—would you be up for that? I know it's rather throwing it at you, but we can't afford to stand still. Nigel would have been the first to approve, I know."

"Of course, I'd be happy to. That is, not happy. I'm only sorry—"

"Quite," said Sir Frederick, brushing aside Venner's apparent embarrassment.

No one was going to dissent. Around the conference table, heads were obediently nodding.

"I'll call a special meeting of the Board next week," said the Chairman. "One item agenda. Bring your thoughts along, ladies and gentlemen. Meanwhile, Celeste will liaise with Nigel's family about the funeral." He dismissed the group with a wave and turned to Venner, indicating he should wait.

Once the Board had dispersed, leaving Venner alone with the Chairman, the latter let out a huge sigh. "I hate this sort of thing," he growled. "Just when we'd got ourselves nicely re-grouped. Listen, Michael, are you really okay with the double post? It's been done before. I'll give you a good deputy for some of the foreign work. Got anyone in mind? How about Tom Morrison? He's a grafter, isn't he?"

"Yes, I don't think there's anyone better suited than Tom."

"Excellent. We'll call him in tomorrow. Go and sleep on it."

"That's fine, Freddie. It'll only be for—what? A couple of months?"

The Chairman grinned and Venner was reminded, as he so often was with Sir Fredrick, of a shark, a large, white one. "Initially. But I want you to take it on permanently. Oh yes, I know the Board has to meet and discuss it and so on. I'll see we get the right result. There are enough of them who'll do what I tell 'em to swing the vote. Keep it shtum."

* * * *

"Really?" said Clarissa Venner, her eyes sparkling, her cheeks flushed with undisguised excitement. "Combined posts."

"Temporarily. The Board—"

Clarissa made a moue at her husband's attempt at observing protocol.

"The Board nothing! Sir Frederick will bully them into the decision he's already made. You know what he's like. So—why the glum face?" She put an arm around his waist and pulled him closer.

"I'm not glum, darling. I was just thinking about those three women. How could they have seen this coming?"

"Coincidence. After all, Nigel's health wasn't brilliant, was it?"

"No, I suppose not."

"What is interesting, though, is that they also called you Chairman."

"Yes, they said I'd become Chairman. I can't see Freddie stepping down, though. It's his life. He's seventy, but the old dog's got another ten years at the very least. He'll probably outlive all of us."

Clarissa beamed. "Oh, I don't know about that."

"What on earth do you mean?"

She intertwined her fingers with his and pulled him gently away towards the stairs. "Let's not think about all that now, darling."

* * * *

After a week in his new dual role, the dust was settling for Venner. His colleagues had made the adjustment: if any of them bore any ill-will or resentment, they hid it well enough, and things at Zennor Industries moved on with their customary effectiveness and efficiency. It was exhausting, though Venner pushed himself hard, fuelled by the adrenalin rush.

"Michael, will you do something for me?" the Chairman asked him. "I've double booked some commitments. You know we sponsor that theatre company around the corner? Celeste's little hobby. There's a do on and we can't go—it's a family thing. Could you cover for me? Here's two complimentary tickets. Show's on Friday. Zennor Industries ought to show its face."

Venner took the envelope. "Of course. I'm not much of a theatre-goer, but Clarissa enjoys being seen. What are they doing?"

"No idea. Something highbrow, I expect."

The real reason you don't want to go, thought Venner. He pocketed the envelope.

"Can't say I'm looking forward to my weekend," said Sir Frederick. "It's Celeste's sister's birthday. She always lays on an excellent meal, with all the trimmings. But you know I suffer from anaphylaxis. Every damned thing I eat has to be vetted. One mouthful of anything taboo and I'm finished if I don't give myself a jab. So the doctors keep telling me. Celeste's sister, Melissa, is a bit gung-ho."

"I'm sure Celeste will look after you. She's a very meticulous lady."

"Where would we chaps be without our wives!"

* * * *

"This makes a nice change," said Clarissa, looking out from the theatre box at the assembled audience.

Venner nodded, mildly interested, as the house lights went down and the curtains drew back to reveal a dimly lit stage draped in various other curtains to give it an obvious other-worldly feel. Dry ice leaked its white clouds over the stage to compound the effect. Rising up through the fog, three shapes took centre stage, their faces hidden by long, straggly hair.

Clarissa sat back with a little gasp.

"When shall we three meet again?" said the first of the shapes, the voice sharp and piercing.

Clarissa smothered a giggle. "What is it about Macbeth?"

Venner shrugged. "Flavour of the month," he said, though he didn't feel amused. He watched and listened as the three witches went through their opening speeches, moving this way and that like so much weed shifting on the bottom of the sea. The audience, now silent, was evidently rapt.

Later in the play, when the doomed Macbeth met the weird sisters for the first time, they greeted him, their hair parting to reveal deathly white faces. As they spoke, their eyes stared upwards and Venner felt them fixing on him. They raised their arms in supplication and he felt as though he'd been deliberately singled out.

"All hail, Macbeth! that shalt be king hereafter."

Venner felt himself going very cold. It was impossible not to superimpose the three women in the office who had taunted him that day a couple of weeks ago, with words that were if not identical, close in meaning. In fact—and now his blood was running cold—the whitened faces of the three actresses looked horribly familiar. They were the same three women! No, that wasn't possible. This was a professional West End production. His office workers couldn't possibly be in it.

It was only when he realised his wife was shaking his arm gently but insistently that he came to. The witches had left the stage and events at Dunsinane castle were unfolding.

"Are you all right?" said Clarissa.

He mentally shook himself. "Yes, of course. I think I know how this one ends."

"Well, don't tell me!" she whispered. "I imagine they kill the king, though."

Venner frowned, but said nothing. In fact, he hardly spoke a word until they were back at home.

Clarissa brought coffee and sat down with a flourish. "Very interesting. I'm not one for this arty stuff, but I thought it was rather good. You haven't said much. Did you like it?"

He nodded.

"It's funny," she went on. "Those witches and their prophecies. And the three women in your office. Do you think that's where they got the idea? They had a damn cheek."

"Undoubtedly. A bit of a sick joke."

"And then Nigel died. The joke backfired a bit, didn't it? Mind you, what if it wasn't a joke? What if it was a prophecy—or a premonition?"

He stared at his coffee on the table top. "Coincidence."

"What about the other bit? You know, when they called you Chairman to be."

"One day I may be. Not exactly magic to predict something like that."

"I loved the way in the play Lady Macbeth worked on her hubby. He was a noble, valiant hero, but she knew him better than anyone else." Clarissa leaned a little closer. "She knew what was in his heart."

Venner looked at her, his eyes meeting the deep mischief in hers. "He wanted the crown."

"Oh, yes! Didn't he just. She worked on that. Right up to the point where he did the foul deed." She giggled. "It's actually a very good story. But, those times are long gone. No one runs around with daggers and stuff these days."

"God forbid."

"It just seems such a pity that Sir Frederick is in your way. I mean, you'd be the obvious choice for Chairman, right now. There's no one else. Tom Morrison—"

"The witches—I mean, the three women—said he'd be more important than me, through his kids. Like Banquo, who fathered the royal line after Macbeth. One of Tom's sons has just finished university. Top honours graduate. He'll undoubtedly join Zennor Industries."

Clarissa's eyes turned cold for a moment. She and Venner had no children of their own. It wasn't something she liked to be reminded about.

"Sir Frederick's health isn't good, is it?"

"No. What of it?"

"I'm quite friendly with Celeste. In fact, I've made a point of it. In your best interests, darling. Corporate wives love to get together. Par for the course."

He knew something was coming. Clarissa had a mind like a wasp's sting.

"I know all about Sir Frederick's anaphylaxis. And his diet. And those little pen-things he keeps near at hand."

"What on earth are you talking about?"

"He has to avoid certain things. If he—accidentally eats the wrong food, even a tiny bit of it—he could go into shock and, well, at worst, it would kill him. The pen-things are the antidote. A quick jab and the effects of the allergy are nullified. I've been reading up all about it on the net."

"Why are you telling me this?"

She sipped her coffee slowly and beamed at him over the rim of the cup. "It would be very convenient if he did eat something he's allergic to."

Venner laughed. "I see! You want to play at Lady Macbeth. Not with daggers, but with food! That's preposterous."

She joined in with his laughter, though much more softly. Unlike his, her nerves were not on edge. "Is it?"

* * * *

The dinner party was in full swing. Even though Sir Frederick's huge mansion would have been fit to service a king's extravagances, it was tightly packed. The top men and women from Zennor Industries were all there, of course. No one ever refused an invitation from the boss. And there were people from rival companies, too, carefully chosen so they could fawn and preen, although knowing they were in the presence of one of the Big Players.

Celeste had brought in the very cream of the caterers, no expense spared and they knew well enough the rigorous demands Sir Frederick's wife would put upon them. However, they prided themselves on their unique and totally professional approach to their work. Men like Sir Frederick and his allergies, were nothing new to them. All that would be specifically prepared for. A team worked scrupulously in the huge kitchen and Celeste hovered, constantly fussing over the various elements of the banquet. Nothing got past her hawk-like appraisal.

She was delighted to have a few well-chosen friends to assist her in her inspections, among them Clarissa Venner, who was now elevated up the social ladder as the wife of Zennor's new number two.

"You'll have to prepare yourself for entertaining guests on a grander scale," Celeste had told Clarissa. "This sort of do will become more commonplace for you two now."

"I don't know how you do it, Celeste."

"I'm sure you'll cope admirably. Now—I need to arrange Freddie's food. Would you help me? He can have most things and I'll make a selection. You and I can take them to him. You don't mind being a waitress?"

"Heavens, no. It's an honour."

"Freddie loves to be fussed over, especially by attractive women."

And indeed, the master of the house was flattered. He sat at the head of a huge dining table, which seated the most privileged of his guests and received his food, beaming like a teenager.

Michael Venner sat close at hand, relieved when his wife joined him. He leaned over and whispered, "Did you have to go that far? Made to act the part of a waitress. Bloody pomp and circumstance."

She smiled sweetly. "Oh yes. It was necessary, darling. I was perfectly happy with the role."

Sir Frederick ate well, working his way through a number of side dishes his wife and Clarissa had set beside him, before starting on the main course, a particularly rich *ragout*, the speciality of the caterers, which he adored, and in no small quantity. After several mouthfuls, he leaned back, coughed and turned a decidedly unhealthy red. He coughed again, clutching his chest, his breathing ragged and stertorous.

Celeste gasped, knowing immediately what had happened. "His anaphylaxis!" she cried, getting up, her chair tumbling behind her as she fought her panic. "I need his pen."

The guests immediately around the couple all looked agog, none of them understanding what she meant. She pushed through them as they stood, ignoring the sprawled figure of her husband and made for a small annex and a tall chest of drawers. People watched, stunned, as she rummaged first in one drawer, then in another.

"Whatever's wrong?" said Clarissa beside her.

"The EpiPen! For the antidote. He has to have it. Immediately. Where is it? It's not here. It's always here. There's two of them. Where are they?"

Calmly Clarissa searched through the drawers, which held a few papers and other small items. Evidently the EpiPen was not there. "Could you have left them somewhere else?"

"No, no, they're always here!"

"What about Sir Frederick? Could he have moved them?"

Celeste rushed back to her husband, where several of his guests were desperately trying to succour him. Venner stood behind them, watching in horror. His wife looked at him across the utter chaos. Her face wore a grimace that mirrored those of the appalled guests, but Venner sensed something behind those eyes—a smile, perhaps.

* * * *

They didn't get home until the early hours. The police had crawled all over Sir Frederick's dining area, kitchen and adjacent buildings and their forensic team would be there for a long time yet.

Venner sagged down on to the settee, utterly spent.

Clarissa calmly brought him a stiff brandy. He demurred, but she made him drink it. He looked up at her.

"Don't tell me you had something to do with that?"

She laughed softly. "Who would know?"

"Meaning you did? Hell, Clarissa, are you mad?"

"Far from it. Sir Frederick's anaphylaxis got the better of him. He ate something he shouldn't have."

"In the *ragout*?"

"If they analyse it and find traces of powdered peanuts, well, who knows how they got there?"

"Christ—!"

"And it was careless of Celeste to misplace Freddie's EpiPens."

"Clarissa, you can't dress it up. It's murder." Venner got up and paced the carpet, his face bathed in perspiration.

"Darling, remember the witches. They foretold all this."

He kept shaking his head. "The police are no mugs. They'll get to the bottom of this."

"I doubt it. How many people were there? How many had an opportunity to slip something into the *ragout*? They'll never prove anything. For a start, what would the motive be?"

"Are you joking? I'll get the Chairmanship. It'll point to me—us."

"But you're not Chairman. Not yet. You will be, of course. It was predicted."

"You believe those damned women?"

She put her hand over his. "Darling, you're a tough nut in the boardroom. Everyone knows that. You never flinch from competition. Inside, though, you're a bit of a softy. I've just given you a little push, that's all. Be a man, isn't that what Lady Macbeth said?"

He sank down in the chair, his mind whirling. "So - what happens next? I'm damned if I'm going to find those women and ask them."

"No need. We'll make our own future now, once the dust settles and they give you the Chair."

* * * *

Venner woke in the early hours. Clarissa snored softly beside him. They'd made love, at her insistence, though he always found it impossible to resist her demands, and afterwards she'd slipped quietly into an untroubled sleep, lulled by the soporific of sex. He'd followed soon after, but now he was awake, he couldn't get back. The play came back to him.

This is crazy. I'm not living a parallel to it! How can I be? Nigel's death was coincidence. And Clarissa murdered—god, yes, actually murdered—Sir Frederick. Is she right? Will it be impossible to prove it was her?

If I am living this play, what happens next? It should be easy to identify it and deliberately chose another path, a fresh, unseen fate. So—what did happen next?

He went back over the play he'd seen, clawing at memories of its plot. Banquo. The witches had predicted he'd not be king, but his sons would be. Tom Morrison was the Banquo equivalent in this farrago. His son, Alistair, would have a career with Zennor Industries—he was a brilliant lad, so maybe one day he'd become Chairman.

Venner chewed it over. So what? Clarissa and I can't have children of our own. Once my days as Chairman are over, someone like Alistair Morrison will probably be an ideal successor. In the play, Macbeth has Banquo murdered. Well, screw that. I've no intention of murdering Tom. I doubt if Clarissa has thought beyond the Chair.

* * * *

The following weeks fled by for the Venners. Zennor Industries had always been at its best in a crisis and was quick to reorganize itself in the face of potential chaos. Venner, despite a few protestations, was made Chairman, while the rest of the Board re-shuffled. Tom Morrison became Venner's deputy. The police finally ended their interviews, the Chief Inspector in the case privately confessing to Venner they had nothing to go on and weren't pursuing things. Ronald Barrowcliffe was an old friend.

"We might have treated it as death under suspicious circumstances, but we don't have the manpower or the time to follow it up. If Sir Frederick was pushed, anyone could have done it."

Venner felt drained. He'd hardly had time to adjust to the situation, his nerves shredding. "You've got more than enough to deal with, I guess."

"How are you coping? You look like hell"

"It's been a nightmare. I've had the press to deal with. "

"They've more or less had you on trial, now that you've got the plum job."

"Whoever took the Chair was going to be in the firing line."

"Quite. Well, good luck. If anything ever comes to light I should know about—"

"Yes, of course, Ronald."

* * * *

Venner finished signing the papers and handed them back to Jago, one of his newly promoted staff. Jago was a cold fish, Venner thought. Never quite knew what was in his mind. He was efficient, bloody good at his job. *Perhaps that's why I held him back, this time round*, Venner thought. Jago had done well enough out of the reorganization, but he'd probably seen himself higher up the ladder, maybe even in Tom Morrison's post. If he was resentful, he hid it well. Venner approved of that. Professional behaviour.

"Anything else?" he asked Jago.

"Well, there is one thing, sir. I hesitate to mention it. I wasn't sure if you knew about it."

Venner studied the cool features, the unflinching eyes. "Go on—what's wrong?"

"It's Tom, sir. You may already know, in which case, I apologise for bringing it up."

"Oh?"

"He's left his wife. They're getting a divorce. I know it's a private matter, but I just thought you ought to know. Sometimes it's better to be forewarned of these things. Obviously they can be stressful."

Venner sat back, slowly shaking his head. "No, I didn't know. Damn, that's a shame. I didn't know they were having problems."

"I hope I haven't stepped out of line, sir."

"No, no. Thanks for letting me know. Is there another woman involved?"

Jago shuffled his feet and looked everywhere but at Venner. "I believe so."

"Bloody fool. Do we know who it is?"

"I'm…not sure, sir. The rumour mill's been turning."

"And what does it say?" Venner fixed Jago with his coldest glare.

"It's nothing, sir. You know how tongues wag."

Venner sat back after Jago had gone. Tom Morrison. The last person he'd expect to get mixed up with another woman. And a divorce? With all that had happened at Zennor Industries, this was hardly the time to be bed-hopping.

Later, after another wearing meeting, Venner was speaking to two of his staff and noticed others leaving the boardroom, some glancing his way, slightly uneasily. *Odd*, he thought. Why should they look uncomfortable?

"Tell me," he said quietly to his colleagues, "is it true what I've heard about Tom Morrison?"

The men exchanged glances, then seemed to be studying something beyond the windows.

"Well," said Jefferies, normally quick to exploit any opportunity to impress his superiors. "I gather he's left his wife."

"For another woman?" said Venner. "Come on, Jeffries, spit it out. I need to know what my senior staff are up to. We've got a tough couple of months ahead of us. I can't steer the ship in fog."

Jefferies would not meet his gaze. "I'm sorry, but I don't know anything."

* * * *

Venner left the offices in the early afternoon. He needed an early night. The events of the last few weeks had worn him out. A long weekend and a bit of relaxation would sharpen him up for next week, when there were several critical issues to tie up for the company.

With one eye on the busy streets and choking traffic, he reached into his pocket for his cell phone. Not there. *Dammit.*

He fumbled through all his pockets. Left it at the office? He didn't remember using it that morning—he'd used the landline for the morning's calls. So where had he left it? He had to swerve to avoid an oncoming vehicle, its horn blaring.

He'd just have to surprise Clarissa. He didn't think it would matter. At worst she'd be entertaining some of her society friends, no doubt regaling them with anecdotes about the events of the last fortnight. The police, as she'd said, had never followed up their initial interviews. Amazingly, she had got away with murder.

As he was approaching the gates of his house, some hundred yards away, he saw a car pull out of his drive, turn left and accelerate away. By the time he reached the gates, it was out of sight. But he'd recognised it. It was a Jag. Tom Morrison's XFR.

Venner parked his car, grinding up the gravel, got out and slammed the door. He opened the front door to his house and walked in, his mind racing. What the hell was going on?

"Clarissa?" he called.

There was no immediate answer. He climbed the wide stairs. Beyond the balcony he could hear water running. Bathroom. He went to the door. He could hear movement inside.

He eased the door open and went in. Clarissa was standing in front of a tall mirror, body wrapped in a pink towel, carefully fixing her hair up.

"Michael!" she said, turning, her expression shocked. "You gave me a surprise. You're early."

"What was Tom Morrison doing here?" he snapped, the words out of him before he'd taken the time to pull himself together.

"Tom? What are you talking about?"

"I saw his car pull out through the gates. He just left. There's no point denying it."

"That's ridiculous!"

"Is it? Is this part of the bloody prophecy? Discredit me so that he can take over and then pave the way for his son."

"I don't know what on earth you mean! Discredit you? How?"

"Or am I supposed to be so enflamed by jealousy that I go out in a fit of rage and kill him? The Banquo figure. Well, it won't work. We're not re-enacting a bloody Shakespearian play!"

"Will you calm down? I've told you, Tom Morrison hasn't been here. You obviously saw someone else's car."

"So who has been here?"

"I had my usual Friday afternoon chat with the girls. Three of them. They work for Zennor Industries, although you probably don't know them."

"And one of them drives a Jaguar XFR?"

"Probably. I don't take a lot of notice. I can't tell a Jag from a Porsche. But yes, it would have been an expensive car."

Venner knew that she wasn't going to change her story. He understood her stubbornness only too well. He turned on his heel and went back to his car.

* * * *

Back at the office, he wasted no time in making a bee line for Tom Morrison's office. To his surprise, Jago was in there, reading through some files.

"Tom asked me to check something out for him," he said, trying not to look embarrassed.

"Do you know where he is?"

"He said he had a meeting with his solicitor, sir. That business I mentioned earlier."

"Who would that be?"

"I could find out, sir."

"Do it, will you."

Jago left the office to consult Tom Morrison's secretary. Venner paced restlessly, glaring at the desk, its tidy papers. Among them, partially hidden, was a cell phone. Venner recognised it.

He picked it up. It was his. What was it doing in here? Why would Morrison take it? So he could use it to contact Clarissa? Covering his tracks? Possible.

Jago returned as Venner slid the cell phone into his pocket. Jago gave no indication of having seen.

"I've rung the solicitor's, sir," he said. "Goldmans. Tom Morrison hasn't been there today."

* * * *

"Don't you think you've had enough to drink?" Clarissa stood over Venner, more than a hint of anger welling up in her.

He slammed the whisky glass down and lurched to his feet. "Enough? Yes, bloody enough. Let's get this business settled once and for all." He grabbed her wrist before she could stop him.

"What the hell are you doing?"

"We'll go and see Tom Morrison." He used his free hand to wave his cell phone at her as if it explained everything. "Now that I've got this back, I'll ring him on the way."

"Michael, you're not making any sense—"

"Well, let's talk to Tom. You can both put me in the picture."

He pulled her through the hall and opened the front door, tugging her down the steps to where he'd left his car. She was powerless to stop him opening the passenger seat and forcing her to sit. If she'd shrieked with protest, no one would have heard her. Resigned, she clipped her safety belt in place.

It was only when he pulled away that Clarissa realised he wasn't at all fit to drive. Now she did protest, but he simply accelerated down the drive and swerved dangerously into the street.

"Michael! Slow down! You'll kill us both."

His face beamed inanely. "Oh yes. One way to end this charade."

Several near misses later, revving the engine up to seventy miles an hour in a built-up area, he drove head on into a double decker bus.

* * * *

In the office, their desks wedged in between banks of redundant filing cabinets, the three women smiled contentedly.

"Well, that was fun," said the first.

"I think we should go on holiday," said the second.

"Yes, I've been looking at these brochures. There's this wonderful old castle. It's been completely modernised. Lovely hotel," said the third.

"Yes, that looks splendid," said the first. "Where is it?"

"Denmark."

▲

Laying The Hairy Book
by Josh Reynolds

"It needs getting rid of, John Bass," Franklin Armstrong said softly. He reached out as if to stroke the square shape that sat on John Bass' kitchen table, but pulled his hand back like a man wary of snakebite. The shape was wrapped in a threadbare pillowcase, but Bass knew what it was well enough, and the thought of it sat on his table set his skin to crawling. His little South Carolina shack, with its rough clap-boards and tin siding, didn't seem big or sturdy enough to contain it.

"So get rid of it, Armstrong," Bass said, not looking at the thing. He didn't look directly at Armstrong either. He knew better than that, from painful experience. Instead, he looked out the kitchen window. Outside, the setting sun rode the tops of the close-set, black-rooted trees that stood sentry over the untilled field like fire.

"I've *tried*," Armstrong said, his voice catching on the last word. "Lord God above, I done tried," he continued. "I said my prayers and done my penance but it's still here."

"Try harder," Bass said. Then, against his better judgement, he asked, "You've done tried to burn it?"

Armstrong moaned. "I burned it on a pile of dry tinder, and I burned it with gasoline. I even threw it in the charcoal pit at Leroy's." Bass nodded. Leroy's was a juke joint down on Corn-Snake Road, south of Wackasaw Bend. They served barbeque on Saturdays, and the charcoal pit was so hot, the devil himself would shy away.

"Can't imagine Leroy was too appreciative about that, for all sorts of reasons," Bass said. He smiled without humor. "You tried drowning it too, I expect."

"I threw it in the river with my own two hands, and dropped it in Maisie Tucker's well, but it just kept coming back. I can't get shed of it." Armstrong reached for Bass, and the other man sat back. Armstrong let his hand fall. He closed his eyes and began to shake.

"I ain't at all surprised, if I'm being truthful," Bass said. There was a salt shaker on the table, and he pulled it towards him. "You know damn well that burning won't do it. Nor water either. Ain't airy an element conjured that can do away with a book as been written by that particular hand."

Armstrong's eyes sprang open, and there was a wild light in them as he looked at Bass. "You got to do it, John Bass. You got to use your hoodoo—"

"I don't hoodoo," Bass grated, standing abruptly, salt in his hand. "And I don't take on another man's burdens, Franklin Armstrong. This is your cross, so you carry it to the mount."

"John, please," Armstrong's voice cracked. "I can hear him coming down the road. The King of the North is running south, coming to carry me home. But if you was to get rid of this here book…"

"I'll thank you to leave now," Bass said, turning away, not wanting to hear any more. He tossed the salt over his shoulder.

Something whimpered and the chair legs scraped on the pine planks and then the door slammed as if caught by a hot storm wind. Bass turned and saw the book still sitting where Armstrong had put it. Cursing, he moved to the door, but Armstrong was nowhere in sight, and maybe he hadn't even been there in the first place, owing mostly to the fact that he'd died two days earlier. Stranger things had been known to happen, and to a man of John Bass' experience in particular.

But the book was there and it was real enough.

The breeze, hot and smelling of honeysuckle and burning rubber rippled through the house and the book stirred like a lion in a cage. Somehow the pillowcase had come undone, and the book looked up at him, hairy and black. The cover flopped open and the pages lazed like tongues and Bass caught words before his eyes snapped shut…*in the red trees there is a red church and in the red church stands a red altar, and upon the red altar there lies a red knife; take the red knife and cut red bread…*

"Hell you say," Bass grunted. Eyes still shut he reached out and slapped the book closed. The hair on the cover curled around his fingers. It was like a cat looking for a stroke and he got a queasy sensation deep in his gut. Bass pulled his hand back as if it had been stung.

"I know what you want," he said. His mouth was dry and there was a pain in his head, way at the back of his skull. "Damn you, Franklin Armstrong."

Truer words had likely never been spoken. Armstrong was damned, though he'd left the object of his damnation behind on Bass' kitchen table. Armstrong had been a witch-man in life, a fully paid up member of a coven, and a coward. In death he was still the latter. Afraid of the thing he'd used, because it was an anchor hauling him down into the deep, dark wells of the world. Every man paid a fair price for the life he'd lived.

Bass sat back down. The book looked at him, and he looked at it. It crouched in the center of the table, the hairy cover swelling ever so slightly, as if in invitation.

"Nope, don't think I'll be doing that," he said, leaning back. "I know what you are, though I reckon Franklin Armstrong knew too. But I ain't him, and I'll get shed of you right enough, I expect."

A book like this one couldn't be drowned or burned or even torn apart. It could only be given away…or buried. You had to as bury it the way you'd bury a man, six by six and say a bit. That was why Armstrong had brought it to him. Dead, Armstrong could no more pray over anything than he had while he was still living. But Bass could, and would.

Something laughed. It was a quiet sort of sound, but he heard it and it made the summer heat drain out of the room and part of him, the dumb animal part that had been to war, wanted to go for one of the kitchen knives in the rack by the sink. They had been his wife's knives. She was dead now, ten years gone, and he hadn't touched the knives in their rack where she'd left them since that day. He wouldn't touch them now. Not for a small thing like this.

The pages of the book fluttered and brought the smell of strange things into his nose and images of lean, long-legged shapes galloping through distant, dead places into his mind. Whether it was a warning, or an enticement, he couldn't say. The book was old and like all old things, it had a temper. Bass had one himself, and it was stretched thin.

Bass picked up the salt shaker. Outside, the birds fell silent. The twilight sky was the color of rust stains on cloth, and the day was slipping on by, leaving only darkness in its wake. It'd be night soon. Bass wondered whether Franklin Armstrong had made it back to his grave, and then he pushed the thought aside and poured a circle of salt around the book.

The screen door banged like a judge's gavel, and the windows rattled in their peeling frames as the first white dots danced across the table. The curtains his wife had made from the lace of her wedding dress danced and twisted, and he could smell something sickly sweet and strong on the air. Night was coming on fast, and he wondered at a distant noise, like his old mule pawing at the hard soil of the fields outside. The animal in question set to braying and wailing a few moments later, its voice echoing out of the barn out back, as the sun slipped out of sight. There was something was out there, waiting for the light to go.

Then, there was always something or other out in the dark. That was why he'd taken up the iron nails and salts, and charged a fair price for his services. A man had to keep meat on the table and fire in the stove for his loved ones, that was all there was to it. Bass had put the dead back into their graves and set pennies on the eyes of things that had taken the low, winding road. He'd never charged folks more than they could afford, and most as paid gladly.

There was a saying around local parts as allowed that a man who'd spent blood barring the devil's way once might bar it forever more. Though Bass held no truck with such sentiments, he knew that was why Armstrong had come to him, bearing his sins. But dead men were notoriously bad at paying their debts. "Your sins are yours, and no responsibility of mine, Armstrong," he said, out loud.

"And such heavy sins they is, for such a little man."

The voice slid on up from the porch like a shadow. Bass grunted, and turned to the screen door. He'd been half-expecting someone to come knocking before too long. "Well, I expect as you'd know, Maisie. Seeing as you one of them folks as led him onto the crooked path."

Maisie Tucker was beautiful, in that Old Testament way. A woman of substance and promise in equal measure, with eyes like hot brass and hair the color of spilled ink. She'd led many a man widdershins, and more besides. She looked like Eve, but she was a serpent at heart. He knew that from previous dealings. Supposedly, she'd hexed Selma Pickney's chickens, so that they forgot how to lay. And Abel Carter swore that he'd heard tell that she'd drawn a razor across a black rooster's throat on Christmas Eve, and laid out a wet feast for something that spoke in a voice like a bell tolling up out of deep places.

Whatever the truth to those stories, Bass could feel the strength in her, beating at his senses like heat from an open stove. It was a fell sort of strength, hard and wild. The sort of strength you needed to draw the dead up out of their sleep, or wrestle things that ought not to be. But it was a given strength, rather than earned.

Maisie leaned against the door frame, not quite touching it, bathed in shadows and moonlight. She laughed—a soft, genteel sound, at odds with everything about her. "Now John, is that any way to speak to a lady?"

Bass shrugged. "I'll let you know, next I speak to one."

Maisie grinned. "Still the same sour, old apple, I see." She licked her lips. "It's awful chilly out here, John. You going to invite me in?"

"I don't think I will, Maisie. But you can come on in, if you can open that door yourself." She smiled, and made to touch the door, but then her eyes caught sight of something, high up on the outside frame—a horse shoe, right where he'd nailed it, the day he and his wife had moved in. He watched Maisie's face turn ugly and then smooth itself back out, quick like. "That's what I thought," he said.

"That horse shoe above your door is loose, John. I'm afraid it'll hit me."

"It ain't either loose. There's one on the back door too, so you'd best watch yourself."

She craned her neck, trying to see inside. "That's some interesting reading material there, John. How'd you come by that, I wonder?"

"I expect you know damn well how I came by it. Otherwise you wouldn't be here." He wondered if Maisie was the reason Armstrong had been so desperate.

"Shouldn't ought to swear in front of a lady, John. Didn't that wife of yours ever teach you no manners?" She laughed again. "Then, maybe she didn't have time, dying as she did."

Bass hunched forward in his seat, causing the legs to squeak against the floor. "You talking awful loud and brave for a woman alone, Maisie Tucker. Who else is creeping round out there, I wonder? They'll find all my doors and windows sealed tight, against your sort."

She frowned then, like a child that's been found out in a lie. "Why, John? You scared?"

"Only a fool ain't scared of the dark," Bass retorted. Out of the corner of his eye, he caught a flash of a head ducking beneath the sill of the window over the sink. A man's head, with thinning hair. How many of them were out there, then? Two or three at least, if the fumbling at the back door was anything to go by. The house wasn't big, and he could hear everything, if he listened close. Right now, it sounded like someone was softly banging on the walls, and gently dancing on the roof. There was even a quiet scuffling below, as of mice, or perhaps something larger.

A verse from the Book of Joel fluttered through his head. *They rush upon the city; they run along the wall. They climb into houses; like thieves they enter through the windows.* Only his windows were sealed tight with iron nails, and the frames rubbed with capsicum and salt. "You come away from there now, you hear?" he called out. "It's barred tight."

The rattling at the back door grew more insistent. On the table, the book's pages flapped, making a sound like a dog smacking its lips. A man could lose time in those pages. There were three colors of pages—red with black writing, white with red and black with writing you could only read beneath the moon or at certain times of the year.

It would take more time than a man ought to have to read them all, and learn all that was in them. Time and more than time; the hairy books were promises bound in skin, and they as wanted to give the man what read them every one. But that was how it happened, how it had always happened. Promises had a power.

Bass had made no promise to Armstrong, but he was bound regardless. There was a right way and a wrong way, and he held to the former as best he could.

"Night comes on, John. Sure you won't let me in?"

"Not tonight, or any other, Maisie." He eyed her. "Best you go now."

She turned away, a slow smile spreading across her face. He followed her gaze, and saw a red light to the north, just visible through the kitchen windows. It was like the eye of distant train, only there weren't no tracks near here. He recalled a bit he'd read somewhere about how Hell was in the north. He recalled too how the king of that place was said to have written all the red pages of all the hairy books, and how he sent those pages out, like hounds hunting wickedness. And hadn't Armstrong mentioned a King in the North, running south? "Is that who you waiting for then, Maisie Tucker?" he said, looking at the woman on his porch. "The King who your sort bow down to?"

Maisie eyed him through the door, her hands not quite pressed to it. "Let me in, John. Let me take that there book from you. Armstrong should never have brought it here, and burdened you with it. That wasn't kind of him."

"Maybe not kind, but maybe right." Bass knocked a knuckle on the table. "Seems to me, he knew as you'd come looking. So he brought it where it'd be safe. If he'd been a better man, or alive, he might've taken it to church. But he was what he was, so he brought it to me."

Maisie shook her head, as if in pity. "And what do you think you going to do, John?" Her eyes flashed suddenly, the first bit of real emotion he'd seen from her. "That book is ours. Armstrong took what wasn't his to take, and he'll pay for it, along and along."

"I expect so. But that's between him and God Almighty."

"And tonight is between you and us." She stepped back, her face lit by that red light. "The King is coming to reclaim what's his, and he'll be here at the dark, just before dawn. That's all the time you got left in this here world, John."

"Then I expect I'd best get to work."

Bass stood abruptly, and there was a soft sound, like the beating of a bat's wings. Maisie was gone from the door. She wouldn't be far, though. He cocked his head, listening. The sounds outside had faded away to stillness.

He murmured the Lord's Prayer as he found his old shovel, walked out of the house and around back. In the barn, the mule was making noise, its hooves beating a tattoo on the wood of its stall. But there was another sound, audible now that he was outside, and he looked north again, his eyes squeezed into slits, listening. It sounded like hooves, not horse hooves or mule hooves, but cloven and sharp and he could feel the sparks they struck from the stones of the dirt road. The sky was deep red where it should have been dark, and the trees that lined the horizon looked like the bristly, black hairs on the book's spine.

Another verse, this one from the Book of Daniel, rose up in his memory and he muttered, "The King of the North who comes against him shall do whatever he wants, and no one can oppose him." He shook his head and frowned. "Well, we'll see about that."

Grass crunched. He spun. Old instincts, honed in the mud and blood of Europe, brought the shovel up and around, and he struck. Something screamed—a caterwaul, a swamp-cat scream that sent shivers down his spine. A black shape retreated in a scattering of shadow. But it hadn't been alone. More shapes, beast-lean and low-slung, crept around him. Eyes flickered green in the dark, reflecting the light from the house. They growled. There were words, jangled up amidst the growling. He backed away, shovel held like a spear.

The shovel dipped, and he carved a cruciform shape in the dirt. Two quick slashes. There was a quick noise, like startled birds, and the black shapes were gone. Bass waited, counting each breath. When he'd counted seven, he bent. One place was as good as another, for what he had in mind. But he had to be quick. He was safe in the house, but not out here.

Bass dug into the hard soil. The skin between his shoulders itched from the weight of green eyes. The sound from the north was louder. He bent forward, digging and praying, until both his hands and voice were raw.

They said that when a man as had given himself up to them hairy books with their red and white and black pages, that when he died the devil would come to collect, not his soul (for he already had that), but the hairy book. Armstrong had extracted no promise, but he'd left his burden on Bass' doorstep regardless.

The sound was steady and gnawing, like the echoes of distant gun shots, clopCLOPclopCLOP, coming faster and faster, running under the red banners of the sky, and John Bass kept his head down and his eyes on the hole he'd dug and off the horizon.

After a time, the hole was as square as he could make it, and deep enough. The moon was high and grinning bone-white, and the trees were rattling like bayonets along the trench-line. He turned back towards the house, ignoring the thunder that he knew wasn't thunder, because the sky was clear and there was no storm.

They were there, as he walked back, creeping on the eaves and peering at him, around the edge of the porch. They were whispering among themselves in soft voices. His grip on the shovel tightened. The whispers stopped.

Maisie stood between him and the porch. She hadn't been there, and then she was. "That was Clyde Spence you hit, if you were wondering."

"I wasn't."

She smiled, sweet and easy. "You learn how to fight with shovels in France, John? Ol' Black Jack teach you that?"

"Never met Major General Pershing, to my recollection." He took a two-handed grip on the shovel. "Step aside, now."

"Say please."

Bass raised the shovel and took a step forward. The only part of Maisie that moved was her smile. It got wide and long and white, like a slash of moonlight. "Let me in that there house, John. Let me have that book, and you'll nary hear a whisper of me again."

"And what about them? I bet Clyde wants him a piece of me, at least."

Out in the dark, something growled low and long. Maisie waved a hand, and it fell silent. "That book belongs to us, John. Armstrong was one of us, bought and paid for. But the iron in his soul got rusty, towards the end. He thought he could pay debt with debt." She cocked her head. "He was wrong, as it happens. But you don't have to share his fate."

Bass grunted. "Don't expect as I will."

"The King is coming, and you don't want to meet him. Be sensible. Give us the book."

Bass peered at her. "Why you in such a hurry, Maisie Tucker?" When she didn't answer, he went on. "I think it's you as don't want to meet the one you bow to. Leastways not without that book you bargained away your soul for."

She stared at him, her face cold and stiff. Her eyes glittered green, and he suddenly recalled a story he'd heard in the trenches, about a certain town where all the folk became cats by night, to dance and prowl as they would. He levelled the shovel at her. "I showed you the cross once, and you had the good grace to skedaddle. I can do it again."

"I'll have the meat off your bones before you make the first swipe," she said. Her voice wasn't soft anymore. She hunched forward, and something like sweat gleamed dark on her skin. Bass took a breath, and then a step. The shovel handle slid through his hands as he swung it. She slid away, hissing and spitting. Then he was past her, and thumping up the porch steps.

Hot breath washed over the back of his neck, and several sharp somethings tore at his back, ripping his shirt wide open and laying into the flesh beneath. He flung himself forward and hit the door, rattling it. Blind, he twisted, shovel lashing out like a club.

A panther-shape jerked back, letting out a wild squall. He fumbled at the door and fell inside. The thing hit the door as it banged shut, and let out another scream. Bass rolled over and stared out. The creature slunk off the porch, tail lashing, looking back at him balefully as it went. He let loose a shaky breath.

A moment later, the fumbling at the windows and roof started up again. They weren't planning on giving up. He groped for the edge of the table, and hauled himself up. He hissed, as pain flared through his back. He fumbled at the wound. It wasn't deep, but it hurt like blazes. He found a bottle of whisky on the sideboard and splashed some into a rag. He groaned as he pressed the rag against his back, and took a slug from the bottle. It burned outside and in, but in a good way. He needed that fire.

Bass dropped into a chair, muscles trembling from exhaustion. He wasn't as young as he used to be, and he'd worn himself out digging and running. He stared out the door, watching as green eyes flickered in the shadows outside. Sinuous shapes danced in the red light, and soft voices chanted. He felt a tugging on his soul as the song crept through the eaves.

Memories fluttered across the surface of his mind, like moths circling a flame. His wife's face was among them. She had been that kind of woman, his Talia. You couldn't not think about her, even when it was better you didn't. His eyes got heavy, and his chin dipped towards his chest. The bottle of whisky fell from his grip.

"You look hungry."

He looked up. His wife set a chipped ceramic plate loaded with a steaming stew of carrots, canned beef and peas over rice down on the table in front of him. "Eat," she said. Her voice was soft, the accent an ocean distant from his tiny shack. She'd been a war bride, the only thing other than bad memories he'd brought home from Europe after the Great Big One. He made no move to reach for the plate.

"You're dead." The words slipped out before he could stop them. She nodded, in that way he remembered. His heart twisted in his chest.

"I am."

"You're not here."

"I'm not," she said, agreeably. "You spilled your whisky."

He closed his eyes. When he opened them, the shadows in the kitchen were thick, and the single light bulb overhead flickered dully. He realized that he'd fallen asleep. The book sat and watched him come like a cat waiting to pounce. A trickle of spilled whisky stretched from the fallen bottle towards the circle of salt. He reached out instinctively to mop it up, but found he couldn't move.

It was hard to breathe. There was a weight on his chest, and something wrapped around his throat. He made to shove himself upright, and something fought against him. The weight twisted around, and the grip on his throat tightened. Something hissed in his ear.

"Found me a crack, John. Just a little one. High up in the stove pipe."

Maisie.

Bass staggered into the table. His limbs were heavy, and his lungs strained. His head swam. He clawed at the air, his fingers finding something that felt like raw meat. The bottle crashed to the floor, and the book slid. From outside, voices rose in a murmur as he wrestled with his unseen opponent. He groped for the salt.

"Just another squeeze more, John, and then you'll be with that wife of yours," Maisie crooned. "I'll dump your body in that hole you so kindly dug."

The world went black and soft at the edges. Maisie's voice seemed to come from far away, and her grip on his throat was like iron. For a moment, he thought he heard his wife's voice, whispering to him. Then his fingers found the salt, and he dashed the shaker over the shape that held him. Maisie gave a cry, like a woman who's been slapped. He ripped her from him, and sucked in a lungful of air. Maisie slipped from his hands with another high-pitched cry, this one long and drawn out and sorrowful. The door banged as she fled.

He collapsed against the table, wheezing. He glared at the book. It was as dangerous in its own way as Maisie. Outside, the singing had stopped. "Almost had me," he said. The book didn't reply. Neither did Maisie. He doubted she'd be back.

Bass shook his head, trying to clear it. They'd hexed him, put him to sleep. The sky was growing light. The dark moment before the dawn was approaching, and the King with it. He'd lost too much time sleeping and wrestling with Maisie.

He took a bag of nails out of a drawer and spilled them on the table, keeping his eyes on the book. He could feel a tremble beneath his feet, the vibrations of a mammoth tread walking the low, winding road up from the fire down below. The King was close now, and coming fast.

"Now we come to it," he said and grabbed the book. Something squealed and then he was pushing one of the nails through the swollen flesh of the cover. The book began to scream. It writhed in his hands and it was like holding a catfish or a snake and he stumbled back, another nail in his hand, iron to pin its hateful pages shut. Something that wasn't blood or ink or anything as pure as either spilled across his fingers and things that might have been teeth bit at his fingers. From outside, voices set up a wailing. Hands slapped against the kitchen window and feet stomped on the roof. But without Maisie, they weren't nothing.

Bass ignored them. He slammed the book down hard on the table. The door was banging hard enough to crack the frame and the curtains tore off of their rods, lashing him across the face. Behind the wallpaper and up under the eaves things that were black and hairy like clutching hands or crawling spiders moved and scrabbled, showering him with splinters or causing the pictures to tumble off the walls.

"Don't care for that, do you?" he said, fighting to keep his voice calm. Nine nails he pressed into the book as it shrieked and bulged in his grip and then, as the ninth sank in, it hung exhausted in his bloody hands. Nine nails of iron, to bind its hateful pages shut. Iron and salt were the only sure remedies he'd learned of, for matters like these.

When he'd finished, he leaned over the table, breathing hard. His back ached. He was tired. The ache climbed and twisted into a knot at the base of his skull, but he ignored it. There was still work to be done. He snatched up the shovel from where he'd dropped it. Shovel in one hand and book in the other, he stepped out onto the porch.

There was no wind, but the air churned nonetheless and the red glow was spread across the horizon, lighting up the night like distant fires. A shape bounced and bounded down the lane towards his plot of land, too far away for him to make out, but it wasn't any sort of man. It might have been a black sheet caught on the air or just a shadow dancing in the moonlight, but Bass knew that neither of those would explain the sound of hooves or why his mule was screaming in its stall in the barn, as if in warning.

He ran towards the grave he'd dug. Things he couldn't see sought to trip him, grabbing at his legs and clawing at his ankles. Maisie might be gone, but the others were still around, and still determined. He could hear them following him, their breath rasping hot and savage across the nape of his neck. He leaped over the grave and raised the book, shouting, "You want your hairy book? Come and get it!"

And then he let it tumble into the grave. It hit the dirt with a sound like a stone striking the water's surface and he raised the shovel. They were all around him, now, and the sky was sliding from black to purple. He could make out their hunched shapes, crawling low across the ground. Clawed hands reached for him, and green eyes blazed like marsh lights. He swung the shovel, driving them back.

Before they could regroup, Bass scooped up a shovelful of dirt and dumped it, before repeating the process. The shapes gave out a sigh as two shovelfuls turned into four and four into eight as he filled in the grave. He recited the Lord's Prayer as he worked, the words tumbling from his lips the way the dirt fell from his shovel. And all the while, that terrible red light grew brighter, until even the green-eyed shadows gave way before it.

Something with a shadow as deep as dark as the pit was striding towards him as the grave was filled in, and sometimes it looked like a flock of crows and other times like a man made out of black corn husks and then like a tattered shroud. Its hooves were striking sparks so fast was it coming towards him. Panic sliced through him like the blade of one of his wife's knives. It was the King of the North, come south to claim what was owed, even as the Bible had it. Its long arms stretched, reaching, and Bass threw down the last shovelful of dirt and shouted the last words and slashed two lines in the dirt. A thunderclap sounded as something wet like a spray of sea-water passed over him and was gone.

And then there was nothing to see but the dawn's light, and his house, and the newly-filled grave at his feet. After a time, Bass picked up his shovel and carefully patted down the dirt and thickened the two lines of the cross. He'd find rocks and cover it up later. But for now the book was buried and dead, and that was good enough for him.

There was no sign of Maisie Tucker or the others. They'd fled before the coming of their lord and master. Like as not, they were still running. Bass considered hitching up the mule and riding out to Maisie's place, to see what he could see. But he decided against it, after a few moments. If Maisie wanted to find him, she knew where he lived.

He wondered idly whether laying the book would make any difference to Armstrong's fate, in the end. Or whether the King of the North would, thwarted, move on to the witch-man's lonely grave to collect on his debt regardless. He hoped not, for Armstrong's sake.

He'd always charged the living a fair price for laying haints and setting things down in their graves. It galled him to think he'd never be able to charge Armstrong's accounts for what he was owed for this particular service.

"And if ever you owed a man, Franklin Armstrong, it'd be me," Bass muttered, dusting dirt from his hands. Then, shovel over his shoulder, he left the grave and what it contained and didn't look back.

▲

Here Is Where Your Proud Waves Halt

by Erica Ruppert

Aster went to the seaside at the end of autumn, to bear her child in peace. No one bothered much with the coast since things had changed. She had not told her family she was going; it was better they were behind her, with their sharp questions, their wants and needs. Their superstitions. Their claims on her. I refute you, she thought. All of you. At the edge of the land she could be alone except for the constant song of the sea, to ready herself as best she could.

She stopped where the pavement disappeared, smothered by drifting sand. Her car still had nearly a quarter tank of gasoline, but she was done driving. The roads were broken, and lonely. She could not escape the conviction that some terrible thing rode with her. She hoped it was only the dread of the new.

The town where she stopped was called Ocean Gate, and it was nearly empty. The houses along the main street stood shuttered against the season, and all but one greasy-windowed convenience store was closed. Before, even this late in the year there would have been more people about. But before was behind her, with her family. Now Aster stood on the sandy pavement, letting the wind push at her back, and looked around as the dusk gathered down. Here and there she could see a dim light come on, a sparse handful among bungalows crowded in like teeth. It was what she expected.

She pulled up to one of the tiny holiday cottages that huddled in accelerating decline on the near side of the dunes. The cottage had once been a seafoam green before years of benign neglect had faded the color to a shadow. It was near the entrance to the long amusement pier that stretched out in rotting grandeur over the beach and into the waves, near what remained of Ocean Gate's town center. She broke the lock and hauled her bags in from the car, and took stock of the shoddy, vacation-home furnishings. From the other lights in town she knew there was still power. The electric heat smelled of burning dust when she turned it on.

* * * *

Her son was born alive at midwinter after two days of labor. He only lasted for a few hours. He did not suckle. She was not surprised. She did not name him.

When his breathing stopped she gathered up the bloody bedclothes and bundled his small body in them, disguising him under layers of cloth, a cocoon for his transformation from being to object. Then she lay down with him on the bare, sagging mattress and finally slept. Her dreams could not cut through her exhaustion, but they informed her.

When she awoke in the afternoon, she walked stiffly to the beach and gave him to the waters.

As the tide drew the small wrapped body down and away the water scraped clean a glistening oval that had been buried in the grey sand. Her grief still too distant to touch, Aster pulled it up and wiped it off on her wet skirts.

It was a mirror, as big as her palm and set in a black frame of tarnished silver. She could see something in the glass, a reflection that was not hers. She held it closer to her eyes, then startled and let it fall from her cold fingers. The image of her infant son's face laughing up at her was erased by a flash of white sunlight caught in the glass.

Addicted, Aster wanted that image back. She scrambled after the mirror, afraid the sea would sweep it away as well. As she grabbed it a sharp edge of the frame sliced across her fingers. Bright blood drew a line that dripped onto the wet sand. The glass reflected only her face and the empty sky behind her. She shuddered, suddenly burdened with a sense of being noticed, being known.

She looked at the sea but the water was empty. Her son was gone. She wrapped her fingers carefully around the mirror and held it against her heart as she walked back up the beach.

She went back to her bungalow, locked all the doors, drew all the shades. When darkness fell she tried to sleep again, but her son's living face laughed at her when she closed her eyes. Aster felt suddenly sure that he knew where she was. It was no comfort.

* * * *

Days passed in slow, solitary motion, became a week, became two. Aster's body still ached from the fruitless birth. She still bled. She slept in fragments. At night the ocean called her, its dull growl the only sound in the quiet dark.

She did not need a lamp with the moon falling bright through her carelessly covered windows. She pulled on loose sweatclothes and left the shelter of the tiny cottage for the wide, cold beach. The wind was sharp. Broken black threads of seaweed sketched the line of the tide. All the shells she saw were shards. The mirror was a weight in her pocket.

As she waded into the tide the wind bit her where her clothes were soaked. She knew she needed to be in the sea. She pulled out the mirror and clutched it in one stiff hand, turning it to catch what it would. All the glass reflected was scattered moonlight. Her legs grew numb, but she felt the warm, wormy trickle of blood between her cold thighs.

I will grow my hair out into hag's weeds, she though madly. I will starve myself down to a whip, beyond the matters of meat and bone, beyond the limits of flesh. I will bring you back. Her lips moved over the words. Her eyes burned with tears.

Still, the mirror was empty. Aster waited for a few more minutes for some sign or direction. None came. She slogged out of the sea and back across the sand to her house.

* * * *

In the late spring, like blossoms, a few families came down from the inland towns to show their children what had been, drawn by nostalgia and old habit. They came with loaded cars, with coolers and sand toys, folding chairs and swimsuits. It was too chill and grey for swimming, but that did not prevent the wide-eyed children from running up and down the long empty beach until the misty sun began to slip away. When it did the sunsets were brilliant, slashes of gold and coral and violet across the deepening sky.

To Aster's amazement a handful of stalls opened on the pier as soon as the vacationers appeared, selling what plastic junk they had left from other, brighter years. A perpetual smell of sweet grease hung over the single food stall.

Aster, nostalgic herself, joined in by setting up her own shop in what had been a fortune teller's booth. She found old nets and draped them on the walls, filling them with whatever the sea threw up to her. She wrapped herself in layers of loose clothes and any bright jewelry she could find. She rimmed her cloudy blue eyes with smeared dark liner, teased her silver-shot black hair into a cloud, turned her dark skin to ash under powder. She felt safer in her costume, less watched.

Enough people still yearned for magic that she stayed the whole brief season. She would lean in to her visitors, and hold up the mirror as if she were taking a selfie with them, whispering nonsense the entire time. Sometimes she saw things that shouldn't be there. More often she invented them, spun stories like candy floss. Her visitors saw what she told them was there. Some hoped for more.

"Sylvia. Ah. And what are we asking for now?"

"I want to know—"

"No. Don't say it."

Sylvia had been to see Aster several times over several weeks, always with vague, empty questions that anyone could nudge into an answer. She seemed attached to the exotic lie Aster offered. It was clear she was lonely. She was very young. Aster remembered being so young, so lonely.

Sometimes Sylvia offered her old dirty cash, sometimes packaged foods. Once, Sylvia pressed a brooch made of dried flowers and Lucite into Aster's hand.

"Look," she had said. "It's your name in there. The aster."

And indeed, the faded blue flower was her name.

Now Aster leaned close, her cheek against Sylvia's. She held the mirror up before them, cupping it safely in her hand, turning it until she looked into her own eyes.

Aster drew a sharp breath.

"What is it? What do you see?" Sylvia cried out excitedly.

Aster hushed her, looking again into the clouded glass. He looked back at her. He had her eyes.

"He is already here," she said.

Aster reached out to touch Sylvia's belly but stopped herself, letting her hand hover.

"Are you sure?" Sylvia asked. "We've been trying so long, and when everything changed I thought we should stop but Tom said we have to go on..."

Aster turned the mirror away, afraid to look again. She shoved the glass into her pocket, silent, thinking. Sylvia began to make small noises, upset.

"Will you be back next year?" Aster said to calm her. "Bring him to me then. I'll prepare something for him. To keep him safe in the world."

"I will," Sylvia said, rising reluctantly from the cushions, her eyes soft. "I promise."

She hesitated until Aster waved her dismissal. Then she pressed folded bills into Aster's hand, more symbolic than valuable, and ran away up the pier.

Aster tucked the money away. She pulled the mirror out and held it up again. Her own face looked back, but from a great and foggy distance. She watched as her mirror image turned away from her, to the sea that roiled behind her. She watched what her mirror-self did then, the gestures, the payment made. She remembered the patterns.

* * * *

When the summer was gone and the chill of autumn rolled in, Aster stood on the rocks under the empty pier and slit open her palm.

As the blood ran she swung her arm up to draw remembered lines in the air, spraying her own red blood into the sea. The drops fell, dissolved, disappeared into the great swallowing mouth of the ocean.

That night as the tide turned she felt it swell within her, felt it rumble and turn. Alone in the dark in the tiny cottage, with only a stretch of sand between her and the vast black sea, Aster grew frightened. She did not know what exactly she had done.

* * * *

The next year Sylvia came, but it was nearly the end of summer when she did. She was alone, and she walked into Aster's sea-damp stall without greeting her. She had done as Aster asked.

Without a word, Sylvia took a seat on a faded cushion and unwrapped her child. The thing was as dark and twisted as driftwood, and waved its thin arms helplessly as the blankets came away. It had no eyes. Its mouth was a pink hole in a wet leather face. It whined like a pup.

"This?" Aster said before she could catch herself.

Sylvia held the damaged thing out to Aster. "Here," she said. "You wanted me to bring him."

Aster kept her hands down, knotted her fingers in her lap to make them useless.

"His name is Ty," Sylvia said. "You said you would have something for him."

Aster stared, nodded.

"Why now?" Aster said.

Sylvia started to cry but choked it back. Ty made his own sounds.

"It wasn't safe anymore." She pulled the wrappings back over her dreadful child. "I should have come back sooner. I think being around them did this to him."

"Them?"

"The things. The things," Sylvia said. Aster did not press. She could not trust Sylvia's needs, now.

"What did you make for him?" Sylvia said after a moment. "You said you'd make something to keep him safe."

"I remember," Aster said. She stood and went to a cabinet on the back wall. She opened the door carefully on its broken hinges, sorted through the bits she had collected over the past year. Her fingers closed around a bottle of multi-colored sand with a cork stopper, the kind of dross children made at booths on the boardwalk. Aster had added seawater to it, and a drop of blood, and when it dried it had made a crust of bright sand on the glass.

Aster held it out to Sylvia. "This," she said.

Sylvia took it, glanced at it, and put it in a pocket. She rewrapped her baby and walked carefully out of the booth. Aster could not help notice the black lines of blight that crawled up Sylvia's wrist.

* * * *

Sylvia came for Aster again in the depths of the following winter, when the sand was frosted in snow and the sea was as grey as slate. She knocked at the bungalow door, and Aster let her in. She had expected this, if not so soon.

Sylvia's nose and upper lip were eaten away by blight, and the disease had begun to work on the lower rims of her eyes. It had moved quickly. She clutched a swaddled Ty to her, or what was left of him. Aster held her breath against the smell of spoiled meat.

She drew Sylvia into the living room and made her sit in a threadbare armchair. Sylvia grabbed at Aster's hand, not letting her move away, and then her dam burst and she cried like a child. Aster stood there until Sylvia stopped sobbing, then pulled her hand free.

"Give me that," Aster said, and reached for the damp mass of blankets Sylvia held against herself. For a moment Sylvia looked at her through glossed eyes, not understanding. Then she released Ty's body to Aster's keeping.

"We'll bury him in the morning," Aster said. The taste of death wrapped around her tongue and seeped down her throat. "He'll be alright on the porch until then."

And without waiting for a reaction from Sylvia, she took the small body out the back door of the bungalow and left it on the cracked slab patio. She tucked the blankets closely around it. She did not want to see.

When she went back in Sylvia hadn't moved from the chair. Her coat was stained like a butcher's smock, and the rotten smell still hung in the air. Aster opened the front and side windows to let the cold wind clean the air.

"How did you get here?" Aster said, breathing deeply, shivering in her nightclothes.

"Drove. Then walked. I have nowhere to go," Sylvia said. "There's no one left who wants me."

Aster gave up and closed the windows again.

"How long have you had the blight?"

Sylvia looked away. "Before I was pregnant. That made it worse, I think."

* * * *

After the morning's silent ceremony Sylvia went back to the bungalow. Aster stayed behind to pray, she said, for Ty's safe passage. Once Sylvia was gone Aster unearthed the sad shrunken body and gave it to the sea.

When Ty had sunk beneath the surface Aster drew her sigils in the sand, calling. The waves came up but would not wash over them, swept in at an angle that left her marks behind. She drew the lines again, further down the sand, but still the sea refused to take them. When she sliced her finger deeply on the mirror's frame and retraced the lines in red, the sea came up, hungry, and wiped the sand clean.

She held the mirror steady to see what it reflected, careful not to smear it with blood. He was there, older. His dark hair was a mess, but his eyes burned clean.

Aster smiled to herself, and put the mirror away.

* * * *

The winter wore on, longer than it had ever been. Aster found she didn't mind having Sylvia there. She was like a ghost in the tiny house, tragic and nearly invisible.

"What's left out there?" Aster asked her.

Sylvia cast her eyes down, shy or embarrassed. "Not much more than here," she said. "Everyone just sort of…went wandering off. The world is getting empty."

Aster went over to her then, put her arms around Sylvia's crumbling, bony shoulders. "We're still here," she said. "That's got to count for something."

Sylvia smiled wanly and shrugged.

"I have an idea," Aster said. "If the car starts, we can take a ride."

"To where?"

"Wherever."

Aster dug through the kitchen drawers until she found the keys. She bundled herself and Sylvia in sweatshirts and sweaters and coats, and tucked an old crocheted afghan around Sylvia once she was settled in the passenger seat.

"Ready?" Aster said. She felt a flutter of excitement at the thought of driving away. She turned the key. Silence. Not even the click of the starter. She tried again, turning the key harder, afraid it might snap. Her eyes blurred with tears, sudden and unwanted.

Sylvia sat quietly, breathing steam into the cold space of the car, until Aster finished crying and brought her back into the house.

* * * *

The next day while Sylvia still slept Aster walked to the rotten end of the pier, where the pilings had broken and spilled part of the boardwalk down into the water. The remaining boards were spongy underfoot. She braced herself, as if her stance could save her if they collapsed.

She slit her palm open across the old scar and threw her blood into the sea, the salt of her veins enriching the salt in the water. A storm swirled up from nothing, the wind a solid force, sharp pellets of ice salting the pier and her hair. The wind caught in her hair, pulling it loose of its clips and spinning it into a twisted crown, catching on her cheap earrings and silver chains. In its howling the storm told her things, dredging them from the muddy deeps, sucking them away from farther shores.

But for all the frenzy of the storm, the sea itself lay calm and smooth before her, its swells as quiet as sleeping breath. Aster wiped ice from her eyes. Through the clear glass of the waters she could see the sunless white face of a young boy, floating up toward the surface like a balloon. The boy's eyes opened beneath a film of water, blue as her own. His mouth opened, a grey oval, and inside the reflection of her face.

She shrieked and covered her eyes, and the wind dropped away, the waves resumed their pulse. Aster climbed quickly back up the slick boards, away from what she had seen.

* * * *

Sylvia died one dark morning, her face a filigree of black scabs and ash. Aster buried her in the wet sand under the pier. She would be safe there. Aster knew that no one would come to the pier any more. There had been no lights in Ocean Gate since summer ended. That part of the world was over.

Sand from the grave clung to Aster's hands. She scrubbed it into the black threads of blight that knit their pattern on her own skin.

* * * *

At last the weather turned, cold grey winter sliding into chill grey spring. Aster had given up on marking time. The mirror had shown her things she couldn't read, her son's face, her own, echoes of each other. She missed her nameless boy. She missed Sylvia. She went back to the sea.

The pier had suffered from the winter's storms. The farthest end where she had once stood had tumbled into the surf, the wood smashed into jagged fretwork. Aster went as far as she could. She breathed deeply. The air was still cold enough to hurt.

She sliced deep into her hand, ready to draw her bloody patterns in the air. But there was no blood. She was dry as salt. The blight had drained her.

The sea needed blood. It fed him. The sea would not return him without it. Her heart fluttered in her chest, the thought of such loss overwhelming.

She stumbled farther down the broken staircase of planking, splinters digging into her black, weathered hands. She had to reach the water. From the slumping end of the pier she threw the mirror into the sea, as far as she could, as deep as she could reach. The water closed over it, hiding it, and became as still as the glass it had swallowed. She waited.

Behind her, footsteps creaked and rang hollow on the crumbling boards as what made them climbed down. Aster stood still, impatient, her eyes on the sea. Sharp breath and the heat of another body fell on her naked neck. The water threw back a reflection of what stood with her. Cloudy blue eyes. Tangled black hair hair. He had grown up. She had read it right.

"Mother," he said. When he embraced her it burned like acid, like an electric shock. His touch charred her skin and blackened the bones beneath. Her eyes stung without tears to shed. She had no more blood in her to quench the fire.

▲

Vicious Circles

by Paul Dale Anderson

"Are you sure I'll be accepted?" I asked Sara.

"Absolutely," she said. "It was the Sidhe who asked me to extend the invitation." Sara pronounced the celtic "Sidhe," or seer, as a very sibilant "She."

"Why me? I thought men were forbidden to attend Lughnasadh circles."

"One man, each year, is welcome to attend. This year you, Samuel, are that man. You shall be the symbolic embodiment of the god Lugh."

"Why me?" I asked again.

"Because the Sidhe has divined it is your time. You have power, and you have skills. This year you are like unto the god."

The Sidhe was the woman chosen to wail the Aos Si from abodes in other worlds into our own world. If the wind were right on those special nights when the veils were thinnest, one might hear the Sidhe's wail with mortal ears. Those who have heard her, named her the Banshee.

I'm a witch. Well, technically, I'm not a witch. I'm a warlock or a wizard. Women are witches. Men are something else entirely.

I didn't think I—or any man—would ever be welcomed into a gathering of witches on Lughnasadh, the day of first harvest. Traditionally, women made sacrifices—oblations—of corn and raspberries and bilberries at exactly midnight on the night of July 31. In days of yore, women—maidens, mothers, and crones alike—were the planters and harvesters of corn and the gatherers of berries. Men, always too busy husbanding or hunting meat on the hoof during warm summer months, couldn't be bothered with trivialities such as planting or harvesting.

Therefore, men seldom, if ever, were said to be present at Lughnasadh festivals. Imagine my surprise when Sara invited me to attend her coven's circle this Lughnasadh eve.

There are four auspicious times of the year when the doors between worlds creak open: Imbolc (em-bok), Beltane (beel-teen), Samhain (sow-wen), and Lughnasadh (lew-nasa). If I were to acquire the magical powers I desired, including the knowledge of when I was destined to die, I needed to be present in the women's circle on the morning of August 1 when the doors between worlds opened.

So, when Sara invited me to attend the Lughnasadh festival in the faery wood, I hesitated only briefly.

We normally think of Beltane as the magical beginning of planting season; Samhain, the day of the dead, as the season's end; Imbolc, the gathering at the well, as the preparatory cleansing time; and Lughnasadh, the gathering at the mound in the woods, as the time of first reaping.

Legends say that if, precisely at midnight on July 31, the Banshee makes appropriate sacrifices and calls out to the Aos Si—the fabled faery folk—then the Aos Si enter this world to partake of the harvest. In exchange, one person is allowed to enter the faery realm and access all knowledge of the past, the present, and the future.

I wanted to be that person. It is truly said that knowledge is power. I desired power more than anything else in the world. I had studied all of my life to acquire what little power I possessed. To attain the degree of knowledge and power I desired, I needed to attend the women's circle and walk between worlds.

"Yes," I agreed. "I will be honored to attend."

"Excellent," Sara said. "I will meet you at your home and take you to the festival on the eve of Lughnasadh. You must cleanse yourself and dress in ritual garb before nightfall on the last day of July."

I could not believe my luck. Had I not labored for years to acquire the knowledge and skills necessary to walk between worlds? All I lacked was a portal to the faery realm. Until now that portal was forbidden to me.

On the night of July 31st, I bathed and dressed in ritual robe. I would wear robe and sandals only until the bonfires were lit. Then I would shed robe and sandals and enter the circle sky-clad. For one to cross between worlds, one had to be as naked as the day one was born.

Sara was dressed in short shorts and a skimpy halter-top, with colorful Converse sneakers adorning her feet. We had met two years ago in an occult bookshop where we entered into a lengthy conversation that culminated with the wildest sex I'd ever had. Sara was a wild woman in more ways than one, totally uninhibited and uncivilized. She experienced multiple orgasms that seemingly went on forever. I'm ashamed to say, I petered out first. Sara refused to continue on without me and she made me lick her all over until my tongue was as sore as my penis. Finally, she shoved my head out of the way and let me sleep while she finished with her fingers.

That was the one and only time Sara and I made physical love.

We remained friends. We did have phone sex once or twice since, and I imagined Sara's naked body writhing in ecstasy each time I masturbated. I heard her moans and, fool that I was, believed she was thinking of me the same way I was thinking of her.

Perhaps tonight, Lughnasadh eve, I would get lucky. Sara kissed me full on the lips and fondled my naked flesh through the ritual robe. I wondered what it would be like to make love to Sara while twelve other women sat naked in a circle and watched. I wondered if Sara wondered that, too.

When we got into her car, Sara blindfolded me.

"The location of the sacred mound is secret," she said. "No man may know the place."

"Will you take off my blindfold once we get there?"

"That," she said, "is entirely up to the Sidhe."

We drove for what seemed like hours, but it may have been considerably less. Time changes dramatically when one's senses—especially the sense of sight which men rely upon—are even slightly altered.

When the car's forward motion ceased and I heard Sara switch off the engine, I knew we had arrived at the secret mound in the wood.

I heard Sara slip out of her street clothes and tennis shoes, and then I felt her lift off my robe. I stepped out of my sandals by myself. The night air on this last day of July was warm. Sara guided me barefoot through thick brush, and I felt sharp brambles pierce and rake my naked flesh like long fingernails. Warm blood dribbled down my bare arms and my legs like streams of sticky semen after an explosive climax. I needed to stop thinking about sex and concentrate on my surroundings. But how could one stop thinking about sex on a night such as this?

"I am the doorkeeper," said a voice as melodic as a harp. Was that the voice of the Sidhe? Could such a sweet sound come from a Banshee?

"If you intend to walk between worlds this night as our champion," she told me, "you must possess both extensive knowledge and skill. Are you a craftsman, Samuel?"

"I am, my Lady,' said I.

"Are you heroic and resourceful?"

"I am, my Lady."

"Are you a powerful sorcerer?"

"I am, my Lady." I told no lies but the last.

"Many men who want to be our champion are capable craftsmen. Many others are heroic, and some are also quite resourceful. A few, even, are well-versed in sorcery. Why should I allow you to pass into the center of our circle?"

"Because I am all of those things, my Lady. I am a master mason and a skilled craftsman, a smith and a wright. I am brave and resourceful. And I am a powerful sorcerer."

"Do you speak true?"

"I do, my Lady."

"Then you shall pass into the circle and be our champion this night."

I would be their champion, whatever the hell that meant. I didn't dare ask what champion meant, didn't dare show my ignorance. I should have asked. Why was I such a fool not to ask?

I felt the heat of the bonfire as women lit dry kindling beneath felled logs. I smelled smoke fill the air.

Had I lied when I swore to the Sidhe I was a powerful sorcerer? The Sidhe—the Banshee—were said to divine truth from lies. Did this Sidhe know I lied? Or was she as blind as I?

Or, maybe, I didn't tell a lie. Maybe I was more powerful than I knew. Regardless, after tonight what I said would certainly become true and no longer be a lie. Once I crossed over to witness the past, the present, and the future, I would be the most powerful sorcerer ever.

More powerful than Hermes Trismegistus, Doctor Dee, and Nostradamus combined.

Imagine knowing what would happen before it happened. What could be more powerful than that?

I would be like unto a god.

I heard women chanting, and then I heard the wail of the Banshee. What had once been such a sweet voice was now the shriek of a harpy.

I felt winds increase to cyclonic force. I shivered as the cold boreal breezes turned my nakedness into gooseflesh. I felt the sudden presence of the Aos Si—the old ones—who were forebears of the fey. I smelled the stink of rot and decay as if the Aos Si had long been buried beneath the mound upon which I stood.

Suddenly I felt fear unlike anything I have ever known. I felt sharp talons sink into my tendermost flesh and hoist me into the air. I reached for my blindfold and ripped it off.

I saw my body fly toward an open doorway that mysteriously appeared in the sky. It felt as if I moved faster than light as I passed through that portal to enter the faery dimension. There I witnessed all that I had done in my entire life displayed in a linear timeline laid out from my conception until today. I saw myself dressed in ritual robe waiting for Sara's arrival. I saw Sara arrive at my apartment. I saw her tie a black blindfold over my eyes. I saw the whole route we followed to arrive at the wood. I saw the mound in the center of the circle. And I saw the Sidhe.

She was the most hideous creature imaginable.

I heard the siren call of the Banshee as the magical vibrations of the Sidhe's wail unlocked doors between worlds without end. I saw the harbingers of the Aos Si—birds with heads and features of women but the feathered bodies of eagles; no, not eagles but vultures!—pluck me up and fly away with me.

I saw myself cross the threshold and enter the world of the present. And, then, I saw my future.

I saw thirteen women caress me and lick me all over. I saw one of the women—the Sidhe—rip off my genitals and shove a spiked spear into my anus and up my rectum. I felt the tip of that spear puncture my intestines, my lungs, my esophagus, the point of which exited from my bleeding mouth. I saw myself roasted over open bonfires until I was crispy brown and dripping with juices.

And I saw all thirteen women dig in with their fingernails, rip off pieces of my roasted flesh and, after offering me as sacrifice to the Aos Si, devour what remained of me.

And I knew then all the ancient legends were true. Appropriate sacrifice made precisely at midnight on Lughnasadh eve allowed one to cross between worlds to view the past, the present, and the future. What was an appropriate sacrifice? Was it the embodiment of a god?

I saw the exact time of my death and knew how long I had yet to live.

Am I one of the gods now? Yes, I am Aos Si. I inhabit the land of the dead. I am always hungry and feel as if I'm starving for human flesh.

I see the future, and I know that some Lughnasadh eve I will hear the Banshee's wail. When that day comes, I will visit your world to partake of the harvest.

Pray you are not standing on the mound inside the sacred circle in the faery wood when I arrive.

▲

Assorted Shades of Red
by Franklyn Searight

Walter fell down the first five steps of the staircase, slowing down his momentum by grabbing on one of the banister posts, then rose to his knees, more embarrassed than harmed.

"O'm'gosh!" exclaimed Gloria, from the landing above. "Are you hurt?"

"Takes more than a little stumble to harm me," he declared, regaining his feet.

"I know you're as tough as they come, but still…"

"I'm okay. Forget it."

Walter renewed his descent down the remaining steps, saying no more about it, and Gloria followed after him, slowly and cautiously, not wanting to become another victim. She was not nearly as afraid of her agility on the steps as she was about what had come over her seconds earlier. Why had she pushed him in the back just as he moved one foot downward, causing his awkward misstep and loss of balance? She adored her husband, had loved him since their teenage years with an adulation certainly more than just a juvenile crush.

But why, oh why, had she so blatantly shoved him?

Or had she? If his tumble had ended at the bottom, with broken bones or loss of life, it would have been only one more tragedy to a resident of the house.

The couple had only recently signed the papers making Herington Place their own, and were now in the final stages of moving in. Friendly neighbors had recounted stories to them about the place, suggesting all might not be as peaceful there as they expected. Tales were told of accidents happening in the kitchen if one opened the refrigerator late at night, or in the parlor if one stood too close to the harpsicord, or in the darkly-paneled library if one moved an antique from one place to another. Former owners had mentioned odious revenants said to cause inexplicable accidents at the most unexpected times. All of the stories were listened to by Walter and Gloria with healthy skepticism, and sometimes outright disbelief.

"Take your time, Hon," advised her husband, waiting for her at the foot of the steps.

"I will… I will. No matter how much of a hurry I'm in, my middle name is not 'reckless'."

Walter took her hand as she reached the bottom, failing to notice the relief in her hazel eyes she had descended the stairway without a tumble.

"How about we have a little snack before starting?" Walter suggested.

"One of your better ideas," was her response. "I'm famished."

"Well, I'm just hungry. I had nothing but toast and strawberry jam for breakfast."

"Then eat we shall."

Gloria stepped ahead, making her way to the kitchen, with Walter close behind, when the sudden yapping of Mitzi, the family terrier, could be heard. For the time being, to keep it out from under their feet, it was being kept in the nearby laundry room, unable to venture out and look around as she was usually free to do.

"I'll take her out, misses," said Molly, the newly acquired housekeeper who had just entered the room, her large, ruddy hands clinching her angular hips. "'Fraid she'll relieve herself inside, if 'en I don't."

"Thank you, Mol," said Gloria. "You're a blessing."

Nearly to the kitchen, they could hear the sounds of a door opening, and tiny paws scratching on linoleum.

It had been a fatiguing day so far. They had arrived shortly before seven to meet with the movers and give them final directions on what they were expected to do. Gloria provided them with a map of the entire interior, along with a list coordinating where certain pieces of furniture were to be placed, and another list where other furnishings in large cartons were to be left. The placement of assorted odds and ends, their voluminous books, dishes, bathroom articles, etcetera, would be taken care of by themselves, another day.

After sandwiches and bowls of tomato soup, Walter went to the library where he dusted off the enormous lengths of shelving spaces, and sprayed copious amounts of Pledge on the dark, aged oak. A dealer in rare books, who intended to sell them from their house, there was a lot of work for him to do. He looked up as his wife entered the room.

"We don't have nearly enough books to fill all the shelving space we have," he informed her, blowing the dust off one of them.

"We can put other things on the empty shelves to use as place holders until you acquire more volumes."

"Oh, sure. That's what I've always wanted: stuffed animals and assorted knickknacks, put on display. It'll be the show place of the town, and book collectors will line up outside our door to examine our treasures."

"Don't be cynical, dear; give it time. Next week you can have some of the more valuable pieces at our New York store brought here, and you can get down to your mail order business without all the distractions."

"It'll be nice to have everything under one roof, but by then there'll be so many books here we'll have to build extra storage space."

"I didn't think of it. Maybe we'll build an addition onto the house, just to hold them all."

"Yuck! Bad idea! Costs money, and our pile of shekels is dwindling."

"Something will come up. Maybe I can sell another painting in a few days."

"You wouldn't mind?"

"Anything to make you a happy hubby. You'll have your mail-order book business to keep you out of mischief, and I'll have the drafty loft in the attic where I can spend endless hours painting landscapes and abstract scenes to dazzle the capricious art world."

"Dazzle is right. You've already achieved more success than most artists realize in a lifetime."

"Luck. Pure luck. I just happened to stumble on a new media innovation the critics seem to appreciate. But enough palaver. The decorators will be here tomorrow; we have to get the furnishings in place today so we can show them where certain pictures and drapes are to be hung."

"And the roofers will be here in a few days to replace some of the broken shingles we noticed."

"I just hope they don't tell us the entire roof will have to be replaced, dear."

"Oh, our aching bank account. You had to mention it, did you? Our leaking wallet is squeaking out of protest."

"Let it complain. As long as the market holds up for my paintings, the green stuff will flow in to pay the expenses."

"And it's a darn good thing, too. Selling books will eventually be a money maker, but until then…well, your pay checks will have to carry us through the bleak times ahead."

"In the meantime, I'm off to the loft. Need to set up my work area if I expect to get anything done. Oh, and can you please check the staircase—three steps from the bottom? Some of the carpeting seems to be coming loose."

"I'll get to it soon. Probably something for our handyman to repair. Jim's the best. Right now, I need to look over the first edition copy of *Wuthering Heights* forwarded today from our New York store."

"Emily Bronte, huh? Sounds like something you'll sell quickly, provided you price it right."

"Well, it's valued at ninety-five hundred dollars on Abe's. I'll begin a bit lower. Depends upon the condition, of course. It's a first American edition with a new cover, hot off the press in eighteen forty-eight."

"Sounds like a very nice acquisition."

Walter handled the Bronte volume with delicate care, not wanting to mar any of the pages and detract from its value, assuring himself it was in at least good-plus condition and able to command a decent price. He put it in the library safe, straightened the assorted papers and invoices on his desk, switched off the light, and headed to the kitchen.

On his way, he stopped to investigate the rip in the carpeting. It was a negligible blemish, but one he should attend to before it became more pronounced. Perhaps Mitzi had found a small end she could grab onto, and worried away at it, playfully, causing the damage. Also, three carmine dots seemed to have been unobtrusively sprinkled onto it. He was fairly certain there had been no sign of the flaws during their initial inspection of the stairway. Gloria or he would have noticed them. He was no expert, but they seemed to be diminutive blemishes repaired without great cost. He mentioned this to Gloria later and the incident was soon forgotten.

The couple was visited at night by Morpheus who brought to them little relief from an exciting and busy day. Walter slept restlessly and experienced disturbing dreams, but the visions were not remembered when he awoke. All he could recall was the stentorian voice informing him he was living in *her* house, and not his own. He had jerked awaked, and wondered for a while what it was all about.

The next morning, Walter was the first to go down the stairs to start the coffee perking, when he reached the third step from the bottom and stopped. Dumbfounded, he saw the dots were gone, and in their place was a large magenta splotch covering half the step. His face blanched as he saw the paw prints within the smear continuing downward and onto the oriental carpet below. He touched the marred area, still wet, and grimaced at its tacky feel.

This simply could not be, and yet it was. He looked at the ceiling high above, and could see no ruby drops trickling down, no cracks or seams through which blood could drip. Troubled and puzzled, he thoughtfully considered the spectacle interrupting his morning routine. He sat on the step above, careful to avoid the colorful wetness.

"What cha doing down there, dear?" came an inquisitive voice from above.

He looking around and craned his neck upward to see his wife on the landing above, still in her robe, looking at him.

"Come on down," he invited, "but be careful where you step. There's a gooey mess here, and it's still wet."

"Oh, m'gosh!" she exclaimed, reaching the step above him. "Did you fall down? Strike your head?"

"Nothing like that, Hon. This is what I found a few moments ago."

"Is it blood?"

"I think so. I poked my finger into it—still a little wet and sticky—but I can't be certain."

"Well, what else could it be? It'll have to be cleaned up, for sure. Wonder what sort of cleaning agent will get rid of it."

"Don't know, but Molly will. She's adept at this sort of thing."

"She is, but what if she can't clean it off? Maybe we'll have to replace the entire carpeting."

"Oh, sure. More expenses we don't need. I think she'll work wonders on it, though, like everything else she tackles. At worst, we'll just have to carpet the last three steps."

"The last three…?"

It was then Gloria noticed the prints continuing downward, and onto the floor below.

"Mitzi!" she exclaimed at sight of the markings. "The naughty dog has walked in the mess."

"Must have," Walter agreed. "She has free range everywhere in the house. Must have come down earlier this morning."

"Probably wanted one of us to take her for her stroll," Gloria conjectured. "She's probably waiting for us at the door, holding the leash in her mouth. Poor thing didn't realize she was leaving a gory trail behind her."

"No, of course she had no idea. But why did she come down so early? She usually waits for one of us to get up first."

"Dunno. She's a dog. Guess she has her reasons."

"Inscrutable cur. Let's get the coffee brewing so we can feel human again."

Gloria laughed, and took the last three steps down, careful not to step in the wide crimson swath, nor the prints made by their little dog, while Walter made his way to the kitchen.

He was holding the coffee pot, and about to put in the filter, when a penetrating scream rocked his senses, reverberating throughout the ancient manse.

Gloria!

Her screaming did not cease, and peal after peal reverberated throughout the homestead. Walter nearly dropped the pot, setting it down, and rushed off in the direction from which came the hysterical shrieks. The cries led him to the front portal where Gloria stood, her hands upraised to cover much of her face.

"God!" Walter began, skidding to a stop as he saw the small mound of fur lying before the door, and realized what it was provoking his wife's outburst of horror.

Mitzi lay there, her body spread about the foyer, her neck chewed nearly through, almost decapitating her. Fur was smeared and matted with an icky claret coloration; one leg was gnawed off at the haunch and half eaten; and her glassy eyes stared off at an angle toward the door. A brief touch revealed the cherry gore had not yet dried; the grisly carnage was relatively fresh.

"It's awful," exclaimed Gloria, turning and burying her head in Walter's chest.

He said nothing for a time. Something had somehow made its way into the house, brutally attacked their pet, killing and feeding off of it. Another dog? A pack of rats?

"Only God knows what happened down here while we were upstairs sleeping."

"Walter, whatever did this was in our house…maybe it's still here. Mitzi never had a chance. Whatever it was, it grabbed her, and it…and it…"

"Get a grip on yourself, Hon," urged Walter, still gripping her firmly. "Whatever did this is no longer here."

"Maybe not—but something is—something causing a tingling sensation to sprint up and down my spines. Is our house haunted?"

"Not likely; not unless you believe in that sort of thing. Do you?"

"Well, no. Of course not."

"Whatever did this is something physical; something I can get my hands around and…and…and, well, I'll have Jim and Molly clean up this mess, and dispose of what's left of the body."

"Dispose of it? Like leaving it for the trash collector to pick up on Thursday? Oh, Walter, we can't set it outside by the curb to be ground up like fifteen pounds of hamburger."

"I'll have Jim dig a hole in the back yard and bury Mitzi there—what's left of her."

"Well, have him to do it as humanely as he can. I'm going back to bed and have myself a good cry. I loved the little sweetheart."

Walter nodded. He was not as attached to the little pooch as was his wife, but he was quite fond of it, too. He watched her as she ascended the staircase, and then went to find their caretaker.

* * * *

A week had passed, but the process of grieving had not; it would come later. The soiled carpeting had not been cleaned, although preliminary attempts had been made with Mollierox and other solvents that did little good.

The rug remained discolored, a distraction and an annoyance with which they would have to live for a while. Fortunately, no additional calamities had threatened their happiness. Gloria had established herself in the attic loft, readying her paintings for a showing to be held the following month, and Walter had been able to move a wide array of volumes from his New York store to his library, shelve them, and send out a series of catalogues to his clientele.

There had been no return of the ferocious animal mangling their ill-fated pet, nor manifestations of any other sort. Even the voice penetrating Walter's sleep period had been silent much of the time. Life was progressing nicely.

It was evening when Walter finished pricing his latest acquisition, a good-plus copy of King's *The Shining*, with "First Edition" printed on the copyright page. It was a volume he would have preferred to keep for himself, but their need for funds seemed to be inexhaustible, and he was reasonably certain it would not take long before one of his wealthier clients snatched it up. He put it on-line for the eyes of his more important speculators, priced it at the highest amount he dared, asking four thousand two-hundred dollars for it, and locked it in his safe for the night, along with his poor copy of Jane Austin's three-volume, eighteen thirteen, first edition set of *Pride and Prejudice*. He checked to be certain the lock was secured, and went to bed.

The following morning, Walter went to his computer, unaware their blissfulness had come to an end.

One of his clients had already accepted his offering of the King book, which both excited and saddened him, but he recovered his perspective, knowing the book would be going to a dedicated connoisseur of fine editions who would prize it as much as he would. Happily, he went to the vault and withdrew the book. Surprised, he noted immediately things were not as they should be: An angry magenta gash streaked across the cover, leaking over onto the binding, as though someone or something had bled all over it. He was aghast at the grievous manner with which his trophy had been altered as he carried it over to his desk,

But how? The book had been sealed inside his safe, and only he and Gloria knew the combination.

And why? What reason could anyone have to desecrate his prized possession?

Would he be able to repair the damage? Yes, it would be possible, but a new cover would have to be made for it, a costly procedure, and the value would be considerably reduced. He would have to notify the buyer and offer it again, but at a much lower price. How could this have happened? A security system guarded the premises, and anyone breaking into their domicile would immediately set off a shrilling alarm, awakening everyone in the house. Had the malefactor been able to somehow silence it? It was extremely unlikely, but not impossible.

The remorse he suffered continued as he opened the volume and carefully turned its pages, only stopping when he reached page twenty-two. The next page should have been twenty–three, but was instead twenty-five. Twenty-three and twenty-four were missing, leaving serrations where they had been ripped from the book. Frantically, anger mounting, he turned the pages until he reached one hundred sixty-six and found where the same desecration had taken place. The next page had been torn out! Quickly continuing, he learned the villain had not stopped with those two pages, but had ripped out another four.

His oh-so-desirable book had been ruined, beyond repair.

He looked around to see if anyone had heard the expletives bursting from his mouth. A loud scream of rage would have followed, but he was able to contain the impulse as Gloria entered the room, carrying with her a cup of coffee.

"Time for a break, dear," she said.

Walter held the book up for her to see. "Thank you, but a good stiff drink, a double or a triple, would be better. Just look at this."

Roughly, he shoved the worthless volume over to her, which she took and settled herself into a nearby chair.

Walter studied her face and noted the gathering horror transforming her pleasant countenance into a tinge of pinkish dismay as she scrutinized the cover and then, at his request, turned the pages to twenty-two. The color drained from her face as she came to the defiled leaf. She looked at the ragged tear and hurried on to the next despoiled section. By the time she finished her examination of the book, her creamy countenance was suffused with a rosy blush. Tears were swimming in her eyes, and her hands were shaking.

"What happened?" she asked, the agony in her voice as pronounced as when they had lost their dog.

"You tell me. I don't know. This is the way I found it when I took it from the safe this morning, not fifteen minutes ago."

Gloria nodded, and her glassy eyes began to moisten.

"Walter, there's a presence in this house—something I can't identify with my five senses, but one causing a tingling sensation to crawl up my back like an army of ants, and makes the short hair on my arms stiffen erect."

"That's not quite the feeling I have, but I understand what you mean. Are you suggesting our house is haunted? Possessed? Occupied by some ancient evil living here?"

As soon as he said those words he recalled the poignant voice he had heard at the edge of his dreams asserting house was not theirs.

"Don't know what it is, dear. If I did, maybe we could find some way to chase it away, make it hang around some other place. I wonder if the previous owner of our house knows anything about it?"

"The only way to find out is to ask him—or her. It would probably be a good first step to take."

"Or, maybe we should just swallow our loss and find a different place to live."

"Nothing doing, my sweet, although it might be the most practical solution. But it would be unethical, if not illegal, not to tell the new buyer what we know about the place. Still, we weren't told anything before we signed the papers for this house. Maybe we can sue the seller for damages."

"Sue?"

"It might come to that," said Walter, ponderously. "In the meantime, I'll talk to the realtor who sold us this place, and find out just who the sellers were. Seems to me we should have been entitled to know all about Herington Place before buying it."

"Could this be why we were able to purchase it so inexpensively? Everyone else knew about it, and no one wanted it?"

Walter did not sleep at all well. The knowledge only Gloria and he were aware of the safe's combination, and she might have had something to do with destroying his valued book, was a troubling thought—but one he could not seriously consider, so absolutely certain was he of her veracity. Besides, there were those phantom visions invading what should have been the serenity of his dreams, frightening him, taunting him, hinting of a bizarre presence chosing not to fully reveal itself.

In his dreamscape, an interminable time seemed to pass during which he wandered about deserted glades filled with shifting, shadowy beings cavorting about an unholy altar in the light of flickering bonfires. High above these unsettling scenes rode a cerise moon making it's nocturnal passage across the darkened heavens. Coming to another of the blazing fire pits, he saw the figure of an ancient crone, silhouetted against the sky. She wore a dark cloak and a pointed hat rearing above a pointy nose and up-thrust jaw. Large lips, painted a deep maroon, smiled at him alluringly, while scarlet eyes glared malevolently at him. She signaled to him to come closer with claw like fingers tipped in awful grisliness.

The last thing he wanted to do in this lifetime was to move closer to the gruesome creature. With a herculean effect of will he opened his eyes, and found himself in bed, alert, but gravely perplexed. He reached over to gently touch Gloria; not to awaken her, only to feel the comfort of her presence.

Gloria was not there.

He sat up and looked over at the rumpled blankets where she had been. She must be off to the bathroom, he reasoned, and lay back, waiting for sleep to claim him once again. His eyes closed and his mind drifted off to consider insignificant matters before falling asleep.

He dreamed again of airy vistas, stunted vegetation evolved on far off planets, teaming with ludicrous creatures stalking elusive prey in the darkness of the night. Once again, the awesome hag made an appearance and talked to him with unintelligible, incomprehensible words. She became silent for a spell, glaring at him seductively, and then began to speak again, her scratchy voice now quite clear.

"I love you," she declared. "I want you, and I will have you. Gloria must die."

Again, she gestured to him with claw-like fingers, and again he violently awoke.

His face was immersed with sweat. He looked about. An hour had passed, and Gloria was still absent from her bed. Had she returned and then left again? Or had she been away all this time? Should he look for and find her? Perhaps, but it was not so much her absence causing his inordinate alarm, but the ominous words of the dreadful harridan still resonating in his mind.

The morning sun crept above the horizon with a roseate glow and crawled ever-so-slowly over the bedclothes to Walter's chin, and then to his face, awakening him from what he considered a most unpleasant period of sleep. He arose and went to the bathroom to attend to his ablutions, assuming Gloria was downstairs preparing breakfast. Walking down the corridor leading to the staircase, he passed along the barrier over which could be seen the first floor below, stopping at sight of the thick rope, tied to the railing and dropping downward. He approached closer, staring in perplexity, and yelled for Molly and Jim to come to him at once.

The bulky rope stretched downward, taut, and attached to its looped end was the neck of his wife, her legs dangling a few feet above the floor. Momentarily, he attempted to pull the body upward, then quickly dropped it, realizing it was a poorly chosen action. He raced down the stairs, reached the bottom and stared at the motionless body for a moment. Her neck hung at an awkward angle, and her eyes protruded outward. He was pulling a side table beneath the body as Molly and the handy-man arrived, almost simultaneously and out of breath, and stared in disbelief at what they saw.

Molly fainted dead away. Jim raised stubby fingers to his face, half covering it, and looked at his employer with a blank stare.

"Quick," Walter directed, "up on the table, Jim. Hold her up by her legs, taking the strain of her body off her neck. She might still be alive."

Jim did as he was directed, and as he climbed onto the table he inadvertently touched her legs, causing the body to slightly sway, back and forth, forcing him to steady it before grabbing onto her legs and lifting.

Molly sat up, fidgeting as she opened her eyes, and at sight of Gloria, swooned again.

"I'll get a knife," Walter told his handyman, who was having a difficult time at his task.

He scurried to the kitchen and grabbed a long and sharp butcher knife, then raced back to the lobby where he found Jim, struggling on the table to support the body.

In a haze, Walter handed the knife up to him and he proceeded to hack and saw away at the rope. Within seconds, Gloria was lowered to the floor and laid on the oriental carpeting.

"Quick," he said to the housekeeper, awake again and struggling to her feet, a pinkish tinge erasing the blanched look on her face. "Call Doctor Molnar, and get him over here quickly.

"And then call the police," he added, as she moved off toward the nearest phone.

Walter turned his gaze toward his wife, lying there, motionless, the severed noose hanging loosely about her neck. One side of her head was caked with a burgundy mess, causing him to suspect she had been hit on the head before being strung up. He learned, subsequently, there was nothing he could have been done to save her life. Gloria had already been dead for nearly five hours before he discovered her, her death occurring at about the same time she had been missing from her bed.

"S'funny," mentioned the police detective later on. "This ain't the first time we've had trouble over at this place."

"What do you mean by that?" asked Walter.

"Means I've been here before when we p'lice were needed. Nothing quite as bad as this, though."

"I should hope not."

"You folks have any enemies?"

"None we knew of," Walter answered thoughtfully. "We just moved here." To himself he added, "Just an old shrew of a witch who wouldn't stay buried in her grave."

What had happened to Gloria, Walter surmised, might have been a reenactment of what had occurred to the hoary witch, possibly strung up by an angry populace for reprehensible deeds, but he was to never learn if his supposition was correct. Nothing of a paranormal nature, so far, occurred again within the walls of Herington Place. The newspapers were filled with accounts of the tragedy, and the general conclusion was the place was crawling with spooks. Neighbors choose to walk on the opposite side of the street when passing by, and when Walter eventually put the house up for sale, no one showed any interest in purchasing it. He found himself effectively trapped there, unable to move away.

He continues to live there even now, a frightened man, looking over his shoulder at the slightest sound, fearful the abhorrent lady would someday make an appearance and claim him as her own.

▲

Strange Days in
Old Yandrissa
by John R. Fultz

An Age of Changes had fallen upon Old Yandrissa. The ancient oaks in the forest broke themselves free of the ground and floated light as clouds in the sky. Their exposed roots sprouted whispering masses of leaves and singing blossoms. The waterfall at the end of the River Oath began flowing upward, losing itself in a pearly spray among the clouds. The lake below the Marble Cliffs dried into a mire, where fish died or sprouted toad-like limbs, then crawled into the high grass to die. New-born babies in seven villages sprouted wings from their backs and flew away like pink doves chased by wailing, earthbound mothers.

Cookfires leapt from their hearths and took the shapes of beasts, raging and burning until quenched with buckets of water. The tops of the distant mountains were no longer covered by white blankets of ice and snow; they danced with sparkling emerald flames instead. Old men and women grew young again and were stoned from their villages, accused of witchcraft or demonic possession. Some of these newly young elders wandered off to live on the green slopes below the blazing peaks.

During this season of impossibilities the king's soldiers discovered a vagrant sleeping in the road. He lay curled in the dust, clutching a stringless harp to his chest. His garments were gaudy rags, and his gray-white beard was long enough to reach his spindly knees. A month earlier every horse in the kingdom had died and rotted into piles of bleached bones in a single day. On the third night following their deaths, the equine skeletons had risen up and galloped into the yellow hills.

The soldiers stopped their march to lift the vagabond off the ground, believing him to be a neglected corpse. When he began to sing in a beautiful voice, they released him and drew their blades. The old man plucked at the empty harp as if it held invisible strings. His rheumy eyes blinked incessantly, but he was not blind.

The troop's captain was young Ligeus Midorus, and he heard ghostly strains of music emanating from the harp, while his men heard only the old man's voice. Ligeus stood enraptured by the harp song until his second-in-command shook his arm, ruining his reverie. He ordered that the singer be bound and taken along for an audience with the king.

"Beware! Do not touch me…," said the vagrant. He stopped singing to brush away the soldiers' grasping hands. His voice carried a foreign accent, and he waved a bony finger at them. "For your own safety, I beg you keep away."

"You walk the King's Highway," said Ligeus, "without fare or insignia. But your strange aspect is of interest to me…as it will be to our king. Calm yourself, and we will do you no harm."

"I warn you," said the vagrant, clutching his dead harp. "I am cursed with three demons that live in my beard. They will let no harm come to me save that which they invent." He stroked his long, tangled facial hair as if soothing a rabid hound.

The soldiers laughed, all but Captain Ligeus. "Take him," he ordered.

They grabbed the singer's arms and tied his wrists with a strong rope. One man attempted to pry the stringless harp from his tight fingers. "No," said Ligeus. "Let him keep it."

They marched along the royal road, winding through dry hills that once were green and capped with flowers. The soles of the singer's feet were hard and dark as leather. Ligeus wondered from what distant land the man had traveled.

"Where are your demons now, fool?" asked a soldier, sunlight flaring off his golden helm.

The singer shrugged. "They must want you to take me. Otherwise…"

"Do you have a name?" asked Ligeus.

"I used to."

"Lost it, have you? Well…I will call you Pebble since we found you in the road." The soldiers guffawed at their captain's jest.

Pebble nodded. "Perchance I might play…and sing…for your king?"

Ligeus smiled. "Perhaps you will."

As they passed beneath the verdant sky-forest, Pebble stared upward in awe. Ligeus remembered the words his cousin King Thamion had shared with him over bowls of purple wine. "This is an age of miracles and curses," said the king. "The priests blame me for offending the gods, though I have done nothing to affront them. The sages say the gods themselves have gone mad. The people…they are too afraid to blame either gods or king. But this precarious state will not last, cousin. If these strange happenings continue, eventually everyone will blame me…and revolution will foam in their cups."

"What can we do, Majesty?" asked Ligeus. "Arrest the priests?"

"No," said the king. "Too rash. No...I need a Wise One. Someone versed in the working of miracles and curses. I need a *wizard*, Ligeus. Go and find me one."

Ligeus led a cohort of men into the mountains, and beneath the green fires of the peaks they sought the hovels of wisemen and chased rumors of magic workers. After twenty-two days of scrabbling and climbing, they found nothing but hungry tigers and moaning spirits that haunted their camps at night. However, on this day he had something to bring before his regal cousin...someone who played a mystic song on invisible strings. Surely this longbeard must be a wizard. A bit mad, perhaps, but who wasn't in these days? He would present his rare Pebble and let the king decide its worth.

Sunlight filtered through the aerial forest. A white dove descended from the floating branches and perched on Pebble's shoulder. Marching straight ahead, Pebble seemed not to notice the bird. Ligeus nearly stumbled over his own spear when a crimson hand with black claws crept out of the man's shaggy beard. It grabbed the bird and pulled it beneath the mangy fibers in a rush of displaced feathers. A faint crunching sound came from Pebble's chest. Ligeus looked at his men for signs of their marvel, but as with the phantom music earlier, he seemed to be the only one who noticed.

He spoke of this to no one as the white spires of Yandrissa rose against the blue horizon. All that truly mattered was this: He would not be returning to the king empty-handed.

* * * *

The city was crowded with thirst and hunger. The marble streets stank of fear. Seasonal crops had withered when the rains ceased to fall, and children went hungry in every house. Even the highbloods despaired as the fruit in their orchards dried and fell like stones. Beggars moaned on every corner and cutthroats lurked in every alley. Now that crimes and murders could be blamed on the strange phenomena of the age, brutal men took what they wanted and blamed it on the gods. Those who represented the gods, the Priests of the White Temple, blamed the king.

Thamion sat anxious on his throne, his jeweled crown heavy as an iron yoke. The finery of his court was muddied by a constant stream of complainants and captives. It was impossible to tell which outlandish claims were true, from "A winged lion appeared and ate that pig!" to "A devil flew out of the well and ravished that maiden, not I!" In the absence of facts and credible witnesses, he sided for the plaintiff half the time and the defendant the other half. It was his last attempt at fairness...and after thirty cases a day, he no longer truly cared. He thought only of the bitter priests and how they poisoned the peoples' minds against him.

When word reached the king of Ligeus's return, he ordered the throne room cleared of all petitioners and prisoners. He wished to banish High Priest Norum from the hall as well, but the head of the Great Temple was within his rights to keep a place near the king. Norum lingered beside the royal dais in orange robes and spiked miter, waiting for the day when his influence would exceed Thamion's. The king had never liked the sallow-faced priest, and now he secretly feared him. If only one of these strange curses would fall upon the White Temple…

Ligeus and his troop entered the hall, spilling dust from their cloaks across the marble floor. The king had ordered them present immediately, giving them no time to bathe or make their "guest" more presentable. Courtiers and fellow captains cheered the return of Ligeus, who met their approval with a polite smile and a raise of his spear. He stepped before the throne and sank to one knee, as did his men. That left the longbeard with the broken harp standing awkwardly among them.

"What is this, Ligeus?" asked the king.

Ligeus rose and gestured at the old coot. "Majesty, I present to you the wizard Pebble."

The king smiled as he gazed upon the ragged man. Pebble stuttered and shook his head. "P-pardon me, sire," he pleaded through his outland accent. "I am no w-wizard…m-merely a singer of songs…a fool for your delight."

The king turned to Ligeus. "What does he mean?"

Ligeus's smile was like molded bronze. "He is modest, Majesty! Ask to hear his song, and you will see his power."

Thamion noted the presence of his young queen, Camryl, who had entered the hall without fanfare. Her flaxen hair glimmered in the light from arched windows, and her large eyes were green as the leaves of the distant sky-trees. She clutched the hem of her golden robe and stared at the stranger. The shadow of fear darkened her sweet face.

"Sing then!" commanded the king.

Pebble bowed again and raised his feeble instrument.

"His harp has no strings!" said the High Priest.

Ligeus raised a hand to silence the man.

Pebble stroked the nonexistent strings and his voice rose fine and tremulous, weaving the story of a beautiful queen in some far land. Her loveliness was such that stars would extinguish themselves in envy when she walked through her gardens at night. Her king was a kind and simple man, yet she did not love him. The curse of her beauty was that it made her dissatisfied, and she plotted against her husband. The king's best friend was a bard who kept him entertained with ancient tales and filled his court with joy. Yet the bard, like the king, was only a man. He succumbed to the beauty of the faithless queen. Together they poisoned the good king and fled, seeking sanctuary in the land of his enemies. In the mountains, the faithless queen betrayed her lover and left him to be devoured by tigers. She married the enemy of her dead husband, who sent his armies across the border to wage bloody conquest. In time, the faithless queen grew tired of her new husband, who was now king of both realms. One night she prayed to the Gods of Darkness and they transformed her into a tiger. She devoured her new king and fled into the mountains, where she still roams to this day, hoping a king will venture near to sate her endless hunger.

When the song was done, King Thamion wiped at his wet cheeks and saw his Camryl doing the same. Even hardy Ligeus was moved, and his men shuffled restlessly to hide their riven emotions. The only member of the court who stood with dry eyes, apparently unmoved by the performance, was High Priest Norum.

"I heard no music, Majesty!" complained the priest. "Only this fool's warbling..."

The king glared at Norum. "His words were so beautifully delivered, so strikingly sung, he did not need accompaniment. All of my court understands that, priest. How is that you do not?"

Ligeus shifted uncomfortably and cleared his throat. "I heard *music*, Majesty. I heard the strings of this wizard's harp clear as day, golden as dawn's first glow." He glanced toward his men, who caught his unspoken command.

"Aye," said a soldier and then another. "I heard it, too! As did I! Sweet golden strings!"

Thamion grinned at Ligeus, his most loyal supporter. Perhaps there was magic in this vagabond. "Welcome to my court, Lord Pebble," said the king. "My court needs a wizard, so I will engage your services indefinitely."

"B-but I am no wi—" Pebble began.

"Outrage!" cried the High Priest, stalking toward Pebble. "This man is a fraud—nothing more than a beggar selling lies to the court. First you offend the gods, Majesty, and now you fall for the falsehoods of this... this..."

All at once, three crimson shadows blew like a great wind from Pebble's twisting beard. High Priest Norum staggered backward beneath a trio of gangly demons. They tore at his robes with black claws. The mouths in their oblong heads opened impossibly wide, brimming with pointed fangs, tongues slavering like serpents. They tore raw hunks from the priest's obese body. Blood spurted across the white marble, a few drops even staining the king's sandals. The panic of shuffling guards, the drawing of steel from a half-hundred sheathes, the clanking of shields, and the screaming of women—all these filled the hall while Pebble stood pale before the slaughter. The king disguised his pleasure as the three demons ripped the High Priest to shreds at the foot of his throne.

Once the demons had rapidly devoured all but Norum's bones, they flowed as oily clouds back into the tangle of Pebble's beard. A few stray drops of crimson stained the snowy locks. A calm of shocked silence fell over the court. The priest's bloody bones lay in a heap, an offering of pulp and gristle for the mighty king of Yandrissa.

"Forgive me, Great Majesty!" Pebble wailed. He fell to his knees on the steps of the dais. "I did not do this thing! Long have I been cursed with these three evil spirits. They deny my will and ride me like a beast of burden. Although they will let none harm me—for they relish my eternal suffering—they take the lives of those they wish. I beg you—do not seek vengeance upon me...or these fiends will slay your soldiers even to the last man." He wept like a broken man upon the royal carpet.

After a moment of deliberation, Thamion rose and helped the old man to his feet. "Fear not," he told the wizard who denied his power. He whispered now so that none else in the court might hear him. "You have done me a great service this day. Go now and rest... Servants will attend you. We will speak at moonrise."

Quivering servants led the wizard toward the guest chambers while Thamion spoke to his court. High Priest Norum was the one who had offended the gods, he said, by speaking against their chosen ruler. "Let all the priests learn this lesson well...as they convene to choose Norum's successor." The word went out, and the hall cleared as the sun sank into the west.

Thamion clapped his cousin on the back. "Good Ligeus, my right hand," he smiled. "You have brought me a great power. I knew you would not fail me."

Ligeus swallowed a lump in his throat. "The man seems ignorant of his own power," he said. "He may be...too dangerous."

Thamion took the hand of his young queen and bade farewell to the warrior.

"These are dangerous times, cousin."

He smiled and left Ligeus standing in the blood-smeared hall.

* * * *

In a cloistered garden at the edge of the palace grounds, Queen Camryl sat upon a bench surrounded by withered blossoms and shriveled grapes. A stone fountain full of dust stood before her, its carved mermaid figure staring with onyx eyes. The queen yearned for a time not so long ago, when the fountain's waters sang for her and fruits hung ripe among the flowering vines.

A hooded figure with broad shoulders approached through the dusk. She trembled, remembering the days of sunshine and racing hearts. She was still young, but she felt so old. As the tall figure neared the light of her candle, a lean face glimmered beneath the hood, and the weight of invisible years fled suddenly from her. It was only in these rare stolen moments that she became herself again, a maiden of twenty with love dancing in her breast like the candle's flame.

Ligeus doffed his hood and wrapped her in his powerful arms. She melted against his chest, inhaling his scent of pomegranate and sweat. She met his lips with her own, and for an instant, the palace, the kingdom, and all their troubles disappeared.

They pulled apart and her worry returned.

"He knows…" she breathed. "The wizard…he knows!"

"Shhhh," Ligeus quieted her, stroked her cheek with a callused hand. "He cannot know. His wits are addled. He does not even know that he is a wizard."

"But the story…the tale he sang…why else would he choose it? He must know. And he killed poor Norum… What does it mean for us?"

Ligeus stared at the parched mermaid. "It means we must be patient. You must be patient. The likelihood of holy revolt has been quelled for the time being. But Thamion's new ally is not so trustworthy… Perhaps the longbeard's demons will devour him just as they did the priest."

"And if they do not?" asked Camryl. She pressed herself against his back, nuzzling his neck with her chin. He clutched her hand against his chest.

"There are other ways," he whispered. "Other means to remove my cousin and give Yandrissa to its queen."

"Shall I…continue?" she asked.

"You must." He turned to meet her eyes. "This Age of Changes must continue until you take the throne. Only then may the land return to its healthy state, and the people will revere you for bringing them salvation."

Camryl stiffened. "I am afraid, Ligeus. So much suffering already. What if I cannot stop these things? What if I unleash something over which I have no control?"

Ligeus grinned. "You sound like Old Pebble," he said. He grabbed her frail shoulders in his hands. "You must be strong. Remember the ways your mother taught you. The magic serves you… You do not serve the magic."

Camryl nodded. He always gave her courage, even made her believe she was every bit the sorceress her mother used to be. But hadn't her mother lost control in the end? Hadn't eldritch forces torn the life from her when Thamion's soldiers stormed the gates of Draza? Yes, her mother had been betrayed by the book.

But her mother did not have Ligeus at her side.

"Be strong," he said, and kissed her again. A current strong as lightning flowed from him into her, and she smiled. She wished he would take her right there among the faded garden, but it was too dangerous.

"Where is he now?" asked Ligeus.

"In his war room," she said, "talking with the wizard."

"Well," he said, pulling her close. "We have some time then…"

Despite her worries, he took her on the ground, bringing her to bliss on a blanket of dead leaves. Here was the vigor she needed to face what was ahead.

In the light of the waning moon, she slipped back into the palace, leaving a trail of desiccated blossoms.

She was no longer afraid.

* * * *

One morning, a storm of flaming hailstones arrived with the dawn. The smoldering rain set fire to several city precincts and a dozen outlying farms. The crops that had survived the drought were now burned, and the specter of famine reared its deathly head. Several wells were drained in putting out the city's fires, adding to the shortage of potable water. The king ordered legions into distant provinces to commandeer water and provisions for his people. Even the palace stores were growing thin, according to bathhouse rumors heard by Ligeus.

The captain was supervising the morning drills when he saw the wizard Pebble walking across the martial yards. The man's beard was back to purest whiteness, his rags replaced by a flowing robe of violet and black silk. Golden bracers hugged his narrow forearms, and a circlet of silver held back his thick mane. The king obviously wanted his new wizard to inspire awe wherever he wandered. Ligeus thought the old man looked rather ridiculous weighed down by such finery. Yet he chuckled when he saw the singer's harp fitted with a fresh set of gleaming strings.

Amid the clash of wooden swords and the grunts of straining soldiers, he heard a clear voice ring out. "Captain! A word if you please?"

"I've no time for your pretty songs today, Pebble," said Ligeus. He corrected a new recruit's spear stance and turned to face the dubious wizard. "Famine approaches, and that may lead to war. My soldiers must be ready."

"Yes, yes," muttered Pebble, staring at the dry ground. He bent and picked up a small piece of charcoal that had formerly been a flaming hailstone. The yard was singed, but not much damage had been done here. "I promise not to sing. But I do have a story you need to hear."

Ligeus was about to deny Pebble's request, but something in the way the man stroked his prodigious, neatly combed beard reeked of menace.

"Very well," said the captain. "We'll speak over there, beneath the olive tree."

They walked together as Pebble studied the barren branches. "Pitiful thing," he muttered. "Needs a good rain…as all things here do, I suppose."

"Do you intend to waste my time telling me what I already know?" asked Ligeus. He dipped a ladleful of water from a bowl set beneath the branches. The taste was cool and sweet, like Camryl's lips. He put her out of his mind.

Pebble looked at him with brown eyes desolate as wastelands. Dark circles hung beneath them, and lines of suffering wrinkled the old man's brow. How old was he?

"I was much like you once," said Pebble. "Not a soldier…but I knew the way of the sword. Yet after a while I tired of shedding blood. I forsook it and took up this harp instead. So I came to serve the king of a land called Aegros. Have you heard of it?"

Ligeus sighed and shook his head.

"No matter," said Pebble. "Perhaps that nation belonged to some other world. I have wandered far. But listen…I fell in love with the most beautiful woman in the kingdom. I was helpless before her. But I served her husband. She was the queen of Aegros."

Ligeus clenched his fists. His jaw hardened. Pebble's eyes bored into his.

"Until I saw her face, I had all that I ever wanted. I served at the court of a king who loved my songs, my jests, my acrobatics. I took pride in being the perfect fool. And so I became a fool for her, if you take my meaning. I betrayed everything I valued in a desperate chase to win her love."

"Your song," said Ligeus. "'The Faithless Queen.' Was that—?"

"Yes," said Pebble. "All of it was true…except for that bit with the tigers…a bit of poetic license."

"What was her name?"

"I…I don't remember," said Pebble.

"Why are you telling me this?" asked Ligeus. Let the man speak plainly if he wished to accuse or blackmail!

"Because I recognize the look on your face, Captain. You love the young queen. Do not worry... No one but I can see it. I will not tell your secret. I wish only to warn you..."

"Warn me of what?" asked Ligeus.

"Let her go," whispered Pebble. "Don't make the mistake that I made. Don't betray everything you have for something that may never be."

Ligeus stared at the rushing white clouds. Could his sword lop off the wizard's head before the demons tore him apart? And if he killed Pebble...would the demons flee?

"You bear a curse," he said to Pebble. "The demons...how did they come to...*inhabit* you?"

Pebble frowned. "I defended my king's life...from a wizard whom the demons served. When I killed him—I set his beard on fire, as I recall—the demons lingered. And later, when I fell into the depths of betrayal and sorrow...I found that I could not get rid of them."

Ligeus rubbed his chin. "Do wicked deeds always follow men so? Even if they are done to serve a greater good?"

Pebble lifted an empty palm. "Who can say what is good or wicked? Who decides?"

Ligeus folded his arms. "Each man must decide for himself, wizard."

He turned and walked toward the dueling men.

"I am not a wizard," Pebble called.

Ligeus ignored him.

* * * *

In the throne room, Pebble stood in the same place of honor the High Priest had formerly enjoyed. He watched peasants and noblemen and thieves brought before the king's judgment, strumming his harp to lighten their weary souls. Between assigning executions, the king often requested a jaunty tune or called for Pebble to sing.

"You will serve me best by doing what you enjoy," King Thamion had told him last night. "Pluck your harp; sing your songs. The threat of your demons will keep my enemies in line. It matters not whether you be true wizard or simply a cursed minstrel. Do you understand?"

This meant that he could once again be the entertainer of a royal house, a dream he thought long dead, especially in light of his three tormentors. Ironically, his curse made this king desire his services even more. He almost wanted to thank the demons, but he knew they were only waiting for the chance to work more evil. Still, he had found a measure of happiness in Yandrissa. And since all happiness was fleeting, he determined to enjoy it while it lasted.

He played the harp with singular devotion, bringing the chamber to solemn stillness or impassioned reverence as he wished. He never remembered being so full of joy, so immersed in the moment, not since… not since he had lived under another name in another land that may or may not exist any longer. In all his years of mad wandering, had the demons dragged him across dimensions into some alternate world adjacent to his own? He neither knew nor cared; he had a king and a court to entertain. It was enough.

At the end of the long day's judgments, the king retired to speak with his generals. Pebble sensed a war in the offing, especially now that Thamion enjoyed the support of such a powerful wizard. Pebble would have laughed if the circumstances were not so dire. Perhaps one day, when the demons tired of this, they would leap out and devour Thamion. Perhaps at the very moment of his proudest victory.

Pebble accepted a carafe of wine from a nervous servant and quenched his thirst. His throat was tired from a day of singing. Tired… but content for the time being. After an evening meal of braised pork, apricots, and fresh bread, he fell to drowsing by the window of his guest chamber. Not long after sunset he woke to a familiar tugging at his beard. "What?" he asked the demons within. "What do you want this time? Haven't you done enough? Leave me alone."

But the pearly beard fluttered and twisted and pulled him toward the door. In the hallway outside, a servant rushed about lighting torches ensconced along the walls. With a heavy sigh, Pebble grabbed his harp and walked into the corridor. He wandered through a dense network of passages hung with rows of stitched tapestries and paced between statues of bronze and marble. He crossed a gallery of paintings that showcased the ancestors of Thamion. A line of conquerors, they brandished silver blades or clutched tall, pennoned spears in images wrought by brush and oil.

"Where are you taking me?" he asked his beard in a hoarse whisper. He crept past marching guards, turning the corner at a moment just before he would have been noticed, all at the gentle tugging of his long whiskers. He considered chopping the beard off again as he had done many times before…but the demons would only flock about him like noisome ravens until it grew back. He had long ago ceased trying to resist the triple willpower that at times enveloped and mastered his own.

A winding stairwell brought him to the summit of a palace tower. He paused before an oak door bound in iron. A single guard stood at attention before the portal. As he first caught sight of Pebble, a crimson hand emerged from the white beard and wove a gleaming sigil in the air. The guard inhaled sharply and slumped upon the stairs, either asleep or dead. Pebble moved closer to the door, and the demon's claw reached out to touch the oak. The door swung inward on soundless hinges.

Beyond lay a chamber lit by guttering candles. Shelves lined the walls, littered with yellow scrolls, blackened skulls, and crystalline vials of liquid. A lone window overlooked the city, through which Pebble saw the glimmering moon and stars. Before the window stood a pedestal, and on the pedestal lay a thick book. Pebble's beard pulled him closer, and he clutched the harp to his chest.

He stood before the book and saw that it was bound in the scaly hide of some great beast. It was a thing of ancient days, and the forgotten language inscribed on its cover was indecipherable...until the crimson claw emerged again and cast a sparkling spell.

Now Pebble read the tome's title as clearly as his native tongue.

The Book of Curses.

A drowsy moan startled him. He turned to find Queen Camryl re-clining in the shadows on a black divan. A brazier of strange-smelling incense fumed beside her. She rose, inhaling the vapors. Pebble moved into the shadows between two bookcases, marveling that she did not already see him. Her eyes were glazed... She walked to the book, lost in some deep trance.

The queen opened the heavy cover and turned its moldy pages one by one, stopping somewhere in the middle. Now she read the words—no, *sang* the words on the page—soft and low, bubbling like pitch in the back of her throat; then a guttural chant spat steaming from the tip of her tongue. Pebble's skin crawled, for against his will he understood those inhuman words. She was calling upon forces that were not of this world, or any world ruled by humankind. Fear swelled in his chest like a desperate fit of coughing, and he cried out.

Camryl spun about and saw him. Her spell was broken. Now the comely face was a mask of fury... Death danced in her eyes. She would tear his throat out with her teeth.

The demons leapt forth in a crimson gust. Two of them grabbed her arms while the third slammed the book shut. It turned and smiled at its fellows with a snaggletoothed grin, eyes bulging like black jewels. Pebble feared they would tear the queen limb from limb. He turned his head away.

Camryl screamed, her trance entirely gone now, terror replacing fury in her green eyes. Her wail rang through the tower window into the wilt-ing courtyards of the palace. One of the demons grabbed her body in its spiky arms and leapt out the window. Another beast followed, gliding on fresh-sprouted wings. The third demon clutched the *Book of Curses* like a lover and leapt back into Pebble's beard.

Then it pulled him out the window too, as if an invisible giant yanked at his whiskers. Instead of falling to his death, he flew toward a distant chamber window. Inside, King Thamion and his three generals sat about a table strewn with maps. But the maps blew away like torn leaves as the demon carrying Camryl hurtled in through the open window. Pebble followed next, his feet touching the floor of the chamber as the generals stood about their king with drawn swords.

Camryl lay in a heap on the floor, weeping and moaning. The crimson beast stood over her, drooling like a hound. Before any words could be exchanged, the demon inside Pebble's beard tossed out the *Book of Curses*. It landed squarely upon the king's table with the heavy thump of a dead body.

Thamion raged behind his guardians. "What is the meaning of this, wizard?"

"I am not a—"

Pebble never finished his denial. It was drowned beneath a rush of flapping, leathery wings. The third demon flew in through the window clutching Captain Ligeus in its arms. It dropped him to the floor, and the creatures leapt back into Pebble's beard, flowing like wisps of black smoke.

Pebble stood before the sobbing queen, the stunned captain, and the furious king. Soldiers rushed into the chamber. A forest of blades pointed at the singer, who laid down his harp and raised his empty palms.

"It is she, Your Majesty," Pebble said sadly. "Queen Camryl has betrayed you with black magic. She brings the curses down upon your kingdom."

Thamion's eyes blazed with fury. "How can you know this?"

The king of Yandrissa met his wife's eyes. The red heat of his face withered her delicate skin.

"It's true!" Camryl cried. "I did it. I used the Black Book… It was my mother's…"

Thamion started as if slapped in the face. He looked from Camryl to the cursed tome. The generals gaped and stuttered. Their blades glittered in the lamplight.

Camryl rushed into the arms of Ligeus.

"Faithless Drazan whore!" shouted Thamion. "Witch's spawn!" He raised his hand to strike her.

Ligeus grabbed Thamion's wrist. "Do not touch her."

The king was doubly stricken. His face curdled.

"You betray me too? *You*?"

Ligeus did not reply, but bent to kiss Camryl.

"Kill him," Thamion said. "Her too."

The nearest general raised his sword, but his blow never fell. A red mist whirled about the room. Pebble stood at its calm center. He watched while the world moved slowly as a dream. A demon leapt upon the table and threw open the book, while the other two flowed about the room, opening soft necks with razory talons. The fiend at the book chanted loudly in a language far more natural on its black tongue than Camryl's.

The earth began to tremble, and the palace walls swayed. Dust fell from massive stones in the ceiling and walls. Chandeliers shattered and rained to the flagstones, marble statuary cracked to shards. Green flames danced along the corridors, and in the king's war room blood swirled like pink mist...and the fleshly bodies therein lost their shapes. They, too, flowed like fog in a windstorm. Circling, circling, spinning about the book and its reader. Pebble held his hands to his ears, but still he heard the demon's booming incantation. The other two joined in now, as if singing a familiar chorus...

Now the gardens and streets of Yandrissa filled with screams. Pebble was glad he could not see what was happening. Terror flowed like a flood from a broken dam. He closed his eyes and endured the whirling, pulsing madness. The stench of blood made him choke. He fell to his knees and the world went black.

He awoke in the throne room. Pillars had fallen and shattered across the wide floor. Grand tapestries hung in tatters, and the entire roof had been wrenched away. An early dawn turned the sky to a pall of scarlet and orange. Pebble found himself clutching the harp to his chest. His beard waved lightly in the morning wind.

Bodies lay at odd angles among the ruins, but Pebble's eyes were drawn to the platinum throne. Upon it sat a pale, three-headed creature with six arms sagging from its barrel-shaped body. A robe of royal silk draped the lumpy, distorted torso. Six legs hung from the front of the shimmering chair. Atop each of the being's three heads sat a crown of gold and jewels.

Tears spilled from Pebble's eyes as he recognized the triple monarch. Its three faces, staring with dull eyes and slack mouths, were those of Thamion, Ligeus, and Camryl. The girl's sweetly dumb visage sat directly between those of her husband and her lover. Three had become one. Pebble noted, too, that four of the arms were strong and masculine while two were slim and fair. Likewise, the six legs.

He pulled himself to his feet before the royal dais and heard a faint chuckling within his beard. Now he knew why the demons had brought him here. The book had called them. Now it belonged to them, and they had used it to wreak a brilliant mischief.

He stumbled toward the fallen gates of the hall and saw the bodies of soldiers welded together, seamlessly, as if they were dolls of clay spun in a furnace by some mad potter. Each consisted of two men melded together into four-armed, double-headed beings. They were alive, most of them. Even as he watched, they stood groggily, discovering how to balance their new bodies, grasping for their implements of war—their swords, spears, and shields. They were now a host of multi-limbed monsters, serving a triple-faced king-queen. How had the change affected their brains, their souls? Pebble wondered briefly if any spark of humanity could survive such a metamorphosis. He wiped his eyes and left the palace grounds, ambling into the streets.

There the people of Yandrissa waddled and scuttled...weeping, laughing, or crying out to oblivious gods. They were all of them—men, women, children—blended in pairs. A kingdom of two-headed, four-armed, four-legged things, drooling and shambling toward the broken palace. Pebble walked faster as they milled about him, moving in the opposite direction.

By the time he reached the sundered gates of the outer wall, a heavy rain broke over the city. Great, cool drops fell across flagstone, field, and roof. A cheer went up behind him. The people were glad for this life-giving downpour, even as their lives had been warped and changed forever. Pebble ran into the storm.

In the distance mountain peaks glowed with green flames, and the sky-forest rustled above the plain. Perhaps these curses or miracles would fade in time. Perhaps not. The people of Yandrissa would survive in some strange new way. Beneath the roaring of the elements, a flash of lightning seared Pebble's eyes. *Run! Run!* hissed the demons, and run he did, leaving behind a city of hopeful monsters.

▲

Fertility Rites
by Glynn Owen Barrass

I'm here again. The simple thought paled against the feelings the scene evoked. It was ethereal, dreamlike, and frightening.

The mossy earth was invisible beneath her bare feet, the ground coated in a thick white membrane of mist. The soil clung to her toes as she stepped forward, between the trees, so many trees. Thick twisted monstrosities, they resembled giant limbs, swollen with disease. Obscene white growths, a leprous fungi, bulged between their many knots, and the branches? Jagged, leafless, they hung above her with cruel intent, hinting at laceration, penetration. Constance hugged her naked form, shying away from the trees as best she could. They meant to violate her, she sensed it most clearly. The sky above was a looming, grey mass of cloud. In the distance, it met and joined the mist.

Within such a wide-open space, why did she feel so enclosed, so trapped?

A rustling sound appeared around her. It was the trees, shifting slowly although she herself felt no breeze. She sent them a look. Yes, they moved, but not from any wind, but rather, they twisted of their own unnatural accord. Their movements were sinuous, like black, oily serpents. Yes, she could see it now, thick dark, ropy lengths, coiled together to resemble pulsing trunks. Their hollows dripped fetid green slime, down to bases bearing large splits. The bloated wood between the cracks resembled thick, bestial hooves.

She looked around in panic. *There has to be a way out.* Then, despite the softness of the earth, the distinct clip clopping of hoofed feet sounded behind her.

The tree hollows hissed, spat filth, moving like obscene mouths.

Unable to endure any more, she ran. The sound behind her transformed into a gallop. The branches reached down, whipping at her, spattering foul smelling gore against her face and breasts. She ducked as she ran, for the reaching limbs became more frenzied by the second, the galloping closing in.

No escape in the distance, just a grey horizon between black, groping trees. No, not trees, she realized, but black tenacled horrors, stamping massive, hoofed feet.

Vibrating footsteps thundered nearer, closing the gap. Hot, roaring breath touched her back and she caught the stink of sweat and sex. Huge talons slashed at her buttocks, and though it burned to breathe, she increased her speed. Then, disaster struck. In her panicked rush, she stumbled and fell. A talon reached her, slashing her buttocks with a pain so intense…

…Its touch awoke her, a gentle stroke above her roughspun cotton sheet. Beginning at her ankle, it brushed slowly past her calf to cross her knee then press against her inner thigh. She moaned as the pressure there mounted. Suddenly, with strange magic, the sensation appeared beneath the sheet, pressing directly against her flesh. She bit her lip in anticipation, for she had experienced this same encounter every night now for two weeks. The warm pressure reached her crotch. Another pressure appeared, and both worked to push her legs apart. She yielded with pleasure. The throbbing, thrashing warmth that followed made her stifle a shriek as her legs and buttocks bounced in ecstasy.

"Oh God," she whispered, and experienced a brief pang of shame from saying the Holy name in vain. She reached down, wanting to embrace the invisible head pressed against her womanhood. As always, she felt nothing beneath the sheets, but the ecstasy continued.

She shuddered wildly, rocked the bed against the floorboards as powerful sensations ripped through her body. The ecstasy sent her legs pounding against her mattress, her limbs growing limp as suddenly, she found herself alone and exhausted. Light headed, unconsciousness followed, a deep, contented, dreamless sleep.

* * * *

Constance entered the kitchen and stifled a yawn. The hearth fire was blazing, the grandfather clock beside it revealing the time as just before eight. She glanced around the room. *Father must be at the slaughterhouse.* Her mother was at the kitchen table, rolling dough; she glanced up, frowned then returned to her work.

Constance felt suddenly wary, worried her mother had heard her in the night.

"There is tea in the pot," she said. "I'd like you to go to the shops as soon as you are decent."

Constance flushed red, felt suddenly naked despite her nightgown.

"And wear your shawl and bonnet out there my dear," her mother added, "There is a chill in the air."

I'm alright, I think. Constance nodded. She stepped around the table and reached for the pot suspended above the hearth.

* * * *

She left the house and turned right, down a dirt track scarred by countless cart wheels. Her mother was right, it was a cold one, and she pulled her shawl closer with one hand, hugging the straw basket to her chest with the other. She passed the Henderson's, more prosperous neighbours that could afford a carriage, and to her father's continued chagrin, three Negro slaves. Constance shook her head as she continued towards the village. Mist carpeted the woods surrounding her, their diaphanous tendrils licking round thick oak trunks. This ethereal scene returned her thoughts to the…entity.

A sinner, I am a sinner, but… Having reached the village path bisecting her own, she set eyes on the church, off in the distance to her right. A large, whitewashed building, it stood upon a circular hill, towered over the gambrel roofs of the village.

The sight recalled the day Pastor Muse took her aside at the end of service, where he had spoken of the upcoming Winter Harvest Festival. "The bible says offer yourselves to God, and offer your bodies to him as instruments of righteousness." His eyes had gleamed brightly after the cryptic speech, and passing her a small folded white tissue, he continued, "open it later my dear, and tell no-one." In candlelight, at her bedside after evening prayers, she had tore open the tissue to reveal a silver chain with a small silver crucifix. No, not a crucifix she had quickly realized, for the naked form on the cross was female, with strangely hoofed feet.

That night, the dreams and the visitations, began.

"Constance." Martha Jobling, the Whitesmith's wife, greeted her curtly. Martha greeted her in return before placing her head down in shyness.

Sinful, guilty of things abhorrent to God. She approached the shops beneath the church. *Or am I, as Pastor Muse said, an instrument of righteousness? He will know. I have to ask him.*

* * * *

"My dear, please come right in." His wrinkled face beaming, Pastor Muse ushered her into his study. "Constance isn't it? Yes, that's right."

His study, built in a basement hewn from the very flesh of the hill, was small, wood panelled, and without windows. Two oil lamps illuminated the room, placed on the ends of a sturdy oak desk. He bid her sit before it, before taking the seat facing her. He nodded and folded his arms.

"Pastor."

"Please, call me Jonathon."

She looked away from his intense gaze to stare at the empty basket in her hands.

"Pastor, I have been troubled by dreams, strange experiences." She flushed and clenched her hands, " and I was…"

Pastor Muse filled the pause. "You were wondering, my dear, if God forgives you?"

She looked up.

No longer smiling, his lips were pursed. "You know Genesis? It says: 'be fruitful and multiply, teem in the earth, and multiply in it.'"

"Yes Pastor, I know the words but—"

"Fertility," he interrupted, "the realization of your womanhood is nothing to be ashamed of." He leant forward, spoke more quietly "You have the icon still?" She nodded. "Beautiful girl, good girl. I have a mind, an ambition, to carve the cross behind my pulpit, with hooves and breasts as black as night." He shrugged and sat back. "I would make all of you fruitful, in the name of the Black Goat."

Constance shuddered, thought of devils and brimstone and incubi.

The Pastor seemed to divine her thoughts, for he said, "I come from a town, Dunwich they call it, where the worship of older gods is not frowned upon. There we offer the gods love, and they love us, in return. They are purer, more primal, than a resurrected Christ and an uncaring Lord Almighty. So please, return in a few days and tell me then if your shame outweighs your pleasure."

* * * *

The forest: ethereal mist and monstrous trees. The Black Goat's children. Brought forth, multiplied.

The hoofed horror, her lover, hounding her.

I will be a mother too.

"Uh, please, no more!" Her plea was half-hearted as the thing within her continued thrashing wildly. Constance shuddered in sympathy, her numb legs soaked in sweat. Then, all of a sudden, the entity was gone. Constance cried in despair at being left unfulfilled, but a moment later, it returned. She smiled. Her body shook again from the glorious sensation.

Halfway through another wave of pleasure, a creaking noise froze her still. The entity disappeared. Constance stifled a gasp, twisted her head to the left, and in the nebulous darkness saw the door to her bedroom stood ajar. The fear came like ice water, the breath she had held remaining trapped in her throat. She had terrible visions of her father bursting in, but no, no sounds followed, no movements in the darkness.

She released the breath but the fear remained until, sweat soaked and uncomfortable, she fell into an uneasy slumber.

* * * *

Constance awoke with a start, and instantly knew something was wrong with her world. She sat up and looked around her room. The curtains were open, but she had left them that way before bed. The oak dresser facing the window, her dried flowers pinned to its upper shelf, there was nothing wrong there. But there was something…amiss. She cast a shameful glance to the door, closed now, whereas last night it had stood open. Still there was something— "The crucifix!" the intuition proved fact as she poked her hand beneath her pillow to discover the blasphemous icon gone. "No. No!" She flung the sheet from her bed. The pillow followed as she pushed her arm past the mattress to check if it had slipped down. Her panicked search found nothing but dusty floorboards.

Her hand came back grimy, her arm white with plaster. Sitting back, she slowed her panicked breaths and considered the options before her.

I had it last night, I'm sure it was here last night. She leapt to the edge of the bed and with frantic movements, searched again.

* * * *

She entered the kitchen in a sullen mood. To her surprise her father was home, sat at the table with his fists clenched against a surface white with flour. Her mother stood by the hearth, staring at her feet. The clock ticked ominously in the silence between the three. Her father opened his mouth, and all hell broke loose.

"Whore! You harlot! I did not believe what Mother told me." Red-faced, he spat as he spoke.

"What—"

"No denials now, I have been to your room and smelled your sheets."

He was in my room as I slept? Feeling vulnerable in her nightgown, she raised her hands, crossing them over her breasts.

"Unclean child." His face grew redder. He kicked away his chair and stood. "And what is THIS?" His hand opened, a small silver object falling to the table.

The crucifix. He had it. He'd taken it.

"I took it while you slept. Explain yourself, whore."

He stepped forward with menace. Her mother, head still lowered, burst into tears. Constance stepped forward too, her eyes entranced by the blasphemous icon.

"I will whip you raw young lady," he said. She saw the slaughterhouse blood beneath his cracked nails as he reached for her arm. "Mother, pass me the poker."

"No." Constance looked up at his face. "That is not what will happen."

Her father's eyes went wide. Not in anger, but in shock. It continued as the hand she had sent to the table swung the rolling pin at his head.

Her mother screamed as he tottered then fell to the floor. His head hit the floorboards and he stopped moving, eyes closed. Taking the rolling pin one-handed, she hiked up her nightdress to straddle his huge form. The stink of sweat and animal blood wafted up from him as she raised the rolling pin over her head. Her mother screamed again. Scrabbling footsteps followed.

She smashed the rolling pin against his nose. He shuddered as blood burst from his nostrils in two red streams. The next blow split his lips, the yellow teeth cracking beneath them.

"Stop this!" her mother screamed in her ear. Weak hands took her arm. She shrugged them away easily, and raising the bloody rolling pin, took it two-handed before coming down with all her strength. The loud crack resounded from the walls. Constance thought of the animals in his slaughterhouse and giggled. Her mother collapsed beside her, then her father opened his lips to reveal broken, blood-slicked teeth. His mouth released a short, liquid death-croak.

Constance stood, stared at his still form, and felt nothing. A whine to her right turned her head. Between her and the table, her mother lay on her side, her hands covering her face. The woman sobbed quietly. Constance looked to the blood-soaked rolling pin and smiled.

* * * *

The day was cold, the morning mist lingering on the dirt track. The chill air quickly cooled the blood on her face and hands. Her breath escaped her mouth in white plumes as the mist curled around her feet. She stepped from the porch, the cold floorboards replaced by frozen mud.

The chilly day didn't urge her back to the charnel house. The crucifix atop her bloodstained nightdress was all the warmth she needed. Her mind felt fogged, her world dreamlike as she turned towards the village. When she heard the Henderson's door open, what she witnessed there neither shocked or surprised her.

Lindsay Henderson stood there, accompanied by her Negro servant girl, Bess. Still in their nightdresses, they stepped hand in hand from the porch towards the track. Something glinted in Lindsay's hand—a knife, bloody at the tip. Constance spied the Pastor's crucifixes around each girl's neck.

She nodded, smiled, and continued on.

Her feet were numb by the time she reached the village. Six neighbours, all girls, now formed a procession behind her.

The gambrel roofs were rimed with frost; no smoke issued from their chimneys. Doors stood ajar, and for all intents and purposes, the village appeared deserted. She passed houses then shops as the church grew ever closer. The cross on the cupola shone brightly against the cloudless blue sky, and Constance thought she spied movement on the Lookout beneath.

It came as no real surprise, when she reached the hill, to find Pastor Muse stood halfway up the church's steps. His thin, elderly form was naked, yet she felt no embarrassment at looking upon him. Instead, her gaze returned to the Lookout. There she witnessed a shimmer of air, an invisible shape barely hinted at.

"My lover," she said.

"Yes." The Pastor's voice broke her reverie. Constance paused. She had climbed the steps without realizing it. "He awaits you," his patrician voice continued. He raised his hands. The palms were smeared black. "I carved the cross behind the pulpit. Painted it with bitumen. It is a mother now, The Black Goat of the Woods."

"Am I to help her multiply?" she asked.

He nodded. "You all will."

Footsteps crunched the frozen grass behind her—the other girls climbing the hill.

Pastor Muse raised his arms. "There is no immorality, or impurity. Just the power of love, and lust."

"Yes," Constance agreed. A warm longing filled her as she ascended the stairs, a longing she knew would be fulfilled.

▲

The Witch's Heart
by Rachel Bolton

Having hair feels wrong to her now. She plays with the cold scissors, warming them between her hands. It takes three snips to cut the hair to her chin. Tara's mother steps into the room and sighs. Tara knows her mother believes she is losing her powers.

It is dangerous to love a witch. It is more dangerous to break the heart of one.

Mother leans next to Tara and strokes the back of her head, her fingers catching on the uneven ends. "You know what must be done," she says calmly, the weight of her words heavy on Tara's shoulders.

"I'm with child." She chokes on the last word.

Tara feels weird to say it while she kneels in her childhood bedroom. Her favorite doll still sits in the corner. The first spell book she opened rests on the shelf. Tara doesn't belong here anymore.

Mother flinches, her pointed nose wrinkling. "You may do what you like with your daughter," she says, not unkindly. "Cast her from your womb if you wish. But please wait until you get your powers back."

Tara covers her face. She knows she cannot take back these words once they are spoken. She has waited to say them until it is almost too late.

"I'll perform the spell."

"You must, my daughter will not die to save a worthless man's life," she says, crossing her arms.

* * * *

There are thirty other witches in the coven. Tara's kind can have lovers of any gender, but only three witches are married to men, Mother included. Father took the risk of becoming involved with a witch, they creatures of passion, giving their hearts fully and deeply. Glory and success follow those who love them with kindness and generosity. Misery and death come to those who dare to wrong a witch. And Tara has been wronged most severely.

News of her situation spreads throughout the coven. She doesn't want to speak to the other witches. They can't give her the sympathy she craves. She refuses to hear their creative suggestions for revenge. The door shut in her mother's study, she speaks into the fire that connects her parents' homes, hoping that Father is there. They are happily married, but Father always maintained a separate residence in town. No one wants to work with a merchant who lives in a witches' coven. People want to believe Father is merely the uncomplicated and pleasant man he appears to be.

On the carriage ride to her father's house, Tara thinks on how she was both lucky and cursed to know a life outside the coven's farm. The other young witches only socialized with one another. Unlike her, their sires were not involved with their lives. On occasion, she worked in the marketplace with her father, going not as a witch, but as a merchant's daughter. How stupid was she to think that someone like her could pretend to be ordinary. Living in the outside was how Tara met her lover after all. He danced with her at the harvest festival when no one else would. He had promised her so much. He left like she was nothing at all.

Tara places a protective hand on her stomach when the carriage hits a bump. While many in the coven are trained to be midwives, witches are not known for their fertility. One woman she knows bore three daughters over fifteen years. Her kind can only have female children, who will share their mother's powers. No wonder Tara's lover abandoned her. She could never give him a son and heir.

The garden outside Father's home is empty. She is relieved that no one is here to do business with him. She doesn't want to explain her presence to his peers. Father opens the door and welcomes Tara with an understanding embrace before she wanders inside the parlor. The smell of lavender and old books is comforting to her. Her lover never visited here. His memory does not taint this place. She has always been impressed with Father's ability to live simply; a lone rug and some paintings decorate the room, how unlike the cramped coven farm.

Father doesn't ask questions and tells her to stay as long as she wants. He says nothing about the hair.

Tara remembers the wedding dress Father paid for, back when her lover told her they'd be wed. She knew it was too expensive, but she asked for one anyway. Tara liked how lacy it was and how long the train could be. The dress still hangs in her bedroom here. She thinks about burning it.

Father offers her a cup of tea, but she declines, not wishing to see the sorrow in his eyes. She tries to go upstairs, but wobbles as her vision blurs. She doesn't feel her father catching her.

* * * *

Tara wakes to voices speaking over her. She can't open her eyes or move.

"She shouldn't have come here," Father says. She feels his callused fingertips brush her forehead.

"Unless she conducts the breaking, she will die," Mother says. "She gave her heart to that miserable man, and since he rejected it her life will fade away."

"He will pay for his mistreatment of her whether she conducts the breaking or not."

Tara wishes that she possessed the energy to feel embarrassed. Her problem has brought the head of the coven out of her reclusive nook. Then again, she is her great-aunt. Many members are interrelated to some degree. She can imagine the Lady Lavinia in her mind's eye. She is small and hunched. Her patchwork robes are too big for her; they trail behind as she walks. She whispers an incantation. Her voice is deep and crackles with magic. The sound of it frightened Tara as a child. She opens her eyes.

"I can only temper your decline for a little while. What comes next is up to you, niece." Lady Lavinia touches her briefly on the arm before leaving.

Tara says nothing while her parents weep over her inaction. She has had two months to conduct the breaking. Two months have gone by since he left her. Two months since her powers drained away. Her magic is barely strong enough to perform the simplest of spells. Her parents explain that she may have a week left to live. Her lover gets married on Sunday. Tara will likely be dead by the time the ceremony ends. She thinks about when she last saw him. He was with his new fiancée down by the lake. From up on the hill, she watched him and that miserable girl he chose instead, listening to her stupid laugh. How it took all of Tara's willpower not to make her eyes melt in their sockets, to use that much magic would've killed Tara that instant.

"What will you do?" Mother asks.

"It shall be done tonight," Tara breathes, saying the words that will make her a murderer.

* * * *

While she gathers the materials for the breaking back at the farm, she decides to keep her daughter. She thinks she is too young to be a mother at her twenty-one years. But the desire to keep a part of him forever overwhelms her. She hopes they look alike to remind her of what she is about to destroy.

Tara weeps while she kneels in front of her cauldron. She can use the tears as part of the breaking. The spell needs to be personalized after she puts in the base ingredients. The deeper the connection between witch and magic used, the more effective the breaking will be. Guilt gnaws at her as she kills the dove needed. She bends the rules by drugging it before slitting the throat. She is creating enough pain as it is. What is dealt to the world always returns in kind, a little gentleness will go far. She pauses for a moment to hold the still-beating heart in her dirty hand. The sight fascinates her, and the thought that it does makes her nauseous. The heart sputters then stops moving. The weight of Tara's actions sits in her palm, waiting. Blinking, she drops the heart in the caldron. She stops to the wash the blood from her fingers. Magic cannot come from nothing.

Tara breaks the tea set he bought her. She smashes it piece by piece on the stone floor, enjoying the sound it makes each time. Tara's lover surprised her with it on her birthday. The china was hand painted and delicate. Even now, she doesn't know why he got it. Tara never considers putting it back together again. She adds it to the cauldron, turning the boiling water from yellow to red. She keeps one of the teacups. Tara will give it to her daughter when she is old enough to understand.

She tries on her wedding dress one more time. It doesn't feel as good on her skin as before. The gown is itchy and constricting, the fabric heavy. Tara is grateful for the sensation, as it makes it easier for her to cut it to shreds for the breaking.

At last, she pours the tears in. Tara collected them one by one in a vial while she worked. Only a few drops were needed to make the spell truly hers. Blue steam hazes above the cauldron. She invokes the incantation, saying his name one more time. It is done. She is being merciful, really. A certain witch in the coven conducted the breaking a few years ago. Her former lover died by having his bowels turned to snakes. He died slowly as they crawled up his throat, choking him. His wife went mad after witnessing it. She makes sure to conduct a protection spell as part of this. No one else is to be harmed.

She sighs, tucking the frayed ends of her hair behind her ears. She starts to feel healthier already.

* * * *

Sunday arrives. Despite their protestations, Tara tells her parents to take her to the church. She still struggles to walk on her own and merely consumes broth and bread. She needs to see it happen. Tara needs to replace the memories of his love and kindness with revenge. She will never move on if she doesn't. Tara refuses to tell her mother and father what the breaking entails, only saying that it will happen during the wedding.

Mother gently laces her into the loveliest green gown Tara owns, hoping to distract her, while her cousin tries to style her butchered hair. The sky is bright and the breeze warm. She wishes that the weather matched her miserable mood.

Tara nods when Father asks if she is prepared to go. She doesn't let him or Mother see the handkerchief she hides in her sleeve.

* * * *

Her parents don't speak in the carriage. Father fiddles with his beard, while Mother makes flower petals appear and disappear in her lap. The knowledge that people will be nervous at the sight of two witches at the wedding keeps them all silent. People are only comfortable with witches when they need their help. Tara guiltily thinks that the townsfolk's fears will be well founded when this is over.

The three settle in the back row of the church, they were not invited. But no one turned them away. The church has done its best to be welcoming to all, witches included. The other guests don't make eye contact with Mother, not that Tara blames them. She is dressed in the traditional witch garb for the occasion. Her black robes make her stand out against the bright colors of the festivities. The guests talk amongst themselves when they see Tara, wondering why she is attending. They probably thought she would never appear in town again. Everyone is polite to Father. Tara hopes that the events of the breaking will not affect his business, even though it certainly will.

Tara sees her lover standing with the priest at the altar. The air has been pulled from her lungs. Mother rubs her back as Tara catches her breath. She shrinks down in the pew, hoping he doesn't notice her. Instead, she peers through the heads of the guests to watch him. He seems neat and happy, his blond hair combed away from his face. It angers her that he is wearing the blue cloak he promised he would wear at their wedding.

As for his fiancée, Tara doesn't want to look at her during the ceremony. Tara shuts her eyes when her rival walks down the aisle. She can't stand the idea of seeing her happy before the breaking takes him away forever.

Tara tears nervously at her dress, the service moves too slowly. Mother tries to hold her hand. Tara flinches at her touch. Mother and Father exchange knowing looks. She never should have brought them here. Tara should have attended the wedding alone. But the pain of knowing what is about to occur makes her regret coming all together.

At long last, the priest declares them husband and wife to the applause of the congregation. Tara can't stop trembling. It is moments away from happening.

"You may now kiss the bride," the priest says joyfully.

Time slows as he kisses her. Tara's heart feels as though it will beat out of her chest. She wants to cut it out as she did to the dove. The instant the couple's lips part, a spark cracks in the air between them. He bursts into flames, burning by the strength of her grief and rage. His hair and blue cloak soon disappear in the fire. The church dissolves into chaos. Tara wasn't expecting his screams to hurt as much as they do. He begs for it to stop. He cries for his mother.

"Someone help him, please!" his bride shrieks.

From a magic practitioner's point of view, Tara is relieved to see that her protection spell worked. The bride hits her husband frantically, trying put out the flames with her bare hands. They do not harm her, nor does the church burn alongside him.

The priest impotently douses him with water. Men leap up to try and beat the flames down with their cloaks. It won't work. Tara's former lover will burn and burn until there is nothing left. Black smoke billows into the rafters. She gags into her handkerchief. Human fat crackles in the air. The stench is more than she can bear. His features have burned away. His ears are no more, nor are his strong jaw and nose. The breaking is impersonal now. The stump of smoldering flesh could be anyone. The screams are over. All Tara hears is his wife's sobs, begging for him to return to her. Tara stares as she claws at the ashes, as though she could bring him back if she tries hard enough. The spell complete, Tara's powers return. Her body buzzes with energy.

The fire gone, the congregation has attention to spare. A man screams as he points at Tara and her parents.

Mother does not wait. She spreads her cloak wide, instantaneously transporting her husband and daughter back to the safety of the coven's farm. She needs to lie down afterwards as it is exhausting to use so much magic at once.

"It was a brilliant piece of spell work." She holds Tara tightly before departing. "I'm relieved you will live. He never should have abandoned you," she adds before kissing her daughter on the cheek.

Seconds after Mother leaves, Tara runs and vomits in the washroom. Father gives her a cup of water and dabs at her forehead with a wet cloth. Tara thanks him, but she can barely stomach his expression. His face is white in horror at what she has done.

When she finally leaves the washroom, Lady Lavinia and the other members of the coven congratulate on Tara on her achievement. Her cousin tells her no one will dare to cross the coven again, not after what she did. She doesn't want to be near these women, even though they are her family and have been part of every important day of her life. And life she will have now, but what sort will it be? To her fellow witches this is not a tragedy, but a victory. Tara wants to lock her door and weep.

She can't stand to stay at the farm. She can't listen to the younger witches' requests for details about the breaking or the unintentional condescension of the elders about the matter. Father helps Tara escape for a little while. Mother understands and gives her blessing. Tara stays with her uncle in the next village for a few months. Uncle does not ask the reason for the visit. Behind his kind words and actions, Tara knows he is afraid of her and her powers.

Sooner than she expects, Tara starts to miss her parents and friends, dancing at the full moon with the other witches, conversations about magic with Lady Lavinia. Tara is not brave enough to run away forever. When she comes back the coven's farm, her belly is swollen and she is not happy, but content for the first time in ages.

Her late lover has been reduced to fantastical tales. Tara hears a rumor that he made a pact with the devil and was burned to death as a consequence. She believes that the coven shaped the stories told with a spell or two. Or perhaps it was her protective spell, the magic transforming to defend herself from the townsfolk's persecution. Still, people whisper when she walks by. But Tara finds she lacks the energy to feel angry about it. Any other time they will ask her for wisdom and help as a witch. Mother tells her that the coven and Father did not participate in the community while she was gone. The residents are grateful when the witches returned. People do need magic in their lives, as brutal and dangerous as it may be.

In the early days of fall, her daughter is born. She loves fire a little too much.

▲

Hag Race
by Andre E. Harewood

[[Now Available In Described Thought]]

"Previously on Jean-Paul's Hag Race…" a perky voice heralds.

Several festive tea lights burn gently on a long white table as wind blows through the willow trees in the middle of an ancient cemetery. Chief judge, Jean-Paul Tiresias, sits at the table flanked by two other judges: a pale, large-breasted woman and a dark man in a classic undertaker hat and suit. An hourglass with its sand almost expended rests before Tiresias, a brown-skinned man in a sequined black suit with ridiculously wide padded shoulders, a garish purple tie set against a sky blue shirt, sporting a hairdo that would make a resurrected Madame de Pompadour envious. Two women stand on the grass before the judges with a broom between them: one crying hysterically in a red stained apron, the other with resting bitch face in an extremely short and extremely dishevelled haute couture dress.

"Régine Heaux, the self-proclaimed baddest witch of them all," Tiresias says to the stone-faced one. "Your love potion was supposed to bring two lucky souls together, not have random people getting lucky in an orgy in downtown Lima. Still, you didn't almost kill your targets like Mary Jane did. Confabulations, you're safe this week. Hop on your broomstick, baby, and fly free."

"Grâce à Dieu," Régine whispers in a thick French accent while bowing slightly. The broom next to her levitates, she straddles it in a most unladylike fashion, and she flies off into the starry sky.

"Mary Jane Strange, our resident apothecary," Tiresias announces to the weeping woman. "Your blood marmalade should have been a classic… but it put you in a jam."

Tiresias touches the top of the hourglass as the last grain of sand falls.

"Your time is past. Light the faggots… and burn away."

A pillar of fire descends from the sky, completely engulfing her screaming body before disappearing.

The perky announcer chimes in, "It's time for the season two finale of Jean-Paul's Hag Race!"

A flood of colour, feathers and entrails, graves and epileptic fit-inducing strobes flash, revealing an aerial shot of a beautiful island resembling an upside down Africa. Quick images of the bustling city streets, lush beaches, exotic party nightlife, and smiling faces dissolve to the side profile of Jean-Paul Tiresias in the same outfit as before standing at the edge of an infinity pool at high noon. The scene is completed by a brilliantly white coral stone pool deck with palm trees and tropical flowers all around, and nothing but the expanse of Caribbean Sea beyond. Tiresias turns, revealing a feminine other half with a shaved head, a green bathing suit, and a black high heeled shoe. Tiresias is split perfectly down the middle between masculine and feminine.

"Hello, hello, hello, my little witches!" Tiresias says, both commanding and sweet. "It's been a long and winding road but we're finally here on location in breathtaking Barbados for the season finale! Our little coven has been whittled down to the top three vying to become my disciple for the next lunar year, a position that will take that lucky witch or warlock around the worlds and beyond! Let me introduce the fiendish finalists!"

Three people are tied to white stone pillars raised in the middle of the pool. The pillars have small ledges on which they stand.

"We were just in his hometown last episode. From La Nouvelle-Orléans, Louisiana… Hollis Schiti, better known as Bubba Yaga."

"I prefer New Orleans. I don't wanna sound all Old World [BLEEP]y like some people," the large black man in jeans and a red flannel shirt on the left says with a smile.

"Fresh from almost being eliminated last week and originally from Marseilles, France… Stuck in the middle is Régine Heaux!"

"Brûle en l'enfer, salaud," the pale woman with unshaved underarms in a strapless, animal print Roberto Cavalli evening gown that has seen better days retorts to the man beside her. She emphasizes the remark by rolling her eyes.

"Oh no, Heaux," he replies. "I'm a carnivore. I don't eat 'salad'."

"And finally," Tiresias adds, "on walkabout from Queensland, Australia… Kimberly Shane, Wandjina."

The over-tanned white woman with flowing blonde hair in a sequined silver pants suit smiles broadly.

"I'm just happy to be here, Jean-Paul."

"And it's funny Régine should mention burning in Hell…" Tiresias pours the clear contents of a vial into the pool, almost instantly transforming the water into raging fire. The witches groan and wriggle against their pillars and their bonds as the flames come within a foot of them or closer.

"Feel that, witches? That's something worse than burning in Hell: burning into nothingness, into insignificance, into obscurity. You three have survived when your ten coven mates perished... metaphorically speaking. Do you have what it takes to enter the crucible and come out stronger? A winner?"

A second vial's sky blue contents return the pool to normal, much to the witches' relief.

"I have to thank my current reigning disciple, Henrietta Mann, for being a special guest oracle last week. Now let me introduce the oracles I will be consulting for the finale."

The tall, thin black man in undertaker wear from the previous episode and a short, well-muscled white man with flowing black hair and no shirt walk around the gorgeous pool deck to stand beside Tiresias.

"You remember Conrad Hartman, born here in beautiful Barbados, haruspex to the stars, and descendant of the infamous and much maligned Tituba."

"I hope you're enjoying my island and my home. I'm looking forward to seeing what they have to offer this time, Jean-Paul."

"Of course I invited you back, Conrad. I didn't want you using my liver to see who would win!"

"I does only use animal parts. You know them just vicious rumours."

"Of course they are, Conrad. Of course... And my best fiend forever, the master of the arcane invocation, the beautiful and buff Feguel Barrage. What's the word on our winner?"

"Still a secret, JP. My lips to The Dark One's ears."

"With your loose lips, you never could keep a secret... but it's no secret that it all ends here for two of you, so to speak. This live Halloween aetheric broadcast will announce the winner but we've got lots to show you experiencing this before then. This time around, our witches had to perform two impressive feats: a small, intimate one and a larger, more public one of their own choosing. First up: Régine Heaux!"

The ropes binding the French woman disappear, allowing her to move her hands, but she is still confined to the small raised area on her pillar in the middle of the pool.

"Oui, Jean-Paul. For my first challenge, I decided to... eh... do something small yet important. So much history has been... eh... lost due to ignorance and fear. I have decided to... eh... help recover some of it."

The pool becomes a screen showing the image of grimoires and other old tomes.

"In one of these, the Wið færstice, I found a recipe for fighting gout may be able to... eh... treat and cure herpes. I..."

"Wait, witch. Wait," Bubba Yaga interjects. "You went searching through old books from the Dark Ages to find a cure for an STD? It don't get more Eurotrash than that."

"It is… eh… necessary, responsible for us to do this, to bring back old learning as Wicca goes on."

"Wicca? Witch, please. I'm a 45 year old man who steals bone dust from graves, puts curses on penises, makes you fall in love again with your ex, and raises old rich men from the dead because they died before changing their wills to leave everything to their twenty one year old hood rat wives. All for money. Do I look like some Earth goddess worshipping, hail to the watchtower of the north vegan who couldn't summon a bath if her pumpkin spice latee'd, coconut oiled, dreadlocked life depended on it? No offense, Mary Jane Strange, wherever you are. [BLEEP]ing Wiccans, going around ruining [BLEEP] for real witches an' warlocks."

"Comme j'allais dire… I… eh… left the recipe with doctors who can… eh… research it deeper."

"Very well," Tiresias comments. "And your major challenge, Régine?"

"Russia… eh… banned Wicca recently, calling it… eh… extremist group but that is only first step. Chechnya has been… eh… torturing and killing witches for a long time."

The pool shows naked men and women driven by armed soldiers out into the deep snow of a dark forest.

"A lucky few survive, magicks protect them. Most freeze or, in warmer time, are shot. Witch hunts are more common every day but there is… eh… underground movement, oui? Border security is heavy. There is almost no way out. So I… eh… create diversion."

Soldiers and government officials scratch themselves until they are bloody, others vomit and convulse on the ground, some dance and jump and laugh and cry as though possessed.

"Mass psychogenic illness. Conversion disorder. Call it whatever. They were… eh… under extreme stress, already afraid of what the evil witches might do to them. It did not take much to… eh… push them over edge. I communicated with Chechen witches using… eh… entrails, sometimes livers. You appreciate that, Monsieur Hartman. Witches and allies act in strange ways around authorities. Soon authorities act like them and it spreads. Some even believed their… eh… penises were disappearing. Our people escape during that week, that mad season."

Dozens of people, sometimes entire families, run across border checkpoints, sometimes stepping over incapacitated soldiers.

"C'est ça. C'est tout."

"Thank you, Régine," Tiresias said. "Now… Bubba Yaga!"

"I wasn't as flashy as Ms. Ghetto Fabulous Paris over here but I think I done good," Bubba says as his ropes disappeared. "Scary things are happening in America. The alt-right is gaining more and more support for destroying anything not straight, white, Christian, male, and 'American'. Now they're making a run for the presidency."

The pool shifts to show a middle-aged man with a wrinkled, prune-like face, stark white hair, pale skin, and a smile that makes you feel uncomfortable the more you look at it since you can't seem to make yourself look away.

"Michael Pound is the underdog but we all saw what happened the last time sensible people underestimated someone in the election. He represents everything that's wrong with America, from being in bed with big business to hating minority groups, the environment, and science. The only thing he isn't is a part of the Illuminati. Or so you'd think…"

A much younger Pound is shaking hands with a man with dishevelled long hair in black leather who is sticking his tongue out and making a sign akin to devil's horns with his free hand.

"That's dark metal band Behæmaggot's lead singer Nergal Marduk with Governor Pound on The Latest Show back in 2001. The real story is that the Latest Show's production team thought it would be funny to book a right wing conservative politician and Satanic performers on the same night. It was [BLEEP]ing hilarious watching Pound squirm while Marduk talked about philosophical Satanism and the ultimate meaninglessness of existence. Clips from the show with Pound and Narduk shaking hands were always paired with clips of Nergal expounding on Luciferianism and growling out songs about burning down churches, so it was easy to make the connection between Pound and the Left Hand Path. Memory is a tricky and malleable thing, Jean-Paul, especially when the bits are already in the mind just waiting for something to cross-connect them. It didn't even take magick at all to do that. I just found the old clips on üTübe, repackaged them a bit, and watched them go viral. So many people now 'remember' seeing Pound agree with Marduk on that show, even throwing up his own devil signs along with the band. Sometimes the mind can perform wonders without the need for a spell. I don't know if that's enough to make him lose the Republican nomination but a few hundred million views on üTübe and millions more across other social media platforms later, I've done my bit."

"But that's not magick, Bubba," Wandjina comments.

"Listen, witch," Bubba retorts, "I went back to school at 41 and got a degree in network security with a minor in social media marketing. I'm not some one trick unicorn. Who needs to scry when I can just hack your Snapchat? Memes are magick."

"Very well, Bubba. Trickery and misdirection have always been mainstays of magick through the millennia." Jean-Paul pronounces. "And your major challenge?"

"Thank you, Jean-Paul. Carlos Ortega, the man behind a few multi-billion dollar telecommunications and textiles companies, the man with a net worth almost equal to Bill Gates, the man who can't have the only thing he truly wants: a kid."

"Un cabri?" Régine jokes.

"Un enfant, ton imbécile," Bubba replies in his thick Louisiana drawl, much to the amusement of the judges.

"What?" Wandjina asks.

"Do not worry, child. It was…eh…good one," Régine concedes with a smirk.

The pool shows an older man of Latin descent and his beautiful and very young Nordic wife.

"As I was saying… Ortega can't have kid… children. A genetic mutation means science is, at the moment, not an option for him in getting Vigdis pregnant. Where money and medicine fail, that is where the basic principles of magick succeed. He wants nothing more than to carry on his family name. He grew up dirt poor in Honduras, barely getting by on what money his father sent home for his wife and only child from working illegally in the US. His father was doing some other things in the US, too, like having another family."

The pool shows a rundown home in a Los Angeles barrio. An old Latin man stands on its porch shouting at a teenager who looks very much like him and Carlos.

"Pops was smart enough to know he couldn't afford more than two sons, especially when he might have to hide from Immigration, so he only had one other child: Marco. But Marco was as rebellious as Carlos was studious, in prison as much as his brother was in school. When their father died, Marco was in the middle of five years in jail for robbery, and Carlos was in the middle of his master's degree in international business. An old friend got together enough money to ship the old man's body home for burial but didn't think it was right to tell Carlos and his mother about his half-brother and the other life his father had lived. So Carlos never knew about Marco and Marco never knew about Carlos. When their father's friend in the States died, there was no way for them to find out about each other… until I came along. Carlos open sourced his unique DNA out to scientists to see if they could find a way to let me him reproduce. I was the only person who ran that DNA through the International Forensics Database."

"So you reunited… well… united the family?"

"Yes, Jean-Paul. I let Carlos know that I could provide him with the continuation of his family name for a price."

"And did you?"

Ripples reveal a private jet landing at a nondescript airport, Carlos being helped down to the tarmac to cautiously greet five men who look very much like him.

"Marco got around when he wasn't in prison or getting murdered. Five sons from five different women, and all of them kept on the straight and narrow. The Ortega boys were doctors, lawyers, radio announcers... and good fathers themselves. Carlos got a version of what he wanted while I got what I wanted in return."

"Which was?" Fequel Barrage chimes in. "This family drama has been interesting but not interesting. How does this all tie in with witch-craft?"

"There are witch camps in Ghana filled with men, women, and children shunned and violently thrown out of their communities either for real or imagined witchcraft or real or imagined charges listed as witch-craft so that the superstitious would reject the victims. These camps have existed for hundreds of years, providing some measure of safety for those in them from the sometimes violent masses but keeping their inmates from truly living or getting the help they need. In exchange for giving him flesh and blood heirs, Ortega has secretly provided [BLEEP]ing mil-lions of dollars to the Anti-Witchcraft Allegations Campaign Coalition of Ghana. He's almost singlehandedly paying for the dismantling of the country's witch camps. He's funding mental health drives and education initiatives to help improve the lives of witches, the poor bastards wrong-fully accused, and the general population."

"I applaud what you've done so far, Bubba Yaga," Fequel interjects again, "but I'm not sure how anything you've done in either challenge counts as magick. I know what JP has ruled before and JP has the right to that view but I don't think you've fulfilled the criteria of using magick to resolve your challenges."

"I must respectfully disagree," Bubba replies. "I used the magick of the mind before. I used the magick of the machine here, tugged on the strands of chance, and followed the ghostly footprints left in the aether of cyberspace. How many true witches have read a palm or consulted a crystal ball while using their observational skills and understanding of human nature to make a mark believe the witch knows their thoughts, their past, and their future? Witches were the first detectives, mixing gut intuition with keen investigation and subtle manipulation. I accom-plished everything in these challenges without having to sacrifice an ant. If that ain't magick, I don't know what is."

There was a brief silence before Conrad Hartman speaks, "I gotta agree with Bubba Yaga. Consulting guts or performing a summoning can be easy ways out sometimes. In the end, it's all witchcraft. It's all magick."

"I agree," Tiresias pronounces. "Well done, Bubba. And finally, Wandjina."

"Thank you, Jean-Paul," Wandjina begins in her sickeningly sweet Australian accent. "In the southern Pacific, twenty seven hundred kilometres from the nearest land, there's a place that has many names. The spacecraft cemetery, Point Nemo, the oceanic pole of inaccessibility... It's barren, mostly lifeless, and you may get a satellite falling on you if you're not careful, mate."

The pool around her swirls, taking on images of the seemingly endless ocean and a super tanker floating in the vastness.

"Sensitives all over the world started having fitful dreams six months ago, nightmares of a ship whose crew prayed down into the abyss and the abyss whose darkness answered, reaching up to meet them. I walk in dreams so I followed the strands of somnolescent horror to the hijacked TI Oceania super tanker floating at the point in the ocean farthest from any land. The crew had been killed once the ship reached its destination so only the cultists remained."

Men and women in filthy clothes slice apart and place the limbs and organs and blood of the crew in a pattern akin to diagrams of the Earth's magnetic field, marring the ship's brilliant white with lines of offal red.

"I don't know what rite they were performing, what abomination they were invoking. Maybe it was something that caught a ride to Earth on a decommissioned spaceship, maybe it had been down there all along, I don't know and I don't want to know. Whatever it is, I reckon the cultists were almost ready to wake it and bring it up."

Two destroyers bearing United Nations markings approach the super tanker.

"Satellite images showed the carnage on deck but there was no way to be sure if any crew were still alive below. Any Peacekeepers trying to get aboard would have been killed by the wards erected by the cultists or simply shot or stabbed or savagely torn limb from limb by them. I couldn't do anything about what happened on the super tanker but I could get them to it safely. They needed something to get them through the apotropaic velleity safely, and I gave it to them in dreams the night before. It was a simple lorica, a shielding prayer I repurposed from an old ditty... 'Do not brood upon the chaos dark and rude, but bid its angry tumult cease, and give, for wild confusion, peace.'"

The soldiers mouth the words as their patrol boats approach the super tanker and pass through an almost invisible web surrounding it, fatal strands trying to cling them but futilely falling into the boats or water and disappearing.

"They boarded the ship and had to kill all the cultists. Most of the Peacekeepers survived, and whatever's down there is still down there waiting for its next chance at freedom. That's someone else's problem now but I think it'll turn out OK. She'll be right, I reckon. She'll be right."

"And your second challenge, Wandjina?" Tiresias asks.

"Islamic State fighters in Syria have been…"

"Les millénaires," Régine scoffs just loud enough to be heard.

"…in Syria have been murdering 'witches', and the numbers are increasing. Whether real witches and warlocks or people with mental illnesses or unlucky enough to make someone angry at them, over fifty have been beheaded so far for the year."

The pool shows devastated Syrian cities and the homeless about to become refugees fleeing with little more than their lives.

"I decided to do my part to stop the fighting. The dreams of insurgents are filled with gore and glory. They are very easy to track. I just put that one such location into the mind of an American general when they were planning to bomb the ever-loving [BLEEP] out of the bastards."

The stark landscape of a Syrian city is obliterated by a string of massive explosions.

"Nom de Dieu!" Régine shouts. "Qu'avez-vous fait?!"

"Seven bombs each with a blast yield of ten tons of TNT. Over two thousand IS militants killed in a matter of seconds."

"[BLEEP]," Bubba says softly.

"You know that killing… especially killing on such a grand scale… is against the rules of this competition, don't you, Wandjina?"

"I know. I have to do whatever I can to be a force for good in this world. If that means I get disqualified, so be it. I can't rest on my laurels anymore."

"Witch, please," Bubba interjects. "Like you have morals."

"I said 'laurels'."

"I heard you… and I saw you blow up two thousand people. You don't have any of those, either."

"You don't understand."

"That's fine. We'll never see eye to eye… and not just 'cause we're different heights."

"Witches, please!" Tiresias interjects. "While the naiad familiars bring you some local rum punch, I will consult the oracles and inform you of my decisions."

With a finger snap, Tiresias makes the water of the pool form an opaque dome over the three contestants while she, Fequel, and Conrad retire to polished mahogany deck chairs under a white umbrella.

"All three did impressive work that will further their own reputations and help witches and humanity in general. With that out of the way, let's start with Régine Heaux. Fequel?"

"I applaud her finding and repurposing an ancient potion but Régine and Bubba were almost in the same boat on the last challenge. I think we can speak about them together. They used trickery and played mind games but was it magick? At least Régine talked with her witches through hepatomancy."

"After the last twelve episodes of bringing it to reach the finale," Tiresias says, "they achieved their most potent and wide reaching effects by not using spells at all. That's impressive."

"I agree," Conrad Hartman adds. "As was said earlier, manipulating memes and machines and minds? That's old school meets new school magick. You don't have to summon a demon to achieve what they did. Hells, a summoned demon would probably have given them instructions on how to do exactly what they achieved by themselves."

"Maybe but it seems very basic, Conrad," Fequel points out.

"Your shtick is controlling people with your voice. You size them up, read their body language, interpret their responses to your questions or comments, and then you formulate your magick words to make them do what you want. We can go back and forth on this but Bubba and Régine successfully took the intrinsic non-arcane aspects of magick almost to their logical extreme."

Fequel scoffs. "I'd hate to see what they could accomplish if they had fewer morals."

"Is that possible?" Tiresias jokes.

The three laugh heartily before Tiresias brings up the final contestant.

"Speaking about morality… What about Wandjina? Feguel?"

"Her first challenge was well done. She stepped in to solve a problem you told me had been on the Planar Coven's watch list for a while. She helped stop it before it escalated… but her second challenge? Saving their lives so soldiers can stop deranged cultists versus giving directions on where to drop bombs? In both cases, she gave used dreams to give information to get people killed. Our rules preclude murder… I should say the rules of this show preclude murder, much less mass murder."

"She technically didn't end anyone herself," Tiresias points out.

"You're splitting that hair mighty thin, JP," Fequel says with annoyance in his voice. "If I discovered a serial killer in my neighbourhood and whispered in a cop's ear that Buffalo Jill lived at the end of my cul-de-sac, aren't I responsible for whatever happens next? If Buffalo Jill maims and kills a few cops before being blown away, isn't all that blood on my hands? On my vocal cords?"

Conrad scoffs. "Stop lying, Fequel. If you discovered Buffalo Jill in your neighbourhood, you'd tell her to confess then kill herself."

"Probably but I wouldn't be doing that as part of a show with a strict policy prohibiting killing."

"If we can put aside the killing game for a moment," Tiresias interjects, "we can focus on what I think are the biggest issues here. We have one contestant who showcased her specialty for the umpteenth time while the other two contestants showed their versatility."

"But it's a magick competition!" Fequel shouts.

"And there are many forms of magick!" Conrad shouts back. "We all know that poor horse has been beaten to death in the last few minutes."

"Not as dead as Wandjina's victims."

"Cultists and terrorists, Conrad. Not exactly innocents… but I'm not surprised you're concerned about their deaths. You're a descendant of the woman who caused the Salem Witch Trials. I've heard you're not above vivisecting young children in sugar cane fields to make the best predictions, either."

Fequel and Conrad stand, facing each other angrily. Three loud hands claps from Tiresias get their attention. They sit in silence. "This is why I become a woman sometimes. I can't stand all the testosterone. Silence. I have made my decision. Let's see what our remaining coven has been up to."

The watery shell shimmers, revealing the witches inside still standing on their pedestals.

"…a pity you're not… eh… hag queen," Régine says to Bubba. "Your name could be Holli Schitt. I worked with old enchantress named that in Prague years ago."

Three naiads, water spirits able to assume a basic human shape, step through the dome with tall glasses of bright pink rum punch complete with little umbrellas in them. The contestants happily take the tropical alcohol. On inspection, the glasses and umbrellas appear to be water in a very rigid but not frozen form.

"Thank you. Yup, I can see that. I'm from down south and love eatin' chicken so Bubba Yaga works."

With drinks delivered, the naiads become one with the watery dome.

After a sip, Wandjina asks, "You always have that little hip flask, Bubba. Wanna spike these drinks with a little Louisiana Special?"

"Nah. That's my special brew. For emergencies."

"Fair enough, mate. What do you think each of our chances are? Régine"

"I am... eh... proud of my work. If I win? Très bon. If not? Ça ne fait rien. Bubba?"

"I came to [BLEEP]ing win this thing. I think the oracles will appreciate my minimalist approaches that yielded maximum results."

"I am... eh... in the same boat. I believe I have... eh... shown that I can do anything with almost nothing."

"Well, I stuck with what I know and can do best," Wandjina says.

"And what you do best is get people... eh... blown up, oui?"

"I'm not up myself as much as you are, Régine. I want to use the Dreamtime to help others, not just get myself designer clothes."

Bubba sucks his teeth. "Straight outta Oz, huh? You're pretty. That's good, but spend less time on the beach without sunblock, OK? You're almost as brown as I am. You walk in dreams and influence people's behaviours. That's also good, but I think you made that magical unicorn you summoned [BLEEP] you up the ass with its 12 inch horn a bit too hard a few too many times since you seem to believe this whole Australian Dreamtime fantasy you're milking. What you do is oneiric manipulation, swimming on the top layer of what the real Dreamtime is. You can't dive down far enough to grasp its true depth and power. Arcane [BLEEP]ing appropriation."

"Stop being a [BLEEP]ing sook. You're always whinging like a little [BLEEP] about hex equality and interhexonality."

"Looks like all my hexplaining hasn't helped you any, huh? And you're the Millennial. She's a lot of things but at least Régine here knows her eldritch history and what she's drawing on."

"Merci... for what felt like... eh... microaggression."

"We're're too old to use these words, Régine. It's a good thing we're in this nice safe space, though."

"I've tried like a galah to be nice to every witch in this competition," Wandjina says angrily, "and I'm not going to take [BLEEP] from either of you anymore!"

Régine put her non-drinking hand in the air while taking a large gulp of her rum punch.

"What happened?" Bubba asks with a smirk. "Ride your broom so hard you got splinters in your nethers? It's a joke, witch, not a dick. Don't take it so hard."

Wandjina throws her fruity rum punch at Bubba. The warlock quickly weaves a sigil in the air that pauses the alcohol in mid-flight.

Bubba smiles. "That's a trick I learned from a real wandjina near Kata Tjuta, by the way."

The water dome morphs back into a pool again. The naiads rise from the restored waters to retrieve the glasses. Bubba and Régine quickly down their drinks and join Wandjina in giving back the glasses. One of the naiads merges its water form with the floating pink liquid and all three again become one with the pool. Tiresias, Fequel, and Conrad have gone back to the edge of the infinity pool. A deathly pale blonde woman with sizeable breasts in a tight black dress stands with them.

"Witches," Tiresias announces, "I have made some decisions. Régine Heaux! Bubba Yaga! You two look to the future while embracing the past. Wandjina! We wrestled with the morality of your actions more than you seem to. Once we put that issue aside, we felt that, for a magician who deals in dreams, your efforts were largely unimaginative and monotonous."

Wandjina lets out a quick yet violent gasp.

"I'm sorry, my dear, but your time is past. Light the faggots… and burn away."

The pool once again catches fire, its flames avoiding Bubba and Régine while engulfing the crying Wandjina in a blinding flash. Once the others open their eyes, she is gone.

"Henrietta Mann, one of my oracles last week and my current disciple, is here for the handover. She has excelled at everything I have asked of her, and I know she is ready to go out into the worlds as one of the baddest witches alive or undead. Is there anything you'd like to say to the final two before I announce who will be my new disciple for the next lunar year?"

Henrietta smiles, revealing shark-like teeth and a slithering tongue. "Gendered pronouns are difficult when you're in your half-and-half mood, so… I must thank you for the opportunity to have served and learned from you, Tiresias. I travelled across Earth, ventured beyond Ultima Thule, danced with the Seelie and Unseelie Courts, followed songlines in the Australian Outback, shopped at African Markets of the Dead… So many wonderful experiences. So much time spent learning and growing. I used to be that creepy hemomancer cutting herself to power her spells. Now, thanks to you, Tiresias, I don't have to do that anymore."

Small drops of red liquid appear on everyone's skin but Henrietta's, quickly forming into small streams that flow into Henrietta's now crimson eyes.

"You [BLEEP]…" Tiresias curses after falling to the deck. Fequel and Conrad are similarly incapacitated, Fequel being speechless for the first time in his life. Régine and Bubba barely hold onto their pedestals in the middle of the pool.

"Now I can use your blood, too, the blood of the most powerful mages I can get my hands on at the moment. I learned this one when you sent me to Prague from… What was her name? Ah! Holli Schitt."

"I see… that name is… now free, Bubba," Régine tries to joke.

"I know another… name that's… about to be free! You knew Schitt. Can you… disrupt this draining?"

"Not much!"

"Do it… on me! Quick!"

With a weak wave of her left hand and the middle finger of her right, Régine unleashes a blue wave over Bubba that slows his blood loss. The life is still literally being drained from him, from all of them, but Bubba manages to find the strength to reach for his silver hip flask and throw it Henrietta. The blood mage effortlessly pauses it in mid-air a foot from her face.

"I learned that in the Outback, too," Henrietta explains.

"I know," Bubba says. "You… killed the wandjina who… taught you that. Her sister's the one… who taught me that trick. She also… taught me… something you never learned."

"And what's that, Bub?"

"How to… defend… against it."

Henrietta's blood-filled eyes shoot back from looking at Bubba to the flask, its silver turning green hot. She is about to weave a teleportation spell for the flask when it explodes, imbedding silver shrapnel throughout the front of her body and covering her in acidic bile. She screams and tries to throw herself in the pool but the naiads move the water out of the way, leaving her to crash into the tiles of the deep end. After a few more seconds, the blood drain from the others stops as there is nothing left of her body but a yellow-green stain in the general shape of a human being on the bottom of the pool. Within a minute, everyone is almost back to normal.

"I'm gonna be the one associated with drinks getting thrown in witches' faces this season," Bubba predicts coldly.

"Merde! How did you know, Bubba?" Régine asks as she catches her breath and clutches her pillar.

"Hacked her private email server when I got the call to be on this season. I wanted to see what her experience as the disciple of Tiresias was like. I saw a [BLEEP] ton more than that. Conrad helped me make sure I was ready to stop her when the time was right."

"That was my pleasure," Conrad says in a strained voice, "but this certainly is not."

"And you didn't think to [BLEEP]ing tell JP that his disciple was [BLEEP]ing insane?!" Fequel shouts while helping Tiresias up.

"They told me last night, Fequel," Tiresias explains. "I just didn't tell you. I know how bad you are with secrets, even mortal ones. Loose lips and all that. We weren't sure exactly when Henrietta would make her move but we knew it would be sometime today. None of us were prepared for how vigorous her enervation would be. Bubba, you prepared for this moment for a while. You played the long game, consulted with other arcanists, used quick thinking in the heat of mystic battle, and ultimately saved us all. I don't think anyone here would be surprised or upset when I say that I've chosen you to be my next disciple!"

The water in the pool becomes a rainbow of surging, churning colour that still avoids where Henrietta's puddle is. The pillars and pedestals form a walkway for Bubba and Régine to reach the deck, and they hug as they walk. Once they reach the others, Tiresias embraces Régine.

"I just want to say to you, Régine, that you had an equal chance of winning this competition. We didn't know when Henrietta would strike. My decision would have been based solely on the challenges if this hadn't happened now. And I also want to thank you for helping save all our lives."

"D'accord. Je comprends. I was not the one with... eh... exploding bottle."

"Since I assume it's okay to tell me [BLEEP] now," Fequel says angrily, "what the [BLEEP] was in that flask, Bubba?!"

"Day old piss, battery acid, and Flint County water. Guess which one was most dangerous."

"The most dangerous thing here is you with a computer!" Tiresias says before hugging him. "Confabulations, Bubba Yaga! You're the winner of Jean-Paul's Hag Race!"

"Thank you so much, Tiresias. Does this position come with full medical insurance?"

As they all laugh and hug, the rainbow effects from the pool grow brighter and brighter until only two words flash in your mind...

THE END!

▲

Best Friend Becky
by Wayne Faust

Sammy slept fitfully in her small bed in the attic room. Downstairs a clock chimed twice. Outside the grimy window, the October air had turned cold, and an early frost descended on the small town. A wood fire sputtered in the Franklin stove by the far wall and amber firelight danced around the edges of its doors. A small stack of apple wood rested in a wicker basket next to the stove, in case Sammy awoke during the night to a cold room. Dr. Brooks, Sammy's cat, lay by Sammy's pillow and poked his gray and white head in the air, firelight reflecting in his powder blue eyes.

Sammy had fitful dreams for a child. Her Mom told everyone that her daughter was a 40 year old in an 8 year old body. She was always posing questions to adults, questions that no one her age was supposed to even think about. Maybe that explained why she slept so lightly, and why she awoke in the middle of this long autumn night, even though the voice that spoke was muffled and soft.

"I'm Best Friend Becky, and I love you."

The voice came from a doll perched atop an antique, oaken bookcase next to the window. Sammy had gotten the doll from her Aunt Cynthia on her birthday in August. It was one of those dolls where you pulled a string on its back and a mechanical voice recited one of several phrases. But this time, no one had pulled the string.

Dr. Brooks meowed and arched his back. Sammy's eyes fluttered open and she lay there on her side, facing the bookcase, head still on the pillow.

"Best Friend Becky wants to be your best friend. Will you be my best friend?"

Sammy tried to sort the last of the dream voices in her head from the real, waking sounds of the room. Moonlight silhouetted the doll and Sammy saw it move slightly, cocking its head to the side.

"Best Friend Becky wants to play. Do you want to play?"

Sammy slowly raised her head. The doll's voice hadn't sounded like the tinny, machine voice she had always heard before. This voice sounded more like a real voice. It sounded like a grownup woman's voice, like maybe someone was hiding behind the bookcase, making the voice for the doll. But the bookcase was all the way against the wall so that couldn't be.

"Best Friend Becky wants you to wake up. Best friends don't sleep the night away."

The doll only had seven phrases and Sammy had never heard that one before.

The fire inside the Franklin stove flared briefly and illuminated the doll's face. The doll turned its head side to side in a jerky, robot-like way. At the same time it moved its hands up and down in a chopping motion.

Dr. Brooks hissed. Sammy sat upright and stroked the cat's back. Fully awake now, she stared towards the bookcase. Huge shadows played on the walls in the flickering light. From that angle the doll could have been one of those dinosaurs that glared down at you from the halls of the natural history museum.

"Best Friend Becky doesn't like to sit alone all night. Best friends shouldn't make their best friends angry."

Outside, a gust of wind blew a few brown maple leaves against the windowpane. A nighthawk shrieked in the distance. Sammy swung her legs down to the floor. Dr. Brooks rubbed against her hip.

"Best Friend Becky is very bored."

The doll sounded impatient, like Sammy's Mom got when Sammy didn't clean her room.

Sammy touched her bare feet to the cold, linoleum floor. She reached for the pink, fuzzy slippers she kept by the night stand. She put them on and carefully stood up.

"Best Friend Becky is very upset. Best Friend Becky is gonna do something bad." The doll moved its hands faster. It was less jerky now and there was a peculiar, fluid motion in the way it turned its head.

Sammy took a short, reluctant step towards the bookcase.

"Best Friend Becky wants to play now!"

Sammy took two more steps. She was nearly at the bookcase.

"Best Friend Becky is going to be naughty!" The doll's eyes gleamed red. It pointed its flesh-colored, plastic finger at Sammy and bared its teeth. Dr. Brooks spat at it from under the bed.

Sammy gritted her teeth and reached out. She grabbed the doll by the neck and shook it. It shrieked and tried to bite Sammy's hand but her grip was too tight.

She quickly moved across the room to the Franklin stove and opened the door. She threw the doll into the flames and slammed the black, iron door shut behind it. She heard a few more shrieks and then the soft sound of fabric and plastic burning. Then it was quiet.

Dr. Brooks crawled out from under the bed.

"Why can't I ever just get a doll like the other kids?" asked Sammy to Dr. Brooks. "Why do they have to come to life all the time? Did Aunt Cynthia think I'd be scared? I'm like a hundred times bigger than a doll. Duh! Why do we have to have witches in the family?"

Sammy climbed back into bed and fell quickly asleep, wishing her family could be just a bit more like everybody else's.

▲

The Rat in the Rabbit Cage
by Ashley Dioses

"I'm telling you, it's that rat. It grows patches of fur that are the same color as my pets, but only after they go missing." Theodora gripped her tea cup tightly.

My sister was waiting for me to say something but I didn't know what to tell her; I stalled by taking another sip of tea. I could hear my daughter, Annabel, upstairs in the guest bedroom reading to her Calico rabbit, Clarence. I neglected to tell her that Theodora didn't have any game consoles for her to play with until after we were in the car and on our way. Thankfully, she settled for the books I brought for her to amuse herself with and, of course, the rabbit.

"Emily," Theodora whispered, drawing back my attention.

"You're being ridiculous. What you're suggesting is crazy. Why would Meredith hurt your pets? She's an old crone who barely leaves her house to tend her garden," I said.

"A garden full of belladonna and oleander. Poison! Along with other strange herbs I've never seen before," Theodora said.

Meredith Murray was an ancient woman who lived alone in the house next door for decades. Strange lights were often seen coming from the home's small-paned windows at night, strange noises were also reported from the house, at the time no one from town ever remembered seeing any guests visit; rarely had anyone seen Meredith leave except to work in her garden.

Theodora was well-versed in the knowledge of herbs, vegetables, and plants, but I thought she was overstretching it a bit to accuse the old woman of something nefarious.

"What about the rat? He's proof enough, isn't he? I think it's the same one," Theodora said. There was no rat. At least not anymore. When I had arrived here, she had no animals, including this fabled rat.

When I read her hastily typed email, it was clear that she was in a state of panic.

I never had to worry about Theodora being alone. She was an independent person and very capable of taking care of herself. Now she seemed paranoid and afraid. It was a side I'd never seen before.

When Annabel and I arrived, Theodora looked frazzled. Her brown curly hair was wild and her blue eyes were red with weariness. After she opened the door, she froze upon seeing Clarence; it was only after a long moment of silence that she forced a smile and welcomed us in.

I didn't let her emotions shake me.

"Last fall, Edgar, my black cat, brought me a white rat when I stepped outside one morning. I could tell by the way its head drooped at an odd angle that it was dead. I didn't know it was a pet until I saw its collar. When I read it, I knew it belonged to Meredith.

"I was so crushed, because I couldn't even imagine losing a pet like that. I found a nice little box to put him in and I went next door to give it to her." She fixed her gaze upon me and continued:

"Meredith was so frightening, Emily. She was just a skeleton with yellow skin dripping from her bones. It was a wonder she was able to walk to the door unaided. But it was her eyes that made my skin crawl. They glistened like faceted emeralds." Theodora gripped her arms and visibly shivered. A sweet melody came from the guest bedroom as Annabel sang to Clarence. Theodora seemed to notice it for the first time. She listened for a few moments before turning back to me.

"I kept apologizing, but she said nothing. She just took him and closed the door in my face. Then everything went wrong."

Theodora took a few more swigs of tea and upon draining it, fumbled with the tea pot to pour some more, but it was already empty. She got up to make some more and I took this opportunity to check on Annabel, who had put a little straw hat on Clarence and was pouring him imaginary tea into a doll cup.

I returned to the chair and waited patiently for Theodora to come back.

Theodora lived alone on a small old farm. The house had faded with age, so creaks and sounds of the house settling would be expected, but it seemed there were none to be heard. Shadows crawled from rickety columns outside and roof tiles littered the surrounding patio. The white steps were little more than fragile bone, ever fading in the hot California sun.

A sea of green corn stalks stretched across the yard. A desolate wood was visible beyond the stalks, casting languid shadows from cypresses by the border.

Theodora returned with a steaming cup of white tea. Theodora looked to be on the verge of a nervous breakdown. She took another drink and continued.

"I made her a corn basket, but before I could walk out my door to give it to her, I had a gift of my own. An old metal cage was sitting on my doorstep with a skinny white rat sitting in the middle of it, on some hay. I found him odd, obviously, and somewhat familiar, not simply for being on my doorstep but because he had green eyes. I didn't know rats had green eyes. I never even considered owning a rat as a pet, so I looked for a note or something, explaining why he was here, but there was nothing. I assumed it was from Meredith.

"I went to Meredith's house to give her the basket and to politely refuse the rat, but she never answered the door. I left my basket there but I felt uncomfortable leaving the rat. I didn't know when she would return, if she was out, and I didn't want to just leave him. So I took him home." Theodora closed her eyes and slowly shook her head. "I never should have done that."

She was struggling to tell her story but knew it needed to be said, and mustered the strength to continue. I knew that if she lost momentum, she might not be able to start up again.

"When I returned home, my golden Labrador, Shelly, came to greet me as usual, but as soon as she saw the rat, she whined and backed away, afraid. Edgar had crept closer from atop a chair and hissed at the rat, but he made no attempts to get closer. I tried to calm them down but they would not go near me as long as I had the rat in my hands. So I made a space for him on his own little table in the kitchen and set him down. I then named him Howard, after our father, because they both had green eyes.

"I had to move Edgar's and Shelly's bowls to the opposite side of the kitchen, for they refused to eat or drink near Howard. Edgar would maneuver his bowl so that he could eat while facing Howard, and Shelly barely ate without chancing nervous glances at him."

I noticed that Theodora's hands began to twitch as she held her fresh cup of tea, and that she had trouble meeting my gaze now. I tried not to be so direct in my stare, so I looked out the window and kept her in my peripheral.

"I slept horribly that night and Shelly eventually woke me up with her barks. When I went downstairs, Shelly was standing at the far end of the kitchen barking madly at the rat. I turned on the lights to look at Howard but found nothing wrong with him. He sat comfortably on top of the hay, yet looked at Shelly with a peculiar expression. He looked at her with a sort of ill contempt and his eyes seemed to gleam unnaturally in the kitchen light.

"I then noticed that Edgar was missing and I made a light search of the house. I opened the back door and called his name but he did not come. It was unusual for Edgar to be away from Shelly for long and not to come when called.

"I looked out the window again for a last look, but as soon as I turned away, something crashed behind me. I screamed and turned to see Shelly growling and scratching at Howard's cage, which she knocked down. Howard scrambled away as best he could and squeaked loudly. Shelly had managed to get her mouth part way through the bars and was dangerously close to biting him. I grabbed Shelly by the collar, dragged her upstairs to the guest bedroom, and closed it. I then went to check on Howard.

"I immediately rushed to the cage and saw blood dripping from the bars. Shelly must have sliced her muzzle as she tried to get through. When I held Howard, I could not see any cut on him except for some blood on his mouth. I held him for a while and noticed that he was not entirely white. He had a black spot right behind his head and I saw that he seemed a bit fatter than I had originally thought." Theodora choked as she said these last words. The horror of these mysterious spots was renewing itself within her and she was struggling to keep calm. I was at the edge of my seat, waiting to hear more on this rat.

"I picked up his cage and after I calmed him down, I placed him back inside. I entered the guest bedroom to check on Shelly and shut the door behind me. Shelly still barked and ran around the room. She jumped up on me many times and scratched at the door. I barely got her to calm down so I could check her muzzle and wipe it clean. After a while, Shelly slowed down and curled up at the foot of the bed. I left her in there and went to bed." Theodora tried to hold back her tears but failed. She grabbed the napkin from her lap and wiped them away. She took a few more sips of her tea and cleared her throat.

Her normally light skin grew paler, almost waxy, and her blue eyes were magnified by her tears. When I first arrived, I knew she was over-reacting, but this was the first time I realized that she was hurt. Her pets were her only company and now they were all gone and she had turned to me for help.

Theodora continued. "I still slept uneasily and woke up the next morning with a start. The house seemed unnaturally silent and a sense of alarm overcame me. I went down the hall and immediately opened the door to the guest bedroom. Shelly was gone. The window was half-way open, which I was sure was closed, and a few drops of dried blood smeared the window pane.

"I hurried outside and began calling to Shelly, and then to Edgar, in hopes that they would both come, but neither did. I searched the old barn and the corn fields and even the gardens surrounding the house, but they were nowhere. I gazed toward Meredith's house and halfway thought she might have done something to them, but I dismissed it. Shelly was far stronger and faster than she was, and the gift of the rat was proof enough of her sincerity, I thought." Theodora looked down at her tea cup as if ashamed at her quick dismissal of her initial thought.

"I went back to the house and looked at Howard when I entered. Ice entered my veins as Howard stared at me with those horrid emerald eyes. And then a knot tightened in my chest when I realized that there was something else strange about him. Something was different, something had changed.

"I started tea and tried to turn my attention away from him, but he seemed to watch my every move. Now that my pets were gone and I was really alone, I wondered if something was now going happen to me," she sighed, her voice slightly quavering. "I felt those beady green eyes boring into the back of my skull, but I found the strength to feed him. As I scooped a few spoonfuls of pellets in his bowl, I saw that he was noticeably fatter than in the night and as he moved to eat, I saw that he had a golden spot on his right shoulder."

Theodora abruptly looked up to look me straight in the eyes. I could tell by her expression that this was the part she had built up to tell me. The mystery of the strange colorization of her new rat. But what did she want me to think? Did she expect me to make some sort of connection between this rat and his colored spots that happened to match that of her missing pets?

I dared not make an expression to cause her to retract or think I did not believe her. I remained expressionless and nodded so that she could go on, but I knew that this was ridiculous. Theodora breathed a small sigh of relief and continued.

"I was now sure that when I got him, he was entirely white. Each spot he grew was the same color as one of my missing pets, and Howard got each one right after they disappeared. I didn't know what that meant, but I knew that Meredith was behind it." Theodora closed her eyes and took a deep breath.

"Emily, you know me, I never believed the nonsense that the townsfolk said about Meredith being a witch or summoning demons or what other outrageous things they cooked up, but there was one thing I did know, and that was that I did not want that rat anymore.

"So I grabbed the cage and went to Meredith's house. When I got there, I noticed that my corn basket was still there, though knocked over. I knocked on her door but it went unanswered again. I called to her and told her that I didn't want the rat and hoped that we were still on good terms." Theodora let out a shrill laugh which caused me to jump. "Foolish," she muttered. "I left Howard on her doorstep and left. I never even chanced a look back.

"The quiet of the house got to me, so after a few weeks, I got a new dog. She was a brown German Shepherd named Jezebel, whom I instantly fell in love with.

"Jezebel took to the house immediately, except for when she entered the kitchen. She would not go near the part of the kitchen where Howard used to reside. Now that disquieted me, so I kept Jezebel upstairs with me during the night, something I never did with Shelly. I finally got to sleep soundly for the first time in weeks." Theodora snorted and took another long gulp of tea. She drained it and poured herself another cup. I wondered if she would upgrade to something stronger if she eventually ran out of tea.

"Then I woke up one morning and my bedroom door was open and she was just… gone. Disappeared, like the rest of my pets. I went into the kitchen and found a few tufts of brown fur leading outside through the doggy door. I went outside and called to her, but I knew in my heart that it was pointless.

"That's when I emailed you. I went to my desk and noticed that there were small black drops on Jezebel's bed. When I took a closer look, I saw that they were rat droppings," she finished. She looked at me over the top of her cup. "I want you to come with me to Meredith's house. I need to confront her and find out the truth."

I thought she was overreacting, and that her pets had just run away. The woods were just beyond the corn fields, and any wild animal could have attracted the attention of a dog, but I kept that to myself.

"Alright, Theo. If that will ease you," I said, and Theodora nodded.

"Thank you, Emily."

I told Annabel to stay in the house and to read to Clarence to keep him involved, and I left with Theodora to go to Meredith's house.

When we reached the porch, a cage lay off to the side of the door, open and empty. I suspected that it was the same cage Howard was in when she left him there. The corn Theodora left in her gift basket looked like it was eaten by an animal or animals such as mice or rats. I knocked on the door but no one answered, so I let myself in. I looked at Theodora, who stiffened, and I turned back and called to Meredith through the open doorway.

A stench like the horrid decay of meat wafted out from the living room, gagging me into a fit of coughs. Theodora grabbed my arm in warning but I shook her off. The old woman was probably long dead in the house somewhere and Theodora was overreacting for nothing.

I took a few more steps and stopped abruptly as I saw the opposite wall. Red symbols and crude yellow signs were painted on the wall, with writings from a strange language unfamiliar to me beneath. Under them was a table covered with glass vials of various sizes that contained different muddy-colored liquids. Next to them were bowls filled with strong smelling herbs, perhaps coated with oils or juices. Their scents were nauseating but they did not take over.

We cautiously walked further into the house and both froze as we entered the kitchen. Theodora issued a scream which pierced into my very core, while my blood became frigid in my veins as I gazed onto the scene.

A horde of fat feasting rats scrambled atop crimson-painted bones that littered the yellow floor. I only knew that Shelly and Edgar were among the bones by their distinguishable matching collars, for their bodies were completely eaten away. Jezebel was not yet fully devoured, for her eyeless head still had fur as it lay at an awkward angle on the floor. Maggots seemed to make her body pulse as they pressed against her body.

I could do nothing but stare, and barely even remembered Theodora behind me. My eyes trailed to the center mass amid the graveyard of bones and saw the body of what must have been Meredith. Her sunken face was turned toward us and my insides twisted at the sight of the bits of flesh that still hung from her chin and cheeks. Her flesh had turned gravestone-gray as it dripped from stained bone, while her thin hair loosely clung to her scalp.

A sudden movement startled me, and I stepped back as a white rat with different colored spots jumped on top of Meredith's head and crushed it beneath his weight. His emerald eyes gleamed for a moment before he scampered past us and out the front door. I knew that it was Howard.

Theodora had said his spots appeared after one of her pets went missing and I was sure I saw brown in his coloration as well as the black and gold.

I spun around and grabbed Theodora by the shoulders and told her to call the police. She started mumbling something about Meredith having green eyes and Howard having green eyes and something about it being the same dead rat, but I shook her hard and she snapped out of it. She nodded and ran back to her house.

I exited the kitchen but became immediately entranced again by the wall of symbols and signs. A strong force pulled me closer, and I was sure I heard whisperings coaxing me to go nearer. They were unlike anything I had ever seen, and as I looked about the table beneath it, I recognized the titles of forbidden books of ancient arcane lore that I was warned about as a child from the local townsfolk. They had said Meredith was a witch and had managed to get her hands on many rare and evil books and artifacts, but I never thought that was true.

The symbols, the herbs, the vials all pointed to a ritual. Meredith must have performed one to get back at Theodora for killing her pet, but it surely went wrong. Whatever evil necromancy she had bestowed upon that dead rat had turned on her, and ultimately destroyed her.

Almost by a will of its own, my head turned and gazed upon a crimson tome lying in the center of the table. This was surely where the ritual came from. The book mesmerized me, and before I knew it, I reached out to open it. Before I could touch it, however, another piercing scream brought me back to reality and I realized it was Theodora. I turned around and raced out of the house and back to hers.

When I entered, Theodora had clawed her own face and walked around in circles in the living room. She stared at the ceiling as she muttered in fear to herself, so quickly that she was incomprehensible. I grabbed her, shook her again, and asked her what happened, but she acted as if I was not there. She had finally snapped. I followed her gaze and saw a crimson stain form on the ceiling below the guest bedroom.

▲

Two Spells
by Neva Bryan

"Will it leave a scar?"

"Maybe." Henry wrapped a strip of clean cloth around Cathleen's wrist and secured it with a safety pin. He lifted his wife's hand and kissed it. "That cow is a menace. You're lucky all she did was nick you with her horn. She should have been dehorned years ago."

She threw her arms around his neck and kissed him on the cheek. "Thank you."

"Tis nothing." He pulled away and gazed into her face. A lock of his hair, black as a crow's feather, fell across his blue eyes. "I've got her tied up at the side of the house. Don't go near her."

She pushed his hair behind his ear and smiled. "I won't. After you go to work, I'll walk up the hill and tell Granny Moon that Ole Sal is here."

"Make it quick, Cathy. I don't like you spending so much time with that old witch."

"She's not a witch! She's a healer and a midwife."

"She's a *cailleach* if ever there was one. Her and her sister, too!"

Henry curled his finger beneath her chin and tilted her face to his. He touched his lips to hers. The gentle peck turned into a deep, lingering kiss.

Cathy wanted to pull him back into bed and crawl on top of him. She felt her face grow hot at the thought of it, wondering if other women had such wicked desires.

But it's not wicked if I love him. And I love him more than anything.

"Cathy."

"Hmm?"

"I'm going to be late."

After she released him, he pulled on his cap and tucked a carbide lamp under his arm. Cathy tightened the galluses on his overalls, then kissed him again.

"Will you take Ole Sal up the hill when you get home?"

"I'm a coal miner, woman! I didn't leave County Clare and cross the wretched waters to be a farmer."

"Granny Moon's getting awful feeble."

He sighed. "Aye. I'll do it." He grabbed the tin pail that held his lunch and opened the front door. "I love you, my sweet Cathy."

She followed him to the porch, wrapped her arm around the post, and watched him walk down the steps. Just before he disappeared into the darkness, she called out to him. "Henry! I love you. Please be careful!"

The sun wouldn't be up for several hours, so she crawled back into bed and wrapped her arms around his pillow. She inhaled his scent and smiled. Cathy's heart had belonged to Henry since the first moment she laid eyes on him.

Three years ago her family had hosted a secret meeting for union organizers. Her father was one of the first men in the county to call for a local assembly of the UMWA. Cathy, bored with all the talk of working conditions and legal tender, had huddled in a rocking chair in the corner. While organizers tried to persuade fence-sitters to join, she had let her attention wander. That's when she spotted the finest looking young man she'd ever seen.

He had shaggy black hair, a strong jaw, and blue eyes that seemed to look straight into her heart. When he had noticed her staring at him, his mouth turned up at one corner and he winked at her. He came courting a week later. Six months after that he slipped a ring on her finger.

Henry's all I've got.

Her mother, brother, father, and grandparents—her entire family—had passed last year, victims of the influenza epidemic.

I couldn't live without him, she thought before drifting back to sleep.

Cathy woke up a few hours later. She heated water on the cast-iron stove to clean the breakfast dishes. When she was done, she carried the dish pan to the back door and flung the dirty water into the back yard. Ole Sal bellowed from the corner of the house and Cathy shushed her.

After she finished her housekeeping chores, she pulled on her shoes and set off to visit Granny Moon. A dusty Model T approached her from the opposite direction as she walked up the rutted dirt road. Its horn sounded and Cathy waited for it in the ditch. When it came to a stop, Dr. Stanley Daniels leaned his head out the window and greeted her.

"Good morning, Mrs. Hogan. How are you?"

Dr. Daniels served the coal miners and their families, but his loyalty rested with the company. Even so, Cathy was fond of him.

"I'm good, I reckon. Are you heading to town?"

"Mrs. Wright called a few minutes ago. I've got a baby to deliver."

"Bless her heart." She nodded to the doctor. "Give her my best."

He tipped his hat and continued down the hill. Cathy headed to Granny Moon's home.

The old woman lived with her sister in a rickety wooden house on the ridge behind Cathy and Henry's home. She was coming out of her chicken coop when Cathy arrived. Shifting a basket of fresh eggs onto her hip, she greeted the young woman. "I declare. I ain't seen you in a week of Sundays. Come on in. Sit a spell."

Cathy followed her to the porch swing, where they both rested. She watched the old woman wipe off the eggs with the hem of her apron. Granny hummed as she worked.

I wonder how old she is.

Granny's wrinkled face looked like a brown paper bag that had been folded too many times. She wore her white hair in a thick plait that hung down the center of her back. It swung back and forth when she walked.

As the old woman cleaned the eggs, Cathy stared at the thick blue veins on her hands, fascinated and a little repulsed.

"Did you need something, child?"

She lifted her eyes to Granny Moon. "I wanted to tell you that Ole Sal got loose again. She's tied up at my house."

"She's an ornery beast. Not worth the milk!"

A husky cackle floated out the door, making Cathy jump. Another old woman stepped outside and stood with her knuckles on her bony hips. She looked very much like Granny Moon, only older. *And scarier*, Cathy thought.

"I been trying to tell Sister that for ever so long. Ought to kill Ole Sal and tan her hide!"

Cathy stood and greeted Granny Moon's sister. "Here, Auntie Maggie. Take my seat."

"Thank'ee." The old woman dropped into the swing, then cocked her head at Cathy.

"You're with child."

Cathy gasped. "How do you know? I've just suspected it myself."

Auntie Maggie bared her teeth in a grim smile. "I always know."

Cathy rubbed her belly. "I want to know when it'll be born."

Granny Moon laughed and extended her hand to the young woman. "Come inside and we'll figure on it."

* * * *

When Henry returned home that evening, he called to her from the yard. When she ran out to greet him, she saw that he was covered in coal dust from his head to his boots. The whites of his eyes stood in stark relief against his dirty face, making his irises seem even bluer than usual.

"I'm going to try to wrangle that cow up the hill. Would you heat some water for my bath while I'm gone?"

Cathy wanted to tell him her news right away, but he looked dog-tired. *I'll tell him at dinner.* Now she felt a little guilty about asking him to take Ole Sal home.

After going inside and setting two pots of water on the stove, she stepped to the porch and grabbed his lunch pail. She cleaned it with a rag, muttering at the black muck it left on her dress.

"Damn it all!"

Her husband's voice floated across the yard. Cathy smiled, but when she heard the cow bellow, she jumped up and went to help him. Just before she turned the corner of the house, she heard a loud thump.

Ole Sal had pinned Henry to the wall. Before Cathy could get to him, the cow rammed her shoulder hard into his chest. Even through the coal dust, she could see the blood drain from his face. When the animal moved, he slid to the ground.

When Cathy saw Ole Sal lower her horns, she grabbed a stick and prodded her. The cow bawled at her, then trotted away. Cathy ran to Henry and helped him into a sitting position. He grimaced and pressed his right hand hard against his chest.

"Mother of God, that hurts!"

He tried to stand, but immediately sank to his knees.

"Should I fetch the doctor?"

"No. I'll be alright. Just knocked the wind out of me."

"I could go get Granny Moon."

"And have her feed me a potion or say a spell over me? Thank you, no." Henry shook his head. "She'll have to find someone else to herd that damnable cow."

Dusk had fallen by the time he was able to stand and limp to the house with her help. Inside, Cathy found the water boiling over onto the stove. Henry leaned in the doorway, his face pale as clabbered milk, while she pulled the long metal tub into the middle of the kitchen and filled it with hot and cold water.

She helped her husband undress. When he struggled out of his shirt, she gasped at the sight of a giant black and purple bruise that covered the left side of his chest.

"I think you need a doctor."

"I'll be fine, my love. Just help me into the bath."

She held his arm as he stepped into the tub, watching him wince as he lowered himself into the water. He groaned, then sighed.

"Tis better."

While he soaked, she bundled his dirty clothes and dropped them into a box on the porch. Usually he undressed there so he wouldn't get the house dirty.

Black coal dust was the bane of almost every woman in the coal-fields. It seemed to settle into every nook and cranny of the houses, no matter how far from the mines they sat. Cathy was proud that she managed to keep their home so clean. It had been her brother's house. After he died, she and Henry had moved here to escape the coal camp town in the valley.

After he finished his bath, Henry pulled on a clean night shirt and said, "I need to lie down a while."

"What about your dinner? Aren't you hungry?"

"No."

"Okay." She rubbed her belly.

I don't know how much longer I can hold it in. I'll tell him when I come to bed.

But when she joined him, he was already asleep. Cathy snuggled up next to him, hoping he would stir, but he didn't move. Sighing, she closed her eyes and thought about their baby.

Granny Moon said it will be a boy. Henry will be so happy. He'll be a good father.

She hoped their son had his father's cool eyes and black hair. She rubbed a lock of her own bright hair between her thumb and forefinger.

Any hair color but red.

* * * *

Sun slipped between the curtains and warmed her face. The light behind Cathy's eyelids was orange, waking her in degrees. She squinted at the sunlight dancing on the walls and realized they had overslept. She turned to shake Henry.

He lay on his back, one arm thrown over his eyes. His lips curled up in a slight smile. She wondered what he was dreaming.

"Wake up, my sweet." She laid her hand on his arm. His skin was cool.

She jerked away from him. "Henry?"

He didn't stir. She brushed her trembling fingers against his face. His arm fell from across his eyes and his knuckles hit the wooden bedframe with a thump. The sound reverberated in her head, bouncing from one side of her skull to the other.

Leaning over him, she pressed her hands on either side of his face and lifted his head. "Henry?"

His skin was smooth and white, his lips almost blue.

"No. No. No."

She climbed to her knees, sinking into the featherbed, and pulled his head and shoulders to her chest. She hugged him tight. Her throat closed against the wail that had wound itself tight inside her, a sound that tried to spring from her soul. Easing him back down onto the bed, she patted his face. Her tears dropped onto his skin, covering it with translucent streaks.

"Henry? Wake up. I need you!" The wail escaped her now.

She pressed her fists against her temples and shrieked. "Don't leave me now!"

Cathy plucked at his nightshirt and bunched it into her hands. When he didn't respond, she rubbed her thumbs across his eyelids, willing him to open his eyes. She wanted to see those blue eyes bright as the Irish sky.

She kissed him, first on his forehead, then his cheeks, and in the hollow of his throat, desperate to feel his pulse there. There was nothing. She pulled up his nightshirt and stared at his chest. The bruise was darker now.

"I'm sorry, Henry. It's my fault." She leaned over him and pressed her lips against his.

Did you fall into a deep sleep and just slip away? Or did you call to me in the night?

Cathy slid onto the floor, crying so hard she vomited. A few minutes passed before she was able to compose herself and stand up. Walking on stiff stalks of flesh to the kitchen, she slipped into her shoes.

Granny Moon can help. She'll know what to do.

* * * *

"I can't do what you're asking, child."

Granny Moon sat in the porch swing. Cathy stood on the top step clutching a porch post with one trembling arm.

"I've heard stories about what you can do. You can't do this? Or you won't?"

The old woman sighed. "It goes against all that's right. To do this thing…it would be an abomination in the eyes of the Lord."

"Henry died before I could tell him he has a son. I'm all alone!" Cathy fell to her knees and laid her hands on Granny Moon's bare feet. "I beg you!"

The older woman clucked her tongue. Finally she leaned forward and grasped Cathy by the shoulders. "By my soul, and for the sake of yours, I'll not do it."

Granny Moon rose and went inside. She shut the door behind her.

Weeping, Cathy stumbled away. Before she could take two steps, Auntie Maggie called to her from an open window.

"Hey, girl!"

Cathy swiped at her tears with the binding on her wrist and hurried to Auntie Maggie.

The old woman extended her hand and handed her a lumpy flour sack and a folded piece of paper.

"Follow the directions on that note."

Cathy pressed the sack to her chest. "How can I pay you?"

"I want nothing."

She started to pull her head inside, then paused and said, "Whatever happens, don't come up here no more."

* * * *

Henry lay on the bed as she had left him. She leaned forward and stared at him. His eyelashes were dark against his pale skin.

He's beautiful. She touched his face. Finding him cooler than before, she burst into tears again.

Still crying, she opened the bag and removed the items it contained. She understood why the bag had been so heavy when she saw a large river stone amongst the contents. She set the things on the floor next to the bed, then unfolded the note and read it.

Afterward she removed Henry's nightshirt, then folded the quilt down to his waist. Morning sun shined on him through the bedroom window, making the dark bruise look worse. Clenching her fists, Cathy took a deep breath and held it for a moment. She offered a silent prayer for forgiveness before beginning the spell.

She followed the directions exactly as they were written. After pulling the cork from a glass bottle, she dribbled its clear tincture onto her index finger and dabbed at his nostrils and on his lips.

The directions instructed her to place the leaves of an herb unknown to her on Henry's eyes. Cathy panicked when she didn't see leaves among the materials she had arranged on the floor, but when she stuck her arm into the bag, she found them clinging to the bottom of it. They were still green, but curling at the edges. She laid them gently on his eyelids.

She checked the note, then laid the river stone on his chest, directly over his heart. She removed the lid from a small tin and found a fine brown powder that she was instructed to sprinkle across his waist and groin. Another tin held a pungent salve which she massaged into his legs and rubbed on the bottoms of his feet.

Finally, she lit a candle and recited the words written in the note. When she finished, she held the note to the flame and watched it burn down to her fingertips. She gathered the ashes from the floor and cast them out the window.

Suddenly very tired, Cathy shuffled into the kitchen and dropped into a chair. She laid her head against the table and fell asleep.

* * * *

She awoke with a stiff neck and a dry mouth. Night had fallen and the house was completely dark. Cathy fumbled around the kitchen until she found an oil lamp and lit it. Shadows stretched from the corners, grasping at the flickering light.

She walked through the house and stood outside the bedroom door. The bed creaked. Holding up the lamp, she stepped into the room, then stopped short.

Henry was sitting up in the bed, holding the rock in his hands. His chest heaved as he took slow, deep breaths. The bruise had disappeared. Leaves still clung to his eyes.

Bile climbed up her throat. She swallowed hard against it. Slowly she walked to the bed. She removed the leaves with trembling fingers, letting them flutter onto the quilt. When her husband turned his head to stare at her, his eyes were dull. He didn't seem to recognize her.

What have I done?

She raised one hand to her collar and bunched it in her fist.

He blinked, then looked down at his body. Henry dropped the stone and it thumped against the floor, making her jump. He brushed the powder away, then swiped at the potion on his face. He spoke with a flat tone and a voice full of gravel.

"Draw me a bath, Cathy."

She shuddered at the sound of her name in his mouth and rushed out of the room.

Silently, from the corner of the kitchen, she observed him bathe. His movements were slow and tentative, as if he had forgotten how to use his limbs. His face seemed fuller, his features softer, and his eyes…*that's not my Henry looking out from those blue eyes.*

He clambered out of the tub and dried himself. He turned his cold gaze to her now and motioned for her to come to him.

"Help me. My love."

She hesitated a moment before moving close to him. After helping him into his pants, she handed him a shirt. He slid into it, then looked at her expectantly. She fumbled with the buttons. When she was done, she attempted to pull away from him, but he caught her up in his arms and squeezed her so tight she couldn't breathe. She struggled out of his grasp and backed away from him.

"Why do you shy away from me, Cathy?"

"I'm not." She crossed her arms across her chest. "Henry. How do you feel?"

"I don't know." He shook his head. "Am I sick?"

"Yes. In a way."

"I don't understand."

"What is the last thing you remember?"

He closed his eyes, for which she was grateful.

"Walking home from work. I was going to take Ole Sal up the hill." He shivered. "I'm cold."

"We'll go sit by the fireplace." She took his arm and steered him to the parlor.

Maybe it just takes time, she thought. *He'll be more like my Henry after he warms up.*

* * * *

"Henry, I have something to tell you."

He stared into the flames without responding to her, so she plucked at his sleeve.

"What is it?"

"You're going to be a father." She tried to stretch her mouth into a smile, but it felt all wrong. "A son."

When he turned his head toward her, she thought she heard his neck creaking. "How do you know that?"

She shifted her eyes to the floor. "Granny Moon told me so."

"A boy?" His expression didn't change. He turned his gaze back to the fire. "*M'aonmhac.* My son." There was no emotion in his voice.

Feeling sick, Cathy started to rise, but Henry clasped her by the wrist. He pulled her to his side.

Without looking at her, he asked, "What's wrong with me? I don't feel…right."

His fingers were cold and hard, and she wanted to jerk her hand from his grasp. Instead, she forced herself to sit still. *Tell him the truth. Part of it.*

"Ole Sal attacked you. You were hurt real bad. You've been…in a fever."

He let go of her wrist and stood up.

"Where are you going?"

He didn't answer her so she followed him outside. Henry staggered like a drunk, but by the time he got to the edge of the yard, he had found his feet. She heard twigs and branches snapping as he crashed into the dark woods.

"Henry!"

Only the peepers and the night birds responded to her cries.

* * * *

When the sun crawled over the mountains the next morning, she found him asleep on the porch. Leaves littered his hair and dirt rimmed his fingernails. His palms and his face were covered in a dark substance.

She reached for his shoulder to shake him awake but stopped when she heard a noise in the nearby woods. It sounded like a low groan with intermittent snuffles and snorts. Cathy stepped over her husband's prone body and followed the sounds to the nearest line of trees.

Ole Sal lay on the ground, her gut split open, her shredded udder mingled with a steaming pile of intestines. She lifted her head to look directly at Cathy and groaned again. One of her horns had been ripped from her head and used to disembowel her. It was still embedded in her belly.

Cathy gagged, then spit. She backed away from the dying cow and tripped on a tree root. Rolling over, she crawled out of the woods and across the dew-covered grass. When she got to the steps, she curled up in a knot.

She heard Henry stir. She looked up and found him standing over her. He pulled her to her feet, then smiled at her. His teeth were stained deep red. Her vision narrowed to a pinpoint as a black circle expanded in front of her. She fell backward into darkness.

* * * *

They never discussed what happened to Ole Sal. At first she convinced herself that it had been a nightmare. But when she returned to the woods and found the cow's remains, she put away the idea that she had imagined it.

Cathy began to fear Henry for the way he looked at her. Most of the time he was stone-faced, but on a few occasions she caught him staring at her as she performed her chores. In those moments, his expression wavered between pain and rage.

April gave way to May, then passed into a long, hot summer. They fell into a routine by silent agreement. She couldn't bear his touch, especially when he turned over in the bed and brushed against her swollen belly. Now she slept alone while he bedded down on the sofa.

He didn't seem to mind. He was no longer a man who desired carnal pleasures. But she missed the old Henry's touch. She missed his warm breath on the back of her neck.

There's nothing warm about him now.

His body was cold, and so was his manner. She knew that people in town had noticed something off about him, as had the miners he worked alongside. Men cast queer glances at Henry as he walked beside her down the street. Women whispered behind their hands when they shopped in the company store.

That's what the women were doing on this bright October afternoon, so Cathy waddled out of the store and stood on the sidewalk. As she waited for Henry to finish and join her, she spotted Granny Moon standing outside the bank across the street. She waved to her but the old woman turned her head and stepped into the building. Cathy sighed and rubbed her tight belly.

"I expect you want her to deliver our wee one."

She started, for Henry had walked up behind her without making a noise. Shivering, she shrugged away from him.

"She doesn't do much of that anymore."

That night she began to worry about birthing the baby. *Granny Moon and Auntie Maggie won't help me. Who can I ask?*

She shuddered at the thought of Henry touching her, pulling their son from her depths. Cradling their baby boy in his frosty embrace.

Dr. Daniels will help me when the time comes.

She slept in fits and starts, and woke early, just as Henry left the house for work. Remembering their last warm morning together, when she wanted to pull him back into bed, she burst into tears. She got up and wandered into the kitchen.

Cathy was halfway through breakfast when she heard it. *Boom!*

The sound bounced across the hills and valleys. She knew at once what had happened. The mine had exploded. It was every wife and mother's fear, though most every miner, deep in his heart, expected it to happen someday.

She got dressed and started down the mountain. It took longer now that she was so ripe with child. Halfway down the road, Dr. Daniels pulled up in his car. He pushed open the passenger side door and invited her in.

"Mrs. Hogan. You're not fit to be walking down this mountain!"

"I have to see about Henry. Are you going to the mine?"

"Yes. Got the call about two minutes after I heard the explosion. I was just grabbing my bag when they called me." He touched her arm. "Everything will be alright."

She felt blood rise up her neck and into her face. *He would be shocked at what I'm thinking.*

It'll be a blessed relief if Henry don't come out of that hole.

She turned her head and cried quietly for herself and the husband she had loved too much.

The mangled bodies of three men were pulled from the rubble immediately. Then friends, family members, and other miners set to work trying to dig out the others. They found five more bodies over the next two days, but seven remained in the black pit. Henry was one of them.

Dr. Daniels gathered the families around a fire blazing in a barrel and told them to prepare for the worst. "It's unlikely they'll find the others alive."

He drove Cathy back to her house. "I'm sorry, Mrs. Hogan. Losing your husband must be a terrible thing, but think of your baby. Take care of yourself. Don't let your grief make you do anything foolish."

Too late.

"I'll be fine. Thank you."

"Do you have a phone? No? Just do the best you can to get in touch with me when the time comes."

Once inside, she threw off her dusty clothes and climbed into bed. She wondered how she could be so full with child but still feel so hollow inside.

She covered her head and welcomed darkness.

* * * *

Cathy woke up shaking. It took her a full minute to get her bearings. The house was dark and cold, but that was not what had pulled her from sleep. It was a strange noise.

She sat upright and pulled the blanket up to her chin. Cocking her head, she listened but heard nothing. *Maybe it's the house settling.*

She started to slide back down into bed when she heard it again. *Thump!* This was followed by a sliding sound. *Thump. Skee. Thump. Skee.* Someone was walking in the kitchen.

Cathy climbed out of bed and pulled her dirty dress over her head. She tiptoed to the parlor and pulled a poker from the hearth. Holding it with both hands, she crept to the kitchen door. Something moved in the darkness but she couldn't make out what it was.

Suddenly an oil lamp flared, its flickering light highlighting the haggard features of her husband. His eyes shined bright against the coal dust on his face.

"My sweet Cathy."

She screamed.

"I figured out what's wrong with me. Sitting there in the mine, listening to all those men gasping for air. Hearing them choke on dust until they passed. Alone in that black hole with corpses, I remembered. And when I did, I clawed through the black earth so I could come home."

Henry stepped forward. His right leg had been crushed, so he dragged it.

She retreated.

"I'm dead. I've been dead a long time. You and those witch women conjured me back, but not to life. I am cold and empty."

He took another step. She stepped back.

"Why would you do that to me? I thought you loved me."

"I do love you! I did. I just wanted you to be here with me and our son. I'm sorry, Henry!"

He reached for her, so she raised the poker above her head. When she did, a white-hot bolt of pain streaked through her core. Gasping, she dropped her weapon and fell to her knees.

"God help me!"

"God shall strike you." Henry crouched over her.

She gripped his good knee. "Please. Don't you feel anything?"

He said nothing.

"For me?"

"For our baby?"

"*M'aonmhac.*" He paused, then raised his ragged hands to his face and covered his eyes. "I'm so tired." His voice was forlorn.

Severe cramps forced Cathy to curl up on the floor. Henry lifted her into his arms and limped through the house.

"Where are you taking me?"

"To your witches."

* * * *

Henry and Cathy returned from Granny Moon's house just as the sun peeped over the ridge. She held baby Liam bundled in her arms. When they got to the house, she told her husband to take the child into the bedroom.

"Go lie down with him. I'll be there soon."

In the kitchen, she grabbed a coal bucket and stepped outside. Frost was burning away beneath the morning sun but the air was still cold. She could see her breath.

She wandered around the hillside gathering branches and leaves from the trees and shrubs that surrounded the house. After placing them in the bucket, she carried them to the door. She limped to the garden and gathered what remained of the fall harvest: pumpkins, squash, and greens. Cathy pulled apples from the tree in the back yard and grapes from the fence. When she gathered everything she could find, she took it all into the house.

Henry reclined on the bed with Liam on his chest. Cathy pulled the blanket away from her child's face and though she touched his perfect nub of a nose, he didn't stir. He was pale and still, his lips blue. He reminded her of Henry many months ago as he lay in peace.

Peace I took from him.

She wept, thinking of that night and the one that just passed.

After Auntie Maggie had opened the door to them, she cursed and retreated to her bedroom.

Granny Moon had to tell Cathy what to do.

She followed her instructions exactly.

She rested Liam at her husband's side. Henry extended his arms so that his palms rested flat on the bed. His skin was still black with coal dust and it smudged the bed. *It doesn't matter,* she thought.

Cathy found the Bible that he had carried from Ireland and placed it beneath his right hand, then she laid the garden bounty at his feet and the fruit around his head. Weaving together leaves of maple and sweet buckeye, she sang to herself: "Black is the Color of My True Love's Hair."

Satisfied with the wreath of orange, green, and gold, she set it on his brow, then made a smaller one for their son. After covering Henry's legs with hemlock, she placed branches of bittersweet on his chest, its berries red and bright yellow.

She returned to the parlor and piled dry sticks in the fireplace. Cathy pulled Granny Moon's note from her pocket and read it once more. It was a simpler spell this time. Only two words.

"Fire purifies."

She used the note to start a fire in the fireplace. After a moment, the kindling ignited.

Cathy grabbed a burning stick and tossed it into the kitchen. Another she dropped onto the sofa in the parlor. She took a third stick and held it to the bedroom wallpaper until flames licked the fabric and leaped to the ceiling.

She joined her family on the bed, resting her hand on the baby's foot. Henry laid his cold hand on top of hers.

She smiled at her husband one last time, but he didn't see it. His eyes were closed.

"I love you, Henry."

▲

Pulled Over
by Paul Spears

Trooper Bob Baratz saw the Jeep swerve as soon as it left the off-ramp. The Arizona afternoon was painted with sunset, and though traffic was nonexistent off the exit, that kind of driving was hazardous. And hazards needed dealing with. Flipping his lights, he radioed in the pursuit and stepped on the gas.

Why don't people ever learn?

He slapped his turn signal as he peeled out from under the overhead bridge. Always use your signals, always cover your ass, that was the Bob Baratz way. Resignation chased him down the dusty road as the Jeep grew larger in his sights. If he'd had a dollar for every drunk who thought the desert was a lawless place and its highways a Mad Max movie… Well, he'd have around a hundred bucks, probably. Maybe two. After twenty-one years out here, he'd seen everything from meth-heads diving out truck windows to kooks who claimed they'd been abducted by aliens—hence the swerving. Of course. And maybe they had. But even space aliens didn't give you an excuse to drive like a dipshit.

The Jeep had picked up speed coming off the highway, exactly the opposite of what you were supposed to do, exiting. "Goddamn whacka-doos…" For the last three hours he'd been content sitting, waiting for a cloud of pot smoke whirling from a truck cabin or for his radar gun to go off, and he would have been happy to sit two hours more until his shift was over. But no, somebody had to be a wise guy.

Even as he stepped on the accelerator, he was surprised to see the Jeep pull over. *Well, that was a piece of cake… Time to cross my fingers and hope they're not cartel, or Tucson bangers.*

As road dust swirled over his cruiser hood, Bob sat tight in his Crown Vic and called in the update. Jodie at the station told him she understood, and recommended he try not to get shot today. Bob advised he would do his best, and stepped out of the car.

Approaching the driver-side door, he pulled his Maglite to counter-act the vanishing light on the horizon. The dusk spread in red-and-gold blooms across his vision, momentarily blinding him as he left a patch of shadow, and his palm hovered over his sidearm as he peered through the window.

There was no one in the car.

His pulse quickened a few beats. Bob swept the Maglite through the vehicle. There were no signs of open alcohol containers, or a ruckus; in fact, the whole Jeep was spotless. He made a note of the plate number, and did a three-sixty around the vehicle. Nobody home.

"Well, I'll be damned," he said.

"Aren't we all," said a velvety voice from a nearby ditch. He whirled around.

The woman wore all black. She was drinking from a flask, heavy Raybans resting on her regal nose. She was Native, and Bob felt his heart sink, drawing an invisible line from her to the swerving of the van. There had always been trouble on the rez, but lately it was worse. Meth, heroin, girls getting pregnant younger than he'd assumed humanly possible. Old workhorses like Bob had no idea how to deal with that crap. It took a subtler, less arthritic hand.

Something odd caught his eye as he approached her: the sand between her and the car was smooth, wind-ruffled, unbroken. *No footprints.* Had she hopped out a side window? Bob scrutinized her: black hair tied back in a thick ponytail, a sharp face, and a leather jacket. Designer stuff, something more appropriate for Vegas or San Francisco than the rust-colored plains of his home state. Native, yes she was—and very beautiful. He'd always felt bad arresting beautiful women, as though their beauty excused some part of their crime. Which it didn't.

Bob approached the driver. Lithe and sinewy, she fit in her clothes like a strong hand in a leather glove. Her cheekbones stood out stark on a face that somehow seemed round and angular at the same time, her cheeks tall underneath brown skin. She showed no signs of aggression; a good sign. In all his years wearing the big hat, Bob had never been forced to draw his pistol, and he preferred to keep it that way.

"Ma'am." Even upwind, she smelled of alcohol. Jack Daniels, if his own armchair connoisseur's taste were to be considered. "Do you own that vehicle?"

"Nobody owns anything." Her words had gone syrupy and loose with drink. She squinted through her shades at the setting sun, and sucked at her water bottle. "You should know that, Officer Baratz."

He squared his shoulders. He didn't recognize her from the local rez, but maybe she was from further out—a drifter, maybe one he'd picked up before. It was hard to tell; he'd eased countless no-name layabouts into the cracked and weathered backseat of his cruiser across the years. She could've been anyone, a Jane Doe, or maybe a relative of some pissed-off Native kid he'd put away. Her attitude certainly yelled "drifter," even if her outfit didn't. *No drifter has a car that clean,* his police logic instructed him, and he ignored it. *Not unless they stole it.* "I'm sorry, do I know you?"

"Nah." She swigged water, then spat, leaving a dark scar in the dirt beside the road. The local DPW had been saying year after year they were going to put gravel down out here, but they never had, leaving the sand and sun and erosion to scrape away the edges of the blacktop into cracked and jagged fragments. "Not in this life."

His patience began to erode. When accosting a suspect, even for a misdemeanor, everything had a procedure; it was how he kept things orderly out here. He did not like deviating from routine. She looked at him, and her sunglasses slipped, long enough for him to glimpse eyes that glimmered dark and wet in the dull yellow glare bouncing off the desert. "What's it to you, Bob? Gonna tow me?"

"As a matter of fact, I was thinking an arrest might be in order." He reminded himself he was doing this for a good reason. He had to remind himself. Keeping drivers in their lanes, keeping them rattling back and forth over the border and through the dusty border towns. Keeping the state's lifeblood, tourists, safe and happy—that was his job description. "I'll ask again. This vehicle belong to you?"

"Arrest me? Aren't…" She paused. Belched, loud and wet. "Aren't you supposed to ask for my license?"

He tugged his notepad from his belt and began taking note of the charges. "Driving under the influence. Reckless endangerment. Oh, and I ran those plates. They don't show up on the database, meaning they're likely fabricated. Meaning you are in possession of a stolen or otherwise ill-gotten vehicle."

"Ill-gotten!" She snorted, and brayed laughter with a volume that made him put his hand on his holster. He was not a hair-trigger man, but she was a strange one; it didn't seem possible that a woman so small should be able to laugh so loud. "Buddy, *all* of this is ill-gotten." She gestured at the scrublands as a car whooshed by at Bob's back. The Doppler effect of it whirred away into the distance as she drank, rinsed her mouth, spat again. "Every grain of sand."

He sighed and reached for his handcuffs. "Ma'am. I'd prefer not to add resisting arrest to your rap sheet today."

She frowned at him, and her forehead was like a gathering thundercloud. "Hey, woah there, big boy. I'm cooperating, right? I'm being non-violent and shit. You apes should be grateful." She nodded at the crumbled asphalt beside her. "C'mere. Sit, I need someone to talk to."

"Ma'am, you're not in a position to be making—" And then something bizarre transpired, something Bob would remember for the rest of his days. It would give him chills, and nothing after that—not the prostate cancer scare, not the gunman firing blindly at the barricade outside of Topeka—would ever frighten him so deeply. When she beckoned, her nut-brown finger curling, his entire body seized up as if it had been electrocuted. He walked, unwilling, like a puppet. He went to her side.

Officer Bob Baratz sat down.

Trembling, he looked at her. She'd dropped her hand, and was drinking from the water bottle again. It was almost empty. "See? That wasn't so hard," she said, and pushed her sunglasses up her nose. As she did, he saw a glimmer of golden-black irises beneath them. Bob decided he was not eager to meet those eyes. "I'm cooperating. You're cooperating. We're just a couple of real cool cats, see? Real cool cats, just having a chat."

I should go for my gun. Yet he couldn't. Something this woman had done—hypnotism, maybe, or weaponized hallucinogenic bath-salts, God only knew—was stopping him. Bob forced himself to stay calm. Stranger things had happened on the road. Not to *him*, of course, but hadn't Officer Kendall once sworn she'd seen a fifty-foot snake cross the road, outside Tulsa? Anacondas couldn't survive in Arizona, but Kendall said it had happened all the same. True, there was a difference between a ten-foot snake and god-damned *mind control*, but it was the point that mattered. Strange things happened. A good officer would operate within the limits of that strangeness, when the need arose. *Is she making me think that? What else can she do?*

"What," he asked, cautious, "would you like to chat about?"

She snickered. "That accent. I love that accent. You know, I've seen it evolve, since the first limeys came over on their boats. It's amazing what living here does to speech. To the brain." She rubbed her forehead. "Crap, I'm hungover."

Bob decided to get down to brass tacks. He had no body cam, and he couldn't seem to reach his radio for backup—he might as well do a little Sherlocking while he was here. "Lady, what the sam-hill do you *want* with me?"

She turned to him and grinned. It was a feral grin, and Bob saw with concern that most of her teeth were incisors, even the ones that should not have been, like molars and eyeteeth. *Sweet Jesus*, thought Bob. "Relax, big man. I'm not the devil." She drained the last of her water, and hurled the bottle into the desert. "Had a drink with him once, though. Nice guy. People don't give him enough credit."

"Hm. I … see." Bob did not see. "So, you're some kind a' monster." It was not a difficult leap. He'd reported to church every Sunday for most of his life, with one or two exceptions for hangovers or marital obligations. His pastor, Pastor Andrews, was quite serious about the existence of monsters. The Beast of Revelations, the whale that had swallowed Jonah, that sort of thing. He'd once joked with his wife that Pastor Andrews' sermon length was the real monster in town. That'd been before Sarah passed. Now the United Methodist Congregation were strangers to him.

It came to Bob, with an awful suddenness, that he had lived alone for almost fifteen years.

The woman waved a hand dismissively. "Nah. Nothing like that." Apparently unconcerned with present company, she fished a small silver flask from her pocket and unscrewed the cap. There was a leather thong looped around the rim; along its length, painted seeds rattled against one another. "I won't keep you long, Bob. Just got a question for you."

"Oh, yeah?" He was still thinking of Sarah. His blood seemed to churn slow and frigid in his veins. He still couldn't seem to stand. The radio on his hip squawked—Jesse, back at dispatch, asking for status. The woman ignored the shrieking interruption, watching the golden fireball of the sun meet the horizon with a splash of light. Bob had always loved that moment: the sun seemed to stain everything. Road, trucks, endless scraggly desert, all of it was now soaked in the red-yellow glow, bathed in it. Baptised.

"This is going to sound rude," she said, waving the flask. "And I don't mean to offend."

"At least you're polite about it," he groused. His sidearm sat on his hip, heavy and useless.

"Why'd you have to steal it, Bob?"

He blinked as the sun lanced its fingers into his eyes. He couldn't seem to look away from it. The smell of blowing dust filled his nostrils. "Beg pardon?"

"All of this." She gestured with slender figures at the cresting hills beyond, the gullies and ditches carved into the earth by time. "What did you even want it for? It's dirt, Bob. Just dirt."

"I have no idea what…"

"But you just had to have it, didn't you?" An unpleasant growl had entered her words. She grimaced; her teeth were long and yellow. "All of it. Every grain of sand."

"Ma'am," said Bob slowly, "I have done no such thing."

"Oh, not *you*, you!" She waved again, and there was an abrupt chill over his heavy limbs, as if a wind had passed. His hand went to his firearm immediately. Whatever had held him was gone—he was free, he was himself again. It was immeasurably relieving. "It's okay. It's not your fault. I can't blame children for the sins of their grandfathers. Or I can, but I shouldn't." She rubbed at her nose, and he saw her eyes were wet. For a while, she didn't say anything, just turning her flask around.

Bob considered his options.

He should bring her in. The woman was clearly drunk, and set on getting drunker. Now that the strange stillness had left him, he burned for action, for movement, a little of the young police cadet still in him. Yet he couldn't bring himself to cuff her. It wasn't just that she had exhibited some kind of mystical voodoo; there was a curious sense of finality to her little speech, as if she were saying goodbye to something, or someone. He couldn't make head nor tails of it, and he still had no idea who—or what—he was dealing with.

All the same, he knew the kind of men he worked with. Any one of them would've been happy to cuff an "uppity" Indian at a moment's notice. Men like that idiot, Arpaio, who thought jackboots and fists were the answer to everything. Bob was not like that. Bob wanted things to run smooth; he wanted people safe. It was a simple goal, albeit one the universe didn't seem to agree with. God willing, he would keep doing his job for quite some time, and enjoy what little good came of it. Today… Today he was witness to something unique. The woman—if she *was* a woman, he thought, remembering those long yellow teeth—was not some swaggering bar-fighter, to be bludgeoned and carted away. She was something different.

Something special.

Going back to the cruiser, he removed a wheel-lock, and placed it on her SUV. (There was a way these things had to be be done.) She didn't move or react as he did so. The splashes of color over the horizon grew darker, even as the air chilled and the headlights of vehicles on the highway became more vibrant and jarring. Night was coming on.

He went back to her. She was still sitting, arms looped around her knees. "I'm afraid I had to impound your vehicle," he said, wondering why he was apologizing.

"'S fine." She shrugged. "Don't need it."

He grunted, and sat down next to her again. He couldn't say why he did it; at his core, though, he was a curious man. Some part of him wanted to see what happened next. "Are you… gonna be alright, then?"

"No," she said.

"Ah."

They sat, for a spell. The sun oozed over the rocky edge of the world in a garish blaze of fire.

"I don't suppose," Bob asked eventually, "you'll tell me who you are?"

"Nope. Not part of my job." She chuckled. "Funny. I get told and re-told for thousands of years, and now no one's ever heard of me."

"Job?" asked Bob, leading her on a little. Sometimes you had to do this, with drunks.

"Yep." She swigged. "My story is very old, Bob. But it's dying. Soon I'll just be a whiff on the wind."

He frowned, trying to parse out her words. A scholar, he was not— but he got the gist. "The folks on the rez, are they a part of your story?"

"Not anymore." She sounded as if something had burned her, hollowed her out. He'd heard the same tone of voice from beaten wives, emergency callers who decided before the cruiser arrived that everything was fine. That they'd just fallen down the stairs. "They've forgotten it. Most of them, anyhow."

"I could…" He boggled at what he could do. It wasn't just that his knowledge of the local Apache folk was scant and poorly constructed; somehow he felt it wasn't his *place* to offer help. It was one of the things he just sensed, as he'd sensed she presented no danger when he stepped out of the car. No danger for the moment, at least. "Someone might help them remember."

"It's too late for that." She sucked at the neck of the flask, then stuck in the sand just beyond her feet. "Don't worry about it, Bob. Not your problem."

"Seems like it is." He sighed. "I don't really know what to do with you, ma'am."

She smirked. "At least you can admit it." The darkness was growing complete, now; the endless dome of the sky had warped to purple-black in the wake of the day. The cars above them on the interstate hissed and roared and chundered their way through shadows, as they always would. The nation they lived in never truly slept; amphetamines and artificial dopamine kept hearts pounding and eyelids peeled all through the twenty-four chimes of the clock. It was a shame, Bob had thought; perhaps if people were able to get some peace and quiet, they might get along a better. Shoot each other less often.

The light was nearly dead in the west. His 'suspect' somehow looked bigger and more unsettling in the dark. Her leather jacket seemed to bunch into hackles in the flash of halogen headlights; her hair looked less smooth, more shaggy. Matted, even. "So what happens now?" he asked.

"Now?" She stood, a little unsteadily; he went to hold her elbow, but stopped. Somehow he did not think touching her would be a good idea. "Now, I go back where I came from. Maybe forever." She nodded at the desert. "Home, sweet home."

"I can't let you do that," he said, and it was true. Countless men and women—backpackers, hikers, drug dealers, and the merely lost or insane—had perished in the flats over the years. "You'll die."

She threw her head back and laughed. It had a little too much howl in it. "You're funny," she said, and pinched his shoulder. It sent a jolt through him, as if he'd been electrocuted by a low-volt cattle fence. "I can't die, Bob. Not so long as *someone* remembers me. Doesn't have to be anyone special," she said, looking him up and down. "Could be a no-name cop who lives alone, talking to himself. Could be anyone."

"Ma'am," he said, still clinging to his rationality as a drowning man clings to his life-vest, "stories ain't real. That's why they're *stories*."

She nodded, sage-like, as if reflecting on this. Then she drained the flask and hurled it over the other side of the road. He heard clunking, as it struck a stone. "I set the world on fire, once, for you guys. The whole goddamn world. That's how you got your roast beef, bacon, your crispy Colonel fried chicken. And here you are, telling me I'm not real." She sniffled a little. "I'm not saying *every* story ever told becomes real, Bob. That'd be ridiculous. Do you understand me?"

"Right," he said, thinking twice about those handcuffs.

"But some linger, if you tell 'em long enough. Some stay." She took a step, staggered, and straightened herself with the ponce dignity of the intoxicated. "I'm not going anywhere, you hear me? Just... Don't forget."

She was moving out into the desert. He couldn't allow that; the desert was death, without a car. The desert had taken Sarah.

He reached for the woman and she turned, and there was a wilderness of color in her suddenly huge eyes. Her teeth were long and yellow.

"Back off, Bob," she said. "Go home."

"What *are* you?"

"I'm part of your story, now." She marched stiff and straight, cowboy boots kicking up dust. "Keep telling it."

He watched her go, and in his head he remembered Sarah, laid out just before the porch, her hand grasping for the rickety wooden steps. Buzzards circling overhead. The sun, so brutal and hot. She had only gone to water the horses, and the heat had done something to her mind, had shattered some crucial cerebral highway, and that was how Bob had learned that you don't get to hang onto anything in this life, not here and not hereafter. Heatstroke. They'd lived together in the desert for decades, and it had been heatstroke. Bob prayed every day, but it wasn't enough, it would never be enough to apologize for coming home late that day. Late enough to see a buzzard picking at his wife's supine back. Late enough to have nightmares for the rest of his life.

He knew about ghost stories, alright. His dreams were full of them.

Yet, in a horrible way, it was comforting to meet another narrative. Another monster, outside his wife's sun-stricken corpse. "I'll try," he said, and in the years after when Alzheimer's claimed him and his remaining family forgot him, left him to rot in a nursing home until he finally managed to swallow his tongue in a fit of delusional spite, he still hadn't forgotten her. He still remembered the story of the strange woman and her coyote's teeth in a human's skull. His last words were not about her, but his thoughts were: the thought of her story enduring, living on, living like the sunlight that slashed over the earth and disappeared but came back again, always come back again. That female boogeyman in cowboy boots, stalking the sands. That trickster.

Bob did as he was told, in the end. He told her story in his crude, fireside way, and it lived. It endured.

For a time.

▲

The Witch of Skur
by L.F. Falconer

I was born a lynx, but that didn't last long. Darkness invaded my life early on. Argent clouds gathered overhead, threatening rain the day the swine devoured my mother and littermates. I was but a kitten, my life spared only because a lion intervened. It swooped in through the hovering gloom, its wings flapping so furiously the wind bowled me over and sent me tumbling down a dusty incline, out of reach of the swine's blood-smeared jowls. The lion shook his mane and snarled. The swine snorted, prancing backwards, black hooves clicking against the stony earth. The lion crouched, pounced, swiped, fracturing one of the swine's tusks and forcing it into a cowardly, squealing retreat. My winged savior then gathered me by the nape into its jaws and flew me through the misty gray vapors that enveloped the top of the mountain, to nestle in the safety of his lair. That was the end of my innocence.

My birthright may have been stolen, yet despite everything, I still retain my feline reflexes. I still enjoy toying with my prey before the kill. I still hunger for fresh, warm meat. Dark magic altered my appearance, but deep down inside, I am still all cat.

For five hundred years, the realm of Skur, this cursed mountain on which I dwell, has been ruled by a fabricated dragon. A most powerful creation, this shapeshifter is known to invade the minds of others, easily raiding the vaults of their thoughts, able to stay one step ahead of any coup set against him. Yet for all his prowess, this magnificent dragon is woefully paranoid. That's why, to guard his realm, he employs the swine. He employs Seret, the lion who rescued me. And that is why he employs me.

It wasn't my idea, but I do derive great pleasure at being his first line of defense—protecting him against the men who would destroy him in order to lay their claim upon the wealth he is rumored to possess. But let me make myself clear. I do this for my own satisfaction, not for any love of my master. This dragon—he is not one to defy. I obey him. But I would betray him in the pulse of a hare's heart if given the chance.

You see, as I outgrew kittenhood, I fell deeply in love with Seret, the only one of the dragon's guard whose mind is safe from intrusion. Yet our love was not to be tolerated. I'm certain it was jealousy of the lion's new loyalty to me that caused the dragon to send me into the underworld, into the land of shadows to undergo metamorphosis. He wished me to become an abomination to Seret's sight so that Seret would love me no more. To ensure that we both might serve our master to the extreme he demands.

As a naive young lynx, at the dragon's behest, I was forcibly taken down into the bowels of Skur—into the murky labyrinth of the dark queen, a creature whose beauty is far too terrific to behold. To do so brings blindness to the eyes—madness to the soul. Attended only by her sightless wraiths, for time untold I endured agonizing tortures until my transformation was complete. My beautiful pelt was sliced and peeled from my flesh. My body ripped to shreds. Boiled in the sulfuric waters. Pieced back together and wrapped into webbed cocoons by golden spiders as large as wolves, then freed from my shroud by the wraiths to begin the process anew. Eight times I perished in this cycle, only to be reborn. And with each incarnation, my powers developed and grew.

Finally, I emerged once more into the world of light, hailed as a thing spectacular. I had become a creature irresistible to the eyes of men. A woman of human form. Forever young. Forever beautiful. Forever alluring and deadly. And the dragon sent me down mountain to dwell upon the border of his realm. To guard. And to feed.

They call me Larque, the witch of Skur. And I am a man-eater.

Despite the cruel transformation the dragon forced upon me, the love Seret and I share could not be broken. Secretly, we still rendezvous, away from the dragon's prying eyes and intrusive mind. No matter what I have become, our love endures. And we still manage to serve our master well.

For over two hundred years I have feasted upon the silly little men who hear my song and are drawn into my nest. My song is the enchantment. My body, the lure. My eyes, the trap. My touch, the poison. No man who ventures into my domain has ever resisted my wiles. No man has ever departed. Why should I allow any to pass further uphill? To feed the swine? I despise the swine. So I do my duty and I do it with excellence. For all I care, the swine can starve. And yes, I do enjoy my job and I proudly display the gathered treasures I earn. Yet my treasure is nothing that men would seek. It comes not from a dragon's trove. The interior walls of my humble home are well insulated with the hides of all those sweet tasting men who have wandered too near.

I often pet these leathery sheathes, calling each one by name. I remember the men, their odors, their flavors, and the unique nuances of the games we played together.

Pleasure is my life. Despite my master's demands and the occasional up or down, time has been fairly consistent in providing me my thrills. And then came yesterday....

I was simply passing time in the meadow, plucking sunshine daisies to string into my dark mane, when a lone wolf loped up beside me. I shot to my feet and dropped my blooms. I have no power over the beasts.

"There will be two warriors approaching," the wolf warned, but it wasn't a wolf who spoke. It was the dragon, shifted in disguise. I hate it when he does that. I never know it's him until he speaks.

"One of these men wears a crystal talisman," he told me. "You will not be able to kill him as long as he wears it. Convince him to relinquish it and surrender it to me when I return." Then he trotted off through the grass without so much as an "if you please."

It didn't seem a difficult task, but truth be told, I would feed the dragon to the swine if I could, yet dared not entertain such a thought until the wolf was hours away. If he knew such a thing he might just allow the swine to dine upon me. Over the course of two centuries, I have learned when, and when not, to entertain my treasonous thoughts.

As predicted, this morning, two young men clad in armor and bearing long blades, answered to my song. Knowing well how to play to a man's desire, I allowed the song to wither on my lips. I pretended coyness, to increase their bravado and lessen their inhibitions, thus casting my initial enchantment. Then, deliberately slinking across the meadow in full nakedness, I approached their position. With a merry laugh, a sultry look, and a bewitching touch, they now belonged to me, to do with as ever I pleased. Taking the older one, a brawny charmer named Jink by the hand, I led him into my home. There was no rush. Like I have said, I enjoy playing with my catch before the kill.

To my dismay, I quickly discovered Jink did not wear the talisman, but I so enjoy games, so played with him for a time. And when I tired, I left him sweaty and spent upon my bed before I sauntered to my doorway. With a long stretch of my arms and back, I spied the other. So young. So tender. Silly lad. He sat in the grass right where I left him, oblivious to everything but me. I am often intoxicated by my own power. This was one of those moments. A chuckle built upon delightful anticipation of the games to come coursed through my belly.

I sidled out onto my stone stoop and summoned him forth.

He was rather plain as far as men go, and told me he was known as Fane. Plain Fane. Soon to become a sweet delight. Indeed, he possessed the dragon's desire, a crystal talisman on a chain around his neck—a stone of blue which cast wicked sparkles in the sunlight. Deftly, I relieved him of his confining armor, petting and purring with a promise of pleasures to come. Yet my attempts to seduce the talisman away were all met with resistance. Somehow, he had failed to become completely enamored. If he was to end up in my cauldron, he must be free of the stone. He refused to give it, therefore, I made the decision to simply take it.

I ran my wet tongue over his sturdy neck. My fingers skimmed across the warm, inviting skin of his chest. They inched toward the stone until they met its hardened warmth. And it bit me!

I snatched my hand back from the fiery jolt, a growl rumbling in the back of my throat. What new challenge was this? I could not feast upon this man until the protection of the talisman was removed. Yet I could not bring myself to attempt touching it again.

Strengthening my gaze, I kissed and purred and rubbed against him believing I had him at the point of no return, but when it came to surrendering the stone, no amount of seduction seemed to lessen his resolve. In no uncertain terms, he told me, "no."

Since my transformation, never have I experienced rejection. Eight lives I had to relinquish. Eight times I died. Eight times I was reborn until I finally reached this powerful state of being. And he has the brass to tell me "no"? I cannot say I was angry—I was livid!

Hissing and snarling, I left him alone and in want upon my stoop, returning to the dark womb of my home. I played roughly with Jink once again while pondering the situation. There had to be a way to retrieve the talisman. I had no certainty what the dragon might do to me should I fail, but I was most certainly certain of what my master was capable of when displeased.

I had no choice in this matter. I had no lives left to live.

All my games with Jink left me bored and restless. My belly reminded me of its hunger. Across the room, my cauldron sat empty as the dragon's soul. This warrior who currently stank up my bed would fill it nicely for now. Or perhaps I could use him as a bargaining tool. Jink's life for the stone. Of course, once the talisman was in my possession, all truce would be canceled. My cauldron could easily accommodate two.

As I contemplated my choices, from beneath the pillow I withdrew my favorite dagger, stolen from my first kill centuries ago, the haft carved from a boar's tusk. Not the particular swine I detest, but I do appreciate the symbolism it represented. I licked the handle before tracing the blade across Jink's bare chest, watching his skin quiver deliciously in the dark. Subtle movement caused a streak of sunlight to dance across the room. It glanced off the blade. In the doorway stood Fane. He wandered inside, uninvited, his sword drawn, moving too freely. Too warily. Somehow, he had managed to completely break my spell.

Shoving my dagger back into hiding, I rose from the bed, once again attempting a bewitching gaze. But wisely, the lad averted his eyes, refusing to meet my own, and spied the skins which adorn my walls. Carrying on like a banshee, he called to his companion for aid, rousing Jink from his slumber. As Jink grabbed his own sword and stumbled to his feet, I held no fear. The man was still spellbound—still under my control.

"He's trying to kill me," I shrieked with my best distress. "Save me!" Jink rushed toward Fane and my heart thundered with thrill. I had convinced him to kill his friend. A simple solution to my dilemma. I would eat hearty and the dragon could then claim his prize.

Induced to fight, the two men began such a parody of battle, I could not contain my squeals of glee. Such jesters. Their pathetic attempts had me nearly beside myself. That is, until Fane persuaded Jink to take a good look at my festooned walls. Only then did he see the skins of all the men who'd come before him. The fighting stopped, never to start again. The spell I'd twisted began to unravel.

I surged beyond livid. Without thinking, I chose to pounce.

Talk about bad timing. At precisely that moment, Fane reeled around, swinging his sword with him like a scythe, and bam! Off with my head!

It smashed against the floor with a hollow, ear-ringing thunk.

Now I'm really torqued. My bewitching body stands there with no head, smoking and flaming like a brand, foolishly clawing at the air. And all I can do is scream and helplessly watch it all from down here on the floor. And if I don't do something fast, I'm going to die. Forever this time. I have no lives left.

My spirit will be sucked back down into the world of shadows and void that gave me this cursed existence to begin with, and I shall be forever imprisoned in the dark, a thrall to the dark queen. At least serving the dragon I can live in the light. There's only one man in this room who's still bound to me in the most miniscule way, so off I go—my spirit vacating one body to take up residence inside another.

It's a painful fit. We join together with a united, agonizing squeal and collapse to the floor.

Trembling.

And now …

The breaths come hard.

And now …

I am a man.

Neither of these two warriors know it yet. They're too shaken up by my untimely, unexpected demise and the dreadful knowledge of how close they came to ending up in my cauldron. I admit, it's going to take some adjustment and a lot of strength on my part to take control of this body I'm now trapped within, but it'll come about in time.

How am I ever going to explain this to Seret? Is he still going to see me as the cute little lynx he fell in love with? It took him long enough to adapt to my human womanly form. Now I'm a brawny swordsman? I do hope our love is strong enough to survive.

Nonetheless, I believe this transformation could be fascinating. I can already feel the distinct improvement in my muscular strength.

Ah, Fane, you unsuspecting, murderous fool. I may be lurking deep inside your friend at the moment, but the day will soon come when Jink will be the one hidden deep inside me. I'm still a man-eater. And I still like to toy with my food before the kill.

▲

Cat and Mouse
by Duane Pesice

"He's been tomcatting," her announced in the Voice of Death. "He doesn't know me very well."

I licked my paw, which had a little bit of breakfast still on it, and waited. Her ran hot water.

"He just doesn't." Him doesn't, either. I have heard him say so.

Her commenced scrubbing dishes. Me stayed around to hear the rest, even though my brothers were outside and I felt like playing. Me hid my intent by going by the rainy room. Noticed that him's hairbrush has content.

Me thought about pulling it out but reasoned that it wouldn't be entertaining enough. So me prowled around in the hall for a few minutes while her finished her monologue.

"Bring a strange woman into my house unannounced and expect me to like it. I don't think so," her continued. "Old friend, my ass. Well, old, I buy." Her scrubbed furiously. Me could hear the Velcro squeak from fifteen feet away. "And expect me to agree to put her up, and just assume it was fine. I'm certainly not in agreement with that, Beltane."

Oops. Too far out into the room. Mama eyes. My mama had them too.

"It's okay," her resumed. "I knew you were there. I heard you in the bathroom, too. You need practice.

"Anyway, he's not getting away with this. I got something with his name on it."

Her dried the dishes and fixed herself another cup of coffee. Me opened my mouth experimentally, hoping she'd notice and give me something to chew on.

Her ignored me and continued into the comfy room. The needles came out and her fished a bolt of cloth and a bit of linty yarn out of her stuff box.

"This will do nicely," her announced in the Voice of Impending Doom. And her went and got the hair and made a little him, and drew a face on it. Her stuck the needle in his mouth.

Her put the little him in a desk drawer, rolled it closed, opened it again. Her moved the little him back to her table and sat back in her comfortable chair.

"Enough for now," she said in a voice that would slice diamonds. She grabbed her yarn thing.

The back door was open. I went while I could.

My brothers were outside, lying in the sun. It's starting to get hot out. My furs aren't as thick as theirs and I abstained. I went instead to lie in the grass on the side of the house, where it's cool, and not so coincidentally, beneath the kitchen window. I took a power nap since him wasn't due for a couple hours. Drama is so exhausting. But I love it so.

Me heard those two hims run up the fence and out into the world and then I was in dreamtime. Me had a fine time in the library, heard the news about the star-nosed weasels, drank a little moonwine, relaxed wonderfully in a velvet hammock strung between two birches, played for a while in the Park of Boxes, and finally had some nip and a bit of fresh cream before heading back to the daylight.

The brothers were back with greetings from our other brother, who ran away because the older cats made him bleed after Fatboy won the leader post. He's doing well, they tell me.

Me knew this much because me am carrying his kittens. But him and him can't smell that yet. Me won't let them anyway. Them need to find their own tail.

"What a day!" Him hollered in the Voice of Dead Tired. "Oh my tooth." Him came stomping out of the back door. "And I have such a bruise!"

Him rubbed his shoulder, which was purple. "I blacked out and fell into the corner of the grill. Sharp! Hard! Pain!"

Me could *feel* her grin. Me heard the click of the needles onto the side-table, the sounds of coffee-fixing. Got up and moved to just around the corner, behind the clothes basket.

Her sat down on a plastic box. "Tooth bothering you?"

"More than bothering me," him said. "It's KILLING me."

"Maybe you should drink the other half of the bourbon," she said, warming to the discussion. "That would deaden the pain."

"And my shoulder," he whined.

"And that, too. I can make canned ravioli, that's fine."

Him looked at the ground.

"I'll cook," him volunteered.

"Of course you will. And then you'll get drunk and I'll watch Practical Magic again. And listen to you snore."

"I'm sorry," him said, still looking at the ground.

"You certainly are," she said, and got up and went back inside.

"I need this," he muttered.

Her opened a can, and that delicious smell summoned the crew. The brothers lagged behind for appearance's sake, and the tuxedo sisters ate first, as usual. The mama cat didn't get up.

The long-eared salad-eaters hopped up to get their leaves and roots. Her fed them, poured our dish full of chewies and crunchables, and went to sit down on her chair and watch the screen.

Him ruined some fish, warming it in oil and squeezing fruit on it, and they ate some roots. In silence. They looked at the screen.

We fur people all went outside after supper. Over the fence and out in the world. I saw my brother and the barrio cats, and we chased the pigs and saw the flying mice go back home.

Her was not very pleased about that, and let us know by giving us a can of ick food in the morning when we returned, but it was worth it for the entertainment and the exercise. We don't get many chances to go catting and might as well take advantage of every chance we get.

"You kids need to stay inside at night," she told us. "Beltane, you're supposed to be in charge."

Actually, Fat Boy is. But he's lazy. Papa cat mostly runs things. But me am assigned to the Cat Mama, and her believes this gives me rank.

Him came stumbling out of the rainy room, rubbing his jaw. "My tooth still hurts," he tried.

"You're going to work," she told him. "Suck on a teabag to get that poison out and suck it up."

Him grunted.

"We need the money," she finished.

Him fetched a bun from the cold box and left, biting on the bun.

Her followed him as far as the front door, picking up the little man on the way. She jabbed a needle in its butt.

"Ow!" We all heard.

"I'll torture him more later," she said, and pulled all the needles.

The tuxedo cats went back to bed. The brothers went to go nap on the birdcage and the mama cat came out to have breakfast.

"Meow," she said, glancing in my direction.

"Mew," I answered, remembering her position. "Mew." I licked a paw. Cats only have so many sounds. The mama cat was telling me that it was hell to grow old, and not to try it. She's going to last a while yet, though, I'd bet. Her is tough. Small but tough, like me, and gray stripes like me, too. We all love the mama cat, but the tuxedo sisters are closer to her.

Them are old, too, the cat-ladies. Agatha is tall and dignified, with a sneer on her face, and Hermione is stout and doughty. One does not tangle with them, for they are not enfeebled and will hurt you. Their years have not yet worn on them as they have on the mama.

"I don't have that choice," is what I said to the mama.

"Mew," she answered. "True."

Me went out for another trip to the dreamtime, met up with my sister, who lives a little ways away but stays inside, talked to her housemate, who looks like my orange brother. He seems a nice fellow. Used to stay with our crew until Cat Mama and Cat Papa started living apart. Our papa cat is very fond of him, and they exchange scent messages when they can't meet in dreams.

This time, by fortune, they met. Papa cat slumbered in his seat in the sun, and dreamed his way with us. The tuxedo sisters and the mama cat all dreamed then, and we adventured far, almost to the edge of the desert, following the flying mice to a fine row of burrows, where we flushed a fat warm thing and enjoyed a bit of sweet water before boarding a carpet to the mountains and jumping and climbing the afternoon away.

Even the mama cat came up a little bit, though she stayed on a low ledge and didn't jump about. It was good to have her with us though.

Me woke and stretched luxuriously and padded onto the tiles. Her was scritching and scratching on the little man with a pin.

Her phone belled.

Him was writing to her. Her smiled and poked the little man in the stomach with a finger, and then put it on her side-table.

Her made more coffee.

Him arrived shortly after that, complaining about a tummyache.

"Poor baby, " her said.

Him didn't speak. Him picked up the little man from the side-table.

"This is me, isn't it?" Him asked.

"Of course it is," her said. "So?"

"That means you have been causing all of my troubles."

"Not all of them," her said. "You create many of your own. But, yes, I have been poking you with pins and needles."

"I should make one of you," him said.

"You lack the ability," her answered. "It takes more than you know."

"I suppose it is something passed on between mother and daughter only," him said.

"Of course it is, and all of the mothers and all of the daughters. I imagine it is part of the mitochondrial DNA," her said.

Him had no answer for that. "I brought home burgers."

"How nice to have been asked. But thank you."

He put the little man down gently, and they sat down and ate.

Later, her went out to make a fire. It was one of *those* days. A mantic night.

Him drank water.

Mindful of her warning, we stayed in and played and dreamed.

▲

Last of the Ashiptu
by Paul Lubaczewski

He was positive one of the reasons that he had worked this hard in life was to avoid life's little annoyances. You struggle to climb the corporate ladder, you have no time for close friends, you put off having a family, all for a reason. He was the youngest company President on the market right now. Companies vied for his services, even though none of them were sure if he was worth it, but a good hype man is better than all of the background checks on earth. He made damned sure that he was in every magazine out there, selling the wondrous product of himself. But the point was, you did all of that to achieve something, to be able to afford to not have the little blasts and bothers that made other people so miserable with their lives.

This week, though, he had been "other people" all week. Today it had been the ticket and a flat tire.

He didn't HAVE to drive, he could be limo-ed, he certainly had the money, but he LIKED to drive. He bought cars because he liked to drive them. At least normally. Today, he was positive he had paid the meter, he was positive he hadn't been in the Design Center very long, he was sure of all of that. He was also just as sure of the ticket waiting for him on the Mercedes when he got there.

Not to mention the flat tire, it had just been that kind of a week.

He climbed into the car to consider his options. He could call Triple A, but they wouldn't be here for forever, he had a meeting to get to, and he really couldn't wait. He considered fixing it himself for a few moments, he'd changed a tire for the love of god. A cab whipped by at roughly the speed of sound just then, the whole car rocked from the wind of its passage. Nix that. He decided that he'd just drive on the flat, and deal with replacing the whole rim later. Maybe he'd send some gopher down to change it while he was in meetings. Slowly, he pulled the car out into traffic.

That, was when the bike messenger plowed directly into the door. It had just been that kind of week.

As he pulled into his parking garage, the guy in the booth leaned out, "Hey, you know your tire's flat?"

He just sighed and said, "Thank you for pointing that out" and limped it slowly to his spot.

Williams Bryant, 34, single, moderate height, blond, blue-eyed, hot shit executive. President of SZN Holdings, second only to CEO Aran Nagi, and his chosen successor. Every year someone made an offer to buy him off to their company, every year he stayed put. In other words, living the good life. His politics were strictly mercenary, his music tastes a weird hodge podge of rap and rock that he listened to in college.

It was in his senior year of college that his mentor and boss Nagi found him. He didn't know why the successful Arab man had taken him under his wing (it would turn out Aran was Iranian, his family having fled to America with all of its money mere months before the Islamic revolution). But here and now, he thought he saw it, Aran needed an American just a soulless and driven as he was, a kindred spirit. It was hard to argue, life had one goal and one measure, money. At first, it had just been simple laziness, life was easier if you had money, but now, it was score-keeping.

But wasn't everything? Women, cars, houses, having them was boring. Getting them was part of the fun. The real fun began after you'd gotten them. Knowing that someone out there was gnashing their teeth in jealousy, that was the joy. You might not drive the 1970 Ferrari even once a year, and it might not even be your favorite car, but you kept it anyway. Just knowing that some poor sap out there couldn't have it kept you warm at night.

It was one of the reasons he remained unmarried, never own anything that can take itself away from you. It was a frame of mind Aran would have done well to consider. There was a party one night and Aran had left it to go deep sea fishing in the middle of the night with some of his friends. Which is a privilege of having enough wealth, you can go deep sea fishing no matter how late, or drunk you are. Will had begged off, citing his own intake of alcohol which he had exaggerated.

Which left him alone with Noora. Noora who he had secretly lusted over for the five years since he had been Aran's best man. Aran had married her because he thought his fortune should have a physical heir, and she had been from a prominent Iraqi family that he had business dealings with, so she was easy to acquire. She was also gorgeous her dark hair framing a strong yet feminine face that showed strength and beauty at the same time, and eyes you could practically swim in. Will, as he was known to close associates, couldn't have helped himself if he had tried. And he hadn't tried.

And while Aran fished, or most likely passed out below deck, Will, his trusted partner wooed his wife. It had taken him hours, plying her with alcohol and lies. He found what she was lacking in Aran, and found a way to provide it. Her marriage was a loveless passionless arrangement, so first, he flattered her with compliments, and then he gave her lust and passion. He acquired her for one night, the same way he acquired everything. Once he had her, her only value would be to hurt Aran, and strangely he felt bad about that.

Both of them agreed to pretend it never happened by morning and to never speak of it again. Her for fear of her situation, and him out of a desire to not cuckold his mentor. That was five months ago.

He spent his time in the executive elevator getting more bad news. Word of the takeover he had organized on a rival had somehow leaked out to the press. This was going to cost, the shareholders had mounted a vigorous defense of the food maker, which left him few options. He could either mount an expensive campaign to force it through, every second of which was going to cost them profit when they dismantled the damn thing, or he could sell out of it now while the stock prices were up which would make him look foolish to the market.

Either way, he was boned when he'd have to explain it to Aran.

Every single day this week had been like this, every day and in every way. One of his cars had gone in for a tune up and was still in the garage as the mechanic hunted for the rare parts it would need for a transmission rebuild. At his California house, his caretaker had called to tell him that a very, very expensive chandelier was now being swept up and that he, the caretaker, had needed stitches. This of course just upped his insurance on that place, he'd have paid outright for the Doctor's visit for the guy, but since he had been bleeding out at the time he'd ended up taking a ride in an ambulance. He'd met a girl at a very exclusive club a few nights ago, he thought he was moments from closing the deal until her boyfriend showed up, the ex-heavyweight champion.

It felt, personal.

Which was stupid, he knew, life didn't operate that way, but it didn't help his feelings for the knowing of it.

He sat at his desk trying to get his head straight before this meeting. He clicked on to Facebook. He kept a fake page on there just for friends. You just don't keep a page under your own name to goof off on Facebook or Twitter, where everything you say, can and will go right to the press. He was just about to close it out when he noticed a message request. The profile had no picture with it, from someone named Agnes Sampson. He didn't know anyone by that name, so it was weird to see it on his private profile. He didn't bother to open it, he didn't have to. It only consisted of one word, "Ezeru".

For some reason, he was weirded out by it. He had no idea what it meant and didn't have the time to look it up before his meeting with some of the underlings from a newly acquired energy concern. He found himself not even listening, really just nodding at the appropriate moments, while they were going through projections.

Until something caught his attention, "Wait, what was that last thing?"

"We're hung up getting a clearance on a set of fracking pods?" the nervous looking exec repeated.

"Why in the hell are we hung up, I thought for sure we BOUGHT the seats for the local reps there?" he demanded irate and heated.

"The local didn't stay bought Will, he went to the press with water concerns," the other fidgeted.

"Why in the HELL did our bought and paid for state rep do that?" William demanded.

"Apparently one of our other pods cost his cousin his home, and he developed a conscience and a spine because of it."

"Jesus CHRIST!"

It had just been that kind of a week.

* * * *

It was Thursday, it was his last meeting for the week, and he was getting out of here before anything else could go wrong. Especially before Aran found out about the pod going south on them. They'd get the land eventually, and the clearances, but this was going to devour their profit margin for a while. He sure as hell didn't want to be here to explain it.

He told his secretary Ellen to not forward him anything until Sunday night unless it involved an actual fire. Even then she was to consider if there was a possibility that it would go out on its own. He needed a weekend away, he wasn't sure where, but it was going to be nowhere near New York City. THIS was the kind of problem money could solve.

He was already in the parking garage when he remembered that he hadn't left instructions to have the flat repaired. He had choices here, he could have an assistant get another car, and then have this one delivered. He could call a repairman. But none of it seemed right, part of owning cars is the manliness of tinkering with them. The entire day seemed powerless, at least he could handle this on his own.

A text buzzed him as he walked. Taking out his phone he looked down, "Unknown Number" but he could see what it said, it said, "Ezeru"

He almost broke a knuckle changing the flat tire.

* * * *

He got to his condo early that day and grabbed a bottle out of his beer fridge. Almost everything in there cost more per bottle than a case of normal beer. He sometimes doubted it tasted any better, but appearances needed maintaining. He couldn't allow a guest to go in there and find something plain, it wouldn't look right.

He had called in a meal, he kept a chef on retainer and went to his study. He wanted to check his messages and watch some TV. After he ate he'd figure out where he was going this weekend other than that magical place, "Anywhere but here" that people often dream of. He didn't have to dream, he just needed to make arrangements.

He turned on the TV but kept the volume low, some football, he didn't really need volume for it. The announcers annoyed him half the time anyway, just talking to fill space mostly. They'd contradict each other one play to the next. "Boy I love the way this secondary never gives up!", the next play going for a fifty-yard touchdown with nobody anywhere near the receiver, "You just CAN'T give up on a play like that in this league!" He wasn't really going to be paying that much attention anyway.

He sat down on the couch and opened up his tablet and his beer. Time to clear out his messages in his private email. He had a private email almost nobody knew, even with spam blockers working their magic it would still fill up amazingly quick if he didn't stay on top of it. It filled up to the point where you had to be careful you didn't accidentally delete something you actually wanted, so he was dutifully scanning his way down.

One of the emails was labeled "Ezeru", he deleted it without opening it. Someone was fucking with him. It was either that, or he'd gotten on the weirdest mailing list. He wasn't having it, not tonight, not ever. Whoever it was, would sooner or later figure out that they weren't getting to him, and when they tried to goad him further, they'd slip up, and let on who they were. When that happened he would ruin that prick!

He went to swing his legs up onto the couch in annoyance at the whole thing. There was a thunk, and a bubbling hiss, he looked down to watch his white carpet begin to soak up about fifty dollars worth of beer that he'd just knocked off the table. Thankfully he had a lot more, his plans for the rest of the night included more anyway. Time to eat dinner, and drink himself to sleep. Tomorrow would be another day. The rest of the night went fuzzy soon after.

* * * *

The next morning he got up slowly, and carefully, thanking all things holy he had remembered to darken the windows before he had passed out last night. He hadn't drunk that much, and he wasn't old enough for a hangover to be an automatic consequence of drinking, but light hurt regardless. If the windows had been letting in full sunlight right now, that would have been considerably worse.

Coffee, the smell of the Jamaican Blue already filled the kitchen as he wandered in. It presented the hopes that the day would not be as awful as he'd suspected when he opened his eyes. Coffee, a couple of hits off the oxygen tank he kept for just such an emergency, ibuprofen and some eggs, and maybe things would be fine.

He sent down an order for his breakfast and toddled off to his study, steaming mug in hand. Flicking on his tablet he opened up a news page. It was amazing that in a world where they had part ownership of one of the major networks there would still be news he hadn't heard about already, but god bless the world, it still found a way to be surprising. God damnit! Their little paid for state rep had made the news whining about poisoned drinking water. Time to get the local papers to publish some dirt on him. If he'd sold out to them, there had to be enough of it, and if what they had wasn't sufficient, it was amazing what people would swear to for the right amount of money.

Annoyed, he flipped open his email and started scanning through deleting. He almost deleted one marked "IMPORTANT" because everyone knows that nothing that is actually important is actually marked that way in the message line. But he took the check off of it when he saw who it was from, Noora Nagi. After hitting it with quick scan he found there weren't any virus's and opened it. "I understand that you are having bad luck lately. I think I know why. Meet me at the Great Falls in Patterson at 7 tonight, and I will explain. Please do not tell anyone. Aran might get angry, you understand. -Noora p.s. Do not call for the same reason."

His brain twitched to full awake now! Any lazy easing into consciousness had vanished and he was now on full alert! He kept re-reading the message like it would suddenly crack under his scrutiny and relay its hidden meaning. But it remained inscrutable as ever. Did Aran know? Was that it? Was he just trying to make his life a living hell now? Get him to quit on his own without a public scandal? Make his deals look so bad that his value went down? What if it wasn't that, what if it was someone else, and they were trying to blackmail Noora? What if nobody knew at all and she just wanted to talk to him about his guilt and was using office scuttlebutt about his recent string of bad days as an excuse? He could already concede the only way he would get an answer now was to meet her. He answered the email back asking if she could just call him or text him back to tell him whatever was so important, but he didn't expect an answer. He wasn't getting away today, at least not far away.

After breakfast, he researched what he could on Noora Nagi, trophy-wife. Most of what he found, he already knew, she came from a well-known family after all. As far as he could tell digging through, her family had been in some prominence as long as there were records to track. Normally not the type to fall in with a con-artist like Aran, they probably would have looked down on him for his family fleeing, but the US invasion had screwed with their holdings significantly. They knew they needed friends in the US to put their portfolio back together, and Aran would do just that. Very, very mercenary.

With nothing in there to prepare him anymore for the meeting than he already was, he went and got a shower. He could spend the day puttering around the place and be sure to get to Patterson early. He was actually not completely dreading it, he'd always wanted to see the falls themselves. It might be weird circumstance, but he'd see them today. For all, he knew this wasn't anything major she just needed to talk.

* * * *

In his entire life, he could only remember coming to Patterson, maybe twice, and by limo both times. He'd always been curious to see the falls up close, but never enough to go out of his comfort zone to see it. He was not happy to see all the trash on the streets surrounding parts of the park as he cruised around it. It made him thankful that his Benz was fixed, it was heavily insured and frankly, Benz's were easily replaced.

He decided to find the most exposed looking lot he could find and park there. It would at least take some measure of daring to break into it there. The car itself had enough anti-theft devices they wouldn't be able to drive it off anyway, maybe location would discourage outright rifling through it for anything. He didn't want to drive back to the city on broken glass.

The day itself felt brisk. He couldn't help but reason that it was the mist coming off the falls, which he could hear over the noise of the surrounding city and the nearby highway. But there was no denying the pleasant air it gave to the park, brisk was the word for it. He was almost smiling as he locked up the Benz and strode in down the path. Once inside the gates, he realized the place was actually slightly bigger than he'd been prepared for. Not that much of a worry, though, Noora always dressed spectacularly, an Arab woman dressed at the absolute pinnacle of fashion shouldn't be too hard to spot, even in New Jersey.

It ended up taking him longer than he expected, she was actually dressed in a Hijab. It was even more striking because he had only seen her ever wear top of the line high fashion before. "Noora?" he called out hesitantly still unsure it was her.

She smiled at him, gave a wave and said, "Will, so good of you to come."

"Well," he said with a shrug, " you did say it was important."

"It is," she nodded. "But first, let us look at the fall. I have had few opportunities to see something like this. Iraq has falls, but travel to the north for something like sightseeing has been difficult in my life."

With that, it seemed like she was shutting him off for now. His need to find out what this was all about was to wait until they had both seen the falls. Considering the urbanization on all sides, he had to admit it was a spectacular thing to have right there. There was a large foot bridge across the front of the gorge the falls were in, they walked across side by side. The atmosphere gave it all the feel of two kids on a date.

Once they had crossed the bridge, Noora led them down the steps closer to the falls themselves. They water was oppressively loud now, the noise had become an all-encompassing thing, totally moving past sound into tacit sensation. You could feel the pounding it was so endless and enormous in its nature. You'd have to practically shout to be heard by the person right next to you, he suspected somehow that this was what Noora had in mind in choosing the place.

She looked over, staring at him with her surprising blue eyes sparkling in her dark face. It was one of the things that had made her so irresistible to him. "So, Will, how much do you know about my family?" an odd question he wasn't expecting.

He rebounded from his surprise quickly, "The basic stuff, established family, used to be loaded, the war wasn't kind to you."

"Yes," she smiled at that, "that's all that really is available without snoops on the ground. But my family goes all the way back to Babylon itself, you can trace the entire lineage all the way back to where records cease to exist."

"That's pretty amazing really," he actually meant that.

"Let me ask you, Will, do you know what the Ashiptu is?" she said looking into his eyes.

"No, I mean why should I?" he asked oddly irritated by the question.

"In ancient times, it was a witch, or a warlock is what your English would call it," Noora said her face oddly placid and calm as she spoke, despite the volume it took to make oneself heard.

"Oh, OK" he answered trying to figure out where she was going with this.

"The women in my family have always been treasured, which I suppose as an American you would be incredulous at. We are treasured because we have always had abilities as Ashiptu, and it has brought much wealth to our family over the centuries," she said.

"You brought me here to tell me you were a witch?"

"Not entirely. What I really needed to tell you first, is that I'm pregnant."

It took a moment for the full force of the shock to hit Williams, "Wait, what?"

"Before you ask, you are indeed the father, the only one capable of having done it. Which is why, in my rage and upset I cursed you," she said staring placidly into the sucking void of the falls.

He grabbed her shoulders and twisted her to face him, "Noora, what in the hell are you talking about?" She stared at his hands for a moment, and remembering himself he removed them, "Look I'm sorry but…"

She smiled sadly at him before continuing, "Aran is incapable of it, so that leaves only you Will. That is what Ezeru means Will, it is a hex or a curse. You have felt maybe, like everything you touch lately has gone to hell? It has, and it will only get worse for you I'm afraid. She looked briefly out over the spray again, "But I realized to my shame that I was being unfair. I know what Aran will do to me when he finds out, and I already heard you refusing to fight to save me in my heart. Would you do that Will? Would you risk your career to be a father and a husband?"

She watched his face carefully, examining it until she was sure she was seeing the denial that she had expected. His hangdog look of "But I can't" spoke louder to her than if he had opened his mouth. "I know, but it is still unfair and wrong to put the Ezeru upon you, it is out of your hands. So, I want to make things right, I want to take the curse away, to offer you the Right Of Maqlu."

Something about it all exasperated him, and he just snarled, "Well do it already!"

"Would that it was that easy. The law of the gods and the world, offer one solution. You must plunge into a holy river at a spot of my choosing," she pointed at a spot in the middle of the falls, where it flattened out briefly before the water's final plunge into the river, "and I chose there."

"Are you out of your mind?" he practically screamed, "What in the hell am I saying, your talking about magic and curses, of course, you're out of your mind! No way am I doing that!"

She smiled as she reached into her purse, a beatific smile, like the one a mother gives a child who is being dangerously foolish. He looked down and he saw the meaning to the smile, it was given enforcement by the hard lump of murderous steel she drew out. Her mandate had the strength of burning death behind it, she could afford to grin at his childishness.

"I think you will, one way or another. If I shoot you where you stand, you'll fall in. That would most likely be certain death from here. But it does fulfill Maqlu. If you're careful making your way across the rapids, there is a spot where maybe you climb down, and only get wet and bruised. If I shoot you, I will just tell Aran that you raped me and that I was ashamed and did not want to get in the way of men and business so I said nothing. He thinks all women from the old world are brood mares good for nothing but getting children upon. He will believe I am so dutiful I would rather hide my shame in silence until I could bear it no longer. He will welcome your death."

Williams looked at her, he could see immediately there was no hint of a joke, or levity in her face now. She had also somehow moved out of his reach, there would be no grabbing the gun. He didn't know a damned thing about guns except they made a good wedge issue in a tight election, but he had no doubt it was loaded.

"But, why Noora?"

"Will, I'm doing you a favor don't you see? If I let it go on the Ezeru would get worse, and worse until it killed you. It is the only way to remove it, this is your only hope now! But you HAVE hope!" her face actually looked sad and pitying as she spoke.

"Why here?"

"It is beautiful enough to be sacred."

He looked in the direction she indicated, he realized he didn't have much choice in it. He could just tell someone and have her committed after this, or Aran would. She was only supposed to be a trophy wife, and trophies weren't to wave guns at your partner. Heck, how did he even know she was actually pregnant, for all he knew she'd just flown off her nut being cooped up by Aran so much. But never antagonize a crazy person with a gun if you had options, even bad options.

Now that he looked at it, he thought he could indeed see a way down. It looked dangerous, and normally he wouldn't even consider it. But dangerous compared to what? The woman behind him talking about magical powers and waving a loaded pistol around?

He turned to implore her to think about it when the gun exploded behind him! There was a second noise as the bullet ricocheted off the hard stone next to him! He heard her behind him say, "Please Will, I'd feel terrible about it, but the next one is going through your thigh."

"SHE'D feel terrible? What about me," he muttered to himself as he inched towards the water. Getting there wouldn't be AS bad as he'd thought at first, it was dry rock most of the way. But, there were spots he'd have to jump or wade. He was still trying not to think about the crevice climb down with its slick rocks and pounding water! Thank god he'd dressed casual, that meant he had sneakers on at least, the beginning was just light bouldering. Within very little time he was past the point of any safety, he could hear the roar of the water right below him! Every step was terror now, he wasn't an outdoorsy sort of guy. He liked adventure, but in a clipped off to a rope sort of way, not a slip and die one!

He could see he was getting close to where he was going to have to jump. He had considered wading but he doubted now up close that he could stay upright in the current. Hopefully, he turned to see if maybe Noora would relent. She was watching him with the gun pointed at him still, with what he was afraid looked like pinpoint accuracy. It dawned on him, wealthy young woman who lived through a war, she could probably hit a fly at fifty yards.

As he turned back to look at the upcoming jump, his right foot suddenly slid out from under him on a patch of algae that made the rock like ice! With no time to stop himself, he only desperately twisted to direct his fall to make sure he didn't plummet in the direction of the rushing water! His shoulder slammed into the hard rock knocking the wind out of him! His neck whipped in pain at the sudden stop in motion! His entire body racked itself in hoarse gasps as he tried to get any air back. Desperately his mind kept telling him not to move, any move he made that wasn't carefully considered could lead to death! He opened his eyes, as he felt the water tugging at his foot which he realized had slid into the water!

With utmost care, he got his arms under him and pushed himself up. He was if anything maybe a foot further back from the falls then he had been. As the adrenaline faded he felt the intense pain of his shoulder where it had slammed into the rock! No time for standing still, if he sat too long whatever damage he'd done to himself in the landing would stiffen and he hadn't even hit the hard parts. It could cost him everything on the climb down! Keep going, get it over with!

Pulling himself upright, he shook his head clear and walked the rest of the way to where he had to jump. There was nothing for it, there was a wide plane of rock on the other side. If he landed partially in the water he'd have to fall towards the rock and scrabble up. He took a few steps back and started running as fast as he could and leaped! His heart was in his throat for a moment as he flew over the rushing water beneath him! He was trying to keep his eyes on the rock ahead and not even glance down. Landing hard, he let himself stumble a step or two forward, before standing there gasping for air.

In front of him was a wide flat plain of rock here that led directly to the ravine that went down. His eyes squinted through the mist that filled the entire thing. There WAS a way! It was dangerous, but he could see it now! He risked another glance at Noora and seeing no help there, he concentrated on the climb.

Will dug in his first footholds and began. The blasting water right next to him now sent up a spray that soaked him almost immediately! He could feel the slick rock, thankfully blasted free of algae. One hold after another, that was the way! He grasped for a hold as he lowered himself down again further, and felt the rock gash his hand! He looked to see blood pouring out down his arm now, washing away in the spray! He had to hurry! He could see there was pool directly below him now, just a little further!

Will had to use the hand, no other way. He made it a bit closer when he felt another stabbing pain in the hand from a rock jabbing into the wound! His hand jerked back automatically! He felt himself slip! He was going over! Both hands scrambled to regain balance and.....

There was a smack as he hit the water below him! He heard it as he hit. Will felt the water already taking hold of him, spinning him out over another void surrounding him with droplets of water and then slamming again into the river! Even in his daze, he knew that he needed to get to the surface. He fought his way up to the dancing and flickering light above himself plunging out into the air gasping sucking back life into himself!

He looked up, there was Noora standing on another prominence staring down at him as she stood at the edge.

"There! I fucking did it! Good enough?!" his words echoed up the ravine.

She smiled as she stood there, her hands cupped around her abdomen and she smiled at him looking like an angel now. The way she held her stomach was almost like she was cradling a child, their child. "And now, to FINISH THIS!" she yelled, her voice echoing everywhere.

She waved at him, he would always remember that she waved a light little happy jaunty wave like a wife to a husband taking a train ride. She smiled wider, she closed her eyes, and she took one, step, forward.

The noise when she hit was enormous, it echoed for minutes afterward through the ravine.

* * * *

He sits in his office, alone, always alone. No boss, or mentor, or friend anymore. That man went mad after his wife's suicide, especially after they told him she was with child. Aran never checked on the genetics of the girl in the womb. He runs the company now, alone. Alone, with the memory of his tryst with the Ashiptu and the death of his daughter, who would have been the next one.

* * * *

"If a woman has put a spell upon another man and it is not justified, he upon whom the spell is laid shall go to the holy river; into the holy river shall he plunge. If the holy river declares him innocent and he remains unharmed the woman who laid the spell shall be put to death. He that plunged into the river shall take possession of the house of the one who laid the spell upon him."— Code of Hammurabi, 2000 BC

▲

Firestorm

by Richard H. Durisen

In Spring 1946, Lloyd Phillips, known as "Phil" to his Lancaster Bomber squadron, hoped to flee his personal terror by moving to a remote cliff-side cottage in Donegal, Ireland. On the fourth day after his arrival, the banging on his door in the early morning hours demolished that hope. Phil wasn't sleeping, just lying in bed to get through the night, but the noise made him launch upright as if startled from deep slumber. Acid billowed into his throat.

His legs dropped mechanically to the floorboards. Inevitability, not volition, drew him to the door. He knew what was there.

A hooded figure, vaguely female, stood in tatters on his threshold, illuminated by the Moon. She held a swaddled bundle in her arms. As waves smashed against the base of the nearby cliff, the woman's skeletal hand swept her hood away, revealing a blackened face and bared teeth. Pieces of seared flesh with bits of hair clung to her scalp. She smelled long past rotten in the salty air. Despite the devastation of her features, her eyes were intact. They had a soft look and were moistened with tears.

She held out the bundle to him.

Phil fell to his knees and screamed.

* * * *

The scream echoed off the surrounding hills. A third of a mile away, the reverberations jolted Sean from dreams of fairies and spells. He knew immediately it was the Brit who had moved into the nearest house, the cottage previously owned by old Tom O'Malley. Sean felt the Englishman's anguish wash over his own body as the howl faded. With a sigh of reluctance, Sean resolved, then and there, to do what he could to relieve this man's pain.

* * * *

Sean McLaughlin had been a fisherman before his sister, Rose, bequeathed the Book to him in her suicide note. Studying the Book transformed his life. Town folk noticed his newfound familiarity with the old ways. Father O'Connell and the Faithful kept a wary eye on him, but, in an uneasy truce, they let him be, as long as he did nothing public to undermine the Church's authority.

Sean was a barrel-chested man of ruddy complexion, well liked by most for his caring soul. Despite his affinity for alcohol, Sean's physical prowess and skill with the knots, nets, and tackle had made him welcome on most boats even before Rose's death. These days, though, he could ship out with anyone any time, because of his uncanny knack for knowing where the best catches could be had and when the bad storms would roll in. Those who had no qualms about powers outside the Lord's province also sought his help with their love quandaries and other ailments. His ministrations proved surprisingly effective.

The day after being awakened by the scream, Sean studied what the Book had to say about troubled souls. Because there are so many causes of turbulence in the human spirit, it was well past three in the afternoon when, tired of reading, he decided to cull more information. He hopped on his bicycle and headed to the village along the coast road. As he passed old Tom O'Malley's place, Sean noted that the Brit's car was gone, and so he'd likely be in town.

At about four o'clock, Sean rattled down the cobblestone hill toward the docks on Donegal Bay. With his enhanced senses, Sean could see a pod of seals chasing a school of mackerel and, far beyond the horizon, a nasty swirl of clouds.

Sean road up to the Squealing Pig, parked his bike, and entered the din and smoke of the pub. Finn, wearing his threadbare fisherman's cap and smoking a pipe, waved him to the bar. Finn ordered two fresh pints and handed one to Sean.

Sean had been counseling Finn for some time, because Finn's softness proved awkward for him, even though he was a giant of a man with fists meatier than most. Finn confided indifference toward women, not something Sean had thought possible, but the Book described it as being as natural as the sea and stars.

"Hey, Finn. Tell the mates I see a bad blow coming in from the west. It'll be here tomorrow noon."

"Will do for sure, Sean. Thanks. We could use a day's rest, even with the money to worry us."

"Say, what do you know about the Brit who bought O'Malley's?"

"A mousy man, name of Lloyd Phillips. Drops a lot a coin here. Not much on talking, but sometimes he'll buy a round for everyone, just like that. Sits in the corner with his head in his hands, mostly."

"Have you talked to him?"

"Not much. Bought him a pint, so he let me sit. Thought, maybe, we had something in common." Finn raised one eyebrow slightly.

"What'd he say?"

"Ah, he's locked up tight. Had it rough in the war, he says. Dropping bombs on folks. Then he closed up like a mussel at low tide. He's sitting back there now." Finn tilted his head toward a dark corner.

Sean nudged Finn. "I'll give it a try." Sean downed his pint, ordered two more, and walked over to the Brit's table.

"Hey, me man. Mind if I join you?"

Phil looked up. "I'd rather you didn't."

A frigid wind from Phil's eyes blew through Sean's body, but Sean maintained a smile as he sat down. "Here's a fresh pint. I live by Imeal, the cliff south of Old Tom's place. Let's tip one, neighbor." They drank after Sean offered a saluted to peaceful times and mercy on Old Tom's soul.

"Welcome to Donegal. Lloyd it is, right? I'm Sean."

"The draoi. Yes?"

"That may be going a bit far, but I take the compliment."

"Finn told me a little."

"Good man, Finn. Say, if you don't mind me mentioning it, I heard a bit of a ruckus from your way last night."

Phil visibly cringed.

"Bloody war dreams. It's why I live out of town." He drank down half the stout and set the glass on the table. He took a moment to study Sean. "Chums call me Phil after my last name Phillips." He swirled his beer and looked at it. "Might as well call me that, since we're neighbors."

"Saw some bad stuff, Phil?"

"I was a bombardier. I just saw flashes and fires from high up. Watched a lot of mates go down in other planes, though. The flak and fighters were bad, but my plane never took a serious hit. Damn bloody lucky, I guess."

Sean searched Phil's eyes. Shadows flitted in them. "So what's with the dreams then?"

Phil looked down at his hands.

"I was rotated when my tour was up. Continued in the RAF until '45, assessing effectiveness. Saw pictures... of the Hamburg firestorm. 1943. They were civilians mostly who died... Hamburg was my last drop before being reassigned."

"'Twas a nasty war all around, from what I've heard." Sean pulled at the shadows with mental fingers.

"I hated the bloody Nazis as much as anyone. My mum and sister died in the Blitz. So when I dropped incendiaries, I told myself the Krauts got what they bloody well deserved... But the pictures... I keep one with me." Phil reached into his leather flight jacket. The photo was folded, worn, and stained. It showed a woman charred beyond recognition, lying in the rubble, cradling the blackened skeleton of a baby. Several gritty German men with shovels stood over her with their hats off. The picture felt hot to Sean, like the fire was still burning.

"So I have… bad dreams."

Sean leaned in. A specter leapt at him from Phil's eyes. The dead woman hovered around them. "Maybe a wee bit more than dreams, now?"

Phil looked at him with a blend of surprise, suspicion, and appreciation. Eventually he admitted, "Yeah, maybe so."

"Be right back, me man, with more pints. I have my own hard stories to tell."

Sean and Phil talked on into the night. Phil told war stories—the deaths of his mother and sister, vengeance delivered through a bombsight, the clatter of flak on the fuselage. Sean shared the complicated tragedy of his family—a father lost at sea, his mother's mysterious disappearance, two sisters killed in a brutal love triangle.

Phil confessed that the burned woman haunted him at night, and Sean offered to confront her with him.

"I've learned to trust the Irish magic, Phil. And you got nothing to lose, even if you think I'm daft."

After midnight, Sean piled his bicycle awkwardly into the back of Phil's car. The Guinness made it a perilous drive back to Phil's house, but Sean gave Phil psychic nudges to keep the car on the road. Safely arrived, Phil broke out a fresh bottle of whiskey, and the men drank into the wee hours.

Then came the heavy, insistent knock. Phil's face went white. Sean felt a buzz in the air. Everything sparkled vividly.

"I think you best answer it, Phil. I'm right beside you."

They both sobered going to the door. They locked eyes for a moment, as Phil reached for the latch.

In addition to fairies, Selkies, and other odd creatures born in ancient times, Sean's preternatural senses also revealed the occasional ghost or specter, usually a wispy thing, more like a lingering memory than a real presence. The woman standing on the threshold was as real and solid as his hand. She extended her bundle toward Phil, and he fainted into Sean's arms. The woman stared at Sean and cuddled the bundle back against her chest. While it was impossible to read a human expression on her ravaged face, Sean felt an ocean of sorrow.

The woman reached out a hand to Sean. Where she touched him, her finger burned like a hot iron poker. "Hilf uns," was all she said. Then she pulled up her ragged hood, turned, and stepped slowly back toward the shadows like a nun reading vespers.

Shaken to his core, Sean carried Phil to his bed and dozed uneasily in a chair until the Sun came up. Phil showed no sign of rousing anytime soon, and the air held no trace of the specter.

Back home, Sean ate sausage, eggs, and toast before collapsing on his mattress.

He awoke in mid-afternoon and retrieved a box from under his bed. Inside the box lay the Book, splotchy with age, nestled in a soft, wool lining. The Book was bound in brown sharkskin leather. Embossed on the cover, lavish Celtic patterns were interwoven with other more ancient and eldritch symbols. The pages devoted to cases like Phil's specified that no simple herbs or spells would suffice. To be helped, Phil would have to be fully opened emotionally. The draoi needed to have physically intimate contact with the person he or she was trying to help, best done soon before an apparition of the haunt. Sean felt he was in way over his head.

After twilight, Sean took a lantern down to Rose's grave overlooking Imeal. Being a suicide, she could not rest in the so-called sanctified ground of the Church cemetery. Sean laid a cloth on the dirt and opened the Book. He mumbled some runes. Although sprinkled with a few Gaelic and Finnish words, the earthy, guttural language was intelligible only to the few adepts like Sean left in the world. A glow appeared over the mound of the grave. In the middle, a seal appeared. As it swam toward Sean within the glow, it contorted into a captivating young woman with black hair, large dark eyes, and swarthy complexion.

"Ah, darling sister Rose. Where are you now?"

"Sean, it tickles my whiskers. Mum and I are living in the Hebrides, way north. It's not so good to be conjuring me so. Must be a serious thing."

Rose died to the human world, but, with her mother's help, joined a pod of Sami finfolk who had all returned to the sea as seals. She knew the Book and the old ways better than Sean. In fact, her misuse of the Book in a jealous rage caused much of the trouble in Sean's family and led to her self-imposed banishment to the sea through suicide.

"Rose, you gave me the Book and the gifts that come with it. It's a great wonder, but also a burden. I've got a bit of a problem here. For sure, I need your help."

Sean told Rose about Lloyd Phillips, what he had seen at old Tom O'Malley's, and what the Book said needed to be done.

"So, Rose, I need your skills… and your feminine ways, if I may say so."

Sean blushed at what he was asking Rose to do. She noticed his ruddy face and laughed. "Ah, Sean, I love you so. I'd have thought by now the Book would've burned Father O'Connell's shame of the flesh out of you." She sighed and continued, "My spirit's free to move, Sean. I can come to you, but I need a body. To do a loving spell with a man, I need a woman's body, a woman with finfolk in her blood who knows the receiving spells."

"Rose, you know it's only me here."

"Sure. So, you have to do the shape shift."

Sean turned to the relevant page of the Book and read.

"Bloody Wounds of Christ, what a thing you're asking of me. It's unnatural!"

"Dear brother, nothing that can be done is unnatural, and who is it that's doing the asking here, anyway? I'm minding my own business, feasting on cod and mackerel... Oh, and watch the blasphemy, now, or Father O'Connell will give your ear a twist."

They chuckled together at that and spent the better part of an hour discussing what was required.

* * * *

Later that night, Sean, Finn, and Phil sat in a dingy nook of the Squealing Pig, hunched over pints of Guinness. Finn's pipe filled the alcove with conspiratorial haze.

"Phil, I think I can help you, but it'll take me to another place, shall we say, for a couple a days. I took the liberty to tell Finn here about your visitor, hoping you don't mind. He'll stay with you tonight and tomorrow instead of me. The storm'll keep his boat in anyhow. Are we agreed?"

Phil and Finn nodded.

"Phil, I've got some herbs here might give you a little sleep, better than the whiskey can, but they will not stop the visits. Finn, I hope you got the stomach for a scare. Shook me, it did."

"Can't be worse than those men I saw burned up in the oil slick after that damned U-boat blasted their ship."

"Brave of you to rescue the few you could, Finn, but Phil's specter is not a true living thing and powerful grim. Anyway, Phil, I'm trusting in you. On the night after next, Finn won't be with you, but I'll send a healer. You do what she says."

"I'll try."

"Good, then I should be back the day after that. A toast to courage and fortitude! Sláinte Mhaith!"

Finn replied, "Sláinte agad-sa!"

Phil proffered a "Cheers".

All three men downed their pints.

"It's done then," said Sean and banged his glass on the table for emphasis.

* * * *

The next day, after locking his door and windows, Sean sat down on his bed, cracked the seal on a bottle of Kilbeggan Whiskey, poured some in a glass, and took a respectful nip.

"Aye, courage and fortitude. I'm needing them for sure."

Sean gulped down the contents of the tumbler, while the storm outside rattled his windows with driven rain.

He opened the Book and connected to Rose, much as he had at her grave. The seal pod of finfolk were prepared to protect Rose's seal body when her spirit left, and Sean and Rose began to chant the shape shifting.

Within the hour, Sean's features began to morph—a softening of the skin, changes in complexion, in hair and eye color, loss of body hair. These were easy. His body tingled, but didn't hurt.

By dusk, he was losing bulk. The transformation began to be painful, like dozens of little people inside scraping substance from his bones. Some of the fat simply relocated itself by slithering around. Sean's breasts, hips, and buttocks ballooned and rounded.

The true agony began at midnight with the skeletal changes. In effect, many of his bones had to break and reset in multiple places. Sean took frequent swigs of whiskey. His overall dimensions shrank while his pelvis widened.

As sunrise approached, the major alterations were complete, and his bottle of whiskey empty. Sean lay moaning in bed, as the pain receded. But before Rose could enter Sean's body, it had to become feminine in more than overall shape.

"Sean, my dear brother, are you enough recovered yet?"

"Darling sister, I need another swig o'liquid courage, if you don't mind." Sean pulled a second bottle of Kilbeggan from under the bed, sucked down a few fingers worth, and lay back down.

"I tell ya, Rose, now I know what Father O'Connell's hell must be like, and he'd have me in it for sure for what's to happen next."

With that, Rose, recognizing Sean's exhaustion, chanted the rest of the shifting spell alone from her glowing ball of light.

When Sean's genitals sucked inside him and morphed into their female counterparts, he experienced the blend of pain and pleasure that follows strenuous sex, and his bowels twitched as if invaded by a family of hyperactive voles. The feminization of his brain proved subtler. As the nerve connections altered, he had an involuntary orgasm that was so intense he gasped.

"Ah, gone my lovely manhood," he said aloud. It startled him to hear it come out in the soft, enchanting voice of Rose.

When the orgasm faded, Sean became aware of changes in his emotional landscape. It's not that any feeling was present that did not already exist, but the balance shifted. Emotional tinges in the background traded places with what had once been foreground. States of mind came and went in turmoil. For a while, he even experienced a compulsive infatuation with Phil, like an adolescent girl.

"Darling sister, I'm all wrong inside."

"Aye, Sean. It's time."

The glow that held Rose's likeness drifted to the bed and spread over Sean's body like the aura around a saint, then soaked in. The brain kept enough of the masculine and feminine to accommodate both spirits. There was a brief confusion about who was who, until enough nerve pathways were altered for Rose's personality to coexist alongside Sean's. Both selves cohabited the body. Brother and sister knew each other in a way that all their past family tragedy could never have communicated. Rose thought a spell for transference of spirit and took sole control of the body's voluntary muscular system.

Sean's part of the collective mind reeled at the content of his sister's soul. Although no longer able to act or speak out loud, he was able to converse with Rose in their shared mind.

Rose, truly? This is what it's like to be you?

My dear brother, you're quite the revelation yourself.

Rose ran her hands over the borrowed body, lingering over the more pleasurable parts.

My God, Rose, do you mind?

Brother, let it be. I know we're sore from the changing, but it's exciting to have all the human parts again. Haven't you ever wondered what it feels like to be a woman? It's not such a bad thing, is it now?

I just need time, Rose.

But it's time now we become one thing, Sean.

Rose recited a powerful rune. With that, their consciousnesses merged. Although each maintained a separate focus, Rose's female spirit was the active principle, while Sean's masculinity remained in shadow.

With a burst of exuberance, Rose got up and twirled spirals around the room, celebrating her brief revisit to human life. This lasted until the body reminded her of all it had been through. She lingered for a while at the window admiring the stormy sky. Always a heavy drinker herself, she downed another tumbler of Kilbeggan. Then she got back on the bed, pulled up the covers, and slept until the late afternoon of the next day.

* * * *

Naked at the kitchen table, Rose enjoyed a hearty meal, while admiring the drapery of clouds from the played out storm. Rose relished every ordinary human sensation. Because her body was ravenous from the punishment of the shape shift, every mouthful of human food ravished her palate. The Sean inside her was at first embarrassed by the brazenness of her sensuality, but came to embrace it as Rose's raw natural innocence.

After lingering in a sudsy bath, Rose pulled on a plain, light blue, piece-dyed taffeta dress she found among belongings Sean had saved. It was tight in a way that emphasized all the features most appealing to men. She also donned the simple necklace her mother had given her—a carved wooden Celtic symbol for infinity that hung from a leather cord. It had once signified a tragic love, and it graced her bosom with dark, primitive charm.

Except for the rising Moon, it was dark by the time Rose walked along the cliff trail leading to old Tom O'Malley's. She let her spirit beam and the fairies flocked to her. The seal island off the coast erupted in boisterous welcome. It felt good to be back. Rose lingered at the place where she had jumped to her death only a few years ago, the same place where she had fought with her sister over a trinket from the man they both loved, the fight in which her sister stumbled over the edge. Thanks to the ancient magic, all had in the end been forgiven. It now seemed like just another of the beautiful, sad songs that the fairies sang.

When she arrived, Rose knocked gently on Phil's door. She heard footsteps on the other side. Phil spoke, after a long pause, "Who's there? Is it Sean's friend?"

"His sister, Rose."

"Rose? But Sean told me you were dead."

"Well, that was not the whole truth of it then, was it? Open the door and see."

The door opened a crack. Instead of the specter he feared, Phil saw a beautiful young woman. He opened the door wide. Rose's gaggle of fairies were invisible to him. When Rose stepped into Phil's cottage, the fairies tittered and flew away.

"Bringing people back from the dead? I'm having enough trouble with dead people who won't stay dead. What kind of Irish magic is this?"

"A most powerful kind. You have to trust how it is. Sean and me have gone through a wee bit of trouble over this, I might say. Might I call you Phil?"

Rose moved close to Phil and gave him a flirtatious smile. He took an awkward step back, looked down at the floor, and muttered, "Well, can I offer you whiskey or some tea? Please sit at the table."

Sean, is there something about Phil I need to know?

Well, Finn, he wondered if Phil might be, you know, well...

Now you say it?

Well we don't know one way or the other. He's had it rough with the specter and all. Give him time.

"Whiskey, please, for the dead Irish lass."

There was already an opened bottle of single malt Scotch whiskey and a tumbler on the table. Phil retrieved another glass from a press, sat down across from her, and poured her a couple of inches.

"Phil, I'm here to help ease your troubles if I can."

"So I'm told."

They clicked glasses. Rose took a healthy gulp, while Phil sipped.

"Sean told me I should do what you say."

"Don't make it sound like laundry chores, Phil. There'll be some fun in it. "

"Did Sean tell you about my visitor?"

"Aye, but let's not think of her right now. Let's be us."

Phil stared down at his glass. Finally, he looked up and met Rose's eyes. "Sometimes I think you folks are having a bloody joke at my expense."

"Well, dear man, maybe this will help?" Rose muttered a few sentences in the ancient tongue and a glitter like fireworks covered the center of the table. In a few moments, the Book appeared there. "Touch it. Open it. We'll be needing it, and this little trick is easier than carrying."

Although used to his personal ghost, Phil had not witnessed such conjuring before. The effect was like a slap on the face. He picked up the Book, eyes wide, and his hands tingled as he leafed through the pages. After a while, he asked, "What now?"

"Well, if I'm not being too forward, I say we take the Book and the whiskey to your bedroom. We have to become real good friends if I'm to help."

Phil's face took on a helpless expression. "I'm shy with women, though I like them well enough." Blushing, he added, "You see. I went to a boarding school. Boys only. I'm, well, more comfortable with men."

Sean!

Well now, Rose, I didn't know for sure.

Well, we're healers, brother. We'll do what we have to do.

Ah, Rose.

In the bedroom, Rose and Phil started slow, with proximity and talk. It was a while before they undressed. Rose played a dominant, directive role, while Phil remained passive. Rose whispered infatuation spells to help things along, and the alcohol cleared many inhibitions. The climax satisfied all three of them, though Sean had a hard time admitting it to himself. Rose snuggled into Phil's side and stroked his face.

"Phil, you're not the only one carrying the guilt around."

"No, I suppose not… But they burned to death. Thousands."

"Well, I don't know about the thousands, but let me tell my tale."

Rose explained about her sister and the love triangle.

"Sean told me about that."

"But I bet what he didn't tell is what happened to the man we both loved. Paddy."

"No."

"He spurned me, he did, when my sister died. So I cursed him, with the Book there, and Nazi bombers blew him off a ship in Norway with a hundred others. I did that. I really did. So, I jumped off the cliff."

"Oh, Rose. That's horrible."

"It was the penance. Then Mum gave my spirit up to the seals."

"You're really a seal?"

"Somewhere out in the Hebrides."

Phil paused to digest that. "What do you think my penance will be?"

"Let's hope your visitor knows, Phil. When does she usually appear?"

Phil looked at his clock. "In the a.m. hours. It's not quite midnight now."

"Good, we still have time." Rose jumped up and shifted to her hands and knees. "Why don't you take me like I was one of your school boys?"

Jesus, Mary, and Joseph, Rose!

Shush, Sean.

An hour later, Rose got out of bed and slipped on her dress and necklace. "Phil, it's time."

After he dressed, they sat together on the bed. Phil had his arm around her shoulders. Rose opened the Book near the middle and began to recite. The symbols on the pages rippled with color, and the room buzzed, as if the agitation of the molecules in the air and walls became audible. The ocean sounded loud, as if the breakers were at Phil's doorstep.

In what seemed like minutes, another hour past. Then, Rose and Phil sensed the specter approaching the cottage. There was a loud pounding on the door. Rose left the Book open on the bed. As they moved toward the door, arm in arm, Rose continued chanting. They had no candle, but a brightness like noon moved with them.

Sean, it's more powerful strong than anything I can remember!
I told you, Rose.

Rose could not be certain what Phil saw on his threshold, but, to Rose, it was not simply a burnt corpse. At least two personalities shimmered around it, and faces flickered over the blackened skull. Rose felt dizzy. The brightness in the foyer took on texture. It whirled around the specter and Phil and whooshed like a tornado. The woman extended her bundle.

"Phil, take it." Rose had to shout over the noise.

Phil opened the blanket and saw a live, sleeping baby. He looked up at the woman. A face with angular Germanic features solidified around the skull. She was no longer scorched.

"Danke," was all she said.

"Oh, god, I'm sorry. I'm so terribly sorry." Phil secured the baby in one arm and put the other around the woman. The wind howled louder and burst into flames. Sweating, Rose pressed herself against the wall. She could only witness the center of the fiery maelstrom using her preternatural sight.

Be strong, Phil.

When Phil backed away to look into the women's eyes, the face had morphed into his mother's. Weeping, Phil buried his head in her neck.

"Lloyd, you're a good man. Let go of all this. You need to be yourself again."

Phil felt the baby tear open his shirt. Phil backed away from his mother and looked down to see the child plunge into his body. His chest rippled like the surface of a lake as the baby disappeared. Phil screamed and gyrated and dropped to his knees. Rose leapt into the inferno and put her arms around him. Before she realized it, she found herself holding a baby who smiled up at her. Rose shouted out the strongest spell of motherly love she knew.

The wind and flame dissipated. When she opened her eyes again, Rose had her arms wrapped around the adult Phil, who was on his knees and sobbing. The doorway was empty. The only other sound was the booming of the surf.

* * * *

Sean had expected to become himself again the next day, but Rose lingered. She had fallen in love with Phil and, more important, Phil needed her spiritual midwifery to nurture his rebirth. Of course, Rose also enjoyed human life—the sex, the emotions, all the sensations. It was hard to let go.

Finn stopped by to look in on Phil and was noticeably chagrined to find a woman around. He was even more shocked when he finally recognized Rose. Out of reflex, he crossed himself a few times.

A week passed until, finally, Rose stood at Phil's door at sunset, prepared to leave.

"Phil, I don't want to go, but I must return to the sea. My seal body's dying. If it dies, I will too. Aye, the strangeness of it all."

"Rose, I don't know what to say. Your leaving hurts."

"Ah, you're a man again, Phil. You're not needing dead people anymore."

"Rose, you're more alive than anyone I've ever met."

"You'll meet others, for sure. There's one already seems very smitten with you. And, please, as long as you're in Eire, which I hope is a long, long time, listen for the fairies. They'll sing to you at dusk and break of day. I leave you with the gift of hearing them."

Several fairies twittered around her head. A look of enchantment swept across Phil's face.

"Rose, I hear them."

With that, Rose walked down to the trail along the top of the cliff, the Book under her arm. The wind whipped the dress up around her thighs, and she beamed a broad Sami smile over her shoulder.

"Stay away from the priests, OK?"

"No worries. Safe travels, Rose."

On her way back to Sean's cottage, Rose stopped again at the top of the cliff where she had jumped to her death.

I could just jump again, and we'd both be dead for real.

Dear sister, I'd surely rather you didn't.

The spirit being set free is a beautiful thing. When truly dead, we flow around like the air and water.

Thanks, all the same.

Rose stood on the edge enjoying the stiff, salty breeze off the ocean. The red in the clouds turned the color of blood.

Rose, I'm wondering. Have you heard of the big bomb the Yanks dropped on the Japs?

Yes, all Nature knows. There was a terrible chatter about it in the sea.

Well, if ordinary bombs twist the spirit so, like Phil, what about that?

Sean, what I feel in the sea says bad times are coming that will put to shame this little war we just had. As much as I love this body, I belong to the sea now. I'll do what healing I can from there.

Guess I need to do the same, from here.

The last of the Sun slipped under the horizon.

Sean, dear brother, I hope you live yourself a proud life. I do not want to leave you, but it must be so.

Rose, how can I live with all this inside me now.

Sean, the more inside, the more you have to share.

Give my love to Mum, now, won't you?

* * * *

As the Moon made another cycle in its orbit, Sean's life returned to a semblance of normalcy. He noticed that Phil was spending a lot of time with Finn. Truth be told, Sean had fallen in love—with Rose, with being Rose, and, as Rose, with Phil. He still grieved these several losses and had been keeping pretty much to himself, hiking the hillsides and sitting for hours at a time gazing at Donegal Bay.

This particular evening, when Sean walked into the Squealing Pig, he saw Phil and Finn in the back alcove, seated on the same side of the table. As Sean watched them from the bar, they seemed preoccupied with each other, whispering, shoulders touching from time to time. He asked the bartender to bring a round of Guinness for three and ambled over. "Finn and Phil, it is! I ordered us some pints."

Phil looked up smiling, "Sean, please sit. It's me who should be buying the pints."

"No more specters, me man?"

"None." Phil glanced sideways at Finn. "Finn and I have some news. We decided to tighten our budgets and throw in together. Share O'Malley's place."

Finn winked at Sean. Since learning about Finn's preferences, Sean had noticed there were several bachelor households, and spinster households too, sprinkled around the nearby villages. It was always a matter of economy, to be sure.

Sean felt a twinge of jealously, but his smile broadened. "Well now that's reason to celebrate!" When the pints arrived, they clicked their glasses and downed healthy swigs.

Wiping his lips, Phil said, "Say, Sean, Finn says you had a wife once upon a time."

"Still do. When Rose jumped off that cliff, I was besotted all the time. My wife got fed up and moved back to her mum's in Letterkenny. Haven't seen her since, but there's been a letter or two."

"A shame, that is, Sean, I always thought," said Finn.

Sean's innards warmed in a way they hadn't in a while. He could feel Rose smiling inside him. Sean remembered this as the moment in which he resolved to go to Letterkenny and bring his wife home.

Sean's otherworldly vision noticed a fairy chirping near his left ear. Phil was tapping his finger in time with the melody. Sean looked at Phil with deliberately flirtatious mischief and raised his glass.

"To my darling sister Rose! As she always said, the fairies sing to us at dusk and dawn!"

Phil's eyes widened. All he said was, "What?"

Then they all smiled, clinked glasses, and downed the pints.

▲

The Witch of Pender
by John Linwood Grant

Eastern Seabord, USA. 1926

"A long night coming," said the Dark Man. He stood easy on the edge of a field, red earth between his toes as he sucked on a piece of sugarcane.

Mamma Lucy didn't hold much with visions. And as visions went, this wasn't greatly encouraging her. She didn't recognize the place her left eye was seeing. A great field spread across the valley bottom, and that field was sown with fingers, knuckle-end in the deep soil. Most were black fingers, waving without a breeze, though here and there a white one grew. Some had cracked, hard-worked nails, and some had none at all. Near to where she stood, one finger had died where it was planted; a crow was tearing strips of rancid flesh from the small, pale bones.

"How long?"

The Dark Man pushed back his straw hat.

"Long as a mule kicks; long as cane is sweet."

She reached across the floor of the lean-to shack and took up the largest candle, her grip marking the soft wax.

"Don't you game me now, boy," she said, a husky rattle in her throat. "This ain't New Orleans, and I ain't one of your mamaloi, Sant-eria la-dies, liftin' their skirts when you come callin'."

"Maybe I forget, sometimes. Long time since we talked."

She loosened her grip on the candle.

"True enough. Ain't been need to find you, is all. Lord knows, don't rightly 'member askin' for you this time."

"Pender County," he said. "They'll be needing you there, by and by."

She ran memories across the candle flame, through the scorch of hyssop burning in the bowl at her side. The name would come.

"Might've just said that."

"I might." He leaned on the sugarcane, now a bent stick with a silver head. His crumpled suit was brown, red, or maybe neither, and though he was taller than oaks, it fitted him well enough. "But I don't get to speaking with so many folk these days. It's all kerosene, steel and burned rubber at the crossroads. Every soul in a hurry, always in a hurry."

He tipped his red straw hat, and her milk-and-honey eye twitched in its socket.

The vision was gone, and she was where she'd been. Four plank walls and a broken roof. A place for the night, and straw to rest her bones on. She licked finger and thumb to snuff the candle, and then it came to her.

North Carolina. That was the place…

* * * *

Mamma Lucy hadn't meant to go to Pender County. She hadn't meant to go to North Carolina at all, but between a vision she didn't want and an itch up her back, there was trouble on the dry wind. So she huffed and sighed, and turned her path thataway, because it was what she did.

She took what she could—a lift in the back of farm-truck, a short-cut with a traveling man, and finally, the bus from Wilmington to Burgaw.

It wasn't a new bus, or a clean one, but she found a few cents in her old carpet bag. Rows of seats at the front, sparsely dotted with white folk looking elsewhere, and a packed huddle of black faces at the back. She stood by the driver a moment, and smiled.

"Get along down," he said.

The old woman's horse-teeth clacked, but her smile stayed.

"Must be hard on you, lady." She glanced at the woman in the first row, a hard face under a blue bonnet.

"I'm sorry?" The woman scowled.

"Havin' to sit up front here. Dust and clatter from the doors, and all us good people pushin' past you, like you wasn't nothin', on our way to the comfy seats."

Mamma Lucy nodded, polite as Sunday, and made her way down the bus. Those at the back grinned as they shuffled to make room for her.

"Have my seat, ma'am." A young man in dungarees got to his feet.

"No need, young feller. Jest need to stand awhile, let the dogs stop barking."

Several looked down at her big, splay-toed bare feet, and noted the battered silver coins on a string around one ankle. They took in her milk-and-honey left eye, and someone muttered "Conjure-woman".

She slipped into the rumble of the journey. She could doze as easy on her feet as she could on goose-feathers. There'd be a time to be awake.

It came slow and light, like the breath of a man down her back, though she sure hadn't felt that for many a year. She jerked, and looked out of the bus window. Despite the grime, she could see flat woodland and a curl or two of smoke.

"What's yonder?" she asked the young man.

He peered out. "Bluegill Creek. A farm or three, scratching away. Share-croppers, mostly."

"Guess that's where I'm headin'."

She shuffled to the front of the bus.

"No stop hereabouts," said the driver.

"Better if there was one."

It was clear that he had a hard word coming for her, but it stuck in his throat. He turned it into a cough, and braked hard. His petty vengeance was to point at the tattered sign above the door. No refunds.

The land around was tobacco fields, spreading in the July sun. A broad trail led between two fields and towards the trees, so she took it, humming as she went. Carts had been this way, and a truck or so from the gouged earth. There'd be something at the end, sure enough.

One of the smoke curls came from a sprawl of a shack on the edge of the woods. A man maybe as old as Mamma Lucy sat outside, grey curls on mahogany skin.

"Howdy," he said, not looking up from the skillet he was holding over an open fire. She smelled fish, and remembered a hungry belly. A goose honked by the trees; a goat was tied up next to the shack.

"Fine place you got here." She put down her carpet bag and breathed in the smoke from the fire.

"Enough in this pan for two, iffen you hungry."

"Mighty kind."

He dragged a low saw-horse forward, and bid her sit.

"Ethan Brown," he said. A deft twist of the wrist turned the big fish over in the pan. "And this felluh here's fresh-caught."

She glanced at the bluegill, one side already crisp-skinned and ready.

"They call me Mamma Lucy."

He nodded.

"Thought that might be the sortuh name you carried, when I saw you. Witchcraftin's a close game, I'd guess."

"Ain't no witch," she said, though without concern. She'd been called worse. "Mostly get known as a conjure-woman, where it suits."

The old man split the fish, handing her a portion on broad tobacco leaves, fresh from the field.

"No disrespect. That's what they mostly call it round here, 'specially the white folk."

The fish was firm and sweet, the best thing she'd tasted for days. She gave him a flash of her big horse-teeth.

"You crop these parts, Mister Brown?"

"Ethan. This here's mine, such as it is. Long as I keep to the edge, the big felluhs leave me alone. Do some tobaccuh, beans, goose or two, and the creek is lively with these boys."

"Ain't you I'm feelin' on the air, then. I heared tell there was a need, hereabouts."

He licked his fingers.

"Only trouble round here…" He paused and took in the sight of her, a tall, scrawny woman in a faded print dress, a broad nose over lips that barely covered those teeth. Something must have satisfied him. "Mebbe the Coopersons, down by Bluegill Creek. But you mayn't be welcome."

"Used to that." She stood up. "Thank you kindly for that feed. I'd best go see what ails these Cooperson folk."

Maple and birch swayed above her as she followed the trail. The dimes jangled on her ankle, but stayed bright. A mile or so along, past a stand of swamp bay, she saw it. Five stones on the road, laid between ruts. Others would have seen nothing; Mamma Lucy knew a five-spot. Conjure work.

She knelt down and dug under one of the four corner stones. It came up easy—a flannel wrap of black dust and roots. Whatever was fixed there, it hadn't been done well or proper. The powder tasted sour, milk in a thunderstorm.

"Half a trick, too much guessin'," she muttered.

She went on with more interest. Bluegill Creek was a deep flush of water, but easily forded where the trail crossed it. And there was the place she'd been looking for—a low timber house in a clearing. A family place, with chickens and a rough barn; a battered truck was rottening by the barn, rust on the grille.

There was welcome and there was welcome. Mamma Lucy spat and smoothed her frizzed grey hair. She reached into her carpet bag and took out a battered flask. A swill of whiskey for her throat, and then a few drops to feed the green felt mojo bag in her dress pocket. That would do.

"Mornin' to all good folk," she said, loud, and walked towards the farmhouse.

A woman came to the open door, flour on her hands. Thin-faced, white as the flour.

"Wonderin' if you had any work, ma'am. Passin' through, but I'm fair handy, in or out."

Hesitation.

"Bake a mean pie, as well," she added.

A weak sound came from inside, and the woman nodded.

"You'd best come in. What's your name?"

"Mammy Lucy does me fine, ma'am."

"Esme Cooperson. Mrs Cooperson to you. Where you heading?"

"Travellin' to see some kin, yonder past Burgaw."

"Two days work, maybe three, if you do it fine and keep your place."

Mamma Lucy gave the sort of nod and shuffle that an old black woman in need of work and board might offer a white lady.

The door opened onto a big room with a table fit for eight or nine, a cast-iron range and a sink. The far wall was propped up by a stone chimney, but it was the cot in the corner that caught her eye.

"That there's Suzie." Mrs Cooperson didn't look that way.

Sixteen or seventeen, the girl was sprawled out, humming without sense, her long blonde hair lank and tangled.

"She sickenen', Mrs Cooperson?"

"Ever since her belly started filling." The woman didn't seem inclined to go further on that score. "You sleep in the barn, get a portion of supper, and all the milk you can wring from the cow out back. Got my hands full. No slack round here, so you earn that, you hear me?"

"Yes, ma'am."

There was work. Mamma Lucy fed the hens, cleared a row of early beans in the plot round back, and washed shirts and sheets in a shed. The firebox under the copper took some starting. There were menfolk somewhere, from the size and number of the patched cotton shirts. She was allowed inside the house, but not near the girl. Her neck hairs rose within a few paces of the cot. If there was need here, it had to do with the youngster, she was sure.

The wringer was stiff, and the load heavy, but she was a strong woman. She turned and hauled, singing to herself.

"Got on the train,
Didn't have no fare,
But I rode some,
I rode some…"

The shed door creaked, breaking her song, and a shadow covered the copper. She turned, seeing a plain-faced man with corn-coloured hair.

"What in hell you doing?" he said.

Mamma Lucy let her horse-teeth show proud.

"Keepin' busy, sir, keepin' busy. Lady of the house said she could do with a strong arm to this here wringer."

"Did she?" His expression was closed. "We'll see."

She watched him stalk off. No worse than many men she'd met, white or black. Back to the wringer.

It was supper-time when she got to measure the Coopersons. Jed Cooperson, the big man at the wash-house door, made it clear she would serve the meal and clear up afterwards if she wanted her board.

"Esme could do to set awhile," he said, and in that she saw a touch of tenderness. Seemed to her that the four menfolk could have helped, but she wasn't here for argument.

Jed was the master. His younger brother Daniel, leaner and close-mouthed, had the other end of the table, flanked by Jed's sons, Abe and Jim. Neither were above fifteen. Mamma Lucy laid out creamed corn, potatoes and fatty ham, settling herself back against the hearth when she'd done.

They talked of tobacco and crops, grudges and the price of seed. Ethan Brown wasn't a bad neighbour 'for a coloured'; someone called Nielsen was planning to take a portion of their land away next year. And brother Daniel only came for his meals and washing—he had a shack of his own near the fields.

She watched Esme Cooperson feed creamed corn to her daughter, a spoon at a time. Suzie took it, swallowing in big gulps like a catfish. The girl's pale grey eyes had no focus, but the conjure-woman felt that this wasn't how she'd come out. This had been done to her, one way or another.

When the men stepped out for a smoke on the porch, Mrs Cooperson gave a weak smile.

"Help yourself to what's on the range. There's eggs in the barn, too."

Mamma Lucy stroked the mojo bag in her dress-pocket. She pitched her voice low, soothing.

"Seen my share o' sickness, Mrs Cooperson. Sure there ain't nothin' I can do for your girl?"

A sort of story came out, with the men gone. Suzie had started 'show-ing', and a few days later her wits had gone, it seemed to her mother. Less than two weeks back. They'd had a doctor out from town, not want-ing others to know, but he'd been no use.

"Said she was weak-minded." Mrs Cooperson gritted her teeth. "My Suzie was never weak-minded. Had her schooling."

"But she ain't talkin' about no daddy?"

Almost a push too far.

"The boys think it's a coloured." She glanced at the conjure-woman. "Lige Nixon's son, Willie. Nixon's the seed-merchant, set up in Burgaw. Elder Clark at the church doesn't credit it, but Jed and Daniel are close to taking the boy, beating it out of him. Or worse…"

"They got reason?"

The woman shook her head.

"Won't be much doubt when it comes," Mamma Lucy said.

Mrs Cooperson blinked, as if puzzled at saying so much. "Best you see to those dishes soon."

The matter was closed.

In the barn, Mamma Lucy had hens and her thoughts to keep her busy. She wasn't rightly sure if she was here for Suzie Cooperson alone, or for Willie Nixon as well.

She settled down, said a psalm, and let the soft cluck of the hens soothe her to sleep.

* * * *

Two or three days became four or five. The cow gave more milk when she went to it, easing the cracked teats; the chickens laid eggs like it was a race. The men were out on the fields for long days, and when they came back they talked more openly when she was around.

Only Daniel Cooperson kept himself close. She watched his thin face, and saw worse there than his older brother's blunt tongue. He was calling for something to be done about Lige Nixon's boy, close to saying his niece had been raped, and she knew the tone. Lynch-mobs started that way. There would be men in Burgaw who'd listen to that talk after a drink or two.

Mamma Lucy found a certain herb from her old bag, and let it steep in Esme Cooperson's coffee the next day. By the afternoon, the woman was yawning, hardly fit to stand.

"You go rest up, Mrs Cooperson. I'll shell peas, and keep an eye on things."

Little persuasion was needed. The sun stood halfway between noon and dusk, plenty of time for Mamma Lucy with Suzie before the others got back from the fields.

"Ain't rightly sure what's in there, girl," she said as she eased away a soiled sheet. The nightdress was stained with urine. Her mother changed her, but not often enough. The men treated her like an embarrassment, and chose not to see her—except Daniel. Mamma Lucy had seen him give a strange glance that way when his kin weren't looking.

There was certainly a curve to the girl's belly. An egg did for a cleansing, with a psalm, but as she rubbed the egg against Suzie's skin, Mamma Lucy saw the yolk inside growing dark and tainted, sure as if the shell had been crystal. It wasn't enough.

"Talk to me, Suzie. Tell Mamma Lucy what's ailin'."

The girl moaned, her eyes focussing on the broad, black face.

"Can't tell… mustn't tell."

"Willie Nixon said that? Or some other?"

The moment had passed. Mamma Lucy wrapped the girl in fresh linen, and took herself back up the trail, striding over the dust of a clear, hot day.

Ethan Brown was hoeing a patch by the trees.

"Got your feet under, then?" he said, smiling. "Must say I'm surprised."

"Folk take to me," said the conjure-woman. "Or they don't."

"Imagine so. You come to jaw, or passin' by?"

"Come to jaw."

They sat in a swing-seat at the back of Ethan's shack, and shared a plug of tobacco. Occasionally he spat at the goat.

"You lay a five-spot on that track yonder, Ethan Brown?" The conjure-woman spread her toes, watching ants trickle by.

The old man laughed. "Heared o' them. Wouldn't know how."

"And you don't know no 'witch' hereabouts?"

"Do now."

She laughed back, hoarse and strong.

"Tell me 'bout Lige Nixon."

He shrugged. "Tight-fisted felluh, but no real harm in him. Don't trust the weight o' seed he offers, and don't expect charity. But he don't beat his wife or gamble."

"And the boy?"

"Willie? Fell far enough from the tree, that one. Smart and kindly. I told him, 'Willie, you a clever boy. Go North, leave us tar-heels behind. Don't end up in tobaccuh, scratching the dirt.' "

Mamma Lucy put her hand in her dress-pocket and stroked her mojo bag, thinking.

"Coopersons think he may have laid up their Suzie."

Ethan spat harder, bringing a bleat from the goat.

"In Pender County?" He chuckled. "This ain't Nuh York. Never touched hand nor lip, Willie and Suzy."

"Someone got in there, stirred the pot."

He shrugged. "A jar of hard cider and a big moon. Places dotted all over round Bluegill Creek. I couldn't guess which boy you'd look for."

"Time to stop guessin', then."

She hurried back to the farm. Her rootwork would keep Esme Cooperson settled for a couple of hours, but no use taking risks.

Daniel Cooperson was in the house when she got there.

"Fetchin' eggs, Mr Daniel," she said, pulling a couple out of her dress. She liked to be prepared.

Thick brows knotted over dark eyes.

"Where's Esme?"

"Restin'. Takes a lot from a soul, keepin' house an' seein' your child like that."

She glanced at the girl, asleep again in the cot. He stepped between them, close to his niece.

"White don't go with black." His right hand stroked Suzie's brow. "Lessen black makes it happen."

She could tell him was wrong, but he wouldn't listen. She could tell him that he was a fool, but then she'd be sent packing, and the long night would come. Had that been Willie Nixon's finger rotting in the field she'd seen, back when the Dark Man came bothering her?

Cooperson's eyes had crow about them, dark and beady. Or Jim Crow, staring back, waiting for an excuse to get the mob moving...

The conjure-woman looked away. "Should I fix you coffee, Mr Daniel?"

"Came back to change my shirt," he said, and was gone, leaving what she knew was a lie on the air.

Esme Cooperson was fast asleep in the small room she shared with her husband. There was one more bedroom, for the boys, which would have normally held Suzie as well. Mamma Lucy flat-footed through the house, seeing no hexes or tricks—not out in the open at least. That left Daniel and his shack. It came on her that she would dearly like to see what lay there.

She laid one big hand on Suzie's belly. It didn't feel right. Suzie Cooperson was sick, and near mute with something. If she had longer alone with the girl, she might know. Witchcraft, they called it in Pender County, but Mamma Lucy knew the difference. Good conjure-work, true hoodoo, was mostly a slow thing, needing respect and thought. Time to gather what you needed, time to lay a trick proper and keep it strong.

In the morning, the men-folk took the truck to town for supplies. She feared what gossip they might spread, and what might come. It felt like haste was prodding at her.

When she seen them nurse the ancient vehicle well along the trail, Mamma Lucy asked for leave to 'go see Ethan Brown', get news of kin who'd never been. Mrs Cooperson, though puzzled by sleeping through the previous afternoon, saw everything in order, her daughter clean and changed. Leave was freely given.

The track to Daniel Cooperson's shack ran close to the creek, stiff-leaved swamp bay on either side of it. The Cooperson's tobacco fields, along with some corn, were a half mile beyond that. Ethan Brown told her that the trees around there had been dynamited and the stumps pulled years ago.

"Before the war in Europe, that was," he said. "My pappy saw it. Thin soil now, but it grows good bright leaf, and that's the thing these days."

Cooperson's place was rough cut lumber and a tin pipe for a chimney. As she came close, she felt a pang for the days when she'd seen nothing but hills and pines, smelled the resin and been young. She turned to look at the woods, and knew she'd be better off there, in dappled shade. She'd head there, and forget the shack...

Mamma Lucy had a green felt mojo bag. She'd made it first in Georgia, long ago, and fed it good whiskey for so many years that it knew her better than the Good Lord Himself. It was the sort of green you might say was blue as well, and it served her for good intentions and a fair parcel of luck in most all of her dealings. It was likely it served her in that moment.

She'd fixed the silver dimes above her knee, to avoid the Coopersons noticing. Sweat or strain had loosened the string, and when they fell to her ankle, she heard the clink. She looked down. One of the dimes was smut-black.

"'The ungodly, they is like the chaff that the wind driveth away,'" she recited, and stepped back, the woods no longer calling.

There it was in the dusty earth, almost covered. A line, hot-foot powder around the shack. She scooped up powder with a stick, and placed it in a thumb-sized bottle from her bag. That cleared the way to Cooperson's door as well.

The rusted padlock gave to a hair-pin. She left the dimes where they hung, though they didn't change colour this time.

"Half a witch, and a mean one," she said to herself, for there was no doubting the beady-eyed man in that moment. His bunk was strewn with pamphlets and powders bought cheap, the sort you saw at fairs. A shelf of roots told her by eye that he didn't know his ingredients—some were labelled wrong, others were dried bad and showing mold.

On the wall was a torn photograph of Suzie.

The conjure-woman had seen enough. What had been done, she didn't know. Who had done it, that was plain.

Mamma Lucy could move, when she had a need to. She took up anything that still held power and wrapped it all in a frayed blanket. That would go into Bluegill Creek as she passed, with a prayer behind it. She would need to see to the girl, before more ill came. And to make a call along the way.

* * * *

The hens told here that something bad had been at the farm. The dirt was churned with tyre marks, and the laying birds came to her, not for food but reassurance.

"Hush there," she murmured. "Soon be done."

Esme Cooperson stood by her daughter, hair mussed and red-eyed.

"They've gone after Willie Nixon," said the woman. "They came back, yelling and cussing, then fetched a rope down from the barn."

"Weren't Willie Nixon, nor any other black boy." Mamma Lucy said that clear, final.

Mrs Cooperson gave her a woman's look, as if for a moment they were equal.

"I… I feared it wasn't."

"Who went out?"

"Jed and Daniel. They sent my boys to the fields, said there was man's work to do. I think… I think they were going to get a few more from town."

Mamma Lucy checked the girl. Suzie was pale and sweating, hands over her belly like she was trying to push something down.

"Did you know that it was kin, interferin' with your girl?"

"You mean…"

"Daniel, yes. Don't reckon that husband of yours saw it, but you?"

"They're close, Jed and Daniel. I… I worried, wondered. Suzie was kind of odd with him, smiles one day, shivers the next, and he'd never settled on a woman hereabouts…"

"Seems he did."

"Oh God." The woman was weeping, and her hands shook like a dry drunk. She sat down at the table, gripping it. It seemed to the conjure-woman that Esme Cooperson had been carrying a truth that she couldn't face or fathom for some time.

"You… you're sure?" The woman made a last stab, maybe hoping there could be doubt.

"On the Good Book. You want your girl well, and this trouble over? There'll be blood in Pender iffen you ain't with me. Shoes."

The woman stared at her. Mamma Lucy sighed.

"I need Jed and Daniel's shoes."

"Why?"

"So as I can be helpin' you out o' this."

Unsteady, Esme fetched out two pairs of worn boots. Mamma Lucy opened up her carpet bag and pulled out what she needed. She tipped a yellowish powder into both boots, and with a broken pencil she scratched out names on scraps of paper. She put them in the boots as well. When white folk had needs, it was always a rush.

"How long they been gone?"

"Less than twenty minutes. The truck's playing up - won't be half-way to town yet."

"Good." She unwrapped two used blacksmith's nails, borrowed from a horse out Fayette County way. "Needs be short and sharp."

"Jed…"

"Brings 'em back, not too comfy," she reassured the woman. "Ain't no real harm."

Not unless she fixed the trick and kept it playing, but she didn't say that. She used a claw-hammer to drive a nail into each left boot.

"Down to waitin'. They won't be reachin' Lige Nixon's boy, that's for sure. Help me move this cot. Had a thought."

They dragged the cot to one side, by the hearth. The claw-hammer brought up the boards beneath easy. It wasn't the first time someone had been there.

Another five-spot had been laid in the plain earth under the house. This one was set out right. Maybe the one on the trail had been a practice.

She could feel the ill-will buried there. Graveyard dust, sulfur, roots and scraps. A half-witch's attempt to do harm. Cooperson was no trained hoodoo-man.

"You seen it?" Mamma Lucy fixed the woman with her straight eye. "Yes."

"He's closed your girl's mouth, so as she cain't name him, and I reckon he's aimin' to empty her belly afore his get comes out. Then the blame's on Willie Nixon, and no one the wiser."

Mamma Lucy took the woman's hands in hers.

"It's a hard thing, to blame kin. And you weren't knowin' enough to be sure. We're strong for Suzie, you feelin' me?"

Esme Cooperson nodded, wiped her face on her apron.

"How… how do you know this, Mamma Lucy? Are you a—"

"Ain't no witch, not like you thinkin'." She tolled the words off-she'd said them enough. "Ain't no voodoo lady, neither. The Good Lord's in my prayers, same as yours."

Trembling, Esme washed her girl's face, made her comfy. They heard the truck growl and shudder home a half hour later. The door slammed open, rattling plates, and Jed Cooperson was there, a red sweat on his face. He was limping, as was his brother behind him.

"What you women staring at?" he snapped. "Truck's near rottened out, and we're sick. Came on up the road, sudden."

"Something in the food," said his brother, scowling at the conjure-woman.

"Least o' your worries, boy." said Mamma Lucy.

She doubted a black woman had ever spoken to them so, from the look on their damp faces. Gangling in her worn print dress, she was near as tall as either of the men, and her tone wasn't deference.

"Seems you need a lesson on talking to your betters, old or not," said Daniel, and he reached for the hickory stick by the door.

"Best hear the lady out, I'd say."

Ethan Brown was behind them in the yard, a shotgun on his arm.

Jed looked shocked.

"Ethan, you and me got no quarrel."

"Nope. We ain't. That brother o' yours, though…"

Mamma Lucy expected to face the Cooperson men down, but it was Esme who spoke up, a meat-knife in her hand. She looked at her husband.

"Tried to tell you, Jed, that Daniel was over-fond of our girl. You wouldn't listen."

"But…"

Mamma Lucy took a piece of paper from her dress, and handed it to Jed. It was the photograph of Suzie from the shack.

"Turn it over."

He looked at the back.

"Recognise the writing?" She knew it easy, from the family Bible that she'd riffled through one morning.

It was in Daniel Cooperson's broad, poor hand. One word: MINE.

Her milk-and-honey eye fixed on Jed, and the man's expression must have been plain to his brother.

"Jed, I swear—" Then he saw the lifted boards, and stumbled back.

"Could use a borrow of that gun, Ethan Brown," said Jed, low.

"I don't rightly know if—"

"Neighbour."

Ethan handed him the shotgun.

"You need to get out of this house, Dan." Cooperson swung the muzzle lazily, pointing at his brother. "I'll show you the way, and tomorrow we'll talk. We'll talk real long."

When they'd left, Ethan turned to the conjure-woman.

"What now?"

She looked at the knife held white-knuckled in Esme Cooperson's hand, the almost blank face of the daughter. "Cain't see it ending well for all. I got me a handful o' healin' to do round here."

There was no need to face Daniel Cooperson with the five-spot he'd made. Ethan made coffee on the range, talking goats to the silent mother—after he'd slid the knife from her hands. Mamma Lucy got down and bruised her knees, moving boards and scraping out what was down there.

"Cain't reach the roof with half a ladder," she muttered to herself. The fool man had tried to lay a trick for emptying the girl's belly, but he'd brought a sickening into her instead. And that got her to thinking deeper than before. They'd all made one assumption, even her...

Jed came back inside, and sat with his wife, holding her hand. They took coffee from Ethan, but didn't drink.

"How long your girl been sleepin' here?"

Esme looked up. "Since her belly hurt, two weeks back. She said she hadn't bled, neither. The boys played up at her moaning, so we moved her here."

"Couple of days later, she stopped talking." Her husband swore. "What did that bastard do?"

"That's when he laid the trick—the jinx. Handy for him. Slipped in some time you two were out, had his powders ready."

Mamma Lucy fingered the dust from under the centre stone.

"Your Suzie ever missed a month before?"

"Once or twice, I recall." Esme Cooperson leaned forward. "But—"

"Hush a while."

The conjure-woman went to the girl, slid her hand under the sheets. She felt the gently curved belly. It was tender, and the skin was too warm, slick with sweat.

"Ain't no child comin'," she said at last.

The three looked at her, confused.

"Oh, that brother of yours sowed his seed, but it didn't take. He thought it had. Suzie here been jinxed, to fix what didn't need fixin'. And to shut her mouth, iffen threats and promises didn't carry him past this."

"Her belly—" Esme started.

Mamma Lucy shook her head. "Man messes with conjure-work like that, anythin' can come—might ha' killed your girl."

Jed Cooperson seemed torn between anger and relief.

"No child."

"And no sniff of Lige Nixon's fine boy, neither," Mamma Lucy pointed out.

"Doesn't change what Daniel did." His wife's eyes were on the knife again. "Can you put it right? We'll pay."

"Whiskey does for me," said the conjure-woman. "If there's any payin', that man will do it. I reckon I can bring her back."

Ethan blew out his cheeks.

"How so?"

"My business, Ethan Brown. But most every jinx can be turned. Got me everythin' in this here mess of a five-spot."

"And... Dan?"

For a wonder, Mamma Lucy managed to fix the husband with both eyes at once.

"He'll sicken. He'll sicken as bad as he crossed your girl, prob'ly far worse."

"Good," said Esme Cooperson, and with such venom that her husband kept his own counsel.

They were out of words for her. She watched them walk from the house, Ethan off to his own place, the Coopersons down to Bluegill Creek. They had healing of their own to think on.

Mamma Lucy drew a half-white candle and a rusty nail from her carpet bag. She lit a fire, gathering up the roots, cloth and powders from the five-spot as the fire took. With the five-spot broken, Suzie already seemed more calm, less pale.

"Cain't say I like Pender County." Two names grew as she scratched at the candle—a man's on the black half, a girl's on the white. She held up the sheet with the remains of the failed jinx in it, and flung it on to the flames. "But it'll be no worse for me havin' called, that's for sure."

* * * *

In a small shack by the tobacco fields, Daniel Cooperson felt the first pains start in his belly…

▲

The Nora Witch
by Brandon Jimison

"Are you saved by God?" The preacher asked.

Kairo shifted in his saddle and set his face towards the bronze horizon. The spirit voices whispered incoherently in his ear.

"Your God or mine?" Kairo answered.

"There is only one God, and we are all His children," The preacher continued.

Kairo gently goaded his horse around a tumbleweed bramble.

"What of the damned, and the dead, the cursed..." Kairo said.

The preacher flashed the beaming grin that Kairo had almost grown accustomed to by this point. He had never met a man, in life or death, more comfortable with a smile then the preacher; Daniel Stane. He hadn't even questioned Kairo's unusual visage; that of an ancient mummy hidden under a wide brimmed Union cavalry hat, dirt and dusty cowboy garb. It was hard to tell where the bandages ended and his skin began or which was which.

"Such are we all my friend, but for the grace of God," Daniel said, "You strike me as a spiritual man, though I may have qualms with your... profession. You may yet be persuaded."

Daniel's horse Pharaoh, sensing the conversation was at an end, veered away several feet to chase a wayward fly, and saved Kairo from any more talk of religion.

Kairo knew when he accepted the job to accompany the preacher on his journey, to deliver money to a congregation in need, the preacher could be talkative and the subject of religion would come up. However, he happened to be headed in the same direction as Daniel for a particular bounty, and was promised a good fee. He also couldn't imagine any real trouble waiting for them, besides the dumb horse Daniel had obtained from a one-eyed Mexican on the trail to El Paso. Could run into Indians, but that was always a possibility in this land. Like the desert bandits of Kairo's home.

The path up ahead grew rocky. Large stones jutted up from the ground as ancient monuments to forgotten desert gods. A gigantic tall cliff loomed like a table for giants. The harsh land was like Kairo's home and unlike it in the same way. He longed for home as he longed for life. He also longed for death on certain nights when the chattering of the spirits, which often accompanied him, would not cease. He was a shambling paradox.

"Do you think we should stop for the night Mr. Kairo?" Daniel asked.

"Alongside of the table cliff," Kairo answered, "It will make good cover."

The sun had dipped beyond sight when Kairo and the preacher arrived at the base of the cliff. The land made a sharp dive on the far side of the cliff into a rock strewn valley that stretched out for miles, a drop too steep for horses. They would need to find their way around it in the light of the morning.

Daniel hopped off his horse and stretched his legs. Life in the saddle was not like life behind the pulpit. He didn't even think to tie up his horse before he rolled out a sleeping blanket and opened his tattered Bible to read by the waning light.

Kairo tied up Pharaoh and Daniel's misbegotten horse before spreading his own blanket out. He had little thought of sleeping since he didn't need any, but it helped ease the living if he acted the part. Having slept for a few thousand years, he didn't mind being awake for every minute of each day.

As the sunlight gave way to moonbeams and the preacher tucked in for the night, Kairo looked to the stars. It was some comfort to know that the stars were always there, no matter your location, they looked the same. Though he counted them as friends, they had failed to help him find his love, his Amunet. The spirits were hardly dependable as well in that matter. They would be reunited in this life or the next, of that Kairo was certain.

"Goodnight Mr. Kairo," Daniel said.

Kairo felt no need to reply. He rolled out his pack and made as if to sleep for the night. As he lay down and gazed out over the wide valley below, a faint glow of light caught his ancient eye.

At first he thought it was the glint of a moon beam off metal, but the glow was too soft and consistent. The light started out alone, slowly others joined it. Three lights in total, all the same faint glow and all the same eerie green hue.

Kairo's curiosity was stubborn. He checked to make sure that Daniel was asleep, and sneaked away from camp to the edge of the valley. It would be a hard climb down as rough as the rocks were.

"Like I've got anything else to do tonight anyway," Kairo muttered.

The spirit voices had nothing to add at the moment. That meant that something dangerous or exiting was going to happen. Either way would be better than feigning sleep for the preacher or battling thoughts of life, love and death.

The distance to the first light was deceiving, the terrain didn't help matters. While scrambling over a particularly tricky rock formation, Kairo managed to snag a stray bandage wrapping on a tiny cactus bloom and nearly fell twice. He would not be delayed at this point.

As Kairo came within shooting distance of the first light, details of wait lay in the valley took form in the darkness beyond. The ground leveled out, and his right hand rested warily on the handle of his pistol. He knew it was loaded and that if he ran out of bullets, the machete strapped to his left side would be anxious to cleave again.

Kairo didn't bring death eagerly or with malice, he brought it when called forth. A man who had walked with death as much as he, could bring it forth pretty quick. Though his profession taught him the value of restraint, his bounty was always worth more alive than dead.

The spirit voices resumed their chattering and Kairo thought he heard a warning to turn around. When he did, he found Daniel scrambling over a tricky outcropping of rocks like a rat on ice, the saddlebag with the money in it slung across his shoulder. Sometimes it paid to listen to the spirits.

Kairo waited for the preacher to catch up and placed a finger up to his mouth to signal silence.

"Sorry Mr. Kairo," The preacher whispered, "Woke up and saw you sneaking off and curiosity won out."

"Keep quiet. Keep close. I'm not sure what we're dealing with yet," Kairo said, "Did you have to bring that bag with you?"

"The church entrusted me with it. It goes into Hell if need be," Daniel solemnly answered.

Daniel stared out into the distance towards the light.

"That's a child out there," He said.

Kairo took another look, and didn't like that Daniel may be correct. Why would a child be standing there with that odd light, whatever it was?

As Kairo and Daniel crept closer to the first light, and the valley setting emerged from the night, things grew clear. It was a child, a girl, that stood before them, but she didn't hold a light as they first suspected. She was the light.

The girl in a tattered dress and boots stood and slightly swayed in front of Kairo, her eyes blank, the green light danced atop her head as if she were some sort of human candle. She couldn't have been more than ten or eleven years old.

"Gives me the shakes looking at her," Daniel said, "At them."

Nearly a dozen children in all were stationed around the valley before Kairo and Daniel. Some merely appeared as farther lights, but there was little doubt they would match the others. The children were of various ages, most around the same age as the first. Not a boy in sight.

The surroundings consisted of a lone slanted house, a chicken coop and a well. A faint light glowed inside the house, and the smell of a dingy brew drifted through the air.

Kairo had thoughts of leaving silently the way he came, but knew the preacher could no more leave these helpless children then he could turn away a soul in need of salvation. The spirit voices wailed and moaned in this place. No place for children. He had no children of his own, but had tended to the children of the Pharaoh during his service in the guard in his previous life. A raven haired daughter would have been good. No doubt she would favor her mother.

"This is the work of Satan. We must save them," Daniel declared.

The sound of the preacher's voice brought Kairo's attention back to the present. A different voice caused his hand to draw his gun.

"Don't be giving the Devil credit that belongs to me, stranger. I take pride in my work."

The voice came from the front porch of the house, which was draped in shadow. A woman's voice that dripped malice and sweet sticky syrup. The kind of woman that would cheat on you and expect you to pour her a beer, which you would eagerly do, and wait all night for a kiss in return.

Kairo had a bead on the shadows. He could see into darkness better than most due to his condition and could make out a silhouette sitting in a chair on the porch. The chair creaked and the silhouette rose and floated out from the porch shadow into the moonlight like a specter. An owl coasted into view and landed on the right shoulder of the woman dressed in black. The bird let out a single hoot as if to herald his nighttime companion.

The woman was pretty to be sure, but showed a struggle with age that had been hard won. Her hair was long and silver like bramble during a hard frost. A patch covered her right eye which seemed to let her good eye shine the more brightly. She wore a wicked smile.

Two flat throwing knives flew past Kairo's shoulder and into a post of the porch in front of the woman in black, landing with a definite THUNK THUNK, causing small fissures in the wood.

Kairo turned to see Daniel with another throwing knife already between his thumb and fore finger ready for flight.

"That was a warning. I intend to take these children away from here," Daniel announced.

"That's a good throw for a preacher," Kairo said, "But let's think about this some."

The woman in black laughed.

"A preacher man and a cowboy who reeks death," She said, "What has the night delivered to me this time?"

"I know you," Kairo said, "Seen your face on the wall. A witch is what they called you."

"A bounty hunter?" She said, "Glad to find that Nora witch is still wanted somewhere. How much am I worth?"

"I don't recall the name," Kairo said, "But even I know names are too powerful to give up freely, especially by a witch."

"You're not worth the ground to bury you in," Daniel said, "May the Lord send you back to the devil's pit that birthed you."

"My phantom eye sees that you are nothing but a two-bit carny with a born again pantomime. If only you believed in your lord as much as you do in your own worthlessness. A pitiful mess. You bring bitter tears and salvation in cash."

Daniel looked as if he had just taken a punch to the gut. He quickly clenched his jaw and steeled his resolve. He reached for the young child closest to him. His hand alight in the strange green hue the girl shone.

"I will devour your soul if you disturb my coven, Preacher," The witch shrieked.

An unseen force pushed Daniel backwards and hurled him across the ground.

Kairo had seen enough. The witch would still be worth plenty dead. He fired three shots at her— BLAM BLAM BLAM.

She stepped down from the porch and threw her head back with a wicked cackle that could only be a laugh. No bullet had pierced her body.

The voices of the dead screamed at him to run, but he had always been more stubborn than would do any good. Something else whispered to him amidst the spirits, something sweet and light that gently pulled at him; the call of death. His hand gripped the scarab charm which hung from the leather necklace around his neck, and which gave him the semblance of life. He was no more truly alive than he was truly dead. This whisper offered him a release, a return to that which he had come from, a return to a home. This new land, far from Egyptian sands, was not home. He belonged in the afterlife of his fathers…the afterlife of his lovely Amunet.

Daniel slowly pushed himself up and recovered the bag of money. He saw Kairo in the thrall of the witch, and drew two more throwing knives from his vest. He prayed for God to guide the aim of his next blade.

Kairo felt the hand of the witch stroke his cheek, but his attention was tugged elsewhere. The tendrils of death wrapped all around him. He heard Amunet call out to him, but he couldn't discern if it was from this world or the next. The soothing whisper in his ear told him that it didn't matter, just let go, give in, and all would be made right again. He almost believed it, but he had caught traces of Amunet in this new land, she was out there, waiting for him, calling to him, he knew it to be true and it was what drove him in un-life. Death would have to wait yet again.

"Amunet," Kairo said, and the seductive whispers of death ceased.

The witch's hand gripped Kairo's throat. He grabbed the handle of his machete and frantically undid the loop that held the blade in the scabbard. The witch was unnaturally strong. She would not budge though he pushed against her with all his might.

Daniel threw one of his knives at the witch and it landed directly in her good eye. She howled with pain and dropped Kairo.

Kairo drew his machete from the scabbard. The witch's owl screeched and flew at him, deadly talons first. He slashed at the bird and sliced a wing. The owl spun away into the night and out of sight.

The witch ripped the knife from the blackened pool of her eye and flung it away like it was a bothersome nuisance, nothing more.

"You will pay for that, Preacher," She spat out, "We will make them all pay, won't we my pretties?"

She slowly raised the patch from her other eye, her phantom eye, and pointed at Daniel.

The children's eldritch green light grew strong, brighter, like roaring fire.

The lips of the witch murmured a forgotten tongue that resembled a babbling brook.

Kairo lunged towards the witch, blade raised, ready to halt whatever foul magic she might call forth.

The ground shook and shifted under Kairo's feet, and he had to stop and kneel so as to not fall. Splits and fissures cracked all around as the earth birthed a gigantic hellish centipede. The insect was at least three feet thick, and long as a train with a head black as coal, and a body bright orange. Its front two legs were larger than the multitude of others and ended in sharp points that punctured the ground with deadly force.

"See what great things my coven summons? Soon, death itself will be my slave. I will be able to raise the dead. Your wonders will be mine, bounty hunter," The witch cried out.

The centipede wrapped a section of its long body around Daniel, and let out a hideous chittering noise which the skies returned in a distant thunder. Daniel didn't dare attempt to struggle his way out from the creature's grasp, and risk losing grip on the money bag, which he held with all his might.

Kairo hesitated for a second between fighting the centipede or the witch. There was a bounty to consider, but in the end, he decided to attempt to free Daniel. Seemed that the preacher man had grown on him.

He flipped the point of his machete around so that the blade ran along the outside of his forearm, and he ran along the undulating side of the centipede. The blade followed the same course as Kairo, splitting the creature open the length Kairo had been able to run, at least twenty feet. Guts and fluid burst from the cavity, the centipede let out a terrible noise, but it was not finished.

The giant insect whirled around and stabbed Kairo with one of its pointed front legs. It pinned Kairo to the ground through the gut. If Kairo felt pain like a proper man, he would have hollered and feinted. As it was, the situation greatly perturbed him. To add insult, the sky erupted with a pelting rain.

The great head of the centipede dove directly above Kairo, its bristly mandibles shuddering in anticipation of coring him like an apple. Kairo pulled his pistol and fired his remaining three bullets into the head of the centipede. The shots tore through the centipede's head, and it reared away, tossing Kairo several yards, and dropping Daniel as it thrashed about recklessly.

After Kairo removed the small cactus that he had seredepishly landed on from his lower back, he scooped up his machete and searched for the witch. This whole incident had left him in disarray and in desperate need of a patch up, which a hefty reward would quickly facilitate. Gold was a vital ingredient in the salve that helped him to look less like a monster and more like your average dusty cowboy. He hoped that Daniel had as open a heart as his Bible often instructed.

There was no sign of the witch. Kairo took his anger out on the still twitching centipede, hacking its head off. It turned into little consolation as the task took longer than expected, messier too.

""What a monster," Daniel said from behind Kairo.

Kairo turned around ready to give a defense.

"I think you pretty much vanquished that witch, this beast as well. Your well worth whatever I'm paying you," Daniel said.

"The witch…"

"This thing landed right on her after you shot it. Flattened her like a pancake."

Daniel motioned for Kairo to take a look. The witch's legs protruded out from underneath the body of the centipede in unnatural positions. She was certainly dead. Things were beginning to look up for Kairo.

"Are you alright?" Daniel asked, "You look like the dead. Where did you say you were from?"

"Originally…Egypt. What about you? I've not seen many throw knives like you do."

"Ahh, yes, well I was a carnival knife thrower before I met the Lord. I lived for the stage. Now I live for Christ. At least that is what I am trying to convince myself."

Kairo nodded his head, "They are convinced."

The children that had previously been stationary had broken out of their stupor and were milling about the valley like they had just awoken from a deep sleep. Some ran towards each other and embraced vigorously, siblings stolen together and broken apart by dark magic. Others searched for signs of their parents or any semblance of home. Eventually, they all gathered around Daniel. They were careful to keep the preacher between them and Kairo.

"Mister, where are we?" One of the older girls asked.

Daniel offered his hand to the girl, "A bad place. However, I'm here to take you to a better place. It's a long trip, but I think you all have the strength to make it. I can't promise you your moms and dads back, but I can promise you kindness and hospitality."

One of the youngest girls poked her head around and eyed Kairo suspiciously, "What about him?" She asked.

"Mr. Kairo agrees, don't you Mr. Kairo?" Daniel said.

Kairo sheathed his machete, reloaded his pistol and holstered it, "Sure," He said, "Now help me roll this off the witch. I've got a feeling she's worth a mess of money."

The spirit voices whispered warnings about the danger inherit in the witch, even in her death.

Come morning, Kairo rode out on a skittish Pharaoh in the lead of Daniel and the children. The body of the witch wrapped tightly in a dirty Navajo blanket. Her heart remained in the valley for the birds to peck at. Kairo would have no more surprises this trip.

A gust of wind danced across the harsh land before them and pelted each of the procession with dirt and dust and heat, though it couldn't erase the smile on every face. Surely a better place waited for them beyond the horizon

▲

The Broken Witch
by Scott Hutchison

Three black-shawled women stood waiting for Effie Mae when she emerged from the back room of the Gasp Cave General store. She'd finished her business with Bertram Stokes—selling the cottonmouth and copperhead poison she'd milked from over a hundred different snakes— Bertram, in turn, back-door selling the milkings to someone he knew at the Kentucky Reptile Project which marketed freeze-dried venom extractions to both pharmaceutical companies and vendors in the Far East. Effie Mae received store credit for her painstaking work, though there was little risk for her in such milkings since she used both a sibilant charm as well as a drawing out spell, sweetly asking the snakes for their fanged cooperation. But that too was a barter: bluegills she's fished from the river and trucked up to the house, live swirlings in five-gallon white plastic buckets. Effie Mae had left her house that morning with vipers lying on the labyrinth pattern of flat rocks she'd placed in her front yard, comfortably warmed by summer heat on their little granite beds, each one lazily impaling a small flopping body, drinking in sunshine and sustenance. That was her sheltered and reliable world—an exchange with ordinary women underneath a somewhat civilized roof was not something she was entirely comfortable with. Effie Mae smoothed her hands down her grey cotton blouse with its homemade bone buttons. There were ground mixes in her shoulder bag she could grab and toss in an instant if need be, pulverized ghost peppers combined with minced salamander skin in the event trouble arose. Her left hand lightly clutched at the polished metal disk she wore at her neck, and when she sniffed the air for trouble, above the constant earthen mud dust engrained in the store's ancient floorboards over the course of more than a hundred farmer-footed years there wafted no present disturbance or trouble. What she inhaled bore the black-rose perfume of grief.

All three women appeared to be similar in age to her—late thirties or early forties, though grey bloomed through their hair and pain spider-webbed at the corners of their eyes. From the looks of their practical clothes and their rough hands they too appeared familiar with working hard to make ends meet. Only the mourning shawls seemed out of place. The one standing in the middle nodded a greeting, and spoke.

"You'd be Effie Mae Warren. Never met you, but Bertram informed us we might find some powerful solace in talking with you." Effie Mae noted that Bertram had not re-emerged through the curtains from the store's shielded back room. "My name's Lenora Chapman, this here"—she shouldered her weight to the right—"this is Earlene Gittleson, and this"—her shoulders swayed to the left—is Lettie Mayhew. Don't know how much you pay attention to the news hereabouts, but we're widows. Lumberman widows, our husbands recently taken from us by twisting trees. And a witch woman."

The back curtains parted and Bertram, his face a jitter of guilt, shakily trundled out, the seat of his rolling walker bearing a tarnished beer tray with four mason jars of sweet sassafras tea, a store specialty. Bertram breathed heavily through his portable oxygen which rode in a holder attached to the walker, plastic nose clips secured just above a tremble of lips. His old humped back crested inches above the bent neck, one red suspender falling from a shoulder and draped across his forearm like the mantel of a pitiful and skinny Roman. He'd said nothing to her about this meeting during their business transaction; Effie Mae had picked up on his fear as it crawled into the filthy corners of the room, but then Bertram was always a bundle of various trepidations and ailments.

"Apologies, Effie Mae. These ladies been through a damnable time…"

Effie Mae allowed her gaze to slice through Bertram's words, a blade cutting soft blue cheese. Her long blond hair, silken with daily baths of goat's milk, drifted lightly from side to side as she shook her head at the wizened old man.

The first woman bore rings under her eyes the color of blood orange pulp. She stepped forward, a slight bend at the waist. "You being… what's that big word Bertram used…ecalectic…"

Bertram rattled the glasses of tea on his walker when the word "eclectic" sputtered from his dried lips and Effie Mae's hand rose with a sun-browned finger twitch to silence him.

The woman pressed forward another step. "Anyway. That Ravere woman, moved into the old mill house down on Newfound Creek two years this July? Well, we let her be, gave her wide berth. We got kids, mind our own business. She was just a wicked seed spit out of the city and now living in the low country as far as we were concerned—up until three weeks ago. Old Lady Haggerty, who sells the woman fertilized brown eggs every week, she says the woman was doing her usual something god-awful and the nightmare things she unleashed apparently spurred and clawed abuse all around her head, and now something's gone broken inside her."

The other two, sisters in sweet pitiful if not in actual siblinghood, stepped forward to add their shuck to the story. The slightly more stooped one whispered, but strong enough to make Bertram's sleeping old hound lying next to the soda cooler perk up his ears: "Our men cut trees, that's what they do. Chain saws. Axes. Big skidder trucks. Chains. The Ravere woman, she crazed up and went after 'em all, and none of 'em even working on the same job lot. She's got it in her broken head they're killing some kind of elemental spirits. Said she'd fix 'em good and final for it."

The third woman, wearing paint-splattered overalls and work boots, held her hands in front of her mouth as she spoke. "Ever hear of a widow maker in the axe game?"

Effie Mae sprouted up aloof and far from the school, but she'd still grown up local in an edge-of-the-woods way to the Gasp Cave Township. "Downed tree occasionally gets hung up in another tree, doesn't fall all the way. Men have to figure out how to get it unhung, and the trees don't always act right, not like the way professional tree men can typically drop one on a solitary mushroom growing on the forest floor. Some twist their severed feet in the earth, while topside they're fighting in the arms of another tree. They kick out, not like they're supposed to, killing the sawyer man." Effie Mae nodded in her thoughts. "I know the term."

Lenora Chapman took the other two, hand in hand. They all looked down as Bertram's old hound rose and slowly paced over to them, leaning his weight into their legs. "The Ravere woman, she come out of the woods while they worked. Different days, same story. They hit the kill switches on their saws and gave her a respectful listen. She called them un-Christian things, threatened each one of 'em with retribution for what they were doing. And on each of the days things went bad she was standing at the edge of the woods when other trees somehow caught the cut ones on the way down. I don't know what's broke in her, but you want to see broken? You got someone you love, been loving for years, love flowing steady like creek water. Your own eyes rupture when you look down at the cracked and pulverized thing that's just been smashed by the barrel trunk of a sixty-foot pine, twisting for no reason other than someone's making it jump. That woman's on the wrong side of night, drawing ciphers against the just-getting-by world. She's killing folk with foul magics, and even though we're willing we're just too unsophisticated to take her on."

Effie Mae let her thoughts delve into the word *broken*. She envisioned the earthenware jug she'd dropped that very morning, the jagged pottery shatters, the squirming spill of bloodworms she'd kept happy inside, feeding them and grabbing handfuls when she needed to toss lines for hungry bluegill.

The paint-splattered woman let her loose hand stray down to the dog, hesitant to stroke it, as if she hadn't patted a dog since having her hand bitten in childhood. "Evil thing. She's even gone after locals for walking on bridges, saying we need to stay on one side or the other, damn us. Now everybody's got the heebies when we go near a spanner." The dog's tail tucked in, submissively.

Effie Mae had detected the edge of a faint coppery taste near a bridge two days earlier but had dismissed it, focusing on the water's brimming laughter. The bridge had been the scene of summer swimming hole mistakes twice in its history, boys not checking the water depth in a dry season, flipping off the edge and catapulting down into cool water and the unseen rock submerged just a few feet below. Bodies shattering up through the leg bones. Effie Mae had passed off the tongue spark as something natural and residual, something splintered into the water, wood, and darkened stone of the place.

* * * *

The hand that opened the chip-painted door writhed beneath its skin, black veins desperate for air or release. The door itself whispered angrily on its hinges, the hissing sound of a mother ermine protecting her young from a hungry fox. Once open, Clarion Revere stood boldly in the doorway, dressed in a deep purple gown that dragged raggedly upon the ancient mahogany floor, her hair a scatter of dark tresses seeking all four points of the compass. Her eyes, one slightly squinted more than the other, did not appear to blink.

"Hello, *sister*. I felt you…squeaking my way." The woman twitched, her arms gyrating at the elbows. Settling, her eyes refocused on Effie Mae. "You're a weak little thing, but what of that? Did the bumpkins…" she paused, looked far away, her face scored with faintly-healed cicatrixes cross-hatched into the cheeks. "Did they ask you to come deal with the bad woman of the mill?" Clarion stood back, arm gesturing her invitation to enter, the hand drifting loosely at the wrist.

Effie Mae smiled confidently as she strode forward, imbibing the lines of power puzzle-etched throughout the room. "The widows? Of course they did, but what of that? Greetings, sister, my name is Effie Mae. I'm sure you've already read my glimmers—so the fact that trees are precious to me, as they are to you, should come as no surprise. I simply thought it time to introduce myself." The front room was filled with glass jars of powders, herbs, pickled creatures and dark liquids, haphazardly occupying shelves and wooden tables. Red candles burned all around, waxen stalagmites littering the floor beneath them. The entire place carried a vulgar bouquet of mold and degeneration. Effie Mae walked over to a large rectangular aquarium set upon warped boards stretched across oaken barrels. Inside, thousands of carpet beetles ravenously cleaned bone, tiny remnants of flesh and bristled hair sticking to their teeming carapaces. There was no top upon the aquarium, and the polished edge of three uniform sides intersected with an incongruous fourth side, jagged as if something large had crunched a single bite out of it. Effie Mae leaned forward to inspect, thinking she would find a deer skull or antlers. She did not allow her face to convey surprise—the skull being overrun with swarming, mandible snipping beetles was human.

"I don't know what I'd do without these little darlings," Effie Mae laughed, straightening and turning around casually to face Clarion. "I have an aquarium much like this one. They make my taxidermy work so much more precise. Boiling tends to allow fats to seep into the bone, turning them yellow. Sloppy work, in my opinion."

Clarion's fingers played across one another feverishly, as if a game of chase were preferable to interlacing. "A whiskey stray from out along the highway. He presumed my invitation to be lonely and amorous." The tall woman moved to a crowded wooden table of leather-bound books and bones, lifted a femur as if it were a club. "Besides introductions, why are you here, little moon-walker?" She slapped one knee and giggled. "Have you been tasting my home? Quite the little tea blend." Clarion's head snapped to one side, clavicle joints popping, and her voice became threatening, a carnivorous growl over territory. "The power in this beastly place far exceeds your innocuous flower-petal spells. Swallow that, if you will." Clarion began to laugh, if it could be called that. The sound mumbled through her skin more than her mouth, cracking out of her ribcage and dying upon contact with the fetid air.

Effie Mae had breathed in the scorch of the containment circle while more than a mile away from Clarion's slanted and shambling house. She could sense its soiled remnants in the next room. Something ancient had scratched and bitten its way into the world through that grim hex-enclosure, barely held back by incantation chains—lingering char still smoldered with the struggle. The air itself remained bruised. But there was more: the Dark Thing's claw and teeth marks now manifested as scars behind Clarion Revere's eyes, two charcoal smudges that bore and reflected no light. Apparently Clarion had possessed the skills to push it back into whatever godless cesspool it had burned its way up from—Effie Mae shuddered to think that in all likelihood she would have been the second meal for such a creature, which would have smelled her across the distance and bounded through the forest for her with its beetle-like attraction for a specific kind of flesh. The widows, all drained and cried-out from their losses, used the word *broken* to describe Clarion. Another word rose in Effie Mae's suddenly dizzied mind: *violated*. She struggled her way back to composure. The one thing she did not dare to do with Clarion was lie. Clarion's perception of deceit would be keen, perceptive, and her reaction to being lied to or crossed might mean that 20,000 pounds of yellow pine came anthropomorphically alive, tearing its veins to shreds, reaching for you with lightning-strike limbs obsessed with kissing you, grasping at your body with a bark-rough sylvan embrace.

"Sister. I stand humbled in your presence. You're a formidable woman, new to this environment. I was born and raised in these parts, and old-mothers passed along their provincial wisdom to me. As you sensed, I do not possess the boldness or authority to wield the dark fissures wishing for release in this world. But you are different. And there are night-shade corners in these valleys brimming with shadow sway, powerful junctions of power that only someone as potent and dedicated as you might be able to...appreciate."

Clarion pressed into Effie Mae, the distortion of laughter slipping along her skin. Clarion's singed and abused aura nauseously muddied into her own as the woman scented her along the neckline. Erratic fingers touched Effie Mae's face, keeping mad-time to a music only Clarion could here. "What could you possibly offer to me?" Her breath squalled in Effie Mae's ear.

"Dragon's Breath."

Clarion backed up a step, ran a finger along Effie Mae's arm, a tender caress made with a cracked nail. She drew in Effie Mae, an inhalation that frenzied the dust motes of the disturbed house. Clarion took another step back, her posture ticking with admiration, the unblinking stare widening above her fiendish smile. "Truth. I like that. Lead me, Little Sister, why wait a second longer? Turning to open the door, Clarion's bones cracked like birches in a howling ice storm. Effie Mae glanced at the human skull nearly submerged beneath a crawling mass, then proceeded out into the stickiness of the summer day.

* * * *

The cave was cool compared to the outside air. Effie Mae and Clarion lit red candles that Clarion had brought with her. Moisture draped the cave walls, glistening in the glow of their passing as they descended. The fetid smell of decomposing guano preceded the chamber that held thousands of tiny brown bats, restless at the intrusion created by light and unnatural voices.

"Little slow-hearts. Now I know where to harvest them with ease—and still, the best is yet to come!" The tiny flame wavered in Clarion's hand.

"We must go deeper." Effie Mae clutched at her shoulder bag, expecting to soon abandon the candle and switch over to the hard-steel Maglight she carried. She pulled breath in shallow draws. "Come."

They bent and wound their way through low passages, finally entering another cathedral-ceilinged part of the cave. Jagged formations in the ceiling caught the dim cast of light. "The Dragon's Teeth!" Clarion laughed, proceeding through puddles without lifting the hem of her long skirt. The candles began to dance and flicker.

The air became raw here, full of the power of rock and earth, water and cold. "Sulphur! I smell the Dragon's Breath!" Clarion's voice, though filled with heated excitement, echoed cheerlessly throughout the cavern. "Little Sister, we may not have to feed you to the Murk Lords after all! You are as good as your weak little word." The half-light illuminated Clarion's fiery face—one of the wounds upon a cheek had somehow opened, and now oozed blackly down her chin.

When the candles finally snuffed out, Effie Mae was ready. She pushed the button on the body of the LED flashlight, and a bright beam stretched into the earthen bowels before them.

"Sister," Effie Mae choked out the words, "I am frightened. I dare not go further. This quest is for you, not for me." She reached into her bag, drew out another flashlight, this one old and small. When she tried to turn in on it did not respond immediately. She hit it a couple of times, and it came to life. Effie Mae handed the second flashlight to Clarion.

Clarion took the flashlight, aimed it into the near-impenetrable darkness before her. "This is the Dragon's Breath, yes?"

Effie Mae whispered, the blackness seeping in all around her. "That's what some people call it."

"What do you call it?" Clarion's jaw clacked with the question.

"Mercy." Effie Mae was shaking. She coughed, barely able to breathe.

In the dual light between them, Effie Mae saw Clarion blink. The woman clutched at Effie Mae's free hand, her rough-scaled fingers pressing carpals and metacarpals insistently, as if to break them. A spark erupted from Clarion's fingertips, ran its way up Effie Mae's right arm before sizzling out at the top of her head. The pressure on Effie Mae's hand relaxed. There was one more brief clasp, almost tender. Clarion blinked again, turned away quickly and began descending. When her light disappeared, Effie Mae heard Clarion's voice quietly call back,

"Thank you, Sister."

* * * *

"Do you have it straight, Bertram?"

Bertram nodded his old doddering head, grey-bristle chin touching his chest with the motion. "The widows are supposed to retrieve a glass aquarium with beetles in it, take them out of the house before burning the place down to the ground. What do you want them to do with the aquarium after that?"

"Release the beetles in Dragon's Breath. Not one of the other caverns, you hear me? There can't be any confusion on that. If they're unsure on which one it is, then they need to ask somebody. And you be sure to tell them not to go in too far."

"You don't have to worry about that. They know better than to go too deep into a bad-air cavern. I'm pretty sure they know which one it is. Those girls were raised here in Gasp Cave. Not like they're greenhorns or carpetbaggers." Bertram took a knife and shakily cut the thin rope that held a smoked ham hanging from a rafter. It tumbled to the floor with a hard thump. It cost him something, but Bertram picked it up and placed it on the counter between him and Effie Mae. "Thank you, Effie Mae."

She reached into her bag, and placed the long green cylinder and tubing on the counter next to the ham. "Here's your extra oxygen tank, Bertram." Effie Mae smiled at the old man.

Bertram flashed a smile back at her, his dentures shiny and white. But the smile dissipated as he stared at her hair. "Effie Mae, you seem to have a couple of strands of black hair in those blond tresses of yours. Now, you don't color your hair, do you?"

Effie Mae squinted hard at Bertram, pursing her lips. The elderly man's fear discharged into the store front, its smell and taste overpowering the strong comforting aroma of the ham. She relaxed her face and took the old man's hand, patting it for reassurance. "How, old man, did you manage to live this long asking women questions like that?" Bertram's smile returned.

Hoisting the ham up under one arm, Effie Mae headed for the door, stopping for one last exchange. "You low on root stock for your tea?"

"I am." Bertram clapped his bony hands together, holding them prayer-like.

"Then I have a piece of work ahead of me. Venom and sassafras. I'll see you next Tuesday, Bertram."

▲

The Desert Rose Inn
by Maurits Zwankhuizen

The innkeeper saw by the flame-fingered door
A sharp silhouette cut the shadows night bore
And a long cloak of sand was the robe which he wore:
It's startling indeed what the desert blows in.
The wanderer sat with a shiver of gold
As the eyes of those gathered grew large but not bold.
It took all their power their greed to withhold
Lest their features grown wild in the desert show sin.

How like to a killer is faith when paroled.
How doubt is forsaken when choice is controlled,
While the purest of faith in the desert grows thin.

Like a shaman come forth from remote Samarkand,
The wanderer daunted, all turbaned and tanned.
Long spirals of sand feathered out from his hand
And doved whitely down in a fine single strand.

Smiling he stated, with humour writ large:
'Assuming this inn is no phantom mirage,
'What luck that this deep in the desert flows gin
'And the fiercest of all the old desert foes grin;
'That a poor man on hajj may rest free of charge
'And say prayers in peace at the Desert Rose Inn.'

'Our fame is widespread', the innkeeper said
Through devilish teeth which the flames painted red
And a withered hand waved at a girl barely bled;
A joy to behold with her desert rose skin.
But her eyes were dark graves where her soul and sin wed,
Where she'd buried her past though her future lay dead
And incubi fed at her torn maidenhead,
Tattooed with the lust of her desert beau's kin.

The wanderer sighed: 'I do seek but respite.
'My journey is long as a scorned woman's spite,
'I ask only that I be roused at first light';
       If the sun deigns to shine on the Desert Rose Inn.
And he moved up the stairs with the softest of prayers,
In the glare of the flames and a dozen black stares
And when he lay down in the forge of nightmares,
       He felt the chill air of the desert close in.

☼

When the birds of dawn spoke, the wanderer woke
And was striding off west ere the spell of night broke.
He farewelled the inn with its saints and its sin
And threw the new sun on his shimmering skin,
Attuned to the silence and bearing within
       The deep haunting notes of the desert's slow spin.
'Welcome, my friends', said his eyes to the hills,
Those fiends of the desert which sunlight instils
With movement and life and a side where dark spills
And soft-soaks the wounds of the desert wind's quills.
Yet come the day's half and all shade melts away
To a searing white hell where the dust devils play
Till time once more touches the twilight to day
       And bleeds out the barbs which the desert throws in.

His eyes, creased and cast 'cross the dead desert vast,
Saw only the dunes in array unsurpassed
And soon tortured tight by the sun's ceaseless blast,
       His pupils blazed bright where the desert goes in.
His face glazed with sweat in the desert's hot air
And his skin cracked and corned 'neath the sun's senseless stare.
He summoned no calm from his spirit burnt bare:
How he yearned for the cant of the Desert Rose Inn.

Alist from the sunlight's remorseless embraces,
The heat of hell shining from heavenly places,
He planted a wide palm, a thick black oasis,
       To shelter his eyes and his desert-blown skin.
His infinite-eyed and unwavering bride
Weakened his wisdom with each stifled stride
And turban nor veil let his seared eyes abide.
No bones mark the spot where the blind dassie died;
       Just the sands where the shades of the desert doze in.

Starved jackals of thought close at his heels followed,
Licking his mind till it lay drained and hollowed,
And heat hugged the air so that both must be swallowed,
    Dry gulps where the fire of the desert flows in.
He stuttered out gasps of delirious thought
Till silence became the one solace he sought
But then the wind roared with its own dry import:
    The goodwill of gods in the desert grows thin.
Each grain was a god upon which he trod,
A grain then returned by a wind wild and odd,
Each hitting his skin with the force of a rod
And scarring and scraping his desert soul thin.

Then, cresting a dune, he would roll into black.
The fickle oasis would welcome him back
And seep full his soul, each sand-scarified crack,
    Till all aches dissolved in the desert's soul gin.

With vigour renewed in a mirage of skies,
His body would rise in its human disguise
But his soul would still leak through his mind's blasted eyes
A sweat-wet brown mass of ubiquitous flies
    Which once was the girl at the Desert Rose Inn.

A statue he stood while his febrile mind hung
Like a droplet of sweat on his cheek and his tongue
Worked away in pursuit, all his mind's folds unslung
    And loose as the sand which the desert blows in.
He knew his soul well and through fever could tell
That his savaged soul did not these fool's thoughts compel,
That fever clutched him as the pard the gazelle,
    Tore him like the wounds in the desert doe's skin.

Sweet night daubed his brow and deep sleep did allow
For his fever to ease. Like a storm-stricken dhow
With the bane tempest passed and the seas becalmed now,
    He would rest as the wind-studded desert rolls in.

The night, come the night, and it was as in death.
The houri anointed and tended his breath
Till sly sleep stole in with its mute shibboleth
    And he lay there alone with no desert, no skin.

Then sunlight would billow as fine as spun silk is,
As bright as a basin which brimful with milk is,
As bright as would only please sun-smitten Bilqis,
  Arms raised to the sun with their desert-glow skin.

Awash with the sun's milk, he wallowed in days,
No markings or signposts met his thirsty gaze,
No fountain of plenty where livestock could graze
  Nor drink from or sink their burnt desert toes in.
Just sand and more sand in a swift-shifting land
Where no human or beast can oppose its great hand,
A far-reaching fiend which no soul can withstand
  But for water locked tight in a desert doeskin.

Yet here rode another, and quite solitary,
Perched high on the rude hump of a dromedary,
An eagle aloof in its light lofty aerie,
  Jet-eyed and hooded, his desert nose thin.
With faith in his heart that Allah had provided
And no more need he tread this wasteland unguided,
The wanderer met him with purpose decided:
  Hands clasping firmly, two desert souls grin.

This other man seemed such a rich tapestry
Of customs and clichés and conceits, all three
Embracing his soul in a thick panoply,
  Concealing a heart where the desert glows thin.
They travelled the dunelands down trough and up bank
But like to a camel this man never drank
And his gaze while direct was shallow and blank,
  A gaze where the force of the desert flows in.

Was this desert merchant all he seemed to be?
Was that hand held up near his blade absently?
Was the assassin's taint in his veins flowing free?
  Just one seed of doubt in the desert sows djinn.
The sickening stenches of foodstuffs grown rank,
The black scimitar which hung down by his flank.
There was blood in his eyes as the honeyed sun sank,
  A much richer red than the desert owes skin.

A second sun burst for an instant at first,
Then glittered and glinted and twilight perversed
And limbs limned in red quenched the sands of their thirst,
The limbs of a human by all the Fates cursed;
  The trunk of trust's tree in the desert grows thin.

The wanderer saw but did not understand:
He cried tears of sand and withdrew his red hand
And bowed and became as if one with the land.

In this pose he remained until daylight had waned
And the stars stamped the sky like wild kulan unreined,
        There raising the winds which the desert blows in.

He felt his face burn and awoke with a start.
Harsh light stabbed his sight but darkness his heart.
The sun felt so cold and the sand burned like ice
As he lay there arrayed like a splayed sacrifice.
        How often in time do the desert snows spin?
        How often in time has the desert froze in?
As often as Fate was too sluggish to act
And a human hand struck with the Devil a pact.
Yet even dark arts in the desert retract
        And as all things die in the desert, so sin.

The heat steamed the cold caul of guilt from his heart;
He rose from his sorrow and turned to depart.
Upon the vast easel where sprawled his vile art,
Three black figures swooped in and tore it apart:
        What the sands fail to hide, the desert crows win.

They loot and they lurch and this man reduce
To a wind-strangled shred of his bloodied burnous
Which flies off in search of a heavenly truce,
        As the three wisest men of the desert close in.

He watched its brief circles high up in the sky
Until it dissolved in the hell-yellow eye,
Then his conscience was sore as his gullet was dry,
        As burnt and as torn as his desert foe's skin.
Replete with remorse, this wretched transgressor
Turned to the blue veil which hid his Confessor.
He wailed of his woes, both greater and lesser,
        Ripping his throat with his desert woes' din.

Yet still just that empty blue bowl and the heat
As mute as the tongue which the black trio eat;
No whisper was formed of his heinous deceit,
        No stares as he'd felt at the Desert Rose Inn.

Though wretched and racked, he saw consequence dead
And all doubts were bested when fury had fled.
He mounted the camel and turned west its head,
       Sat still as the skull which the desert crows skin.

With conscience laid bare by a short hasty prayer,
No more did this murder mean fear and despair,
And the wind burrowed on and the sun's searing glare,
And the dunes and the crows ate the brown blemish bare;
       In silence his sin the deep desert goes in.
The camel he rode never stumbled nor slowed
But ever marched west with its unwanted load,
Till one dawn it stopped despite guerdon and goad:
       Across a vast plain lay the Desert Rose Inn.

The wanderer gazed at its distant white walls
With half of it hid where the desert sand crawls;
He cursed it a play of the light, oft it falls
       Raising ghosts when the mist of the desert flows in.
Dismounting, on foot he approached this mirage,
Circling it close like a pilgrim on hajj
Until it was proven. With eyes lifted large,
       He drank the last drop from his desert doeskin.

A figure in white robes appeared by the building,
A figure the sun caught in thin blades of gilding.
Dropping the weapon her small hands were wielding,
The girl from the inn fell into his arms yielding
       And flames of lust fletched Cupid's desert bowstring.
The wanderer watched as her eyes roved the sky;
Almond-round brown, all her tears had run dry.
In streaks 'cross her cheeks did their urgency lie
       And he summoned this nymph of the desert close in.

With a shifting of sand by a sudden wind fanned,
Their empathy flowed and the deep silence spanned,
While some being's blood in the palm of her hand
       Tore her soul a deep hole where the desert flows in.
All hate liquefied in her pacified eyes,
A remnant of tyrants she'd ceased to despise,
And a cold pallid sweat bathed her arms and her thighs
       Like a membrane of sin on her desert rose skin.

They let all their wrath to the scorched heavens rise,
The spirits of anger, of vengeance and lies,
And clothed them in honour and deep moral guise
　　　By the threshold grown dark of the Desert Rose Inn.
Their tanned fingers linked at the tips of a touch
But lingered no longer, the moment was such
As lasted a blink but concealed in its clutch
　　　The source where these slaves of the desert chose sin.

The girl vanished then from beside the pale stone;
The wanderer stood there a ghost and alone
While ribbons of red sand about him were thrown,
　　　Blood-red were these grains where the desert stows sin.
He lifted his gaze from the sandbanks ablaze,
From creation of life to the dying of days,
Up into the depths where the stars the sky glaze
　　　And all of the light of the desert goes in.
Then he too moved on 'cross the plain and a rain
Of golden-grained drops formed a sun-sprinkled train
Until he himself was no more than a grain
　　　When seen from the door of the Desert Rose Inn.

▲

Salty

by Lucy A. Snyder

Despite what you said, my love,
you only want pale saccharine
magic: a Splenda Glenda

with cheesecake frosting.
Wave your gourmand wand
and she'll be your candyland.

You crave sweet maiden,
not seasoned mother,
never bitter crone.

My saltiness is legend.
I'm no marshmallow
though I certainly burn.

So, baby, just for you: I'll embody
witchy clichés. Skunk your beer.
Wilt your soufflés. Sour your balls.

I hear that tears pair well with crow.
I'll take my broom and cauldron
and sweep away to Avalon.

▲

The Ballad of Blighted Marsh

by David F. Daumit

She who channels Gaea's power
And he who wields forged steel
Rode to the edge of Blighted Marsh
Behind both charm and shield

Shunned as a witch and left alone
Till the king called in despair
For her to join his noblest knight
In a rescue none would dare

She wore but virtue and a shawl
He wore great plates of mail
As they entered the fetid swamp
They heard a far off wail

'Twas the royal princess of the realm
Who under veil of night
Had been snatched away by forms too foul
To look upon by light

The fearful cry spurred on the knight
To charge after the daughter
But for the witch who stayed his run
Anon he'd be lured to slaughter

For imps and goblins tracked them close
And harpies swarmed o'erhead
Together they might ward off the host
But apart they'd soon be dead

As their ranks in the murky shadows swelled
The abominations readied
To attack the mounted heroes whose course

Remained both sure and steadied

When at last the monstrous horde unseen
Forth from the darkness burst
The knight bellowed out a battle cry
And surged on to face their worst

His sword cut a bloody arc through beings
Birthed unholy and so vile
His shield and armor soon were covered
In the dankest blood and bile

As at the minions dread he slashed
The witch behind him drew
Upon the awesome might of Mother Gaea
Empowering her body through

With nimble hands and dulcet voice
She cast a web of light
Each strand of which shone like the sun
And a hellish beast did smite

His furious blade and her arcane spell
Soon banished all to death
Then raced the knight on through the fallen
Before to even catch his breath

The witch was more the wise and knowing
Of the Foe they now would face
And though not hurried to pursue his folly
She nonetheless kept pace

Their steeds galloped through the tenebrous night
Past a black and boiling creek
Then on past trees that howled and moaned
Towards the Fiend that they did seek

A splintering crack of thunder then
Resounded in their ears
And the stench of days-old rotting flesh
Told the witch It now loomed near

She hailed the knight rein in his mount
That battle now impended

They slowed their horses to a cautious trot
And to preparations tended

The Thing coalesced from the putrid mists
Collecting like rancid dew
All horns and claws and jagged tusks
That could run a human through

Limp in Its claw lay the princess swooned
Her gown with blood was smeared
Enraged was the knight by the state of the girl
And by the Beast who at him leered

Then before the witch could caution warn
He charged forward with his blade
The Thing stood fast and laughed aloud
At the challenge being made

Pure of heart the witch knew the knight to be
If brash and full of zeal
Upon this trait she did fix her mind
And enchanted then his steel

Consecrated now and ablaze with flame
Was the weapon of the knight
As he plunged it deep into the canc'rous heart
Of the Spawn that he did fight

The Thing though mortally wounded was
Not till death about to yield
With a single savage slash Its claws
Tore apart the champion's shield

Then into his mount It gored Its tusks
Toppling the hapless steed
Down went the knight to be trapped beneath
Unable to be freed

Upon the princess cast now the witch
As towards her the Thing did start
A charm of protection to keep well safe
And to strengthen her faint heart

Then at the witch with a fearsome speed

The Bane of Blighted Marsh came
The knight pushed hard against his horse
But could not budge its frame

No fear showed the witch nor inclination
To move from the path of harm
She stoically suffered the ravaging Beast
And embraced It with her arms

She smiled as a holy light from Gaea
Around her body spread
Enwrapping her and the Monster foul
In a curtain dense as lead

The Thing shrieked in seething agony
As if caught in a lava tide
And then within the burning light
It and the witch both died

The light faded out and with it took
The bodies it had killed
And the helpless knight who had seen it all
Felt his very soul grow chilled

With the aid of the princess now restored
He against his trap prevailed
Then the two went together from the horrid swamp
For to tell their heroic tale

▲

The Witch-Queen
By S. L. Edwards

She killed her first god at the age of thirteen.
The god was a cold, strong, powerful thing,
With flesh made of clouds and roaring storms,
A crown of blue lightening, cracked and worn.
Eyes of red fire and words of trembling thunder,
But the storm-god inspired no awe or wonder.

She bound it with locks of her long, white hair
Enticing it with songs into her fire-lit lair.
It broke from the sky and descended slowly,
Believing itself summoned by someone lowly,
It could not have known of the plans in motion
That a child could paralyze a god with a potion.

It cursed in claps and spat torrents of rain,
It howled in mercy, It begged in shame.
She ignored It all the while, anointing her knife
Wearing a soft, aloof smile before ending Its life.
She focused on her potions, lest something go wrong
And paid no mind to Its threats as she went along.

She calmly explained that there was no mercy there,
That It would not escape back into the soft, night air.
There was no forgiving beings of Its station
Things that broke apart mankind into nations
And laughed from Their thrones in the indifferent sky
As They set innocent people in Their games to die.

The stone knife handle was coarse in her palm
As she sang the verses of her god-slaughter-song.
She plunged the blade deep into Its ethereal core
It shuddered and shook, bleeding star-light gore.
It subsided into sleep as its fog-flesh faded
And left for whatever oblivion that awaited.

The god's blood pooled into an earthen cup.
She sighed, closing her eyes and lifting it up
She parted her lips and breathed in a moment
There was no going back, no chance for atonement.
She shook her head and refused to think
Deciding it far easier to just simply drink.

The god-blood was sweater with each slow sip
And she took it in deep, long, wonderful drips
It fell from her lips to her flesh in ecstatic fire
And in her frail mind rose an unquenchable ire.
She would break those Things and make a throne
A proud, regal seat made of god-blood and bone.

The gods could not be left alive to thwart her race
So she would expel them from man's sacred place,
Heaven above would shake and Hell would shatter,
As she would make clear that gods did not matter.
She would lead the dance upon their graves and
revel.
For man would make a better god, and a far better
devil.

"See more in Occult Detective Quarterly #3 and the Ravenwood Quarterly: Halloween special."

▲

A Witch's Work is Never Done

by Lori R. Lopez

Beware those paths through wooded places
That lead beyond the jumbled faces,
For in these far-gone clutching spaces
Is where the gnarly witches roam . . .

A house of candy, a cottage of cheese;
The hut may lean and hop with fleas;
A shack of twigs that grope and quease:
'Tis here the witch may call her home!

Upon a wander in moss-draped pines,
Yielding to dark between the lines
Of saner thoughts and madder whines,
An undiscerning folk could meet . . .

The stranger lacking all trace of fair,
A forest of tangles knotting her hair —
Lurking, abiding, crouched in some lair,
Waiting to offer then snatch a treat!

Her wicked work is never done,
Below the Moon, underneath the Sun.
It's a perilous venture in the presence of one,
So avoid every trail the nasties might creep . . .

Those nether reaches, the snaggleteeth wild;
Stay out of sight whether grown or a child;
Keep your distance in case the old bat gets riled
And may swoop for a haggish Midnight reap!

Inspect each shadow for a hidden crone.
Peel your eyeballs to catch every glimmer shone
Of treacherous cusps, her crown of bone.

The Witch Queen awaits a tender meal . . .

Wherever you go, a beldam is near:
That rickety house, the alley you fear;
At the end of a stony walk she may leer;
From the tip of a hat-shaped hill will squeal!

A witch could be squatting upon a bough
Like a cat or an owl, yet no hoot or meow
To give her away, just a moody brow
As she watches through your windowpane . . .

She might skulk down your lane one foggy night,
Be the shape at the base of a dim streetlight,
Or the pale round visage that gives you a fright
In the corner of an eye, that you can't explain!

And no graveyard is sacred enough to be safe
From a conjuring touch, a witch's chafe.
A sorceress will prey on the available naif,
Then carry him home in an earthenware jar . . .

Step cautiously when you have to go out.
Only travel with a group. Don't hesitate to shout
If a suspicious character should linger about.
The spellcaster is craftier than we are!

Unless one encounters the benevolent kind —
Who would sooner cure than strike you blind,
And will always offer a piece of mind.
Such words are bound to be wise, indeed . . .

For a witch's work is not ever done,
Below the Moon, underneath the Sun.
Whether evil or blessed, even dressed like a nun
In the blackest frock, she's a different breed!

In her wake can sprout Witchweed and grass,
Bloodroot, Nightshade, Wormseed most crass;
Devil's Tongue, Bracken Fern, Baneberry in mass;
Witch Hazel, Wolfsbane behind her tread . . .

Gray swaths of wither and trails of brown;
Mildew and mold, paths of dead Thistledown;

A bleak carpet of reek causing angels to frown.
And the devil remembers every word you said!

Refrain from ill speaking or with false intent
Of a witch, for she senses the malevolent
And knows exactly what tattled tales you meant!
Guard well your lips from the heart of gloam . . .

The depths where no candle may pierce the gloom,
And you can't trust anything, even a broom.
The saturnine embrace of a chilling brume —
'Tis here the witch feels most at home!

▲

ORACLE BONE SCRIPT*

by Frederick J. Mayer

«Chapter: Suvannamaccha»

Codex "Oracle Bone Script" Witches lore
told of Suvanamaccha's so Yay kae sigh;
Mo phi read of familiars-cum-succubi
down through China into Thailand's dark core.

She mermaid maemd even god bewitching
He Hanuman succumbs as daayan charms fail;
Be golden Suvanamaccha's nubile tail
corpus Hermeticum body speaking.

Breath fervid bestiaire d'amour seen moon
breasts full mystic sea-witch sings Love it's said;
Caress ghosts of the dead ritual winds fed
chant of man's feral fetish lust soul soon.

Ningyo anthropomorphical Kimon
bring forth shape shifting jellyfish gate oni;
Thing volupte flesh consumed enternal be
Indochina Asiatic beyond.

Suvannamaccha of many names fame
through orient seas bridge Love loss realm taboo;
Wu bequiled lurid leer quenchless as well too
corporal witches skin scripted bone fane.

▲

* "Oracle Bone Script" is considered the earliest known East Asia writing. Clark Ashton Smith, when he would get in his mood of leaving America, usually thought of the Indochina area as where he would probably like his new abode, hence, this is my homage to CAS & his dreamed of locale.

Halloween Witch

By K.A. Opperman

Astride a broom of birch,
Her flowing hair aflame
Upon the cold October air,
A most enchanting dame,
She races with the bats
Across the autumn moon,
And soars wherever witches dare,
Her song a haunting tune.

She swoops down low to search
The ancient town below,
To find a jack-o'-lantern bright
To lend its grinning glow;
And of the green-eyed cats,
The blackest one will do.
She takes them soaring through the night,
Returning whence she flew.

▲

Remembering the Peculiar Effects from the Sugar Witch's Goblin-Brew

by Clay F. Johnson

Her brain-wrinkling seductions of sugar
Unravel the unawakened senses—
That first idle high from vanilla intensity,
Eyes melting with a twilight-gazed propensity
For bloodroot-butter of wicked strangeness:
Cream-filled flavors rich with witchcraft spices
Reviving a languid-bruised imagination

>*Out of my own self-eclipsed shadow I awake*
>>*In profound sleep I dream of external pleasures*

From shadowed phantom worlds to which I clung,
I now stand –alone– with most vivid confidence—
Flying through to pearly paths enchanted
I seek the seeker of once-lucid dreams,
For Her sugared lips once tasted, at once begun

The pale spirit of Her potion-magic
Blooms the closing of unclosed memories,
Strangling the inner eye of dark fascination,
Withering sad-hued petals of inspiration
Turn to dust with a whisper of a breeze—
But may the flowered swirls be re-blossomed
With witch-blistered bark on a draught of goblin-green pearls

>*Though Her potion awakened my sugar-drowsed*
>*brain*
>>*No amount of bat's blood can turn night into day*

The strange effects from Her bone-bubbling warmth

Instill an anxious beating of the heart,
A palm-sweaty shakiness fit to kill,
Fit to murder any dull opiate
Meant for the most bitter of dreams and selfish sleep

In my sleepless quest for supernal climes
I reach the tortured peaks of trembling stars—
Breathless the air reaching the heart's limitations,
Flitting wildly in wormroot-spiced palpitations
I no longer endeavor toward higher skies:
Drowning in fast-flowing scarlet-river rhythms
I now seek the sorceress of sleep-persuading eyes

> *Whispers low in witching rhymes of saccharine white*
> *Voices wicked She sleeps by day and wakes all night*

Her poet's potion of dark-purpled nightshade,
Unpasteurized yellow-bell, old monkshood
Roots, yew-berry essence –necromancer grown–
Fang-frosted wolf's bane with shards of self-torn
Amethyst creates a pigmented hue
Of the most shadowy of Gothic blue:
Hecate's *Queen of all Poisons*

The concoction is thick with frog jelly,
Gore-sludge of newt and shavings of dwarf-beard—
Flesh-bitten globs still attached at the root
Make for a mold-flowered aftertaste—but
It's the pallid eye of salamander
That sweetens its flavor, shimmering white
With an opal-lustrous alabaster

> *Such creature-parts form the swirls of Her goblin-*
> *brew*
> *Shadowing the pearls of Memory's residue*

Mistress of the stars that lights my midnight,
Whom I've sought in star-aligned alchemy,
Let me lose myself in bitter forgetfulness,
Without shadows of moon-silvery hopelessness
Or tortured memories that wander pale—
Undead to the heart's imagination,

Cold to all but the layers of Her livid lips
Closing upon mine She stole that last sugar-rotten kiss

In profound silence I hear no deeper music—
Lingering I'll soon collapse to self-surrender:
The liquid melodies of Her witchcraft still burn
My root-twisted heartstrings like absinthe—yet it's
those
Idle-aching rhythms I long to remember.

▲

Sea Witch

by Vonnie Winslow Crist

Over Corolla, moon carves
an orange crescent in the indigo.
Its light mirrored, mimicked
by the ocean's surface and her eyes.

Salt-wind whips spindrift, hair,
and phosphorescent gown
that drags in the surf,
smells of sharks and drowned men.

At her naked feet,
a storm of gulls whites the sand,
and oyster, scallop, mollusk
shells scatter-clatter like bones.

She chants until static blue
shoots from her fingertips
and gales churn the water
off of Currituck Beach.

Betrayed by a sailor, she sights
his ship, calls forth a funnel cloud.
Then, smiles at the wave of debris
scratching the North Carolina shore.

▲

Little Youkai at the Witch House

by Chad Hensley

Riding the high winds like a bed sheet flapping on a clothesline,
A ghost glides in glaucous light of a monolithic moon,
Elongated eyes shining like bright lights behind emerald glass panes.
Tombstones in the cemetery outside the old house
Smile rows of marbled teeth, rip loose of the musty, moist ground,
And clasp tiny gray hands.
They jig in a wide circle, giddy and exuberant.
Just beneath the deepest grave, an enormous furry belly jiggles.
Awakened from his dream, the Eater of the Dead bellows awkwardly
At the excitement above, toothy maw crunching bone and dirt.
Tending to his perpetually rumbling stomach is forgotten for the moment
As he swims through packed earth like deep ocean,
Anxious to join the reveling of his spirit brothers.
In the old house, a single eye opens in each cyclo-pean turret, perplexed and puzzled, peering down at the ghoulish clamor.
Where the graveyard meets tangled, skeletal trees,
Salamander midget-men stop their feasting on the flayed flesh of a foolish traveler,
Turning blood-drenched snouts toward the laughter echoing through the forest.
Soon, dark hunched forms, grotesque and gibbering,
Frolic within the circle of giggling stones, a multitude of merry monstrosities.
On the rooftop, a little boy bursts into laughter at his

new nightmare friends.
The last tear falls, memories of a mortal childhood
gratefully expelled for the night,
The dusty fate of flesh and bones only a haunting
afterthought,
Buried until morning.

▲

MOTHER PERSEPHONE
by Oliver Smith

On Halloween the vale burned bright,
The way all hung with flaming lights
She hobbled past the hill-top shack
By the post they lit with lantern-jacks,
Gripped in hands of dead men's bones

Welcoming the Witch of Autumn back.
To the little village of Adder's Coomb
Round the winding bend she limped
Leaning hard upon her staff
She hurried down to the harvest home

Beneath her boots the soil burned
The basilisk coiled, and the serpent curled
Her footsteps rang in the deepest holes.
In dim graveyards and the midnight pools,
Among the wallowing ghastly ghouls.

In her green hair vipers were hissing
While by her side zombies walked
Rotting and Wheezing and moaning and whistling.
She danced a gavotte with the animate bones
In the oak woods and round the circles of stone

While the village sat post-card picturesque
Beneath the wicked wide-eyed moon.
Here at the end
Of the snake-tailed year
She stirred a pot on an elder-wood fire.

She added ivy and red autumn sun,
Stirred in a dead dream and wriggling worms.
She called on some warlocks to come
And take turns around barrows and tombs
Leading the dead in a carnival line

Where grapevines droop
And the ivy binds
And lovers lie sleeping in Adder's Coomb
All coffin-bound and sweetly entwined.
At last Mother Persephone felt a decline:

Tired at the end of all-hallows time.
The skull moon was grinning in cold
Starry skies. She opened a door
In a long-barrow mound, made her
Goodbyes, then followed a staircase

Spiralling down.
The witch was last sighted among trolls
And gnolls and kobalds and gnomes
In a goblin cave a lantern in hand
Leading the villagers deep underground.

▲

A WARLOCK SLIPS INTO MY DREAMS

by Darla Klein

A warlock slips into my dreams.
Tall and lean he plies my heart.
Not everything is as it seems.

In midnight forest darkness teems
and blocks me from a wakeful start.
A warlock slips into my dreams.

What does he want as moonlight beams
its ghostly blue gray shadowed art?
Not everything is as it seems.

I glimpse his eyes and quickly deem
our souls shall never breathe apart.
A warlock slips into my dreams.

He stays all night 'til sunlight streams.
In fiery embrace I claim his heart.
Not everything is as it seems.

I bid him stay, my charm supreme.
He vows to me not to depart.
A warlock slips into my dreams.
Not everything is as it seems.

▲

CPSIA information can be obtained
at www.ICGtesting.com
Printed in the USA
BVOW03s1149061017
496968BV00001B/13/P